W9-ACD-073

FORGOTTEN REALMS

FANTASY ADVENTURE ®

THE RING OF WINTER

James Lowder

TSR Inc.

THE RING OF WINTER

Copyright ©1992 TSR, Inc.
All Rights Reserved.

First Printing: November 1992
Printed in the United States of America.
Library of Congress Catalog Card Number: 91-66489

9 8 7 6 5 4 3 2 1

ISBN: 1-56076-330-2

TSR, Inc.
P.O. Box 756
Lake Geneva,
WI 53147 U.S.A.

TSR Ltd.
120 Church End, Cherry Hinton
Cambridge CB1 3LB
United Kingdom

THE HARPERS

Trees crashed to the ground, shoved out of the way as the triceratops charged.

"Run!" Artus shouted.

Calmly, as if he had not heard the explorer, Kwalu lifted his broad-bladed spear and threw it with all his considerable strength. The weapon flew, lodging just below one of the monster's eyes. The wound didn't even slow the beast down. It rampaged forward, closing half the distance between the doomed men with three steps. Kwalu didn't retreat an inch, instead reaching for a small leather box that hung at his belt.

Artus saw then how futile it would be to run. Unless he'd started to move long before the dinosaur broke through the tree line, it could catch him in a half-dozen thunderous steps. The explorer glanced over his shoulder, hoping Sanda had possessed the sense to bolt at the first rumbling footstep. At the same time, he reached back for an arrow from his quiver. Kwalu was right in that much—better to fight until the end.

◉ ◉ ◉ ◉ ◉

THE HARPERS

A semi-secret organization for Good, the Harpers fight for freedom and justice in a world populated by tyrants, evil mages, and dread creatures beyond imagination.

Each novel in the Harpers Series is a complete story in itself, detailing some of the most unusual and compelling tales in the magical world known as the Forgotten Realms.

To my parents, for teaching me the value of the printed word and never complaining when I stayed up late to watch Creature Double Feature.

Chult

completed 1363 D.R.
(not to scale)
A.C.

River Olung (Malina's Domain)

T'Fima's Hut

Mezro

X — Saw Triceratops Here

Batiri Village

Altispinax Swamp

Theron Captured Here
X

Theron Silvermace's Route

Kitcher's Folly
(7 days march)

Port Castigliar

REFUGE BAY

Prologue

The creature had sixteen eyes, and all of them stared hungrily at the man in the center of the circular room. The would-be victim's name—though the creature could not know this—was Artus Cimber, lauded throughout Faerun as an explorer, historian, and seeker of adventure. At the moment, Artus was crouched in front of a short stone pedestal, appraising with a practiced eye the silver statue that rested there.

With slow, careful movements, the explorer circled the pillar. He held an ancient dagger before him, the gem in its hilt casting a soft radiance over the statue. The dagger had been given to him four years past by the centaurs of Tribe Pastilar in Lethyr Forest, a reward for recovering the chieftain's sacred staff of judgment. Magical light was just one of the weapon's strange properties. And at the moment, the bared blade was the only thing preventing the creature from dropping down on Artus, for the hunter's

1

mind was agile enough to recognize such an unusual threat.

"There's no evidence the ring was ever in these ruins, Artus. Perhaps it would be best if we dusted ourselves off and went our way."

Artus glanced up at the lone entrance to the chamber just as a white-haired head appeared around the crumbling stone doorjamb. "Well," the older man asked mildly, his breath turning to steam in the frosty air, "what do you say we head for camp?" His mouth was set in a vague smile, and his bushy white brows hung like clouds over eyes the color of sapphires.

"Come have a look at this, Pontifax," Artus murmured, his attention instantly drawn back to the statue. "It's Mulhorandi from the looks of it, and very, very old, too."

A frown of concern crossed Pontifax's face, and he stepped into the room. "Mulhorandi, you say? For Mystra's sake, don't touch the thing until you've examined it under better lighting. You know what happened to Grig of Armot when he bought that blasted magical model of a Mulhorandi pyramid at the magefair. Still trapped inside, don't you know. Why, his own son—also named Grig, I believe . . ."

Without breaking off his narrative of the elder Grig's unhappy fate, the white-haired man lowered a sack full of less spectacular artifacts recovered from the ruins, then hefted the stump of a torch. The wood burst into flame, filling the circular chamber with light. On the ceiling, the creature tried to shrink back into the shadows. Finding none, it froze, hungry yet frightened by the dagger Artus wielded.

"Pontifax," Artus whispered, "it's absolutely priceless. I've never seen its like." He stood transfixed by the artifact, his gloved fingers held perilously close to its surface.

The glittering silver statue stood about two feet tall. The figure, despite the extra pair of arms extruding from its sides, was human and clad in the sandals and loincloth still favored by the natives of Mulhorand. A simple circlet rested upon its brow, as if to make up for the utterly bald pate. Around the statue's base, a series of complicated picture-glyphs marched in a regulated line.

"Can you read what it says?" Pontifax asked, leaning close. "Maybe it'll tell you why a Mulhorandi statue is sitting in the basement of a ruined keep here in Cormyr."

Artus shook his head. "The glyphs are older than any I've seen. I could make a guess, but . . ." He sheathed his dagger in his boot and rubbed the stubble on his chin. "I think you were right about this being magical, though. The silver isn't tarnished in the least."

At that instant, Pontifax's lower back decided to voice a painful complaint. He straightened with a groan, just in time to glimpse a dark shape dropping quickly and silently from the ceiling high above. "Artus!" he cried.

Sir Hydel Pontifax had been a soldier forty years past, and a mage-for-hire for much of the time since then. His mind knew, therefore, that he should shield Artus from the first assault. After all, the younger man had his back to the attacker and was still resting in a crouch, a terrible position to launch any kind of respectable defense. Sadly, Pontifax's body could only vaguely follow the orders his mind rattled off; he took a single step toward Artus, but instead of shielding him, the mage knocked his comrade into the pillar.

A colorful curse half-formed on his lips, Artus felt his shoulder strike the stone pillar and that stone give way just slightly. It was enough. The silver statue tottered on its base, then toppled. Had Artus's reflexes been as dulled as Pontifax's, he might have saved himself a great deal of trouble. Yet Artus was still a young man, just over thirty-five winters old. His mind told him to save the priceless statue from harm, and his hands did just that.

As the multi-eyed creature slammed into Pontifax, the

statue touched Artus's skin. A flash of silvery light filled the room. The explorer could only hope that he'd broken the artifact's fall, since the flash left his eyes useless and the statue had somehow slipped from his grasp. He didn't bother to grope about for the lost artifact, though. What concerned him more was the sound of a scuffle going on close at hand.

"Pontifax?" Artus asked, stumbling to his feet.

"Behind you, my boy," came the reply. "Seems this blasted creature wants us for dinner."

An animalistic growl followed, as did the sound of a body hitting the floor. Artus drew his dagger and waved it before him. With his other hand he rubbed his eyes, hoping to banish the moving blotches of light that clouded his vision. "Pontifax?"

No answer came, only the scrape of a heavy object being dragged across the dirty stone.

When Artus's eyes cleared, he saw that the room was dark save for the wan light cast by his blade. The smoking stump of Pontifax's torch lay on the ground nearby, next to the toppled pillar. From there, a wide trail of disturbed dust and rubble led to the doorway. Artus tensed for a confrontation, then took a step toward the dark archway.

"Blasted creature," came Pontifax's voice from the hallway.

"Thank Tymora's luck, you're all right," Artus breathed. As he took a step into the hall, he moved to once more sheathe his dagger. "How about a little light, my—"

It was not Pontifax awaiting Artus. The mage was laid out in a bloodied heap, his steady breathing rising from his nose like puffs from a steam kettle. No, the multi-eyed creature squatted there, repeating Artus's name with the voice of his old friend. Fortunately, Artus's dagger was still bared. The light it cast was sufficient for him to get a very clear look at the stunningly ugly thing before it sprang.

Two legs and two arms radiated out from a round torso. Its skin was dark and smooth, as devoid of hair as the silver statue's pate. Like its body, the beast's head was bulbous and bloated, with sixteen heavy-lidded, evil-looking eyes scattered about it. The source of its noiseless flight became clear the moment it moved an arm; a thin, almost transparent membrane stretched from this appendage to its side. The creature flaunted long, dirty claws and needlelike teeth.

Later, Artus would facetiously describe the beast as looking quite a bit like the animals made by street entertainers in Halruaa, using gas-filled bags they called balloons. Actually, the thing was just very well fed, having killed every man, elf, goblin, or orc foolish enough to wander into the depths of the ruined keep. And it was fully intent upon adding Artus Cimber and Hydel Pontifax to that sad roster.

Using the same tactic that had worked so well on the elder man, the creature leaped at Artus in an attempt to bowl him over. The explorer sidestepped the beast's lunge, then planted a vicious kick to its stomach—at least to where he assumed its stomach to be. Anatomy aside, Artus knew he'd hit something vulnerable from the almost-human groan the blow elicited. That noise, too, sounded like Pontifax. The thing most likely picked the noise up when it clubbed the poor old fellow, Artus decided morbidly.

Keeping a wary eye on the glowing dagger, the creature stumbled to its feet. It crouched again, preparing for another go at Artus.

"Just so long as my friend's none the worse for it, we can call this over right now," Artus said. "If the statue's yours, we'll gladly leave it here." He hoped to see the glimmer of intellect in any of the sixteen eyes squinting at him. He didn't.

They circled each other now. Arms outstretched, claws and dagger raised, they looked for all the world like two young hoodlums dueling in a back alley in Suzail or Waterdeep or any other large city in Faerun. Artus gave up hope that the creature might be intelligent enough to reason with when it started repeating the words "none the worse for it" using his own voice. It was most unsettling.

Artus edged toward the door, hoping to catch another glimpse of his friend. He kept the dagger held before him in much the same way a good priest presents a holy symbol to the forces of darkness.

This ploy was too much for the creature. To its limited intellect, it was obvious that the meal with the glowing weapon was going to pilfer its food. Desperate at losing both victims, it let its hunger override its fear. The cry the beast made as it lunged possessed no fragment of mimicked human speech, only bestial outrage and fury.

Artus, too, made an inhuman noise as he choked back a shout of surprise. When the beast charged forward, he planted one hand atop its head, breaking its momentum. With the other he planted his dagger up to the hilt in the creature's chest. The force of the blow lifted the beast off the ground. Artus expected it to shriek in pain or, perhaps, topple over. It did neither. It remained stock-still for an instant and looked at the weapon embedded in its flesh, almost as if it, too, was surprised that the attack had done little except spill some bluish gray blood.

Weaponless, Artus backed away, wishing he had struck at its stomach. The creature knew now it had little to fear, and it grabbed one of Artus's arms with its long fingers. Dirt-encrusted claws tore five holes in the explorer's thick winter coat and five bloody gouges in the skin below. With the flat of his palm, Artus struck the beast in the forehead. Far from being blinded by the attack, the creature growled in anger. Its eyes seemed as immune to damage as its chest. Teeth dripping with saliva, it opened its mouth—wide, wider—and moved toward Artus.

"See here, you damned nuisance," Pontifax mumbled from the doorway. A glowing ball of light appeared near the ceiling, illuminating the entire room.

The creature turned its head just in time to see an azure bolt flash from the mage's stubby fingers. The blast of arcane energy did not strike the beast and paralyze it, as Pontifax had intended. No, the bolt swerved violently around its target and struck Artus in the chest. But it did not paralyze him either.

With a shudder, Artus began to grow.

In moments, he was twice his normal six feet. In an instant more, three times that height. He had to drop to his side to avoid the roof, and still he continued to grow.

Needless to say, the creature was suitably flustered. Its viselike grip broken by Artus's rapid change in size, the beast tried to clamp its jaws down on him. All it got for the attempt was a mouthful of wool-lined leather. Gagging, for Artus's clothing also continued to expand, the creature rolled about the floor. At last it spit out the shredded garment. Without pause, it clambered over Artus's legs and dashed past Pontifax. The magical dagger, dislodged by the creature's haste, clattered to the floor.

"Make me stop before I bring the roof down," Artus shouted, his voice rumbling through the room. His head was propped uncomfortably against one wall, his feet just short of the other. He stopped growing just before his heels touched stone.

"Thanks," the explorer murmured. "Now, can you see about getting me down to normal height before that thing comes back with its friends and family?"

"I didn't stop your growth, Artus, just as I didn't cause it. The spell I cast was aimed at the beastie, not you, and it should have frozen him in his tracks. This shouldn't have happened." Pontifax rubbed his chin, a frown on his jowl-heavy face. "Let me come around and take a look at you."

The mage squeezed through the space between Artus's feet and the wall. His frown was matched by the one on the younger man's face, though Artus's was four times larger. Hydel walked slowly from one end of the room to the other, studying the unfortunate giant. "Ah, there's the culprit, I would imagine."

He pointed at the gaping hole in the front of Artus's coat, where the creature had bitten through. There, dangling on a fine silver chain, was a medallion emblazoned with the image of a bald, four-armed man. The silver disk gave off a wan white radiance, even in the direct glare of Pontifax's conjured globe of light. "You touched that Mulhorandi statue, didn't you?"

"Oh no!" Artus opened the collar of his coat and tried to remove the chain. It wouldn't budge.

"Leave it alone, Artus."

"But we can't leave me—"

"I need to think about this for a moment," the mage said. "Now, be a good soldier and stand down." His command had a biting edge, one gained from years in the Cormyrian army. Though the young man's frown deepened, he did as he was told.

Pontifax nodded and studied the medallion for a time. "Does it burn where it touches your skin?"

"No."

"Tingle?"

"No."

"Hmmmm." The mage steepled his fingers and stared at the silver disk. Then he stepped forward, murmured a few words of magic, and grabbed the medallion's edge. Nothing happened.

That experiment complete, Pontifax dusted a patch of floor and sat down. "The statue itself is gone, so it must have transformed somehow. I don't think it's got a curse on it, so the chain probably won't constrict until it strangles you or some such grisly thing. Still, the enchantment's not altogether friendly. It must have warped my spell somehow, just to make you grow."

Artus examined the medallion. "At least that little stunt frightened away the creature."

Pontifax nodded. "As I said, I don't think the thing's cursed. Still, it would be best if we found a wizard more familiar with Mulhorandi magic before we try to remove it."

"And my size?"

"Will probably be back to normal in a little while, so be a good soldier and wait it out." He paused, considering his next question carefully before asking it. "Has the possibility crossed your mind that there might be another curse at work here?"

"The Curse of the Ring is a myth, Pontifax," Artus snapped. His brown eyes narrowed and darkened, taking on the color of a hard-packed earthen road. "You should know that by now. We've been hunting for the Ring of Winter for almost ten years. If rumors of the curse were true, you'd think it would have caught up to us by now."

Silence hung heavy in the chamber. Ostensibly they had come to the ruined keep, set in the rough foothills of northwestern Cormyr known as the Stonelands, to recover artifacts. Whatever ancient coins or jewelry, vases or artwork they found would then be sold to King Azoun IV for a sizeable profit. Yet the driving motivation for Artus's trek to the desolate and dangerous ruins was the Ring of Winter. Over the past decade, the search for that almost mythical band of metal had become the motivation for the young man's entire life.

All that was known for certain of the ring had been gleaned from ancient histories. It had been forged by a mage of staggering power at a time when the countries that now make up the continent of Faerun were little more than scattered villages. Throughout the ages, men and women had hunted it, for it was rumored to grant unbelievable powers to the person wielding it. Exactly what those powers were varied from legend to legend, but every account agreed upon two things: the Ring of Winter contained the magical might to bring an age of ice down upon Faerun, and the ring granted immortality to anyone who wore it.

"The 'mythical' curse, as you call it, has caught up with everyone who has ever hunted the ring," Pontifax ventured at last. "Someone beloved of the man or woman who hunts the ring died. Princess Alusair lost her one true love a few days after deciding to search for the ring." He unfurled one stubby finger.

"Her lover was killed by bounty hunters trying to return her to her father," Artus scoffed.

"A curse uses many agents," the mage countered. "What of Gareth of Waterdeep? He lost his whole family, every single person who could carry on his name." He unfurled another finger, then two more. "And there's Kelemvor Lyonsbane. He thought he'd found the ring, but all he'd discovered was a deceitful ice creature that showed him a simple band of gold and killed most of his friends. And then there's—"

"But what about that dark-hearted bastard, Cyric?" Artus interrupted.

Pontifax started, then made a gesture meant to ward off evil. "For the sake of your soul, Artus, watch your tongue." He glanced around the chamber nervously. "I'll concede the argument about the curse, just don't mention *him* again."

Cyric of Zhentil Keep had once been a questor for the Ring of Winter, like the others Pontifax named. Yet tragedy had not befallen Cyric. Far from it. During the Time of

Troubles, in which the gods were cast from the heavens for their transgressions of cosmic law and made to walk Faerun in mortal avatars, Cyric had been partially responsible for the destruction of three powerful evil deities. He had then claimed the right to take their place in the heavens, and he resided there still, Lord of the Dead and Master of Strife, Murder, and Tyranny. To take his name in vain was to invite swift and terrible retribution.

"Sorry, old friend," Artus said. "I should know better than to talk about the ring when we seem so very far from finding it." Gesturing to the mage's bloodied forehead, he added, "I hope that looks worse than it is."

"Oh, the beastie did me little real harm—" Pontifax touched the lump on his head and winced "—apart from this egg. It'll take a few days to heal, that's all. Hopefully, that's more time than you'll take to shrink back to size."

Artus mumbled his agreement and settled in for a long wait. "Wounds and disaster all around," he muttered. "As usual."

One

Patrons' pipes and the small, poorly stoked fireplace on the northern wall worked together to create a haze that hung heavy in the Black Rat. Daylight crept into the tavern through two grimy windows, casting long, dark shadows. Regulars of the Rat could tell the time of day by watching those lines of darkness on the pegged floor, but on cloudy days even the barmaids were hard-pressed to tell morning from night without opening the door.

For all its murk, though, the Black Rat offered more genuine hospitality than any other tavern near Suzail's waterfront. The smell of meat simmering in the kitchens, the sounds of unhurried conversations and friendly laughter, the sight of sailors and teamsters, artisans and noblemen sharing tables without complaint—all these were quite common. Fights were few, and those few were ended quickly and without bloodshed by the soldiers who frequented the place, the Purple Dragons of King Azoun IV. It was even rumored Azoun himself visited the Black Rat from time to time, his royal identity hidden by the guise of a commoner.

Artus Cimber was reasonably certain Azoun was not among the half-dozen men and women in the tavern this particular morning. The frumpy, redheaded barmaid who seemed to live in the taproom was chatting amicably with a pair of sailors, twins in fact, from a Sembian merchantman. A few tables away, a man wearing the holy symbol of the God of Justice picked at a meager breakfast; Artus knew him to be Ambrosius, a paladin of high standing in the church of Tyr. Counting Artus himself, that left one other.

"Please sit still and stop looking around, Master Cimber," the sixth occupant of the taproom said. "I cannot be held accountable for any mishaps that might result from your fidgeting." He clucked his tongue. "After all, we wouldn't want to repeat that unhappy incident from the ruins. The owner of the Rat would not take kindly to a giant crushing his tables and chair to splinters, don't you agree?"

The man sitting across the table stared fixedly at Artus. His face was caught up in a look of casual disinterest, though his green eyes revealed the excitement he felt at examining the Mulhorandi pendant. He turned the silver disk over and over in his brown-skinned hands.

"Well, get on with it, Zintermi," Artus sighed. "Go ahead and blow us up."

The man nodded, brushing off his friend's ill humor with a practiced air. He'd known the explorer for almost twenty years, from the time Artus had entered the House of Oghma as a student. The boy had taken readily to the subjects Zintermi taught—the history and lore of Faerun. Sadly, though, he'd lacked the discipline necessary to become an instructor himself. "Close your eyes, Master Cimber," the scholar said. "This should take but a moment."

Zintermi untied the silken cords holding his sleeves closed at the wrists, then rolled the sleeves to his elbows. Gingerly, he took a vial of powder from the pocket of his black vest, then unstoppered it and poured the contents onto the fat tallow candle that flickered between him and Artus. With a hiss, puffs of gold, white, and black smoke rose over the table.

"Grant me the knowledge I seek, great Oghma." Zintermi lowered his voice to a powerful bass rumble. "For I have sought truth and recorded it in your name, bound the past for all to study and captured the fleeting lives of great men on parchment. Allow me the blessing of understanding, that I may exalt it in the transient world of mortals, that I may show others the light of reason, that—"

"That I may drone on forever," Artus grumbled. He gave his former teacher a withering look. "I'm not a yokel at a county fair, impressed by smoke and chanting. If you haven't caught on yet, Zin, I'm really worried about this thing. It may be cursed!"

Artus noticed then that the other patrons of the Black Rat were staring at him. Magic certainly wasn't uncommon in such establishments. It was often in taverns and hostels that traveling mages did their best business. From the frightened looks on their faces, he assumed they had heard him mention a curse. No one in Cormyr took such matters lightly.

Zin cocked an eyebrow. "We will need to continue this exploration out in the street if you don't keep your voice down." He turned a suddenly smiling face to the barmaid. "Have no fear, my dear. The only curse from which my friend suffers is occasional rampant stupidity."

Artus bristled at the insult. The others laughed, returning to their food and chatter.

"Now," the scholar said, slipping into the pedantic tone Artus always found incredibly annoying, "we obviously need to discuss the importance of praying to Oghma before delving into such mysteries. As you should know from your years—"

His hand held up to stop the lecture, Artus nodded. "As always, Zin, you're right. Go on with the service." He slouched back in his chair. "Just wake me up when it's over."

The droning prayer resumed. Closing his eyes, Artus let his mind wander. He had nothing against scholars like Zintermi; he actually respected the man quite highly. Much of what he knew about history, myth, and archaeology he'd learned from the old man. It was Zin's sanctimony that always set him off, that damned mile-wide streak of religious certainty. Artus was certain of only three things in his life: himself, the trustworthiness of Sir Hydel Pontifax, and the importance of the Ring of Winter.

The problem was, the latter two certainties had begun to conflict in the past few months. Hydel had been in favor of the quest for the ring ten years ago, when Artus had first decided the legends were true. They had taken up the hunt eagerly, intent on finding the ring and using it for good causes. Neither wanted the power the artifact granted in itself, but such power was necessary to fight the dark forces that were always threatening to overwhelm the lands of Faerun.

Yet more and more often Pontifax was voicing strong objections to the hunt. He claimed Artus had become blind to the reason behind the quest, that he was seeking the Ring of Winter merely to be the one to find it after it had been lost for so long. Though he disagreed with that assessment, Artus knew the old mage was right in one thing: searching for the artifact had become quite dangerous. The incident with the statue had been the latest in a three-year-long string of misfortunes.

Artus frowned and counted off a few of the more major

unpleasantries they'd faced because of the quest. Let's see, first were the murder charges in Tantras, then the un-dead halflings in Thay, then the frost giants north of Zhentil Keep. There's the Cult of Frost, of course. . . . He sighed. For almost as long as Artus had hunted the ring, Kaverin Ebonhand and his villainous Cult of Frost had dogged his every step.

"You are disturbing my rest, lackey of Oghma."

The voice was deeper than any Artus had ever heard, and it seemed to be coming from him. There was also a rumble of feet on the pegged floor as three people ran for the door. Artus opened his eyes, only to find Zin staring right back at him.

"Most unusual," the scholar said calmly. He saw Artus looking at him and pointed straight up.

There, above Artus, hovered the head and upper body of a ghostly silver figure—the statue come to life. A snarl twisted the bald phantom's lips, revealing a row of glinting teeth filed to savage points. "Should I tear the nosy one limb from limb, O mighty one?" he asked, his voice drip-ping with sarcasm.

"Of course not!" Artus yelped. He glanced at the pen-dant hanging around his neck. A trail of silver smoke rose from it to the apparition.

The spirit snorted in derision, then tossed his head back and laughed, a move that made the interlocking silver rings dangling from his ears bob and jingle. "Another dolt," he chuckled. "That is my curse, I suppose, to be servant to idiots and dolts." With exaggerated deference, he placed the palms of both sets of hands together and bowed. "If that is all, O master of men and beasts?"

The silver phantom disappeared without waiting for a reply.

"Yes . . . most unusual," Zin repeated. He casually rolled down his sleeves and retied them at the wrist.

"Can you tell me what that was all about?"

"It should be obvious, really. The statue you found was a housing for some sort of phantom servant. The four arms make him a better guardian, more dextrous at menial tasks, and so on." The scholar pointed to the medallion. "His name, I believe, is Skuld. The piece has an early forgemark from the city of Bezantur on it, so I assume it to date from, oh, thirteen to fourteen hundred years ago. I wonder how it got to that ruin in the Stonelands?"

Artus took a swallow from the mug set beside him. "So he's very old and has a cheery name. That doesn't help me a great deal. What is Skuld supposed to do?"

Zin sighed. "Their antiquity makes the runes on the back of the medallion difficult to translate, but I managed a few: protect, danger, and eternity."

"Eternity? You mean I'm stuck with this forever?"

"Perhaps. Perhaps not. The word is part of the inscription, but I can't fathom the context. Skuld reared his bald head before I could get that far." The scholar buttoned his vest, then cleared his throat noisily. "Gather your coat if you wish to keep it," he said.

Before Artus could ask why, the owner of the Black Rat stormed out of the kitchens. He was a big man, with wavy black hair hanging into his eyes. Artus might have wondered if the tavernkeeper could see clearly, save that he headed straight for Zin. Grease and ale stains spotted the apron around his waist and the shirt that partially covered his hairy chest. In one massive hand the Rat's owner held a meat cleaver. The other was balled into a fist. "I don't mind magic in my place," he shouted, "but if you scare my customers away, you're not welcome."

Sure enough, only the barmaid remained in the taproom. The other customers had wisely bolted for the street the moment the spirit had appeared. The paladin's breakfast remained half-eaten, and the Sembian sailors had spilled their drinks and toppled their chairs on the way out.

"Sorry for the commotion," Zin offered. He donned his
heavy cloak and picked up his satchel. "The money should
cover any loss." Somehow, in all the confusion, he'd taken
the time to leave a neat pillar of silver dragons in the middle
of the table. The coins more than covered the trouble.
"Come, Master Cimber. I should get back to the temple."

They left the Black Rat, the sour looks of both the
tavernkeeper and the barmaid following them. A few
people stared as they left the place—most notably the
Sembian sailors and a small group of gawkers they had
gathered around them. That crowd scattered when it became clear the Black Rat was not, as the sailors had suggested frantically, going to be blown into the Inner Sea by a
magical explosion or leveled by a rampaging spirit. They
looked vaguely disappointed.

It was getting close to highsun, and the streets near the
docks and the marketplace were teeming with people.
Merchants hawked their wares from storefronts or from
behind the handles of small carts. Servants about their
masters' business bustled from merchant to merchant, filling their baskets or their arms with wares. Grubby children playfully chased dogs from houses and shops, or
not-so-playfully flushed rats out of food stalls. Overhead,
gulls wheeled and shrieked. No one seemed to notice the
chill winter air, though the carts rattled more than usual as
they bumped over the frozen ground. Only a choking
snowfall would slow business, and then only until the snow
stopped falling long enough to be trampled into slush.

Zintermi of Oghma passed through the chaotic thorough-
fares as if he were surrounded by an invisible shield. No
one bumped into him. No overeager merchants grabbed
his spotless sleeves, trying to pass off sawdust for pow-
dered gryphon claw or some other exotic spell component.
Even the children and dogs seemed ensorcelled to steer

well clear of the scholar in their scrambles.

Artus was not so fortunate.

In short succession he was buffeted by a portly woman carrying a sack of flour, a ragman's cart, and a young boy running full tilt after a mechanical toy dragon that had escaped him. As he caught up, Artus grabbed Zin by the arm and pulled him into a doorway. "What am I going to do? The mages I've seen tell me they can't remove the enchantment."

"Skuld probably wouldn't let the enchantment be lifted," the scholar noted. "And I believe he has the power to stop all but the most skilled mages, ones with expertise in Mulhorandi magic." For the first time, his eyes took on a sympathetic cast. "Artus, I know of only one such—"

"Phyrra al-Quim?"

Zin nodded. "Even if you wanted to speak with her, she resides in Tantras now. The murder charges are still pending against you there, are they not?"

"You know they are," Artus sighed, slumping against the door. "I wouldn't bother with Phyrra anyway. That business with the Cult of Frost was just the end of a long feud. She hated me when we were both your students. She thought you gave me too many breaks."

"I did," the scholar said flatly. After glancing at the bright highsun sky visible between the close-set roofs, he added, "I really must get back to the temple. I can do a little research, but it will take some time and some more prayers to Oghma." He smiled at the exasperated look that crossed Artus's face. "Don't worry, though. Skuld may have a bit of an attitude, but I believe his purpose is to protect you from danger. This unfortunate incident could actually work to your favor, just so long as you stay out of trouble until we quantify the spirit's purpose and powers."

Artus watched Zintermi pass unruffled through the bustling, noisy throng. There were few men he respected as

much as the scholar, but somehow he couldn't bring himself to believe his hopeful prognosis. Artus boasted many
strengths and skills, but staying clear of trouble was not
counted among them.

*   *   *   *   *

"Welcome back, Master Cimber. We've missed you."
The butler who served the Society of Stalwart Adventurers bowed his magnificently horned head in deference to
Artus. He took the cloak the young man offered, folding it
gently over his arm. "Sir Hydel is awaiting you in the library." With a red, clawed hand, the butler motioned for
him to enter.

"Thanks, Uther," Artus said distractedly. He barely gave
the butler's demonic features a second glance as he hurried
inside.

The children gathered across the street were another
matter entirely. It was as if the youth of Suzail had posted
a schedule, for there were always at least six children loi-
tering there, day and night. Some begged money from
wealthier members of the society, others picked pockets
of adventurers and passers-by alike. All the ragged ur-
chins taunted Uther whenever he answered the door.

The butler had been handsome once, in a mundane sort
of way. Some women found him attractive still, though only
those favoring a more exotic lifestyle. A spell, cast five
years ago by a young dandy from Waterdeep who'd had too
much to drink and too little training in magic, had misfired
rather spectacularly. The dandy had, in a fit of unoriginality,
decided to punish the butler for refusing to refill his glass
by giving him an ass's head, albeit temporarily. It hadn't
quite worked that way.

Uther had suffered many indignities at the hands of the
younger members of the society, and he took this all in

stride. He shrugged and went laconically about his business when it was discovered the dandy's spell had made him rather resistant to any further magic, especially any aimed at restoring his mundane good looks. The huge trust established by the dandy's family—the extremely wealthy Thanns of Waterdeep—helped him adjust somewhat. Truth be told, though, Uther secretly enjoyed his new appearance. To discourage gate-crashers, all he need do was narrow his slitted yellow eyes and arch one wicked eyebrow. He'd never been forced to use the pair of twisted horns atop his head, the black claws that capped his gnarled fingers, or the pair of fangs protruding from his thin lips. Their very existence was enough to stop any brawl that broke out in the club's gaming room.

This particular afternoon, the butler was in high spirits. He placed Artus's cloak inside on a table. Then, letting his breath puff into the chill air like a snorting bull, he snarled menacingly and took a half-dozen quick steps toward the children. They dropped the sticks they'd been using as mock horns and scattered. Their whoops of fright could be heard echoing from the alleys all around the club.

Uther smiled—a terrible thing to see—and turned back to the door. A thin man in a black, hooded cloak was trying to sneak in through the open doorway.

"Are you a member, sir?" Uther asked blandly. He already knew the answer, but etiquette demanded he not directly confront the stranger with his questionable conduct.

The hooded man stiffened, then leaped for the door. Etiquette neatly put aside, Uther dashed forward to defend his post, grabbing the gate-crasher with one hand. The butler had the strength to match his intimidating visage, though even he was startled to hear a crack when he clamped down on the fellow's shoulder. The man didn't react as if his bone had been broken, but he was as cold as a frost giant's nose.

Spinning the intruder around, Uther was not surprised in the least to find his face hidden by the cloak's sizeable hood. "You are either a very, very stupid thief or an amazingly bold assassin," the butler said. His voice was now little more than a rumble. "Or, perhaps, an attorney of some sort. In any case, you're not welcome here."

Without a word, the dark-cloaked figure slid out of Uther's grip and dashed away at a stiff-legged gait. The butler watched him until he ducked down an alley a few buildings away. Satisfied that he had once again deterred an unwelcome guest to the club, he securely bolted the front door.

Once inside, the butler noted with some amusement that Artus hadn't even got past the entryway. At the end of the long corridor leading to the heart of the club, a young Cormyrian nobleman had cornered the explorer. The man—or, more precisely, the half-elf—was just over six feet tall, with striking black hair and gently pointing ears. In his hands he held a book and a long sheet of parchment. He energetically waved them both in Artus's face as he spoke.

"All I want is for you to sign my petition," the nobleman said. His voice was high with enthusiasm, and it rang in the otherwise silent hallway. "This dratted book of lies has branded my poor departed father incompetent. Imagine the fourteenth Lord Darstan, berated by a commoner! I want the king to know the Stalwarts won't stand for this sort of shoddy history, especially when it slights one of our ranks." He thrust the book—*A History of the Crusade Against the Tuigan*—into Artus's face.

The explorer stared blankly at the massive tome. He was paying no attention whatsoever to the young Lord Darstan's blathering, for he was undoubtedly on a rampage again about his father. The previous Lord Darstan had led a disastrous cavalry charge during Azoun's crusade against the barbarians. All the histories agreed upon that. The young half-elf would not be placated, though. He regularly roamed the halls of the club, jabbing his petition into everyone's face, demanding they help restore his father's good name.

The half-elf was a friend and a powerful political ally, but even that couldn't ease the growing annoyance Artus felt. "Didn't I sign this before, Darstan?" he asked irritably.

"Oh, that was a petition against that other book about the crusade. In that one, my father—"

Uther seemed to materialize at Lord Darstan's side. The butler clamped a clawed hand firmly over the nobleman's head and lifted him from the floor. "Lady Elynna has asked you to refrain from circulating the petition in the club, sir," the butler noted. He removed the book and the blank parchment from Darstan's hands. "And since she is the president of the society, I'm afraid I must enforce her word. I do so with the greatest regret, of course."

Artus recognized a rescue when he saw one, and he smiled gratefully at Uther before hurrying down the corridor and into the maze of rooms that led to the heart of the club.

In a long dining hall, a small crowd of dwarves flipped gold coins at the fifteen chandeliers, trying to make the disks land flat atop the candles, snuffing them out. The room was darker than one had any right to expect; either the dwarves were very good at the game or had been at it for days. The ringing of coins as they fell noisily to the floor, as well as the empty ale mugs and dirty dishes stacked haphazardly on all the flat surfaces, suggested the latter.

"Well met, Artus," one of the dwarves shouted. "Nice to see you back to size!"

Artus groaned and hurried through the shower of coins. Pontifax had obviously been regaling everyone with tales of their trip to the Stonelands and their misfortune with the statue.

The next room was filled with a tangle of exotic plants, so full, in fact, the walls and ceiling were completely obscured. This was the work of Philyra, the ranking druid of the Stalwarts. She didn't particularly like visiting the city and had created this riot of green as a hideaway. As Artus walked along the narrow path between the tangles of vines and bushes, a blur of color caught his eye. The growl from behind a frond-heavy plant made it clear the president's leopard had gotten loose again. The cat, like the druid, favored this room above all others.

Making a mental note to send one of the servants to collar the harmless, if somewhat grouchy, beast, Artus hurried on.

Through laboratories filled with bubbling, gurgling beakers of odd-colored liquids and sizzling arcs of magical energy, tranquil halls lined with white marble pillars where various clerics quietly debated matters both spiritual and mundane—through these and other more unusual rooms Artus passed. He'd never given much thought to the design of the club; like many things in Suzail, it had been created largely through the use of magic. If its architecture seemed out of the ordinary, its floor plan labyrinthine, then the builders had merely succeeded in creating something new to Faerun.

At last he came to the library, the largest room in the club and the central gathering spot for both old and new members. The high walls were lined with books and scrolls of every description, bound in every type of leather or hide imaginable. Ladders reached the highest shelves. There was always at least one person balanced precariously atop them, reaching for some desired tome. A winged monkey and a giant owl fluttered through the air, carrying scrolls they'd retrieved for their masters. Memorabilia of the members' exploits filled every other available spot on the walls—shields, swords, regimental colors, medals, and plaques. There were trophies of rare beasts throughout the room, the most awe-inspiring being the red dragon's head perched over the doorway. Its eyes seemed to watch the proceedings in the room with eternal malevolence.

A magnificent thousand-candled chandelier dominated the ceiling, casting bright light throughout the room. Its candles, brought from magical Halruaa, never needed to be replaced. On the ceiling around the chandelier were painted portraits of four of the five founders of the society, each in a different, remote part of the world. The fifth founder, and first president of the Stalwarts, was immortalized in a life-sized bronze statue in the room's center, directly below the magical chandelier.

Artus's eyes were drawn to this statue of Lord Rayburton whenever he entered the library. Explorer, historian, warrior, Rayburton had been all of these and more. Twelve hundred years past, when Cormyr had been little more than a rough collection of wilderness outposts, he had blazed trails to the interior of the Anauroch Desert and the heart of the Great Glacier. He'd been among the first Westerners to cross the dangerous Hordelands to the ancient kingdom of Shou Lung. His books filled three shelves, and all of them were classics in their field, the basis for a hundred other derivative works.

The thirty or so people in the library were divided into five clusters, with a few of the more studious hunched over books in the far corners. The younger members mostly told tales of their adventures, competing in both volume and exaggeration with everyone else in the room. One group had toppled a table to clear room for a makeshift battlefield. They were reenacting an old skirmish from Cormyrian history with tiny, enchanted soldiers wrought from lead. In the mock war, a line of ogres and orcs charged in a ragged line toward an arrow-straight formation of miniature human infantrymen.

"There he is now," someone shouted. "A giant among us!"

"Better clear the room in case his body swells to fit his ego again."

Artus forced a smile and headed straight for Pontifax.

The older members of the club, white-haired and pompous, encircled Sir Hydel. Their discussion rarely ranged to their own exploits—all were expected to know the merits of their elders in the society, so they had no need to brag. The senior members discussed the glories of long-dead Stalwarts and the foolishness of the youngsters. Artus knew their topic to be his own misfortunes even before he reached the circle of comfortable chairs.

"Well met," he said as he arrived. The half-dozen men and women murmured their greetings over glasses of Tethyrian brandy. In more than a few faces lurked hints of knowing smiles. "Sir Hydel . . . if you don't mind?"

"Any word on the medallion?" the mage asked as soon as they moved away from the others. He gestured to the silver disk. "I see you still have the dratted thing."

The look of genuine concern on his comrade's face lessened Artus's irritation. "I'm stuck with it for now," he replied. "Look, Pontifax, I wish you wouldn't tell everyone about what happened. I mean, the curse on this—"

The mage looked genuinely hurt. "I am the very soul of discretion," he said. "I could hardly call myself a good soldier if I ran off at the mouth about such things."

"Then how did the Raephel and the other dwarves know about me growing? What about all the comments I've been hearing since I came in?"

"Ah," Hydel said, clearing his throat. "I must admit I *did* tell an edited version of the story, leaving out anything about the curse. Replaced it with a misfired spell, you see. The story got quite a chuckle over lunch, if I do say so myself. Why, Lady Elynna even asked if I'd write it up for the society's journal!"

"Congratulations," Artus said, frowning. He wasn't sure if it bothered him more that the mage had told everyone about the embarrassing mishap or that he would never get a chance to tell his own, much livelier version of the battle. "Any luck selling the artifacts?"

Hydel puffed out his chest. "I've secured an offer of three times the amount you estimated. The society will buy all the coins and the spearheads we took from the ruins, and the sergeant of the Royal Historical Office offered to buy everything else for the king's personal collection."

Removing a thin book bound in wyvern hide from his pocket, Artus took a seat at one of the nearby desks. He opened to a page filled with columns of items and numbers, then recorded the exact amount they'd been offered for each of the objects recovered.

"You're not keeping anything from this expedition?" Hydel asked. "You usually take something as a memento."

"I have this," Artus said, holding up the medallion. "Skuld—that's his name by the way—is reminder enough for me, thank you." He clapped the thin book shut and buried it in a pocket. The journal was a prize stolen from the libraries of Zulkir Szass Tam, the undead ruler of Thay. No matter how many pages Artus filled, more appeared without ever adding to the volume's weight or thickness. The book also opened automatically to whatever page he wished to see.

"Skuld?" the mage asked. His puffy eyebrows rose in shock. "You mean the dratted thing's alive? Why, Artus, you should—"

A roar, followed swiftly by a chorus of astonished gasps and a few quite colorful curses, drowned out the rest of Pontifax's suggestion. There was a mad scramble to get away from the miniature battlefield as the reason for the disruption—a fist-sized dragon wrought of lead and painted bright crimson—circled into the air. It screeched and dove back toward the miniature armies, a stream of liquid flame shooting from its jaws.

"Foul!" cried the owner of the Cormyrian infantry. The leaden soldiers were now only so much molten slag burning its way through the expensive Shou carpet. "I say, this is really bad form!"

The other would-be general folded her arms across her chest. "Hardly, Jarnon. The rules clearly state . . ."

Sir Hydel glanced around the room, taking stock of the other members. "Looks like I'm senior," he sighed. "Better settle this before the dimwits burn the place down." The mage waded into the heart of the conflict and, with a casual gesture, cancelled the enchantment on the leaden armies. The remaining soldiers, which had scattered throughout the room to avoid the dragon, froze in place, dull metal once more. The rampaging wyrm screeched, then dropped to the floor with a clatter.

Artus shook his head. The Society of Stalwart Adventurers had been founded as a place for stout-hearted explorers and renowned world travelers to gather in camaraderie and share their findings. To be invited to join, a prospective member had to achieve some noteworthy feat and have it recognized by the society's committee. Over their thousand-year history, though, the Stalwarts had been infiltrated by Cormyr's wealthy. These men and women were often more pedigreed than brave. Their patronage financed the expeditions of the legitimate members, but they lessened the prestige of the society. Artus referred to these members as Warts, not Stalwarts.

It was at that moment, as Artus silently lamented the foolishness around him, that one of the most obvious Warts made the worst mistake of her life.

"Here, old fellow," an elfmaid drawled. "I hear tell

Theron is back from Chult. Had another breakdown, don't you know." She detached herself from a small group of sniggering nobles and sauntered toward Artus. "It wouldn't surprise me if his mind's gone for good this time." As an afterthought, she added, "Poor fellow."

Fighting to hide his surprise at the news of Theron Silvermace's return, Artus said coldly, "The only thing that could drive someone like Theron mad would be to spend too much time around the likes of you, Ariast."

He turned his back on the woman. The eldest daughter of a family that could trace its roots back to the rulers of fabled Myth Drannor, Ariast prided herself on being haughty. She held the workaday members of the club in as little regard as they held her. Like many Warts, she gloried in any gossip that tarnished an older explorer's reputation. Theron Silvermace, in particular, was a favorite target, especially after the crusty old soldier had suffered a mental collapse after escaping from a drow prison in the nightmarish underground city of Menzoberranzan.

"There's no need to be so rude, Artus," the elfmaid said, her sweet voice full of contempt.

Artus heard her stifle a chuckle. This will be trouble, he noted angrily. Ariast was known for casting cantrips on those who slighted her; the minor spells were mostly harmless, intended to embarrass the victim more than harm him. He turned to face her, hoping to give her pause before she made him belch or trip or laugh uncontrollably.

What he saw was not the pretty young elfmaid in the midst of an incantation, but the muscled back of a four-armed man standing well over seven feet tall.

"Skuld, no!"

He was too late. Before either Artus or Ariast could react, the spirit guardian grabbed the elfmaid by the wrists. "You will now know better than to harm my master, witch," Skuld hissed through filed teeth. With a quick flex, he crushed both her wrists.

Ariast's wail of pain brought the room to a standstill, but only for an instant. Within seconds, a dozen mages had launched spells meant to contain the spirit. Glowing spheres of blue and gold energy pelted the silver-skinned giant. A snaking band of light wrapped around him, then fell harmlessly away. Skuld's laughter at the magical onslaught was like the jingling of his earrings, high and musical. He tossed Ariast aside like a broken doll and prepared to defend himself against two swordsmen who were moving warily toward him.

All this time, Artus tried frantically to make the spirit return to the amulet. He shouted orders. When that didn't work, he clasped his hands. together and hammered Skuld's back. The spirit guardian did nothing to stop Artus, but he didn't follow his commands either. It was only when Uther appeared at Artus's side that Skuld paused.

"Please step aside, Master Cimber," the butler warned. His slitted eyes were narrowed as he approached the spirit. He lowered his magnificent horns and prepared to charge. "I will take care of this ruffian."

Skuld dropped his four hands to his sides, a look of surprise on his face. "You, a beast from the pit, call this little worm master?" The spirit looked at Artus and bowed respectfully. "I have underestimated you, O mighty one. Forgive this humble slave."

That said, the spirit guardian faded into a silver cloud and flew into the medallion.

Swords found their sheaths, and mages carefully placed the components for spells back into their pockets. Uther calmly righted a table and went to help Ariast. "Hey," one of the Stalwarts said to the butler, "that thing thought you were from the Abyss!"

Uther studied the man for a moment, then surveyed the chaos in the library. "There are times, sir," he said blandly as he helped the whimpering Ariast to her feet, "when I myself am forced to wonder if I'm not a willing denizen of the pit."

Artus was trying to avoid the angry glares and suspicious looks he was receiving from the other members, but it was difficult. To harm another Stalwart, even unintentionally, was considered highly improper. This would mean yet another conduct review by the president.

"Oh my," Pontifax murmured. The mage was at Artus's side, a hand on the younger man's shoulder. "If that Skuld character respects you because he thinks you're mighty enough to command creatures from the Abyss . . ."

"Then he must be used to dealing with extremely powerful and unquestionably evil masters," Artus noted. "Look, Pontifax, I think it would be best if I just went home and stayed there until Zin discovers a way to get this thing off of me."

"Well, er, that might be for the best," the mage said. He turned away from Artus. "It's just, well, Theron Silvermace is back from Chult and . . ."

"And what?" Artus prompted.

Pontifax lowered his voice to a whisper. "He's asked to see you tonight, my boy. He says he knows where you can find the Ring of Winter."

Two

"It was horrible, Artus, simply horrible."

Theron Silvermace's features resembled a corpse's more than a fifty-year-old man's. His hair was bone white, and it cascaded in long, wild strands around his head. The skin hung in loose jowls from his cheeks. The jagged scar running across the bridge of his nose was a new wound, as was the pulped mass of one ear. Dark circles rimmed his sunken brown eyes, which only heightened the frantic look in them.

"The goblins were the worst of it." Theron shuddered, then pulled the heavy blanket up to his chin and shrank back into the pillows piled behind him on the daybed. "Kwee, can't you get that fire burning any higher?"

"I will try," came the subdued response from the young man standing at the fireplace. The words sounded hollow and tinny in the cavernous room.

Artus swore silently. It was already as hot as a Flamerule

afternoon in the study. He mopped at his brow with a handkerchief and tugged at the collar of his tunic where it was chafing his neck. After the cold evening air, this heat was brutal.

His discomfort was not lost on Theron. For the first time that evening, a tiny spark of mirth lit his eyes. "This heat's nothing compared to the days in Chult," he murmured. "Bearers dropping like coins into a collection plate on a high holy day. You sweat so badly the clothes rot off your back." He looked almost wistful for an instant. "I'd suffer it again to get rid of this awful chill."

"Maybe if you added my cloak to the blankets," Artus offered, reaching for the heavy wool garment.

"No, no," Theron said, then paused. "What was I—oh yes. The goblins . . ." The haunted look swept over his face again as he renewed his tale. "It was five days out of the station at Port Castigliar, on Refuge Bay. We were searching for the ruins of a lost Tabaxi city—"

"Mezro?" Artus asked.

Theron nodded. "The heat had claimed a few of the bearers, and Sigerth, the only one from the club brave enough—or foolish enough—to go with me, died from fever. I'm afraid that's what's got me now," he noted without self-pity.

"The goblins came at night. My guide warned me about them—Batiri, he called the monsters—but we were supposed to be well away from their usual hunting territory." Theron shook his head. "Maybe he wasn't such a good guide after all. Anyway, they ate him first, so he got what was coming to him. The bearers went next."

Now it was Artus's turn to shudder. "Cannibals? Gods, Theron, I've never heard of an entire goblin tribe . . . not unless they're really desperate. Starving, I mean."

"Not in Cormyr or the rest of the Heartlands, but Chult might as well be another world." He nodded. "Yes, that's it. Chult was like another world. Kwee, you might as well give up on that. The fire's not doing me any good."

Kwee finished dumping an armload of wood into the huge fireplace. It was tall enough for a man to stand in without ducking and twice that in width. The blaze contained in this gaping maw cast a monstrously large shadow of the slight-framed man throughout the room. The darkness fluttered across a mummy stretched out in its glass sarcophagus, the dozens of shields and polearms hung upon the walls, the thick, embroidered drapes covering the glass doors, and the stunning self-portrait Theron had painted. The jewel-encrusted statue of a beautiful, fanged woman crouching opposite the fireplace was never touched by shadow. A light shone upon it· no matter how dark the study became. No one knew exactly who the statue depicted—some ancient and long-ago abandoned demigod was the most common hypothesis. Theron liked the woman's looks, so he refused to sell it to any of the collectors or museum curators who bid for it.

Kwee Chan Sen was right at home in the unusual surroundings of Theron Silvermace's study. He was a native of the eastern nation of Shou Lung and had the rounded features, almond-shaped eyes, and night-black hair of those highly cultured people. He wore a silk patch to hide the eye made blind and milk-white by a barbarian arrow. His hair hung in a warrior's topknot, an honor he had gained from five successful campaigns. Kwee had left Shou Lung four years earlier, when his uncle, the former minister of war, was executed for treason. He had joined up with Theron during a trek across the Hordelands; now he lived in the explorer's sprawling home, a setting he found conducive to contemplation of his family's disgrace.

"I am going to make myself some tea," Kwee said softly as he crossed the room. There was a strange, frightened look on his usually serene face. "You should take some,

Theron. Perhaps it will expel the fever."

"Tea," Theron scoffed. "Better bring me some brandy instead. How about you, Artus?" When the younger man shook his head, Theron said, "Bring him one anyway."

After Kwee was gone, Theron pushed himself up on the daybed. "Odd, but he doesn't like to hear about the goblins," he said. "He's fought barbarians and orcs, and all sorts of weird Shou beasts, but these stories really unnerve him."

Artus was certain it was the effect the goblins had wrought upon Theron that was disturbing to the loyal Kwee, but he said nothing. Instead, he asked, "How did you escape?"

"As I said," Theron murmured, "they did in the guide and the bearers. Me and some poor fellow from a neighboring village—a chief's son named Kwalu—they were saving for a sacrifice to some . . . *thing* they worship. Grumog, they called it. I used to hear its roars echoing up from the pit—did I tell you this god-thing lived in some underground cavern? No? Well the goblins intended to toss me and this Kwalu fellow into the pit at the center of their village. We were to be sacrifices to that horrible beast. . . ."

Theron's eyes glazed, and Artus sat back to wait. It had been this way all evening: fits of relatively lucid discussion, followed by periods in which Theron lapsed into silence or incoherent babbling. He'd been at the older man's side since arriving an hour ago. It had taken until an hour before that to settle the sizeable bill for damages to the society's library and healers for the unfortunate Ariast. She'd recover from the guardian spirit's attack—eventually. Fortunately, Hydel had volunteered to write the necessary apology-disguised-as-a-report for the society president. Things would be smoothed over, but at the cost of more than a third of the money gained from their last expedition.

"Snow," Theron muttered. "I never in my life thought

snow would save me in the jungle." Artus turned sharply to
find Theron staring at him. "That's what saved me from
the goblins and whatever it was they worshiped."

Is he rambling again? Artus wondered. Snow in the jungle, in the middle of the hot season? But when he looked at
the bedraggled explorer, Theron's eyes were clear. "Can
you be sure they didn't move you to a mountain village?"
Artus asked.

"When I escaped I was nowhere near the mountains,"
Theron snapped. "I've been through more jungles than
you've been through taverns, so I know what I'm talking
about."

"Someone with an incantation to control the weather?
They're common enough."   ·

Theron smiled. "Oh, it was someone with magic all
right, but no damned spell. It was the Ring of Winter."

"Just because it snowed doesn't mean the ring's there,"
Artus sighed. Obviously a fever dream had granted this de-
lusion about the ring. He rose slowly. "Is there anything I
can do for you before I leave? I'll call Kwee and—"

"Don't be such a dolt!" Theron bellowed. The sudden
exertion left him coughing. He slouched back on the pillows
and caught his breath. "Sit down and listen to this, then tell
me the ring isn't in Chult."

Artus did as he was told, surprised to see the Theron of
old spring to the fore so strongly. "Go on."

"I was standing in the center of the village, tied back-to-
back with the chief's son," Theron said. "The goblins were
milling around before sacrificing us. Then it started to
snow. Not just a little dusting or some freak blast of cold,
but a real blizzard. In minutes, the whole area was blan-
keted. The goblins were frightened out of their wits. They
scattered, some to grab weapons, others to hide in their
huts until the blizzard blew over—which wasn't for three
entire days. No spell can do that."

"So it's some artifact. That still doesn't prove that the ring—"

"Patience," Theron warned. "A man and a woman charged out of the bush and cut us free. Then the goblins who hadn't scattered fell upon us." He pointed to the scar across his nose. "I got this in the brawl, but we pretty well sent the little monsters packing. Before I could thank the people who'd rescued me, they were gone, taking that Kwalu fellow with them. They left me a pack with a map, food, and supplies—enough for me to make it back to Refuge Bay. I tried to follow them. Kept moving north, but somehow I got turned around. Really lost."

"Did they say anything?" Artus asked. "Who were they?"

"Oh, I knew one of them quite well, though he had no way of knowing me." He closed his eyes. "I can still see him, charging toward me with a knife in one hand and a shield in the other. Artus, it was Lord Rayburton. He's alive somehow, living in Chult. That statue in the club is an amazing likeness."

"What!" Artus yelped. Now he was certain Theron had imagined it all. Rayburton must have died over a thousand years ago. "It can't be. In your panic your mind must have played a trick on you."

A crafty grin crossed Theron's face. "I'll admit I suspected that, too, but the old boy left me some hard evidence." Stiffly he reached under the daybed and retrieved a crumpled, weatherstained scrap of parchment. "This is the map they gave me. You've read Rayburton's original journals more often than anyone else in the society. Look at the handwriting."

Artus gasped. It really did look just like Rayburton's unique scrawl—the odd, seemingly random dots over some letters, the missing punctuation. "Have you checked this with the original?"

"I had Kwee take the map to the society's library and compare it to his journals. It's his writing. There's no question in my mind." Theron watched Artus carefully. "Put the two together: Rayburton is still alive, after more than a thousand years. He appears just as it begins to snow in the jungle. . . ."

Artus's silence was all the agreement Theron needed to hear. They both knew the legendary powers of the ring; that would explain both the mysterious storm and the length of Rayburton's life.

With a trembling hand, Theron gave the map to Artus. "I won't even try to talk you out of going," he said, "though you're a fool to go anywhere near that jungle. I told you about Rayburton and the ring because I knew, some way or another, you'd find out for yourself they were there. There's only one thing I'll ask of you. . . ."

But Artus wasn't listening. His mind was already racing ahead with plans for the expedition—supplies he'd need, money to pay for expenses, transportation to Chult. A boat from the Sword Coast would be better this time of year than an overland haul, but even the trip to the coast would take a lot of time. Perhaps there was a way to fly. Hydel knew quite a few mages—

"Artus, this is very important!" Theron had struggled out from under the blankets. He had Artus by the shoulders and was shaking him as hard as he could. "I want you to contact the Harpers. You'll need their help in this. The matter's too big for you alone."

"Absolutely not," Artus said bluntly. "I've had nothing to do with the Harpers for five years, and they've had nothing to do with me." He turned up his collar to reveal a small silver pin bearing the harp, moon, and stars symbol of the secret organization. "I wear this because it might come in useful for getting out of a tight spot with some local government friendly to the Harpers. Otherwise it means nothing to me. I'm surprised the local members-in-good-standing haven't tried to take it away from me by now."

Theron sighed raggedly. "They haven't taken the pin away because they still feel you could be a very useful agent," he said. "And that's why I sponsored you as a member in the first place. You shared the group's idealism once. Now—"

"Now all I care about is finding the ring," Artus finished. "I know that's what you think, but you're wrong. I want the ring to right all the wrongs the Harpers only talk about fighting."

The young explorer grabbed his cloak and tossed it over his shoulders. "Look, Theron, the Harpers aren't an option for me any more. And there's no one at the club beside you and Pontifax I'd trust in a tough spot. You're too sick to go back, but I'll ask Pontifax. I'm sure he'll go."

As Artus headed for the door, Theron said, "You're right. The society'll be of no help to you now. It's too rife with foppery. But the Harpers—"

His features obscured by the dancing shadows from the fire, Artus turned to face his old friend. "I know you'll tell the Harpers about this . . . *for my own good*, of course. But I'll be gone by morning. Even this city's fabled web of Harper agents won't be able to close on me that quickly." His voice was full of cold resolve, but for an instant that icy tone cracked. "Good-bye, Theron. You'll be the first to see the ring when I return."

"Take care of yourself," Theron said, but the steady thud of Artus's boots was already echoing back from the hallway.

Kwee returned to the study a moment later. "So it is as you had feared. He refused to alert the Harpers?"

Theron nodded. "I hope this wasn't a mistake, Kwee. The only thing I can do now is let the Harpers know. They'll alert the few agents they have in the South. Maybe they can help him."

The window blew open suddenly, and the heavy drapes ballooned up, borne on the cold wind whipping into the room. "It wasn't this windy when I let Artus out," Kwee noted as he ran to close the window.

"Carefully," Theron hissed, sliding a dirk from under the daybed's cushions.

As Kwee reached out to fasten the window, a black-gloved hand grabbed him. The young man needed no weapons to defend himself; like many Shou warriors, he possessed deadly hand-to-hand fighting skills. Instead of trying to pull away, he anchored a firm grip on the attacker's wrist and fell backward into the room.

The figure that tumbled stiffly in from the balcony was completely garbed in black, with a long cloak and heavy cowl hiding his features. The young Shou could feel the cold radiating from the cloaked man and quickly pressed his advantage. Before the assassin could stand, Kwee kicked him in the chest, then dropped to his knees and struck at the invader's face with the palm of his hand.

The blow, which would have killed most men, only made a sharp cracking sound and knocked the assassin's cowl back. Kwee didn't know what he expected to see, but a man made completely of ice was not it. A spider web of fractures surrounded the spot where the blow had struck the ice creature's forehead. Below this, two eyes burned blue-white in a rigid, expressionless face.

The moment of shocked surprise gave the assassin the advantage he needed. He lashed out with a rock-hard fist, shattering Kwee's skull. The young Shou dropped to the floor with a grunt.

Theron pushed himself to his feet. The assassin stood slowly and began to walk toward him. A thin film of water now coated his rigid, icy face, running down into his clothes. His wet footprints stained the carpet as he came relentlessly closer. The heat from the fireplace is melting him, Theron realized. If I can keep him at bay long enough, the fire will take care of him for me.

The explorer dropped his dagger and grabbed a boar-spear from the wall, but the polearm was far too heavy for his fever-weakened muscles. The assassin knocked it from his hands with a single blow. It was clear the fire could never finish its work in time.

As the assassin closed its black-gloved hands around Theron's throat, the explorer's mind fell away, spiraling back to the goblin camp. He stood at the brink of a circular pit. Some monstrous creature bellowed in the darkness below, waiting for the savages to push him to his doom. Spears prodded the explorer, slicing bloody ribbons from his back. Without warning the air turned numbingly cold. Theron grew certain the snow had come to rescue him once again. "The ring," he croaked. "Rayburton, use the ring."

With agonizing slowness, the cold of the assassin's icy grip became the final chill of death.

* * * * *

Artus had never been a patient man. That restlessness, combined with a healthy streak of irreverence, had dashed his mother's hopes for his career as a teacher with the clerics of Oghma. It had also done in his position as a scribe for the royal court, a lucrative but incredibly dull job that could only promise him a foothold in better paying, but equally stultifying government service. The Harpers had tried to channel Artus's restless energy into various short-term projects—ridding the road to Hilp of a band of cutthroat orcs, protecting dignitaries in the Dales from Zhentish assassins, and similarly routine tasks—but even those adventurous duties lost their intrigue after a few months.

Now, when Artus stood poised to once more pick up the trail of the Ring of Winter, that restlessness proved to be more painful than any torture.

He sat in a seedy room at the cheapest, most dangerous inn on the Sword Coast. That was quite a claim, but no one with any sense contested the Hanged Man's reputation. Vermin, both human and animal, called the place home, feeding off the transient sailors and criminals who made the inn a more or less safe haven for an hour or a day or a month. Fights were frequent and deadly, the floor of the taproom having long ago been stained reddish brown with dried blood. The government of Baldur's Gate sent notices to the Hanged Man from time to time, condemning the building or revoking their hostelry license; the owner of the inn, a huge half-orc with bad breath and a snoutlike nose, posted these official notices behind the bar. The wall was covered with parchment, but no one had ever come to enforce any of the edicts.

Wanted men were safer than soldiers or bounty hunters at the Hanged Man. It was for that reason Artus chose to stay there, overruling Pontifax's strident objections; even the Harpers would likely steer clear of the inn.

As he had warned Theron, Artus had left Suzail within hours of learning the ring's possible whereabouts. He'd taken only enough time to gather a few belongings from his rented room and track down Pontifax. The old mage had secured them fast passage from Suzail to Baldur's Gate. They had flown much of the way on griffons. But when they could stand the freezing journey by air no longer, they covered the last fifty of the five hundred miles as part of a merchant caravan. In all, the long trip had taken but a few days.

"Gods, I hate this place," Pontifax sniffed. He reached down to flick a thumb-sized cockroach that had just wandered boldly onto the table before him. The daylight streaming in through the broken window didn't deter the bugs in the least. The roach hissed as the mage sent it spinning end-over-end across the room.

"Chult will be worse," Artus murmured vaguely.

"And that's supposed to make me feel better?"

Artus shrugged and sat on the room's sole, ragged bed. "You didn't have to sleep on the floor. Consider yourself lucky." He could hear the sounds of drunken snoring clearly through the wall, though that was less disturbing than the unpleasant human symphony they'd been forced to endure last night when their neighbor had been host to at least three women he'd rented for the evening.

Pushing that vivid memory from his mind as best he could, Artus pulled his notebook from his pocket. He opened to the pages he'd devoted to Theron's wild tales of the goblins and the other monsters he'd encountered in Chult. Artus had hoped to assuage his conscience, bruised by the heated exchange with the sick man, by setting his old friend's story down with the others he'd recorded. Along with his own adventures, he'd transcribed tales told to him by such notables as the great sage Elminster and Princess Alusair of Cormyr.

Unconsciously, he let a few pages flip past, until the book fell open to a section marked with a crude drawing of a harp contained in the arc of a quarter moon. Artus had never been much of an artist, but he'd attempted this rendering of the Harpers' symbol in his enthusiasm just after joining the group. Their ideals were his ideals then—protecting the cities of Faerun from danger; helping to maintain the balance between civilization and the wilderness; recording the stories of those who had passed before. It was all about freedom from fear and the right of everyone to live his life as he wished. Artus shook his head. Was I ever so ridiculously idealistic?

His contact with the Harpers had ended five years past,

with the young explorer storming out of a council meeting
in Shadowdale. He'd been assigned to monitor the activities of Eregul the Freestave, a powerful wizard who had
thrown in with the evil Zhentarim. Even after Artus had
witnessed the mage kill an innocent man, the council would
not allow him to him challenge the renegade. Too dangerous, they had claimed. Too likely to cause an open conflict
with the Zhentarim, one the Harpers were not yet ready to
fight.

But Artus was not one to bide his time. He went off in
search of Eregul, ready to bring him to justice. In the end,
though, he never had the chance to challenge the wizard.
Stalking Eregul through the twisted streets of Zhentil
Keep, he'd been captured by the Zhentarim, brought to
the city officials as a spy, and tortured. It was Pontifax who
eventually rescued him, not the Harpers. Artus had always
assumed that, since he'd given no information about the
secret organization to the Zhentish, the Harpers didn't
consider him a threat. That's why they'd left him alone
these past five years to pursue justice as he saw fit.

A sharp creaking brought the explorer out of his musings. "The door," he snapped. Pontifax had magically
barred both the door and the window, so the intruder had
to be a mage of no small skill.

"Oh my," Pontifax gasped. "Look at the bugs."

The roaches and centipedes, so bold a moment before,
were scattering. They tumbled off the table and the walls in
their haste to find cover. Most raced for the cracks snaking
across the plaster walls. Others went for the window,
abandoning the Hanged Man for a safer home.

The door creaked fully open, and a huge scorpion skit-
tered in. The thing was half the size of a man and as black
as a zombie's heart. Small patches of hair, drooping like a
cat's whiskers, covered its hide. Its tail curled behind it as
it hopped sideways to clear the door.

Pontifax cursed. He'd drawn a small square of grayish ghoul flesh from his pocket; with it, he could paralyze anyone who entered the room, but only by touching them. He hadn't counted on their foe being anything like this.

Artus, too, was at a loss for what to do. He stood little chance of killing the scorpion with his dagger before it stung him. He looked down at the medallion, but it remained dormant on his breast. Where was Skuld? Now that I need the spirit to help, Artus lamented to himself, he doesn't appear. I thought the four-armed thug was supposed to protect me from danger.

"Do not fear my friend," came a reedy voice from the hallway. "He will not harm you unless you attack him—or me."

The man who entered the room matched his thin voice perfectly. His legs were like stems, clad in loose-fitting white pants made of rough cloth. His shirt, which wouldn't have fit either Pontifax's bulk or Artus's well-muscled torso, billowed around him like a sail. One sleeve was pinned closed where he was missing an arm. The other hung loose over a limb that looked like it belonged on a scarecrow. His features were sharp and angular, topped with a mop of unwashed gold hair resembling straw. His blue eyes glinted like sunlight on the ocean.

With his remaining hand, he pushed the door closed behind him. "I hear you gentlemen are looking for passage to Chult," the stranger whispered.

Pontifax stuffed the gruesome spell component back into his pocket, but Artus neither sheathed his dagger nor straightened from his defensive crouch. "Who sent you?" the explorer asked warily.

Chittering, the scorpion took up a position in front of his master. The thin man patted the curve of its bulbous tail, carefully avoiding the wicked stinger. "I'm here on behalf o' the Refuge Bay Trading Company," he said. "Now, put away your dagger, good sir, or you'll be upsetting my companion here. Neither o' us would be too pleased with the results if you got him too riled."

Warily Artus stuck his dagger into the tabletop. It would be easier to retrieve there if a fight broke out.

"I don't begrudge a wise man his precautions," the stranger said, gesturing to the knife. The gem in the hilt glowed faintly, even in the sunlight. "I just can't abide open threats."

"Who told you we need passage to Chult?" Pontifax asked.

"Well, you gentlemen put word out, did you not?" He didn't wait for an answer before continuing. "The trading company happens to have a ship anchored out o' port, ready to be on its way to Refuge Bay. The cost isn't light, but then, we're talking about a fine lady o' the sea, a galleon what made this trip to Chult a dozen times and a captain what made it a dozen more."

The discussion quickly turned to the cost, which was higher than Artus had expected and barely what he could afford. After a few terse exchanges—punctuated by the scorpion's chittering—the amount was decided. Pontifax counted out half the gold coins required and held them out for the stranger.

"Put them in a bag, if you please," the thin man said. He gestured to his missing arm. "This was taken by pirates off Ioma. This—" he held up his hand, which was almost paralyzed into a fist "—is the unfortunate result o' taking more than my share o' the company's money. That's why they gave me the scorpion, you see?"

When Pontifax held out the money, the scorpion scuttled forward. It reached up with one huge claw and took the bag, then backed away.

"Just like a new set o' hands," the stranger said, laughing. The scorpion opened the door with its free claw and hurried out. "I'd better catch him before he spends all the money in the taproom." He winked. "Kind o' a ladies man, you know. Remember, the other half goes to the captain the moment you get aboard. A longboat will be waiting to take you to the *Narwhal* at midnight."

With that he disappeared after his poisonous cohort.

Pontifax walked over to close the door, but stopped short and cursed. "The blasted wards I set upon the door are still in place," he hissed. "Somehow he and his pet strolled right through them."

Pulling his dagger from the tabletop, Artus said, "Use this to jam it shut. No insult intended, but that'll probably slow down any intruders in this place better than your magic." He slumped onto the bed. "Besides, a dagger won't do me any good in a fight here, not with things like that scorpion running loose in the halls."

He tugged at the medallion. "I wonder why Skuld never showed himself."

"Obviously you were never in any serious danger." The mage closed the door and plunged the dagger through the wood, into the jamb. "Perhaps the scorpion's poison had been removed."

Pontifax set about the tedious task of checking and re-checking the three packs they'd stowed in the corner near the window. When he shifted the first, a mangy rat turned its beady eyes to him, then scrambled across the room to a hole in the floorboards.

"Artus, I should make you go through every shirt in these packs looking for unwelcome stowaways. I was against staying here in the first place, and we'll probably get a horde of fleas in our breeches for the bother. . . ."

Artus didn't hear a word of his old friend's diatribe. He'd settled back against the wall, absorbed in his journal once more.

Three

The ship's boat struggled along in the open water outside the sheltered harbor at Baldur's Gate. The wind had picked up at sunset, and the waves were tipped with the slightest caps of white. The eight-man crew didn't seem to mind. They strained against the oars, making good speed despite the rough seas.

As arranged, Artus and Pontifax had met the longboat at midnight, on the southernmost pier, closest to the ocean. The *Narwhal*, it seemed, was anchored outside the port. Artus took this as a bad sign; had the ship been engaged in strictly legal activity, it would seek the safety of the harbor, not shun it. Despite her registration to the Refuge Bay Trading Company, the *Narwhal* was in all likelihood little more than a pirate ship.

"Yer looking a little anxious," taunted Nelock, the only officer aboard the ship's boat. He had the look of a wild ape about him. His hairy arms hung out of his sleeves as he lounged at the boat's prow, his thick features locked in an expression of extreme ill-humor. "Could it be yer beginning to think we're taking ya out far enough to dump yer bodies where no one'll find 'em?"

The thought had occurred to Artus, but he'd dismissed it. The notion was a surprise to Pontifax, however. The old mage blanched, his sudden distress made clear to everyone by the light of the full moon overhead.

"Hardly," Artus said, leaning back against one of their packs. "You could have robbed us on the docks. Two more bodies found in the harbor wouldn't cause a stir, not in a port as big as Baldur's Gate."

The crew's barking laughter rang out over the open water. "Awright," Nelock snapped, "stop yer yapping and put yer backs to it. If the captain hears ya making a racket rowing up to the ship, she'll have the lot of ya under the cat-o'-nine-tails."

Silence fell upon the ship's boat, fear of the *Narwhal*'s captain clamping down on the sailors like a vice. Artus and Pontifax thought better of testing the boatswain's warning. They rested patiently in the stern, watching the dark shape of the ship grow larger and larger.

As the company agent had said at the Hanged Man, the *Narwhal* was a galleon. Such vessels were rare in Baldur's Gate, since ships meant for peaceful trade dominated the ports of the Sword Coast—cogs and caravels and dromonds that mainly skirted the coastline. Not only was the galleon larger than these, it was obviously constructed with more aggressive ventures in mind. At regular intervals, black squares broke the wide stripe of white paint that ran the length of the hull. As the ship's boat drew closer, Artus noticed the holes looked like missing teeth in a giant's smile. He knew, however, that behind each port stood a heavy ballista capable of firing iron-shod spears or bags filled with shrapnel or even more ingenious projectiles.

A few lights winked furtively aboard the tri-master as Nelock guided the small boat to her side. Two crewmen hustled to the task of fastening lines to the bow and stern as the apelike officer pulled a whistle from under his heavy coat and blew a series of four notes. Instantly, a hatch opened halfway up the *Narwhal*'s hull. A lantern appeared, then a blond sailor peered out of the entry port.

Warily, Pontifax eyed the line of steep, water-slick steps cut into the ship's side. He'd never been particularly dextrous, and this obstacle appeared potentially dangerous, even to the most agile of sailors. "I don't suppose you'd allow me to stay in this fine craft until you haul it up to the deck. . . ."

The officer pushed past the old mage and, by way of an answer, started up the twenty boarding steps at a run. He paused partway up. "It wouldn't be wise to keep the captain waiting, gentlemen," he warned, then continued up the steps.

Placing a hand on Pontifax's shoulder, Artus whispered, "You can always use a spell to fly to the deck or climb up the side like a spider."

"Bad idea all around," the mage grumbled. He placed one foot tentatively on the first step. "Magic shouldn't be used to shield oneself from the little challenges of life. It won't win us any respect from the crew, either."

A wave rocked the ship's boat, knocking Pontifax off his feet. The crewmen could have broken his fall, but they didn't. The white-haired mage crashed to the deck. There he floundered about in his heavy robes like a game fish until he became thoroughly entangled in a coil of rope. And still the silent crewmen sat and watched, smirks twisting their faces.

Artus helped his friend out of the rope's grasp and pulled him to his feet. "Look, Pontifax, you—"

"Be a good soldier and get out of my way," the mage rumbled. After pausing for a moment to straighten his robes, he cast a withering look at the crewmen. They received the glare with lazy, indolent faces. Pontifax murmured something as he stepped up to the boarding ladder, his fingers moving in an arcane pattern.

Only Artus seemed to notice the mage was casting a spell. Probably to help him keep his footing, the explorer decided.

Artus watched his friend struggle up the hull. The rolling ship did its best to dislodge the boarder, heaving up and down in the choppy seas, but the mage gamely made the entry port. With a sigh of relief, Artus followed.

The blond elven sailor with the lantern gave Artus a hand and pulled him into the portal from the top boarding step. "Welcome aboard the *Narwhal*," he said, holding the lantern high so it would cast its light evenly over the newcomers' features. "I am Master Quiracus, the ship's first mate. You've already met Nelock." He gestured with the lantern at the hairy officer. "He's the boatswain."

Nelock pulled a battered felt cap from the pocket of his heavy coat. He raised the hat facetiously at Artus, then Pontifax. "We'll be fast friends by the time a tenday's out."

Frowning at the sarcasm, Master Quiracus said, "No need to be discourteous, Nelock." He ignored the startled look on the boatswain's face. "I'll take these gentlemen to the captain. You snap to it and supervise the stowing of the ship's boat. Take their gear and pile it near the mainmast until the captain decides where to put them." He turned from the portal and strode into the darkness of the ballista deck.

Artus and Pontifax hurried to keep within the glow of the lantern. The deck was a cramped, crowded place, smelling of sweat and sea salt. Huge ballistae hunched before the ports, a ready store of ammunition close at hand.

Hammocks slung from the deck-head beams near each siege engine held snoring, muttering sailors. Though he could not see the entire deck, Artus figured there to be at least one hundred men in this part of the ship alone.

The first mate took the steps leading to the upper deck two at a time. When he made to do the same, Pontifax slipped again and fell back against Artus.

"That spell you cast in the ship's boat couldn't have worn off already," Artus said.

"Whatever do you mean?"

"Before you climbed into the ship you used a spell to give yourself steady footing."

The mage snorted. "Hardly." Lowering his voice, he said, "I cast a little incantation·on the lazy dogs who enjoyed my difficulty. For the next few nights, they'll be dreaming of nothing but slightly overweight mages dropping on them from great heights."

"Hurry along, gentlemen," the first mate called from the top of the stairs. "Captain Bawr is awaiting us on the poop deck."

A cold wind blasted over the quarter deck, limning the rigging with ice and setting the masts to creaking. That didn't seem to affect the sailors, who went quietly about their work. Toward the bow, Nelock and a handful of crewmen secured the ship's boat. Others climbed the rigging to vantages high up the masts. From the activity, it appeared to Artus the watch was changing.

"Whatever you do," Quiracus warned as they made their way to the rear of the ship, "be sure not to challenge the captain's word. Go along with whatever she says." He flashed them a warm smile. "If there's a problem, I'll do what I can to straighten it out later."

Artus steeled himself as they climbed to the poop deck. The captain sounds like a real terror, he thought. Luckily, though, the first mate seems friendly enough.

"Captain Bawr, these are the two gentlemen you were expecting."

In his mind, Artus had created his own Captain Bawr—a tall woman with cold eyes and a lantern jaw. Her clothes would be coarse, the sword at her side polished brighter than any smile she could muster. A widow's knot would hold her hair tight. A perpetual air of disdain would lurk in her stance and her movements. Maybe she would bear a scar or two from mutineers—all of whom she would have sent to a watery grave.

"Welcome aboard my ship," Captain Bawr said, her sweet voice like the whisper of an owl's wings. She held out a dainty hand, gloved in kidskin against the cold. "I hope the authorities did not present too much of a bother to you in Baldur's Gate."

Pontifax shook her hand without pause, but Artus stood astounded by the petite beauty before him. She looked almost ghostly in the moonlight, her oval face brightened by an alluring smile. A red cloak, its hood capturing her dark ringlets, hung to her waist. Below that, a white skirt trailed down to silken hose and shiny black shoes. Her blue eyes sparkling with a hint of mischievousness, Captain Bawr reached out and took Artus's hand, which dangled limp at his side. "I'll take your silence as a compliment. . . ."

"Artus, milady. Artus Cimber."

Pontifax stifled a groan. They'd agreed not to give their real names on this voyage, but Artus was obviously too smitten to catch himself. No use bothering now. "And I am Sir Hydel Pontifax," the mage huffed, shooting Artus a gruff look. He removed a small purse from his belt. "This is the rest of the fee agreed upon by the company agent in port."

The captain smiled and gestured to Master Quiracus, who took the purse. As the first mate silently counted out the coins, Captain Bawr asked, "What do you do, Sir

Hydel, when you are not traveling?"

"I have studied the arts, both medical and sorcerous. I've made my living plying both."

The first mate looked up sharply. "A doctor? That's a nice bit of luck, eh Captain?"

The look on her face made it clear the captain had little interest in doctors or mages. When she turned back to Artus, though, a tiny spark rekindled in her blue eyes. "And you, Master Cimber?"

"I, er, mostly travel, milady," he stammered. "I've been a scribe and an explorer and a historian."

Her pouting frown made it clear Captain Bawr found that answer even less interesting than Pontifax's. "Ah, how . . . mundane," she managed at last. "And why are you seeking speedy passage on a ship like the *Narwhal,* Master Historian? Did you mistakenly record the name of a king's bastard in a chronicle? Perhaps you've run off with some money from an abbey." She held up one slim-fingered hand. "I know, you misspelled a wealthy and influential merchant's name in a town record and you're now running for your life. It would have to be something that inconsequential, I'm sure."

The sweetness in her voice had transformed into an unmistakable malice. That was enough to break the spell that had fallen upon Artus. He bristled at the insults, squaring his shoulders and jutting out his unshaven chin. "I've seen a great deal of danger in the last two tendays, milady, and I do not take kindly—"

"The only danger you've ever faced, Master Historian, was your patron's wrath at a bottle of spilled ink," the captain drawled. She idly waved a hand and turned her back on Artus. "Quiracus, take the old man down to the orlop, where he'll be quartered as surgeon for the voyage. Our ink-stained friend will be put in Nelock's charge."

"Wait a minute," Artus snapped. "What do you mean 'in

Nelock's charge?' We're not signing on as crew, Captain. We're paying passengers."

The moment the words left Artus's mouth, his medallion began to glow with a brilliant silver-blue aura. At the same time, Captain Bawr spun around, her face contorted by an unearthly rage. She had grown at least a foot—or perhaps it only seemed that way to Artus and Pontifax. The captain's pale skin had become a mass of blood-red scales, her eyes a pair of glowing blue embers. "Get them out of my sight, Quiracus," she howled. "Now!"

With surprisingly strong hands, the first mate grabbed both men and hustled them off the poop deck. "Gods," he cursed when they were well toward the middle of the ship. "I warned you about questioning her orders." He glanced back to the aftcastle, where Captain Bawr paced back and forth like a caged animal. "I won't be able to change her mind about the assignments, not after you openly challenged her."

"Then we'll leave the ship now," Artus said firmly.

Pontifax nodded. "Right. We'll take the next vessel to Chult. This won't do for a man with my record of service to the Cormyrian army. I refuse to be pressed into service aboard this slave ship like a drunk waylaid in—"

Quiracus clamped a hand over the mage's mouth. "My apologies, Sir Hydel, but you're crew now. If the captain hears you mutter that kind of mutinous talk, there'll be nothing in this world that'll save you from her wrath." He let Pontifax go, then smiled. "Besides, we'll be under sail in an hour, so the only way back to the harbor is to swim for it."

Artus walked stiffly to the mainmast, where the sailors had dumped their gear. "We'll have to make the best of it," he growled, pounding the sturdy wood with a fist. He tossed one of the packs to the mage, then hefted the other two himself. "I'm sorry about this, Pontifax."

The withering look he got in return told Artus it would take more than a simple apology to assuage his old friend's wounded pride.

*   *   *   *   *

"Cimber, need I teach ya the proper way to tie off the topsail halyards again?"

Artus jumped at the sound of Nelock's voice. The boatswain had taken a special interest in harassing him, pointing out his most inconsequential mistakes and meting out ridiculous extra duties for any transgression. "No, Master Nelock," he said, biting back his anger and frustration. It would do him little good to pique the apelike petty officer.

"Well ya done this all wrong," came the expected response. After a moment's pause, the boatswain barked, "Into the rigging, Cimber. I thought I heard a sail tear on the mainmast, so ya better check it for me."

"Yes, sir," Artus managed to reply.

The explorer dreaded the long, unsteady climb into the rigging. Luckily, much of the ice had melted away from the ropes after the first tenday at sea, so they weren't as slick as they had been. The weather, in fact, was fast becoming balmy. Still, the brisk wind hissing into the sailcloth and the not-so-gentle roll of the ship made the duty quite dangerous for someone as inexperienced as Artus. Moreover, he knew the sail to be perfectly sound; unless the cloth had torn from top to bottom, the boatswain couldn't possibly have heard it over the cry of the gulls, the creaking of wood and rope, and the roar of the *Narwhal* cutting through the waters of the Sea of Swords.

Tentatively, Artus climbed into the shrouds. The tar-soaked ropes were sticky on his bare feet, but he'd learned on his first day aboard the ship that his boots were not made for nautical feats. As he went, he scanned the huge sails of the mainmast—at least, he made a show of looking them over for tears. His mind was actually drifting in languid turns over the events of the last few tendays. First the cursed medallion, then Theron Silvermace's news of the ring and the flight from Suzail. Now he was paying for the privilege of being a slave aboard a galleon. He'd been right about the ship being a pirate vessel, but he never could have guessed the rest of its past.

Artus had been told of the *Narwhal*'s short, but astounding history his first night aboard ship. The costly vessel had once flown the flag of Cormyr's navy, but Captain Bawr had gathered a fleet of pirate ships together in the Inner Sea and taken her by force. Next she cut a deal with the villainous masters of Zhentil Keep, who provided her with the services of a group of stupid but extremely brawny giants. The monstrously strong creatures carried the *Narwhal* across the bulk of Faerun, from the land-locked Inner Sea to the wide-open Sword Coast. Now Bawr alternated between outright piracy and high-paying cargo runs for the Refuge Bay Trading Company, carrying supplies to their outposts in the jungles and returning with the ship's holds full of near-priceless Chultan teak and ivory.

Of Captain Bawr herself he could learn little. The crew spoke of her in hushed tones, but always in glowing terms. They were loyal, but fearful, too. They'd all seen her transform at various times, though no one dared venture a guess as to her true nature. The only thing Artus discovered was she never came on deck during the day; when the sun shone, Master Quiracus and the other officers ran the *Narwhal*.

Artus shook his head. The contrast between the sweet young woman and the creature she became . . . He shuddered. It was horrifying to think on the matter too closely.

All thoughts of the captain fled his mind in that instant, driven away by sudden panic. Lost in his musings, he'd taken a wrong step. For a moment, the realization he was going to fall overwhelmed Artus. Then he toppled head over heels down the shroud. The net of ropes burned his arms and legs as he slid. He reached out, but discovered painfully he was moving too fast to stop his fall. It seemed he was going to either roll right down the shrouds and over the side, or slip from them and plummet to the deck.

Fortunately, Skuld was not about to let his master break his neck on the quarterdeck or drop into the sea like so much shark bait. A glowing silver hand shot from the medallion and clamped down on the shroud. Artus gasped, then choked as the chain pulled tight. His momentum gone, he slipped limply between the ropes. The explorer hung below the shroud for an instant, the medallion's chain and the silver arm suspending him like a hangman's noose. Then he was falling again, this time like an autumn leaf drifting slowly to earth.

When the chain had loosened its chokehold and the blood ceased to throb in his temples, Artus tried to sit up. The silver arm was gone, but it was clear everyone near the mainmast had seen his unearthly rescue.

"What's this all about?" Nelock shouted. He stood over the dazed explorer, his hands on his hips. "No sailor's allowed to use magic without the officers knowing about it. The captain will want you—"

"Sent to the surgeon to see about his wounds," interrupted Master Quiracus. The first mate was at the boatswain's side. When Artus looked up, a halo from the sun ringed the blond man's head. "Go on, Cimber. Have Pontifax see to those cuts."

It was then Artus realized his shirt collar was heavy with blood. The chain had dug into his neck, but only enough to draw a ring of crimson. When he moved to lever himself to his feet, he found his hands gouged and bloody, too.

"It looks worse than it is," Quiracus noted calmly. "Still,

better to clean out the wounds before they become infected. Don't you agree, Master Nelock?"

The boatswain muttered his agreement, then turned to the crowd of sailors who had paused in their work. "Awright, back to yer duties, ya bilge rats."

As Nelock looked around, he saw men and women pulling lines out of synch, and midshipmen caught in idle speculation about the strange magic that had saved Artus's life. The crew had been working at top form, like the well-tended engine they were trained to be. Now they were at odds, slowing the ship and making their own tasks harder by working against each other.

In his deep, growling voice, Nelock began to sing. The chanty was an old one and had a hundred variations all along the Sword Coast. The crew soon picked up the song. Its rhythm became the pulse of the ship, and the crew began to once again work in harmony.

> *My love was a lass from Shadowdale,*
> *A beauty with hair of silver.*
> *A pirate from Presper stole her away.*
> *The sea take all pirates from Presper, brave boys,*
> *The sea take the pirates of Presper.*
>
> *My love was a lass from Marsember,*
> *And we were to wed last Mirtul.*
> *A whaler from Westgate stole her away.*
> *The sea take all whalers from Westgate, brave boys,*
> *The sea take the whalers of Westgate.*

"Despite your foul temper, you are quite good at your job," the first mate noted as he came to the boatswain's side.

Nelock rubbed his hands along his hairy forearms. "What I'd like to know, Master Quiracus, is why ya care about them—especially that useless Cimber. This is the third time ya've hauled him out from under a punishment I had in mind for him. It ain't good to undercut me with the men around."

The first mate smiled. "There are reasons for everything, Nelock. You just aren't privy to them." He patted the older man on the shoulder patronizingly. "You should consider yourself lucky."

The boatswain watched the first mate stroll across the quarter deck to the aftcastle, then disappear down the stairs that lead to the captain's cabin and the maproom. "Something ain't right about this," Nelock muttered to himself. "But I ain't stupid enough to get caught in the middle of it either."   .

The boatswain started another chorus of the chanty, and the dark thoughts troubling him flew away with the notes of the bright old sea song.

*   *   *   *   *

Deep in the ship, on the bleak and damp orlop deck, Artus could hear the chanty belted out by the sailors. It didn't lighten his thoughts the way it did Nelock's, but then he'd never been one to appreciate work songs. He much preferred the refined bardic music of Myth Drannor and the Moonshaes.

"How've you been, Pontifax?" he asked somewhat sheepishly.

"Fine. Now be a good soldier and sit on the table," was the somewhat chilly reply. "Take your shirt off so I can get a look at the wounds on your neck."

The mage bustled about the large room, only a small part of which was lit. Two magical globes of light floated at Pontifax's shoulders, but they did little to help dispel the gloom from the place. "I've spent the last tenday setting broken limbs, bandaging gashes received in mindless brawls, and ministering to petty officers with hangovers," he offered as he grabbed a handful of cotton wrapping. "Same sorts of silly injuries I worked on when I served with the Army of the Alliance—until the fighting started, of course. The barbarians dealt in more ghastly wounds. In fact, I spent most of my time on the crusade making men comfortable until they died. . . ."

Artus dropped his bloodied shirt to the floor. Whenever Pontifax was disgusted with things, he talked about King Azoun's crusade against the barbarous Tuigan tribesmen. He had served as a surgeon during the entire campaign and had even fought alongside the royal War Wizards in the final battles. There were few·things Pontifax prided himself upon more than this.

Pontifax sighed. "Did you know there are passengers aboard who don't have to work?"

"What?" Artus leaped to his feet, spilling a bottle of strong-smelling liquid. It splattered on his scraped hands, stinging like a thousand wasp bites. "Gods' blasted . . ."

"Serves you right," the mage said. He righted the bottle, mopping up the spilled liquid with Artus's shirt. "Now sit down before you really hurt yourself."

"But if there're paying passengers aboard who don't have to—"

"These privileged passengers have taken over the captain's cabin," the mage warned, "so don't go making a fuss just yet. Bawr's sleeping in the maproom to make space for them." He glanced at the long slice in Artus's neck, then dabbed the blood away. "They're important ambassadors on their way to Samarach on a secret trade mission. Quiracus told me about them one night after dinner. They paid ten times what we did."

"But I haven't seen anyone who even vaguely resembles a government-type strolling the decks."

"They're more secretive than the captain." Pontifax began to clean the scrapes on Artus's hands, dousing them with more of the stinging liquid. "Besides, you should be glad they haven't seen you. They're from Tantras."

Artus groaned—both from the pain in his hands and the dread in his heart. Government officials from Tantras! Both he and Pontifax were wanted men in that city, for murder and a dozen other charges, all stemming from a battle they'd had with Kaverin Ebonhand three years past. If the ambassador heard they were aboard the *Narwhal*, he might try to take them into custody or even worse, try them on the spot for their crimes.

"There." Pontifax stood back to study his work. "I can't do anything about the cut on your neck. The chain's in the way. The wrap on your hands will keep you away from hard duty for a couple of days, anyway." He shook his head. "Despite our fears, Skuld has been a gift from the gods so far. Maybe this unfortunate voyage will all turn out for the best, too."

"Just so long as we get to Chult," Artus said. "That's the only way I can keep taking the mindless abuse Nelock dishes out on deck—keep thinking about the ring."

Pontifax turned serious eyes on the explorer. "What would you do to get the ring, Artus? I've had a lot of time to think down here, and I've been wondering about that."

"Anything," the explorer replied without hesitation.

"I was hoping you wouldn't say that." Pontifax went back to stowing medical supplies. "I really don't want to believe you, you know, but a little part of me does. I'm frightened for you, my boy."

Artus stood and headed for the ladder to the upper decks. "Don't worry, Pontifax, I wouldn't murder children or do the sorts of despicable things Kaverin Ebonhand would do to possess the ring."

"But you'd let yourself be made a slave aboard a stolen

ship," the mage said, his sapphire eyes clouded by sadness. "That's rather telling, I think, since you say you want to use the ring to preserve freedom." He balled Artus's bloody shirt and tossed it into a bucket. "And if you're willing to stoop that low, you might just be telling the truth. Maybe you would do anything for the ring."

Four

"And you write every night?" Quiracus asked amicably. He rested his pointed chin in one hand and looked thoughtfully across the table at Artus. "I'm almost afraid to hear what you say about the *Narwhal* in that journal of yours."

Artus patted the thin book that lay closed before him. "Actually, I'm getting used to life aboard ship. I'm almost sorry we'll be in Refuge Bay in a few days."

The two sat in the ballista deck. Though it was night, the heat hadn't subsided; the place smelled of sweat and unwashed clothes. Wan moonlight leaking in through the ports and the glow from a lantern atop the slightly swaying table gave the scene an eerie, otherworldly feel, but Artus had grown accustomed to the silent blackness of the lower decks at night. In a neat row all along both sides of the ship, men and women slept soundly, lulled by the rush of water along the hull. The tabletop, like Artus's hammock, was

64

suspended from the beams overhead.

Behind the first mate, the weapon Artus had been assigned to tend in case of attack hulked in the near-darkness. It was like most of the engines aboard the ship, a type of giant crossbow meant to hurl bolts the size of a man. The weapon fascinated Artus; its simple, graceful design clashed intriguingly with his knowledge of its destructive potential.

In the past few days, Quiracus had paid Artus many visits, and they'd discussed the ballistae and a dozen other topics. The elf seemed genuinely interested in striking up a friendship, almost as if he were trying to make up for Captain Bawr's strangeness and Master Nelock's outright hostility. Artus welcomed the camaraderie, especially since the crew tended to stay well clear of him for fear of attracting the boatswain's wrath. The first mate boasted a ready wit and an uncanny knack for avoiding all the right subjects. He'd even given Artus a few fragments of ancient elven tales for his journal, though he was a dreadful storyteller.

"I never tire of life at sea," the first mate offered. He stood and peered around the ballista to get a better look at the water. The breeze blew his golden hair back from his pointed ears. "I mean, just take a look at the moonlight glittering so brilliantly off the water—"

The first mate paused, then pushed his head farther out the port and glanced up at the moon. Cursing, he pulled himself back against the ballista. "Battle stations!" he bellowed. "Man the ballistae! Ready the starboard side for firing!"

The words echoed in the confines of the deck, rattling everyone from their slumber. With amazing speed, the men and women leaped from their hammocks and set about winching back the powerful metal bands that launched the bolts. A few of the younger boys ran along the deck, stowing the hammocks, lighting lanterns, and clearing cups and plates from the tables. Others began to pull the heavy lances from their storage piles, stacking them atop those same tables, which had held the sailors' dinner not so long ago.

"What's going on?" Artus asked as the first mate pushed past, heading for the stairs to the quarter deck.

As if in reply, the *Narwhal* listed heavily to one side. A lantern smashed, spilling its flaming oil across the deck. Before the fire could spread, two sailors doused it with buckets of sand. The plaintive groan that filled the air could be heard even over the shouted orders, the clatter of metal plates, and the clacking of the ballistae as the crews cranked and loaded them. It was the hull crashing against something large and solid.

Artus, like many of those around him, struggled to his feet. The first mate laid a steadying hand on his shoulder. "Come with me," the elf said. "I think you'll be of more value to us on the quarter deck."

As he hurried to the stairs, Artus didn't notice the first mate stop to retrieve his journal from where it had fallen to the deck. Quiracus slipped the wyvern hide-bound book into the pocket of his baggy cotton pants. "Wait for the order to fire!" the first mate shouted to no one in particular, then rushed to the stairs himself.

The scene on the quarterdeck was even more chaotic than below. In a half-dozen places, sailors lay in heaps, broken limbs jutting out at ridiculous angles from their bodies. They had obviously fallen from the rigging when the *Narwhal* listed. Pontifax leaned over one unfortunate woman. Two men held her down as the mage reset her dislocated shoulder. Other sailors scrambled for the pikes strapped to the masts, ready to repel any boarders.

Off the starboard bow, an island had seemingly risen from the sea. The dark, rocky mound was almost half the length of the *Narwhal*. Gorgeous patterns of silver glittered all along the gentle curve of its sides, broken in places by trailers of seaweed. A sharp ridge ran along the center, leading to another, smaller mound—

Artus gasped. It was a head!

"It's Aremag again," Nelock shouted as he ran past, racing for the poop deck.

"I know," Quiracus snapped. He hurried after the boatswain, Artus in tow. This uncharacteristic anger made the elf look oddly nefarious—his arched eyebrows knit together, his gold eyes flashing.

Captain Bawr stood at the starboard rail, a speaking horn held before her. The hood of her cloak had fallen back, and her hair now framed her face in dark ringlets. Artus was struck again with the woman's beauty, though uneasiness at her strange nature overwhelmed any other feelings her appearance stirred.

"We've paid your toll already this month, Aremag," she shouted. "If you've damaged my ship, you'll be the one to pay for her repairs."

The monstrous turtle roared and slowly opened its blood-red eyes. The sounds coming from its gaping mouth at first seemed no more than unintelligible groans and rumbles, but as Artus listened, he discerned a pattern, a clear hierarchy of sounds and a rigid structure of word order. He had learned a few languages in his travels, but this was the first time he'd ever heard any of the tongues related to dragon speech.

Clearly the captain understood the dragon turtle's words. When it stopped speaking, she pounded a fist on the rail. "Master Quiracus," she said, tight reins on her anger, "have the ballistae ready to fire."

"Already done, Captain," he replied. When she glanced at him questioningly, he added, "I saw the silver pattern from its shell on the water right before we hit. The moon's not bright enough tonight to make that kind of reflection. I knew we were near the turtle's territory, so—"

"Fine," the captain replied coldly. "That makes my decision easier." Turning to the boatswain, she ordered, "Gather the men who were on watch tonight and put them in the ship's boat. If Master Quiracus saw Aremag coming, they should have noticed him, too."

"Some are wounded, milady," Nelock said meekly.

"Where they're going, it won't matter." She pointed to the stairs leading to the cabins. "Master Quiracus, get two empty chests from my cabin. Apologize to the ambassador, but assure him we're handling the problem."

The dragon turtle roared again, and Captain Bawr put the speaking horn to her lips. "I'll pay your price," she shouted, "but know the Refuge·Bay Trading Company will be displeased. If you can't be trusted to keep to the agreement we made months ago, our ships will take other routes to Chult."

Artus sputtered a protest, but it was Nelock who spoke first. "Milady," the boatswain said, "the crew might not take kindly to this—sacrificing some of their own to buy safe passage. They might even mutiny."

"They'll be glad it wasn't them I chose, Master Nelock," she snarled. Her skin had begun to take on a reddish hue. "Our ballista fire would bounce off Aremag's shell. We can't outrun him. Our only choice is to pay him the ten men and the treasure he demands. Do you want to be in the ship's boat with those unfortunate men when it's lowered into the water?"

Nelock backed away, shaking his head. He bumped into Artus, then turned and cursed. "Why are ya standing—" He paused and narrowed his eyes. "I should have known."

"Why isn't this man at his post?" the captain asked. She had reverted back to her demure appearance, though her cheeks still held a rosy blush.

"Master Quiracus told me to come on deck," Artus

stammered.

"I did no such thing, milady," the first mate said. The elf was carrying the two small chests he'd retrieved from the cabins below. The burden wasn't heavy, but his face was pale and his voice quavered as he stepped forward. "He must have deserted his post. He's done it before."

"Put him into the boat with the others," the captain ordered flatly. "If the surgeon notices you taking his friend away and objects in the least, send him along as well."

Artus's head swam, and he looked to the first mate for some kind of explanation. The elf was moving toward him, a small sheet of bone-white parchment held before him in his left hand. Nelock grabbed Artus from behind, pinning his arms back. "Sorry," the boatswain whispered, "there just ain't no other way."

Skuld appeared in a flash of silver light. The guardian spirit towered over the apelike boatswain, laughing at the terror in the sailor's eyes. He knocked Nelock senseless with a single fist to the top of the head. As the petty officer crumpled at Artus's feet, Skuld turned toward Master Quiracus. The elf hesitated for an instant, looked at the paper he held in his hand, then ran for the stairs.

"How dare you!" Captain Bawr snarled, leaping at Skuld.

The winsome woman abruptly transformed into a creature more reptile than human. Spiny ridges covered her skull, and red scales ran along her crocodile's snout. Her mouth was like a crocodile's, too, wide and gaping and filled with jagged teeth. Bawr now had the muscled arms and legs of a mountain dwarf. She'd torn through her pretty shoes and hose, but her blouse and flowing skirt still hung in tatters from her leathery body. She might have been truly terrifying but for the absurdity of those dainty clothes.

She sprang for the guardian spirit's throat, but he caught

her in midair with one of his four arms. Bawr tore at the silver limb with her claws and struggled to clamp down with her powerful jaws. Skuld watched disinterestedly as the creature razed metallic slivers from his arm. As fast as the inhuman flesh fell to the deck, the wounds healed over.

"Master?" Skuld asked, lifting the snarling creature higher off the wooden planks.

"Gods, Skuld, just get rid of her," Artus cried.

The spirit leaned back and heaved her over the side. The lizardlike thing that was Captain Bawr tumbled through the air, then splashed into the sea near the dragon turtle's head. Aremag twisted around slowly and gulped down the thrashing creature. After smacking its lips, it bellowed at the boat.

"The dragon turtle wants nine more men," Skuld noted helpfully. He folded both sets of arms across his chest. "Shall I gather them up for you, O mighty one?"

A small circle of sailors had gathered around Artus and Skuld. Since the captain had never kept a personal guard, assured as she was of her own powers of self-defense, no one took up the challenge of avenging her death. If Artus had the might to do away with the unpredictable captain, perhaps he should have command of the *Narwhal*.

"Well," one of the sailors said, "that monster won't wait all day. If we don't give it what it wants, it'll sink us for sure."

Pontifax arrived then, the blood of the dead and wounded spattering his tunic. "Do you have any spells that could help us?" Artus asked.

"Against that thing?" the mage replied. "Only if you want to make it really angry."

Casually Skuld held out a hand. In his palm rested a silver globe the size of a large apple, perfectly round. Mulhorandi picture-glyphs girded the ball—men with the wings and heads of hawks, women with the features of cats, and many other strange creatures. As Artus looked at them, they began to move in stately procession. "This will not kill the dragon turtle," Skuld noted, "but it will breach its shell."

"And the ballistae will do the rest," one of the crewmen shouted. "Shall I pass the word to prepare for firing?"

Artus snatched the globe from Skuld's hand. "Tell the men to hold their fire until this thing, er—"

"It will explode, master," Skuld whispered. "All you need do is throw it at the beast."

"—until this thing explodes," the explorer said. He glanced up and saw the guardian spirit was actually smiling, an odd sort of pride in his eyes. "The men will know what to aim for after that."

The dragon-turtle swam closer to the ship. The waves caused by its slow, relentless movement caused the *Narwhal* to bob like a child's toy boat on bath night. "Once the fighting starts, we'll want to put some distance between us and the turtle. One of you men take over as boatswain." Artus pointed at a brawny half-orc with a broken nose. "You'll do for now."

The crewmembers scattered to their tasks, leaving Artus alone on the poop deck with Pontifax, Skuld, and the three young sailors manning the ship's massive wheel. "Are you sure you know what you're doing?" the mage asked as Artus stepped up to the rail.

"Not in the least," he replied, then threw the silver globe with all his might.

Aremag must have suspected a doublecross, for he tried to dive away from the small missile. He was too large for such a demanding maneuver, however, and the globe flew with magical speed. Skuld's weapon struck the turtle's shell directly over a leg. The explosion sent a flare of light into the night sky and a rumble of thunder over the ceaselessly churning sea. Fragments of shell, sharper than any sword, sliced through the air, tearing through sails and cutting the rigging. Those men and women unlucky enough to be hit by the shrapnel would never know how the battle turned out.

"Fire!" Artus shouted.

Captain Bawr had kept a strict chain of command to handle such battles, but it had disintegrated with her death. Most of the officers were hiding, afraid of both mutineers and the dragon turtle. Yet the crews manning the engines had bested pirate ships and vessels from the royal navies of five countries. When they saw the bloody breech in Aremag's shell, they knew what to do even before Artus's shouted order.

The heavy thud of twenty-five ballista arms shooting forward and the hiss of as many huge bolts slicing through the air came to Artus's ears. He saw the dragon turtle roll in pain. Seven heavy lances had found their mark. The iron-tipped missiles dug deep into Aremag's flesh, turning the water crimson. Most of the other bolts struck the shell and bounced harmlessly away. One well-placed shot blinded the turtle's left eye.

A shout went up on the *Narwhal* as the dragon turtle screamed. The ballistae fired again, though all but one of the bolts struck harmlessly against the thrashing giant's shell. The dragon turtle had taken enough of a beating to retreat, but not without a parting shot. Just before it sank, Aremag inhaled sharply, then breathed out a cloud of scalding steam.

The shrieks of the sailors closest to the starboard rail replaced their victory cry. The steam poured into the ballista ports, searing the skin off the men caught in its wake. In a few places, ropes sizzled and broke. A yardarm, suddenly cut free, fell to the deck and crushed a midshipman.

Skuld shielded Artus and Pontifax from the blast, then disappeared into the medallion. From the rail, Artus stared out at the churning, bloody sea, waiting for the turtle's return. Pontifax, his back to his friend, looked out over the carnage on the quarter deck. "I'd better see if I can help anyone down there," the mage said.

Artus turned and came face-to-face with Quiracus. The elf slapped the piece of parchment he'd been carrying earlier over the medallion, then lashed out at Artus with a right hook. The blow landed on the explorer's jaw, sending him backward over the rail.

No silver hand emerged from the medallion to save Artus from this fall. Only his own quick reflexes stopped him from plummeting into the sea. He gripped the edge of the rail with one hand, his fingernails digging furrows into the wood as he slid. Quiracus reached out, intent on loosening that tenuous grip, but Pontifax tackled him. The mage easily bowled the slender elf off his feet, then hurried to help Artus. Puffing at the exertion, he pulled the explorer back onto the deck.

"Where did he go?" Artus shouted.

"I don't know," Pontifax said. "But we'll find him sooner or later. Not many places to hide on a ship."

Artus slumped back against the rail, then lifted the medallion. The silver disk was completely hidden by a thick layer of hardened white paste.

"I saw Quiracus hit the medallion with that parchment," Pontifax said. "It looks like some sort of magical damper. Unless we can find a way to get it off, I don't think we'll be seeing Skuld again for a while."

Artus looked at the medallion, then dropped it back onto his chest. "Good thing we're just a couple days out of Refuge Bay. Whoever is trying to kill me knew enough to get Skuld out of the way first."

Concern filled Pontifax's eyes. "What makes you think they'll stop once we get to Chult?"

*   *   *   *   *

"Here, let me quote a bit for you: 'I have discovered that the Cult of Frost is led by that blackguard Kaverin Ebonhand.' " The man chuckled. "So I'm a blackguard, am I? How perfectly melodramatic."

Quiracus dropped to his knees in the center of an intricately woven Turmish carpet. It was as expensive and as gaudy as the rest of the trappings in Captain Bawr's cabin. "Please, you've got to hide me. Cimber will kill me if he finds me."

Kaverin closed the small book bound in wyvern hide. "I am wondering, my fine elf, whether you have served me well enough to merit sheltering." He tapped one finger on the book. Like the rest of his hand, the digit was solid jet-black stone, though it moved like one of flesh and blood. "True, you recovered this lovely volume from my vaunted foe. The book, in turn, will tell me everything Cimber knows about our mutual grail. And you did neutralize the guardian of the medallion for us by slapping that parchment over it."

He paused and bowed to the mousy woman sitting in the corner of the cabin. "Plaudits to you, my dear Phyrra, for that wonderfully simple magical damper. The guardian never knew what hit him, as the saying goes." A frown tugged at the corners of Kaverin's mouth. "Sadly, Cimber *does* know what—or more precisely who—hit him. Since you could not kill the blithering dolt, he can identify you as his would-be assassin. That is really quite troublesome, Quiracus."

With one jet finger, Kaverin gestured to the creature crouched atop a lacquered cabinet next to the door. The thing resembled a small albino monkey, though it sported large bat's wings and the talons of an eagle. It swooped across the room and landed on its master's shoulder, then began to fan him gently with its leathery wings.

"This heat is almost unbearable," Kaverin sighed. He wiped the sweat from his brow and from inside the collar of his loose-fitting white shirt. "At least, it would be if not for Feg." The winged monkey chittered shrilly.

Panic shone clearly on Quiracus's delicate elven features. He turned pleading blue eyes on Kaverin, whose face registered no emotion whatsoever. The first mate had seen dark, lifeless eyes like those before, but on a shark, not a man. Quiracus suddenly knew how Kaverin had come to be so infamous, how he could have committed crimes horrible enough to earn him the title "Butcher of Tantras."

"Yes, weighing against all the good you've done for me is this botched assassination. And it is quite a heavy sin." Kaverin closed his eyes to better enjoy the breeze tousling his red hair. "It has most certainly put Cimber on guard. He'll be dangerous now, far more difficult to kill."

From the corner came a coarse laugh. "He's no match for you," snorted Phyrra al-Quim. "Not with the spirit gone."

Kaverin offered her a patronizing smile. "It is a good thing I will be the one to determine when we cross swords with Cimber, Phyrra. He could not have bested someone as bright as you for top honors at that school you both attended if he did not at least possess some native intelligence."

A cloud of silent resentment settled over the young woman. She did her best to hide her emotions by hunching back into the shadowy corner, but Kaverin rarely missed such things. That petty streak will have to be frozen in her soul, he decided, but we'll have time enough for that later.

"No, I'm afraid you'll have to find some way to protect yourself, Quiracus. Our cover as Tantrasan ambassadors will keep Artus himself out of these cabins until we reach Chult, but if you're found here—and Artus will make

certain the crew searches everywhere for you—it might
endanger our cover," Kaverin concluded, making a half-
hearted attempt to appear sympathetic. "That just won't
do, you see."

Quiracus was on his feet, pointing at Kaverin with a
trembling finger. "I swear I'll tell him you're here if you
don't help me. I—"

The elf stiffened, then crumpled to the floor. The bone
handle of an ancient Mulhorandi dagger protruded from his
back. "Thank you, Phyrra my dear," Kaverin cooed. "He
was beginning to give me a headache."

The mousy woman retrieved the blade, wiped it clean on
Quiracus's shirt, then slid it back into her boot. Grabbing
the elf under the arms, she hauled him to the other side of
the small cabin. "Shall we dump him out the window?" she
asked. Daggers of light flashed across the room as her
round glasses caught and reflected the lantern's radiance.

Kaverin pondered the point for a moment. "No," he said
at last, stifling a yawn. "Leave him for my nightly visitors.
They'd love that kind of present, don't you think? Perhaps
they'll go home early, as a show of appreciation."

The stone-handed man tried hard to mask the apprehension in his voice, but couldn't. He was getting sleepy, and
that meant the emissaries of Cyric would soon arrive.
"Perhaps if I read something from this enthralling book I'll
stay awake . . . for a while anyway."

Kaverin sat down next to the lantern and opened Artus's
journal once more. Like his dark eyes, his angular features
betrayed none of his feelings. His mouth was small and tight,
with lips as pale and bloodless as the rest of his skin. Like an
icicle, his sharp nose slashed down across his face from his
forehead. The few who had ever touched Kaverin Ebonhand
and lived often complained that forever after they suffered a
chill where they'd come in contact with him. It wasn't an icy
cold so much as the clamminess of a corpse.

"Are we all comfy?" he asked mildly.

Deftly Feg hopped onto the perch loop standing nearby, fanning his master all the while. Across the room, Phyrra stuffed a towel beneath the elf's corpse to stop the blood from spreading. Then she settled back into her shadowy corner and wrapped her thin arms around herself.

"Another page about me," Kaverin exclaimed. His voice was high and full of excitement, like a child who had just been given a magical toy. "It says: 'Pontifax and I have finally brought Kaverin to justice. As usual, though, he has turned even his punishment to his advantage. . . .' "

* * * * *

Marpenoth 5, Year of the Prince

Today Kaverin Ebonhand of Tantras was found guilty of ordering the murder of Rallo Scarson, a Harper who dared threaten his network of evil agents. I don't feel any relief at the verdict or overwhelming pride in the Lord's Court here in Ravens Bluff. It was the evidence I gathered with Pontifax's help that proved Kaverin was guilty beyond any reasonable doubt; given that evidence, any sane man would have found for the prosecution.

The Harpers will be pleased I've made Kaverin pay for the death of Rallo, even if I no longer consider myself one of their ranks. Theron Silvermace spent the whole trial watching me. I'm certain he was taking notes, gathering proof that I am still worthy of the little silver harp-and-moon pin. It's been two years since I stormed out of the meeting in Shadowdale, and still the Harpers haven't tried to take the pin back. I wonder why.

Anyway, Pontifax and I have finally brought Kaverin to justice. As usual, though, he has turned even his punishment to his advantage.

Since his henchman had been put to death for actually murdering Rallo, the court could not impose the same fate upon Kaverin for the same crime. (Like many of the city-states along the Dragon Reach, Ravens Bluff has a pretty skewed idea of justice.) They decided instead to chop off his hands. How civilized. And when they did, just an hour ago, Kaverin laughed. His hands were lying in the dirt, bloody and twitching, and he laughed.

Pontifax was right—the man is insane.

Before the clerics appointed by the court to heal up Kaverin's wrists could do their duty, the mage who had been serving as his lawyer throughout the trial muscled past. In his hands, he held two blobs of black stone. When the mage touched these to Kaverin's gory wrists, they transformed. Still chuckling madly, Kaverin held his new jet-black hands up for all to see.

Before he walked away—he was free now that the punishment had been exacted upon him—Kaverin pointed one stony finger at Pontifax and me. Not very subtle, but we got the threat quite clearly. He blames us for his conviction. Rightly so, too.

Sooner or later, we're going to hear from Kaverin Ebonhand again. If we do, I'll make sure no mage in the world will be able to save him.

Five

Port Castigliar was a sorry excuse for an outpost. It consisted of seven tin huts, two small plots of vegetables, a large but ramshackle supply depot, and a graveyard. The latter was more densely populated than the land for five miles in any direction.

As Artus and Pontifax stood on the narrow stretch of beach, watching the ship's boat from the *Narwhal* unload its cargo of food, cookware, knives, and weapons, they could not help but wonder if they'd come to the right place. "Are you certain this is where Theron said we should land?" Pontifax asked, wiping his rain-soaked hair out of his eyes.

Artus scowled. "I have the map right here," he said, then patted his pack. "My journal may have been stolen, but I was smart enough to keep the map with me at all times."

Pontifax stared uneasily at the *Narwhal*. The galleon waited impatiently in the deep waters off Port Castigliar, anxious to move on to more substantial stops in Refuge Bay. The lowering sky was dark and threatening, promising worse than the downpour already underway. "Quiracus might have disembarked before we got to the deck this morning," the mage offered absently.

Artus grunted. The crew had half-heartedly searched for Master Quiracus. Not only was the elven first mate wanted for questioning concerning his attack of Artus, but he was next in line to take command of the *Narwhal*. When no sign of him had been uncovered, it was decided he had fallen overboard in the battle with the dragon-turtle—decided, that is, by the newly risen Captain Nelock. Actually, Nelock had made it quite clear he hoped Quiracus never surfaced, and he did all he could·to keep the hunt subdued. Even if he had found the elf hiding somewhere aboard ship, Nelock would have offered him shelter, just so long as he disappeared at the first port.

For their parts, Artus and Pontifax believed the elf to be alive. When the explorer discovered his journal had been stolen—pocketed by Quiracus during the turtle attack, one of the ballista crew had said—he concluded the elf must be after the Ring of Winter. Either that, or he was working for someone else who quested after the ring. That possibility worried Artus the most.

"Well, let's show enough sense to get out of this rain," Pontifax said. "I don't think we're going to catch our elusive adversary by drowning here on the beach." He hefted a pack to one shoulder and started toward the sprawling supply depot.

Artus grabbed the other two packs. Dragging them along, he hurried after the mage. "If we press on after the ring," he said wearily, "Quiracus will show himself sooner or later."

"Quiracus *or* the blighter with whom he's so gainfully employed," Pontifax corrected.

They wrestled their packs into the warehouse. The building appeared dilapidated from the outside, with pocked and scarred tin walls and a haphazardly constructed straw roof. Inside, however, the depot more closely resembled one of the finer shops in Suzail or Waterdeep. Row after row of neatly stacked boxes rose two stories to the waterproof thatch. Everywhere Artus looked lay jars full of buttons, cloth sheets lined with needles, spool after spool of thread, tunics and boots and cloaks, crossbows and swords and arrows. Each shelf was numbered, with a narrow strip of pegboard rising up to the tallest.

"It's cool in here," Pontifax whispered. After the humidity and the warm rain, the cold made him shiver.

"And the floor was clean, too, before you dragged in those sodden packs," came a voice from the polished suit of armor standing at attention next to the door. It spoke in the trade tongue known as Common. "Don't you two know to wipe your muddy boots?"

The armor shuddered, and a child ten winters old walked from behind it. Like many Chultan natives, his skin was the dark brown of fertile earth and his black hair was cropped close. He wore short pants and a loose shirt, both tan and spotlessly clean. "Well?" he asked, gesturing with his polishing cloth to the wet, muddy footprints.

"Oh, er, sorry," Artus stammered. He and Pontifax stepped back to the stoop. "We're here to purchase supplies and to hire a guide and some bearers."

But the boy's attention was on a large package that had fallen into the nearest aisle. "Zrumya!" he shouted. "Pickup in row two, level six!"

From high in the rafters came a shriek, followed by the flutter of wings through the chilly air. A monstrous bat, as large as a man, tumbled down and darted crazily between the high stacks of boxes. Finally it landed with a thud in the aisle, right on top of the fallen package. Using the claws

located at the joints in its wings, it slid the bundle into a
pack strapped to its chest. Then, with slow, spiderlike
movements, the bat crept across the floor and began to
climb the shelving. It hooked its claws into the pegboard
and made it way to the sixth shelf, where it unloaded its
cargo. Job done, the bat fluttered back to its perch.

The boy turned back to study Artus and Pontifax for a
moment. "Father!" he shouted, then disappeared between a high row of boxes.

The boy's father appeared at the end of the long aisle
running from the door to the back of the warehouse. "Pay
Inyanga no mind," the man said. "He is trying to prove to
me he loves the store so he can inherit it some day."

Despite this, Artus opened the door and kicked as much
mud off his boots as possible before treading across the
clean planks. Pontifax removed his shoes completely. The
old mage smiled at the stern-faced boy, who had returned
with a bucket and mop. "It's our mess," Pontifax said,
holding up a hand. "Allow me."

He muttered an incantation. Instantly a blue light limned
the mop, then it jerked out of the boy's hand. As the child
stared, it cleaned up the mud and swabbed the whole area
in front of the door. Finally the mop floated back to the
bucket and lowered itself into the now-grimy water.

"I used to sweep up my father's store when I was your
age," the mage said kindly. "There were lots of times when
I wished someone would come along and make the broom
do the work itself." He patted the boy and hurried after
Artus, his bare feet peeking out from under his long brown
robe.

"This is Ibn Engaruka," Artus said when the mage
reached the long, low counter that ran the entire length of
the warehouse. The owner nodded politely, though his face
was an impassive mask. The young boy resembled him
closely, from the broad nose to the hard-set jaw. Even the

clothes they wore were alike.

Ibn gestured to the wet patch near the door. "It has been years since magic has blessed this place," he said stiffly. "I was just telling your comrade here, a local sorcerer used to trade magic for goods. He placed some enchanted gems under the floorboards to keep the store cool. That keeps my foodstuffs from spoiling so fast, do you see?"

Before either Artus or Pontifax could reply, Ibn clapped his hands. "Inyanga, bring some chairs for these gentlemen." The boy had apparently foreseen the order, for before his father finished speaking, he had dragged two wooden stools to the tired explorers.

"It is best to do business when comfortable," Ibn said, but he did not take a seat himself. Instead, he leaned on the counter, openly sizing up the strangers before him. "What brings you to Chult? If I understand your goal, I can better help you to reach it, do you see?"

"We wish to hire a guide and six bearers, and buy supplies for a few weeks trek into the jungle. But we prefer not to discuss our reasons for being here," Artus began. "There are others—"

"No need to say more. I understand entirely," the shopkeep said, holding up a restraining hand. "I will tell you this, though. The men and women here will do no traffic with slavers. It is something we will not tolerate, do you see?"

"Of course," Pontifax said. The mage nodded emphatically. "We're no slavers. You can count on that."

"Then I can help you," Ibn replied, "but not for a few days. This very morning, before dawn, the only guide in Port Castigliar has gone away with the unpleasant young woman from your ship. It is too bad you could not travel together, but—"

"Young woman?" Artus repeated, shocked. "No young woman got off the *Narwhal* this morning."

Ibn shrugged. "I could be mistaken, but I doubt so very much. Only locals and people from trading ships stop here, and yours has been the only vessel in days."

"Was there an elf with her? A young, blond-haired fellow?" Pontifax asked, rubbing his chin.

The boy, who had been watching the mage from atop a pile of crates, shouted down, "No. She left the camp with the guide. No bearers and no supplies. She was very rude to me and my father."

"She tried to strike Inyanga when he shouted at her for tracking mud into the store," Ibn noted. He pulled a large ledger from beneath the counter. "The guide leaves a record of his destination with me. I am his agent, do you see?" After flipping past a dozen yellow-edged pages, he frowned. "There is no entry here. Perhaps this woman is searching for the same thing you are, for she is certainly as secretive."

Artus was on his feet before the book clapped shut. "There has to be another guide here. You, perhaps? Or the boy?"

"Absolutely not," Ibn said. "Inyanga and I, we will not leave our home, and the bearers, they are slaves freed from galleys along the coast. They work here to earn their passage home, do you see? They do not know this place any better than you." He slid the ledger back under the counter. "You will have to wait for the guide to return. Until then, you can stay in one of the huts. A few are empty now, since three of my bearers bought passage back down the coast aboard a merchant ship last week."

The door slammed open, and the leader of the *Narwhal*'s shore party stuck his head into the depot. "All the stuff is on the beach," he shouted. "Stacked and covered with a tarp. We're going."

"Not until I inventory the boxes," Ibn replied. He vaulted over the counter. "Pardon me, gentlemen, but Captain

Bawr's men have trouble counting their own fingers and toes."

Artus and Pontifax watched the shopkeep hurry outside. "We could risk going on alone," the mage ventured half-heartedly.

"That would be foolish." Inyanga climbed down from the crates. "You would not last a whole night in the jungle alone. There are goblins and wildmen who would eat both of you for dinner." The boy laughed. "And the Children of Ubtao. They do not like strangers roaming around in Ubtao's jungle. Then the bearers would bring you back, and my father would have to bury what's left of you in the ground beside the beach, like the other men who came here and wandered off on their own."

Artus knew many tribes in Chult worshiped Ubtao as the mightiest of gods, the maker of men and animals. Perhaps these "children" were his high priests. "Well, Pontifax?" the explorer sighed.

"What else can we do?" the mage replied. "We take up residence here in Port Castigliar until the guide returns."

*   *   *   *   *

Here lies Wurthek of Tethyr.
He has gone to chart the realms beyond.

Artus pulled a clinging vine off the tombstone. It was as thick around as his thumb, and, when it hit the ground, the vine snaked slowly back toward the jungle. Artus merely stared at it; the rain and the somber setting had dampened his already-dark mood so much that anything less than a charging dragon would have gotten a similarly subdued reaction.

The explorers' graveyard started at one end of Ibn's store and ran behind it for almost its entire length. By the shopkeep's count, it held one hundred and eight bodies. Stones marked most of the sites, though the jungle had long ago reclaimed some of the ground. High, thick-rooted trees towered overhead, their fronds sheltering Artus from much of the downpour. Creepers wound around the grave markers and anything else that stood still too long. Hidden in the wall of green, birds called and monkeys chittered and shrieked. Other, more ominous sounds echoed from the jungle, too, but they were far-off and muted.

Over everything hung a blanket of hot, humid air, thick with the sickly smell of rotting vegetation. Not even the breeze from the sea, only a few hundred yards away, could force the pestilent haze away for long. Like the jungle itself, the humidity soon reclaimed its lost ground.

I wonder if Wurthek's wife knows where he is? Artus pondered grimly, crouching before the marker. He cursed not having his journal; he could have written down all the names—the ones still legible, anyway—and taken them back to Suzail with him.

"He was a mapmaker," came a voice from behind him.

Ibn squatted next to Artus and pointed to the stone. "I cut these myself, do you see? When the men and women from your part of the world make it back this far, but can go no farther, I let them rest here until Ubtao calls them. Then I bury them, as is the custom in the northern lands. They seem safe enough, I think."

"Does anyone know this man is buried here?"

"Ubtao does," Ibn replied, "and whatever gods the mapmaker worshiped. I send a list north with the ships, but sometimes I don't have names to put on the stones or the list." Glancing at Artus, he added, "Since you haven't offered your name, I would only have a symbol to go on your marker—if Ubtao calls you to his home before you leave the port." Ibn opened his left hand. In his palm lay a silver Harper pin.

"I think you're mistaken," Artus said. "That's not mine."

"No," Ibn said. "It's mine. You have one of your own." Before Artus could protest, he dropped the pin into a pocket and held out a calloused hand. "This morning the men from the *Narwhal* told me your name and what you did to save the ship from the dragon turtle. Like many Harpers, I have heard tales of your adventures. I am honored to meet you, Artus Cimber."

There was little else Artus could do, so he greeted the Harper as amicably as possible. "Well met," he said, clasping wrists in a traditional northern gesture of friendship. "I suppose you've been waiting for me."

Ibn smiled and nodded. "The package Theron left for you is inside the store. I have kept it safe, just as he asked." A look of concern washed across his features. "Theron is well, I hope. The case of fever he took away with him was quite serious. I have not heard from him—or anyone else in the Heartlands—for weeks now."

Artus tried hard to mask his relief, but his heart was racing. Theron hadn't told the Harpers after all, or the message hadn't reached here yet. If the guide got back soon, he might actually get away without the Harpers meddling in his quest. "I saw Theron the night I left Suzail," Artus said at last. "His mind wandered back to the jungle now and then, but I think he'll recover."

"He had a terrible experience with the Batiri—the goblin tribe, do you see?" Ibn straightened, his knees creaking at the effort. "There are many horrible things in Ubtao's domain, but many beautiful things, as well. Theron found more terror than beauty, I'm afraid."

"He didn't mention anything about a package," Artus said, following Ibn back to the warehouse. He glanced back at the graveyard, only to see the creeping vine wind its way around Wurthek's tombstone once more.

"He wished you to be surprised." Ibn stopped at the door. "I will get the package, then come to your hut. There is something for Sir Hydel here, too."

In the clearing before the store, there was no canopy of tree fronds to shield Artus from the downpour. He barely noticed the warm rain, though; the humidity made him sweat so much that he was soaked even when sitting inside. His shirt plastered to his back, his boots squishing uncomfortably on his feet, he made his way to the tin huts. As he got close, the steady hiss of the downpour became the loud clatter of raindrops pelting the slanted tin roofs. When he opened the door, Artus was greeted by another sound: the rumbling of Pontifax's snoring.

"How can he sleep with this racket?" Artus asked softly as he entered the hut. The rain beat a fast cadence on the roof, and the walls echoed the rolling sound. But Pontifax was indeed fast asleep on one of the four frond-stuffed mattresses that covered the floor.

The room's accommodations were sparse but clean. Aside from the mattresses, the only other furniture was a low teakwood table, obviously meant to be used without chairs, and a set of four wooden headrests. At first Pontifax had thought these to be chairs for children. Even now, he rested his head upon his pack rather than one of the blocks. The other two packs lay huddled in the corner. Atop this pile rested Inyanga. The boy sat with his legs crossed, watching the sleeping Pontifax with great intensity.

"He said he would teach me how to make the mop work on its own," the boy said in reply to Artus's questioning gaze. "I am waiting for my lesson."

Artus lifted Inyanga from the packs and placed him gently on the ground. "We have to talk business with your father now," he said. "Pontifax will teach you that trick later."

"It is not a trick," the boy said. He narrowed his bright

eyes in anger. "It is magic, like the spells used by the sorcerers of the Tabaxi and the shamen of the Batiri." He crossed his arms over his chest. "Besides, I am also here to watch over the old man, like my father asked."

Pontifax snorted awake. "Eh? Inyanga, you're still here? Don't worry, my lad, you'll learn something from me before I go." He rubbed his eyes and, noting the anxious look on Artus's face, sent the boy away.

"You've just dismissed your guard," Artus said after Inyanga had closed the door behind him.

"Guard, you say? What's this all about? I was just taking a nap."

Artus placed a foot on the low table. "Ibn Engaruka is a Harper. He knows who we·are, too. The crew of the ship's boat told him." He shrugged. "The story of the fight with the dragon turtle will likely be back in Suzail before we are."

"But why a guard?" Pontifax sputtered. "I don't see why—"

"Because someone is trying to kill you," Ibn noted from the doorway. He had a longbow and a quiver of arrows slung across his back and a large bundle of cloth in his hands. "The men from the *Narwhal* also relayed the story of the assassination attempt on Artus, Sir Hydel. You needed your rest, and I thought it best for Inyanga to watch over you. If I have offended—"

"No, no." Pontifax stood and straightened his sleep-rumpled robes. "My thanks for your concern."

Ibn handed the cloth bundle to Artus. "You should keep your voices down, my friends. I heard you clearly from the store's front door. One can never tell who serves as the ears for your enemies."

A silver string held the bundle in a neat square. Artus had only to tug at one loose end for the cord to fall away and the cloth to drape down. It was a hooded tunic. The deep green fabric looked as thick as a heavy cotton weave, but felt as light as a pickpocket's touch in his hands. A folded sheet of parchment slipped from the tunic's hood. Artus caught it before it dropped to the floor. The note from Theron was scrawled in a shaky hand:

Since you are reading this, Artus, I must have survived the trip back to Cormyr. Bully for me. I have no doubt you will make it to this port once I tell you of my extraordinary rescue at the hands of Lord Rayburton. The gifts I leave with Ibn will help you in the jungle. Trust to him for everything else. If you do not know by now, he carries the silver harp and moon.

No matter what or who stands in your way, Artus, you must struggle on. The thing you seek must be found, then turned to good.

Beware the goblins and the dinosaurs—the giant lizards the locals call Ubtao's Children. They are the greatest dangers you will face.

—Theron Silvermace

Below there was one more passage, written in another hand, neater but very small. Artus took his dagger from his belt and used the glow of its hilt to read by.

I have had Ibn sew my badge to the tunic. I hope you don't mind, but I wish to be with you on this expedition—if only in this small way.

"He asked me to add the last part," Ibn said as Artus folded the parchment again. "He had become too ill to write it himself, do you see?"

Artus handed the note to Pontifax. "Burn it after you've read it." He held the tunic up. There, over the left breast, was Theron's family crest. White thread made the diving falcon and spiked mace contrast sharply with the verdant cloth. Artus closed his eyes for an instant, regretting the disagreement that had marked his parting with Theron.

Ibn placed the bow and quiver of arrows on one of the mattresses. "These Master Silvermace bought from me. I purchased them in trade long ago from an elven sailor. They are from Evermeet, I am told, crafted by the bowyers and fletchers of the royal family." He laughed. "Even if that is not true, they are wonderfully wrought."

A gout of flame devoured the parchment in Pontifax's hands. After the mage dusted the ashes from his palm, he sighed. "Thank you for watching over these things."

Ibn bowed. "Any Harper would do the same." He settled back against the wall. "Theron would not tell me what he found in the jungle, saying only that it was not a Harper matter and I would be safer if I did not know about it."

"He was wise not to tell you," Artus said. "There are many who would stop at nothing to gain information about our quest."

He peeled his wet, sweat-soaked shirt off and dropped it to the floor. Old scars—some small, some long and twisted—marred his back and stomach. The medallion hung heavily on its chain, still encased in a cast of solid white paste. Artus studied the now-lifeless medallion, then shrugged on the tunic Theron had left for him. "It's light and very cool. And," he added, flipping the hood over his head, "this will keep the sun off quite nicely."

"You look like a monk," Pontifax chuckled. "Brother Artus of Oghma to the rescue."

Artus pulled the hood down. "Perhaps I should reconsider my calling if I look so dashing in this," he said. "I'm certain Zin would have me back in the order if I asked."

"These men who are after you," Ibn interrupted, "are they Zhentarim? I have seen the marks left by the tortures they employ. Yours are very much like them."

Artus lifted his shirt and traced a puckered line across his stomach. "You're very observant, Ibn. The scars—most of them, anyway—I got in the dungeons of Zhentil Keep, at the hands of the Zhentarim. They aren't the ones who tried to kill me aboard the *Narwhal*, though. They favor magic over brute force, so they would never have been so crass as to push me overboard during a battle."

"You know," Pontifax said, "it could be the Red Wizards. Maybe that's why they took your journal." He gave Artus a stern look. "After all, you stole it from them in the first place."

Artus frowned and crossed his arms. "Or it could be the Slashing Skulls, or the assassins' guild of Iriaebor, or those lunatic halflings from the Shar; or any one of fifty groups that'd like to see me dead." He paused and took a deep breath. "It could even be Kaverin Ebonhand, for all we know. This has Cult of Frost written all over it."

"Wait a moment," Ibn said. "I'd heard Kaverin Ebonhand was dead."

"You're right," Pontifax said glumly. "Kaverin *was* dead, the bastard. We killed him ourselves not three years ago."

"But, if you killed him. . . ?"

Artus picked up the bow, which very nearly matched his height. As he braced it against the wall to string it, he asked, "You've heard how Kaverin lost his hands for murdering a Harper?" When Ibn nodded, the explorer continued. "After that sordid business, he swore to kill me and Pontifax. We clashed now and then, especially after he murdered his way to the head of the Cult of Frost. Anyway, one day in Tantras, he slipped up and we caught him."

"I blasted him to pieces with a lightning bolt," Pontifax noted grimly.

Artus studied one of the arrows and fit it to the bow. "We should have dealt with him sword-to-sword or called in the local watch, but he'd found his way out of their jails a hundred times before."

With a quick pull, Artus fired the arrow across the hut. It split the skull of the snake that was in the process of crawling through a gap beneath the rear wall. The serpent's head was as large as a man's fist. "The end result of all this is Pontifax and I are still wanted for Kaverin's murder in Tantras. The government was annoyed at us interfering with their local problems—even if they knew Kaverin was a murderer and worse—so they tried to haul us in on a dozen different charges."

"But if you killed him . . . ?" Ibn prompted.

"Some say Kaverin made a pact with the Lord of the Dead, but that may be a myth." Artus tossed the bow aside. "We do know that he came back from the dead, as rotten as ever, and he's never slipped up again. The Cult of Frost now shields him from everything. We haven't even been close to catching him in three years, though he keeps trying to kill us."

In the silence that followed, Ibn pulled the arrow from the snake's skull. "This is a fine shot, Master Cimber," he said, "but do not be so cavalier about what you kill in the jungle. More importantly, you must never leave a creature's corpse lying about. If you do not eat it, burn it." He pulled the rest of the snake—all five feet of it—into the hut. "It is too bad Theron chose the menu for dinner tonight. These are quite good when cooked correctly."

"Theron picked the menu?" Pontifax asked.

"That was his gift for you, Sir Hydel," Ibn replied. " 'A good meal for Pontifax before he's subjected to trail rations for days on end.' "

"I always said that man knew how to live," Pontifax said happily. Yet as he followed Ibn out of the hut he warily eyed the snake coiled around the shopkeep's arms. Just what, he wondered, did the natives of Chult consider a good meal?

* * * * *

A clatter on the hut's tin roof woke Artus. He sat up, dagger in hand, even before he realized he was fully awake.

The gem in the dagger's hilt lit the room enough for Artus to see there was no immediate danger. The rain had stopped hours ago, the drumming of raindrops replaced by the soft roll of the ocean and the steady, faraway blanket of sounds of the jungle. It was still dark outside; he could tell that much from the gaps around the door and the hole at the base of the back wall. Pontifax snored sonorously, well-fed upon a meal of fish, koko-yams, plantain, and palm wine. Had he dreamed the noise? Perhaps a monkey had leaped from a tree and—

Something struck the door and a voice cried out, high and filled with fright.

Artus leaped to the door and braced himself against it. "Pontifax, quick!"

Startled from a deep sleep and a pleasant dream of a room in Cormyr's finest inn, the mage was slow to his feet. "What's going on?" he murmured, rubbing his eyes with awkward fingers.

"Help, Father!"

"Mystra's wounds!" Pontifax cried. "That's Inyanga!"

Artus stepped to one side of the door, then pulled it open. A tall figure, pale and ghostly by the light of Artus's dagger, blocked the way. Its body was made entirely of crystal-clear ice. The explorer had faced assassins like this before, minions of the Cult of Frost, conjured servants of Kaverin Ebonhand.

Cursing, Artus grabbed for the door. The frost minion lashed out, knocking the sheet of metal from its hinges. The door crashed to the ground. Swiftly the explorer jumped back, but the assassin grabbed him by the front of his tunic and lifted him from the ground. It raised one massive fist to strike.

A tiny ball of fire hissed across the hut. It struck the frost minion in the side, then burrowed in. The assassin probably didn't feel any pain, but it was sentient enough to sense danger. It dropped Artus and tried to dig the ember out. Too late. The pinpoint of fire exploded, and the minion's clear body filled with flame, then shattered into a thousand shards.

Artus wiped a line of blood from his cheek where one of the larger shards had grazed him. The other fragments had been too small to do any damage.

The mage smiled sheepishly. "Sorry," he said. "A bit of an overreaction."

"At least we know it's Kaverin," Artus said. He gestured to the scattered shards of ice. "This is like an engraved calling card."

There was noise in the compound now—doors being flung open, shouts of alarm, and the clatter of weapons. Artus charged outside and was immediately knocked to the ground from above. The roof! He tumbled, feeling icy hands fumble for his throat.

When Artus stopped rolling, another of Kaverin's frost minions was on top of him, its weight crushing the air from his lungs. Its arms were as thick around as fenceposts, its hands like dwarven hammers. It turned its smooth, eyeless face toward Artus and reached for his throat, but the explorer struck with his dagger. The enchanted blade carved a deep furrow in the assassin's arm. Another frantic blow, and the limb shattered. Water dripped down on Artus as the thing loomed over him, melting even as it tried to choke him with its one remaining arm.

Again and again, Artus dug his dagger into the frost minion, gouging out chunks of ice. Half its head was gone, then much of its torso. Artus felt the thing's grip falter. It went stiff then, and dropped onto him, lifeless ice once more.

Ibn pushed the cold mass from atop the explorer. "Are you all right?"

"Yes," Artus said softly, his throat raw from the attack. He sat up and looked at the hut. Pontifax knelt in the doorway, consoling Inyanga.

"I climbed on the roof to watch over you," the boy said between sobs. "I saw them coming from the jungle, but I thought it was two of the bearers and their child."

Something about Inyanga's words jarred Artus's mind. A child? Artus pushed himself from the ground. "Pontifax!"

In the darkness of the hut, a figure no larger than a human toddler had slipped through the gap beneath the back wall and stolen up behind the mage. The frost minion had been diminished by the heat, so much so that it barely resembled a man. That was to its advantage, though. Its hands were no longer large enough to strangle Pontifax, but they had melted to points at the ends.

It rammed one spearlike arm through the mage's back.

From the compound, Artus saw his old friend gasp, then slump forward. Inyanga screamed. The boy reached for the figure that still stood with its arm buried in Pontifax's back. Stiffly the frost minion jerked free. It disappeared into the hut and out through the hole where it had entered.

Ibn pulled the sobbing child away from Pontifax as Artus stumbled to his friend's side. "Maybe not an overreaction," the mage said. He gasped as Artus removed the ice dagger and tried to staunch the flow of blood.

"Quiet," Artus said. He cradled the old man's white head in his arm. "I'll pull you through."

Pontifax stiffened as pain spasmed through him. "Don't let . . . Kaverin get the ring," he hissed, staring with wide, clear eyes at Artus. "But be careful what you do to get it. You'll become like him if you let the end of the quest blind you to the path you take to reach it."

Artus felt his throat constrict. "Gods, Pontifax, I'm sorry. This is my fault."

The mage managed a smile. "Not your fault," he whispered. "Not even the curse." He closed his eyes. "Be a good soldier. Don't cry till I'm gone."

Artus struggled to hold back the tears, unaware of the men and women looking on in horror and pity. After a moment, the mage slipped quietly away. The tears came then, burning like molten metal as they coursed down his face. But the pain didn't scald away Artus's thoughts and regrets. The only things that offered him comfort were Pontifax's final words and the kindly smile on the mage's lips, a smile not even death could erase.

Six

"Wake up, Artus."

"Please, Pontifax, not again. I'm sorry. You have to know that by now."

"Artus?"

The explorer rolled over and opened his eyes. The sunshine pouring in through the door blinded him momentarily, and he threw an arm up to block the light. "Oh . . . Ibn. Go away," Artus croaked.

"No," Ibn replied flatly. "This is not good." He laid a hand on Artus's shoulder. "To grieve, that is right, but to let someone's death kill you, too . . . that is not the way of the world, do you see?"

"It is just for murderers to be killed," Artus said through gritted teeth. The pounding headache that had been with him ever since he'd finished off an entire bottle of palm wine flared then, egged on by Ibn's low voice and his own angry words. "I'm guilty. That's all you need to know."

"All I need to know is you've been in this hut ever since

we buried Sir Hydel, drinking, but not eating, sweltering away in this little room." Ibn picked up the longbow Theron had left for Artus, then began to batter the tin wall. The din was deafening.

"Gods!" Artus screamed, blocking his ears. "Stop that!"

Ibn paused long enough to say, "You'll have to stop me yourself."

Artus's hand went to his boot, but his dagger was gone. In fact, all he had on was a short, ragged pair of breeches.

"I took the knife away a day ago," Ibn shouted over the racket. "I knew sooner or later you might come to hurt someone—or yourself—with it."

Artus looked up and saw the fiendish grin on the shopkeep's face. The headache was forgotten in the rage that coursed through him. He tried to lunge, but succeeded only in tripping over the low table. Then the banging stopped. The room was once again filled with the sounds of his own heavy breathing, the chatter of birds and monkeys, and the hushed roll of the sea.

"You have tortured yourself enough," Ibn said softly. "Come back to the world." He dropped the bow, and it clattered to the floor. "If you don't, I will send Inyanga here with a drum and a trumpet. He can play them both at once, do you see?"

After pushing himself off the floor, Artus used the sturdy table to pull himself to his feet. He wasn't drunk; the palm wine had given him nothing but a raging headache and a queasy stomach. He never drank much anyway, only in fits of stupid desperation. And he was certainly desperate now. Eleven years of camaraderie, shared adventures and dangers, that's what he and Pontifax had survived. The old mage had been more of a father to Artus than the brigand who'd sired him, more of a brother than the brutish lout he'd grown up with.

Even if Pontifax had brushed off the Curse of the Ring as he lay dying, Artus could not. Just at the point when the ring was almost in his grasp, someone dear to him had died. It was the same story as that of all the other seekers who had paid for their quest with another's life.

"I had dreams about him, Ibn," Artus whispered. "Pontifax came here and forgave me. He was transparent and pale—like a ghost." He rubbed his eyes, trying to ward off the growing ache. "I don't know what to do."

"Did Sir Hydel tell you what he wanted you to do?" Ibn asked. Artus was surprised by the serious expression on his face. "In the dreams, did he talk to you about the future?"

"I drank too much wine," Artus said. "I hadn't—"

"We take dreams very seriously here," Ibn noted. "Maybe it was the wine . . . maybe not."

Artus frowned as he watched the shopkeep look about the room, as if Pontifax's ghost might have left footprints on the ceiling. "He told me I should go on with my quest," the explorer said at last.

Ibn nodded in righteous satisfaction. "Then that is what you should do. I will help you get started again."

"But what about the Cult of Frost?"

"They did not send anyone or anything else after you," Ibn said. "I had the bearers set watches over the compound. Perhaps they think you are dead. Perhaps they know you are not and have given up."

"No," Artus said. "Kaverin can see through the eyes of the frost minions he conjures. He knows he killed Pontifax, but not me." The explorer picked idly at the green tunic Theron had left him; he'd been using it as a pillow. "The elf who tried to kill me aboard the *Narwhal* and the woman who got off the boat and hired the guide, they were both working for him. Maybe he's here himself."

"Is what you seek important enough for Kaverin to come

here himself? You said he hides in Tantras, shielded from danger by the cult."

Artus nodded. "Kaverin is wary, but he's no coward. If he thought the goal important enough, he'd most certainly come." He grimaced and added, "The cult members will kill anyone who stands in their way. That's why I can't tell you more. I don't want to endanger you more than I already have."

"Perhaps I should send word to the Harpers. They might dispatch—"

"No!" Artus snapped. "Leave the Harpers out of this, Ibn. . . . Please." He stumbled a few steps forward. "How many days have I been in here?"

"Sir Hydel has been dead for five days." Ibn slid a shoulder under Artus's arm. "You need to clean yourself up and eat something. Then there is something I wish you to see and someone you should talk with. This will be good news. Do not frown so."

Outside the tin hut, in the fresh air of the sunny afternoon, Artus realized how badly he smelled of sweat and spilled wine. He tried to move away from Ibn, certain he was offending the man, but the shopkeep seemed intent on helping him walk. Together they made their way across the compound to the large barrels of rainwater at the side of the supply depot. A bucket had already been drawn for Artus to use. Next to it lay a cake of soap, a silver straight razor, and a covered dish.

"This will settle your stomach," Ibn said, lifting the round cover from a fist-sized lump of dark bread. "Do not ask what is in it."

Artus sniffed the bread and wrinkled his nose. It smelled distinctly like fish—was that a bit of tentacle peeking out from the bottom? "Er, thanks. I guess."

"Eat the whole thing," Ibn chided. "That is the only cure for the pounding in your head."

Ibn headed back to the depot, leaving Artus to wash up. The explorer scrubbed himself clean, then scratched at the thick stubble on his chin. With a sigh, he lathered up the soap and set to work.

As he scraped away his fledgling beard, Artus watched the activity on the white sand beach. Some of the men and women who worked as bearers in Port Castigliar manned long fishing poles. Others cleaned and prepared vegetables for the evening meal. A few small children raced after the long-legged sea birds that hugged the shore, sending them shrieking into the sky. With methodical care, Inyanga gathered driftwood and spread it in the sun to dry. The port's inhabitants would use it for fires instead of chopping down the living trees nearby.

After rinsing his now smooth-shaven face, Artus sniffed at the bread again. Maybe they chop up the leftover driftwood and put it in here, too, he thought. The explorer took a bite of the roll. As he'd suspected, it tasted fishy. There were chewy bits, too. Squid, maybe. Or octopus. He refused to consider any of the more exotic possibilities. Yet, as Ibn had promised, the bread settled his stomach and drove away his headache.

Inyanga soon ran out of driftwood to gather and wandered to Artus's side. "Have you seen the marker my father made for him?"

"No. Let's take a look at it," Artus said, steeling himself for the sight. When he took a step, he felt as if he were walking in thick mud. Obviously, the bread hadn't countered all the aftereffects of the wine just yet.

At the edge of the graveyard, Artus paused. He knew where Pontifax was buried; he'd helped Ibn dig the grave himself. But there were two plots of freshly turned earth, not one.

"That is where we buried Kwame Zanj, the guide," Inyanga said solemnly. "His brother Judar brought back his body yesterday. He loved the port, so he asked to be buried here."

"What?" Artus sputtered. "The guide is dead? What about the woman who left the port with him?"

"She is dead, too," Ibn said. The shopkeep had returned from the depot and stood behind Artus, a younger man at his side. "Judar says the party from the *Narwhal* was attacked by the Batiri, do you see? Kwame struggled home to his village, but his wounds were too serious. That is why I wanted you to meet this young fellow," Ibn interjected, seeing the shock and confusion play across Artus's face. "He wishes to become Port Castigliar's guide, to earn money for his family just as Kwame did."

The young man nodded his agreement. He was of slight build; that was obvious even through the flowing white robes he wore. Artus had read enough about the cultures of Chult to know that white, not black, was the color of death and mourning here. "Brave Kwame rests in the house of Ubtao now," Judar said in a high, lisping voice.

"And the woman who was with your brother?" Artus pressed. "Did she die in your village, too?"

"No. The Batiri took her away to their camp," Judar said, a tremor of fear in his voice. "She and the other one are surely dead now."

"The other one?" Artus asked.

Judar looked down at the ground. "A flame-haired white man, tall and ill-tempered. Kwame asked me to search for him and the woman, but we found only the remains of their camp. It is a dishonor to our family that Kwame led the strangers to disaster."

Artus pulled Ibn aside. "There's something not right about this," he said. "He's describing Kaverin, but I just can't believe that vermin is dead."

"I can tell you this," Ibn said. "I have met Judar once before, not long ago, and this one seems to be the same boy. He may be working for Kaverin, but you have no choice but to trust him if you wish to get moving, do you see? Without a guide you will be lost in the jungle."

"And with a guide, I may be walking into a trap," Artus concluded.

As Artus turned to Judar, the young man smiled obsequiously. "I will help you, master. I know the jungle for miles in every direction." He cocked his head, and his large, pale eyes flashed strangely in the sunlight.

"Perhaps," the explorer murmured. He looked past the others to the graveyard.

"If you do not go on," Ibn whispered in his ear, "the Cult of Frost will have already won. Sir Hydel will have died in vain."

That statement of common sense jarred Artus's conscience. The despair he'd been wallowing in, the self-pity, fell back before the shocking realization he was doing his old friend a disservice by not moving ahead with the quest. "I have a map," Artus said. "It's in the hut. We can look at it . . . in a little while. All right, Judar?"

Without waiting for a reply, Artus walked toward Pontifax's grave. Clean and white, its edges still undulled by rain, the headstone hunched before the dark mound. Ibn had carved a graceful scroll around the inscription: *Sir Hydel Pontifax of Cormyr.*

The explorer crouched down, feeling the sun pound down on his pale back and shoulders. The medallion's chain seemed to drink in the heat, and soon it was stinging the back of his neck. He ignored the discomfort.

After a time, Inyanga appeared and crouched beside Artus. "It is a good marker," Artus said, "but it's missing something . . . and I think I know what it is."

The boy followed at Artus's heels as he crossed the compound to his hut. Inside, the explorer tore open Pontifax's pack and scattered the mage's clothes. It has to be here,

Artus told himself. Pontifax never went anywhere without it. Maybe it's in with his spell components. . . . Ah, success!

Artus held up a small medal, made of the purest Cormyrian silver, with a lightning bolt engraved upon it. Around the edges wound the inscription: *Order of the Golden Way.* He handed it to Inyanga. "Sir Hydel was awarded this for his service to our king on a great crusade," Artus said. "He was very proud of it."

"My father can set this in the stone," the boy said, nodding sagely.

"And I think I know what other words need to be written beneath it," Artus added.

By sunset that evening, Ibn had set Pontifax's medal beneath the scroll that held his name. Across the face of the white stone, he chiseled these final words: *Healer & Loyal Friend.* Artus could think of no better words to accompany his comrade to the Realm of the Dead.

* * * * *

The expedition set off into the jungle two days later— Artus, Judar, and six bearers. The guide went about his duties, trying hard to earn the explorer's respect. The youth quickly proved his knowledge of the area, or at least the route Theron's map delineated.

Artus missed Pontifax's expertise as soon as he left Port Castigliar. The bearers spoke only their native Tabaxi, and Artus only knew enough of the tongue to struggle through the most rudimentary exchanges. Judar, who spoke fluent Common, was an amiable, if somewhat self-deprecating, conversationalist. He smiled readily and was quick to laugh, though his chuckling was coarse, as if he were amused at some obscene jest everyone else had missed. Artus found it hard to talk with him, so he ordered the guide to march in front once they got underway. Letting the young man set the pace meant he could watch him closely and scan the brush for signs of an ambush.

For the whole day, they followed a well-trodden path, where the vines and undergrowth had been chopped back or crushed underfoot by the local tribesmen. The few natives they passed on the road went silently on their way; the Tabaxi had seen such expeditions before—hunters of treasure or monsters or fame. Such parties offered little threat to the well-armed natives and were rarely interested in trading on fair terms. Artus didn't blame them for their silence, not when ships like the *Narwhal* scoured the coast on behalf of operations like the Refuge Bay Trading Company.

The jungle itself was lush and ominous. Creatures called to one another or warned others off with shrieked claims of territory. The cries were sometimes low and rumbling, sometimes high and piercing. It often proved easier to locate an animal by sound or scent than by sight, so thick was the vegetation.

In the high canopy, dark shapes sailed gracefully from branch to branch, tree to tree. Once, Artus saw a child-sized ape, its dark face ringed by a wild frill of white and yellow fur. The creature hung over the road, suspended from a branch by one impossibly long arm. As the company approached, it bared blood-red fangs and snarled. This was only so much show, for it soon fled higher into the tangle of vines and branches. Artus noted with awe that the ape's back was covered with bristling spines.

The heat drained the life from the party like a massive leech. Artus was hit hardest, though he found unexpected relief in the tunic Theron had left for him. The hooded garment proved to be woven of some magical thread. It kept his body cool and remained unsodden by sweat.

So it went, with the trail becoming more and more overgrown, more and more difficult as they traveled. As dusk called a halt to their sixth tedious day on the winding trail, they set up camp at a crossroads, drawing the tents and foodstuffs from the fifty-pound loads each bearer carried. The cost of the supplies and the wages for Judar and the bearers had taken what little money Artus had left. As the explorer watched the freed slaves struggle with the heavy burdens, he wondered if one day he might be working at the port to earn his way back to Cormyr. More likely, if he failed in this venture, he would be dead. If he succeeded and the ring was half as powerful as the legends told, he'd have no need of a boat to carry him back home. Some claimed the ring gave a man the ability to fly. Others said it had been enchanted in such a way that its wearer need only wish to be someplace to go there.

Artus had managed to keep to himself for much of the trip, but it proved impossible to avoid Judar that evening. The guide came to him as soon as the meal was finished and the watch set. "You are not a talkative man," Judar observed, more a question than a statement.

Quietly, Artus ran his dagger along a sharpening stone. The light from the gem in its grip cast long shadows across his face, making him look quite dangerous. "I just don't have anything to say to you, Judar."

The guide pursed his lips. "I . . . I have heard about the death of your friend," he began tentatively. "I am sorry. I just lost my brother, so I know what you feel."

"Perhaps." Again Artus scraped the blade along the stone. "We'll be at Kitcher's Folly by tomorrow night, if I read the map right."

"If we keep up this pace, we will have time to make camp at the statue before the sun sets."

"And the trail ends there?"

Judar paused. "You know it does, Master Cimber. The map says so." His expression darkened. "I know you do not trust me. A man who has assassins of ice trying to take his life should trust no one." To Artus's suspicious look, the guide replied, "The bearers told me about it. Don't think I could have been in camp a day without hearing of such fantastic things."

"You're right. I don't trust you," Artus warned. "But if you can figure that out, you should be wise enough to leave me alone."

Judar abruptly stood. "When the trail ends, you will need to trust me, Master Cimber." He laughed coarsely, eyes flashing in the firelight. "I do not mean to mock, but you will get nowhere in the jungle without trust."

Artus watched as the guide went back to his tent. *My first impression was right*, he decided. *There's definitely something dangerous about him.*

A swarm of finger-long mosquitoes settled over Artus, and he used the hood of his cloak to scatter them. He retreated from the night, dagger and sharpening stone in hand, for the refuge of his tent. The netting kept the larger insects out, but, as always, a small army of pests had invaded the tent in his absence. He killed a few, which sent the others scrambling for the doorflap.

For much of that night and all the next day, Artus pondered his dilemma. With Kaverin and the cult after the Ring of Winter—for there could be no other reason for their presence in Chult—he could trust no one. Neither could he accept the story that Kaverin was dead. The stone-handed murderer had escaped greater threats than goblin cannibals before. He was crafty and resourceful—resourceful enough to plant a spy in Artus's expedition, just as he had set the elven first mate aboard the *Narwhal* against the explorer.

Yet the guide was right in one thing: Artus would need someone to help him navigate through the jungle. No tribesman had passed them in two days, and the trail had all but vanished beneath a carpet of twisting vines and decaying leaves. The canopy had closed completely overhead, plunging the expedition into a twilight broken only infrequently by slants of pale sunlight. They had passed beyond the lands traveled by any but the very brave or the very foolish.

Artus found himself checking their heading more and more with his dagger. The centaurs of Tribe Pastilar had not only enchanted the weapon to give off a perpetual light, but it could also be used as a compass. By holding his dagger flat in his palm and speaking the centaur chieftain's name, the blade pointed due north. The dagger also allowed him to control spiders—a very real danger in the forest where the centaurs dwelled—but Artus had only had cause to use that particular enchantment once, in the aptly named Spiderhaunt Woods.

"We are at the end of the trail," Judar shouted from the front of the line, startling Artus out of his reverie.

At a word from the explorer, the bearers lowered their packs to the ground. They sat as one, silently rubbing sore muscles. Up ahead, the narrow trail opened onto a weed-choked clearing. In its center, bathed in the light of the dying sun, stood Kitcher's Folly.

The statue was a twelve-foot-high bust of Sir Ilyber Kitcher, an explorer from Scardale who had come to Chult a few hundred years ago. Decades of rain and sun had dulled the features, but enough of the face remained for Artus to see what a sour-looking sort Kitcher had been. His wide eyes looked sternly out from under bushy brows. A drooping mustache hung over a suitably grim mouth, lips drawn into a thin line of resolve.

"So this is the infamous Kitcher's Folly," Artus whispered. He ran a hand along the statue's base, over the dulled inscriptions carved into the stone.

Armed with limited supplies and even more limited wits, Sir Ilyber Kitcher had decided to traverse the unmapped land of Chult from east to west, starting in a small port he'd named after his rich Uncle Castigliar. At the sites of notable discoveries and battles, Kitcher planned to erect monuments to his bravery and fortitude. His funds being nowhere near as restricted as his other assets—thanks largely to Uncle Castigliar—the statues were to be of the magical variety. Upon a traveler's mere request, they would recite the tale of Kitcher's glorious victory, as well as provide useful information about what local fauna to eat, which animals made the best trophies, and so on.

Only one statue had been erected in Kitcher's name. The intrepid explorer had blundered upon a nasty conflict between two warring Tabaxi factions. Instead of skirting the battle, he ordered a mage in his party to draw the attention of the chiefs. He would end this petty bickering, as was his duty as a civilized man. Needless to say, the only thing the magical fireworks attracted was a rain of spears and arrows from both armies. The Tabaxi had miraculously lost track of their own argument in the face of this new and obviously powerful adversary.

Fortunately for Kitcher, two men escaped to tell the tale. In gratitude for the spot of beach named after him, his uncle later paid a small group to sneak into the jungle and erect a statue to the explorer, though one that would do nothing but mutely decry the death of a would-be great man. It soon after became known as Kitcher's Folly.

The bearers had gathered around the statue, talking quietly amongst themselves. "They have heard this is the head of an evil giant, buried here long ago by Ubtao to keep strangers out of his jungle," Judar translated.

Artus glanced up at the rapidly darkening sky. "Well it's too late to move on tonight, especially since we lose the trail after this." He pulled Theron's map from his pocket. "We head southwest from here, through swampland, if the map's right. We can't do that in the dark."

The bearers returned to the packs and hoisted them to

their shoulders. "Stop!" Artus cried in Tabaxi. Fear beginning to show on their faces, the natives paused. One of them began to talk excitedly to Judar.

From the little Artus could understand of the exchange, the bearers wanted to move on until the sun set completely, to put as much distance between them and the statue as possible. Judar's face told his feelings on this much more clearly than his words; he was petrified at the thought of moving farther into the jungle.

At last the guide turned back to Artus. "If we do not move on," he hissed, "the bearers will turn back right now. They will follow the trail home and leave us here."

Leaning against Kitcher's sculpted face, Artus drew his dagger. He held his palm out flat so the blade could turn in his hand. After it had indicated north, the explorer pointed southwest. "That way, then," he said to Judar.

"We must not!" the guide exclaimed.

Artus stared at the man for a moment. "We don't have a choice. There'll be danger in trekking through swamp this close to dark, but it can't be helped, not if we want to keep the bearers. Besides, staying in a clearing like this might make us an obvious target for raiders."

"But we—"

"But we what?" Artus asked, his eyes narrowed in suspicion. "Is there a reason we need to camp here?"

Judar's fear-filled expression softened. "N-no, master. It is just . . . the swamp is very dangerous. I know of many men who have died trying to cross it."

"Well, you'd better prove to be a better guide than the ones they trusted," Artus replied coldly. To the bearers he snapped, "Hurry up, then."

They marched for a few hours more, until night and the jungle itself stopped them. Clouds of biting insects followed the expedition relentlessly. Artus soon found the exposed parts of his arms and hands covered with welts. He must have been bitten by a hundred mosquitoes; he couldn't count how many more he'd inadvertently swallowed or inhaled.

The more immediate concern for the explorer was the terrain. The ground grew more and more soggy as they trudged on. Pockets of thin, watery mud lurked beneath the carpet of fallen leaves and vines, and it wasn't long before everyone's boots were covered in the fetid stuff. Judar had taken to testing the ground with a long stick, but the bearers were less methodical. Soon, their haste proved deadly. As night fell, one of the natives disappeared into a hidden sinkhole. Before anyone could react, the weight of the pack pulled him under, with only a swirl of disturbed mud to mark his passing.

Artus leaned over the edge of the small pool. His arms were soaked from reaching into the murky trap in a vain attempt to rescue the man. "That's it," he said, stunned. "We camp here."

For a moment, everyone watched the leaves settle back over the mud. Then the bearers lowered their burdens and knelt around their fellow's grave, bowing their heads. Their murmured prayer was lost in the calls of night-stalking birds and animals crying out a farewell to the setting sun. Finally one of them took a broad, verdant leaf. With a stick of charcoal he produced from his own small pouch, the bearer wrote his companion's name. One by one, the others spoke a single word of praise for the drowned man, all of which were added to the leaf.

"Just like the tombstones in port," Artus said. "They're writing his introduction to Ubtao." He turned to Judar, but found the guide crouching in the dirt. With his fingers he traced something on the ground.

Artus crouched down, too, his attention drawn away from the solemn ceremony around the pool. Judar ran his fingers around the deep imprint again and again. "It is a footprint," the guide hissed.

Drawing his dagger, Artus held the glowing hilt over the print. It had been made by something very heavy. The tri-clawed foot had to be twice as large as a human hand. "What made this?"

"*Ubtao Zazqura,*" one of the bearers said. Their ritual complete, they had formed a silent ring around Artus and Judar.

"Ubtao's Children?" the explorer translated. "These are dinosaur tracks?"

Trembling, Judar closed his eyes. "Most of them hunt during the day," he said in his high, grating voice. "Most, but not all. We had better pray whatever made this print is sleeping right now."

Once they had cleared a patch of ground large enough for the tents and built up a small fire, the expedition discovered many such tracks. Some were smaller than the first, most were larger. Judar and the bearers spent much of the night staring into the jungle, snatching up spears and clubs at every rumble in the darkness. Artus, too, watched, but not in fear. For years he'd heard tales of dinosaurs, huge, ancient reptiles that once had roamed the entirety of Toril. Some claimed they were the ancestors of modern-day dragons. Other scholars dismissed such theories as non-sense, stating serenely that the great lizards were only mammoth, plodding brutes that had become nearly extinct thousands upon thousands of years ago.

Nearly, but not entirely.

Chult was the one place on Toril where dinosaurs still flourished, though the forbidding jungles kept all but the heartiest explorers from ever seeing one. Artus could hardly contain his excitement. He leaned against a tree trunk that night, lost in imagining how wonderful and in-triguing the dinosaurs might be.

The next morning, he and the rest of the expedition learned only how terrible the elusive giants were.

Seven

The first dinosaur appeared with the sunrise. The creature walked on four thick legs, moving with steady ease over the clumps of turf and shallow pools of swamp water. Its head was broad and rounded at the snout, with large glassy eyes that carefully scanned the area for a likely source of breakfast. Almost eighteen feet of barrel-like torso and stiff, twitching tail lagged behind the dinosaur's head. Spines of bone stood erect along its back, connected by a thick webbing of skin. This sail was mottled with greens and browns and even more subtle strands of dark blue, though the rest of the creature's body was the deep green of the jungle vegetation.

From what he considered a safe vantage, a dozen yards away and halfway up the trunk of a partly toppled tree, Artus studied the creature. It obliged his careful surveillance by perching atop a large cluster of boulders. For a time the dinosaur remained still, head held up to the rising sun, eyes closed.

Artus made a few notes on the creature's coloration and size, using the back of Theron's map. From his studies in the Stalwarts' library, he guessed this to be an altispinax. Little was known about them, save that they were often sighted in Chultan swamps like the one in which the expedition was currently mired.

A gentle tap on his boot made Artus start and nearly lose his grip on the tree. Judar stood below, a long pole in one hand. The guide had discovered a stand of hearty bamboo near camp, from which he and the bearers had harvested walking sticks. "Here is your dagger, Master Cimber," Judar said softly. "We are ready to go."

After one last look at the altispinax, Artus slid to the ground. He took his dagger from Judar, then looked at the tip of his bamboo staff. The end was as sharp as any metal spearhead. "Obviously, this did the trick," he said, slipping the dagger into his boot. Judar had borrowed the enchanted blade because the bamboo had proven too tough for any other knife.

A sound cut through the jungle then, unlike anything Artus had ever heard before. It was the deep bellow of a lion's roar, but trilled like birdsong. Artus spun around. There, atop the cluster of rock, the altispinax sounded out again. Its mouth was open wide, enough for Artus to see it large, sharp teeth.

"The wind is blowing the wrong way for him to scent us," Judar hissed. "What is he doing?"

"I don't know, but I don't think we should stick around to find out."

Artus and Judar hurried back to camp. The bearers had already shouldered their loads, and Artus quickly slid his smaller pack onto his back. He had a pretty clear idea where their path lay, but he checked their bearings with his dagger anyway.

"That's odd," Artus said as the blade stopped moving. "I thought north was more in that direction. . . ." He glanced at Judar, but the guide's face was expressionless. "Which way?"

"South-by-west," the guide said, pointing. "Is that still the way you wish to go?"

The explorer checked the dagger again. It agreed with Judar's directions. "Er, yes," he mumbled. "Lead on."

The bellowing of the altispinax unsettled Artus. It rang through the jungle, silencing all the other animals. He wondered if the dinosaur was declaring its territory. At least he hoped so. Those teeth most definitely identified the altispinax as a carnivore, and one in the area would be dangerous enough.

Judar, too, seemed frightened by the creature's cry. He shifted his pole from hand to hand, even as he used it to test the ground for sinkholes like the one that had swallowed up the unfortunate Tabaxi the night before. As Artus watched the guide nervously push on at the head of the group, he noticed the young man stumble now and then. The trek was taking a toll on Judar; fatigue had made him clumsy and drained the life from his eyes.

For their part, the bearers showed no fear of the sounds. They knew the roaring of the dinosaurs well. To them, the monsters were the Children of Ubtao, the most spectacular creation of the great Chultan god. Unlike many of the other gods in the Realms, Ubtao had little traffic with those who believed in him. The Tabaxi did not plead to him for boons or ask for visions of the future; they went about their lives, secure that events in the jungle unfolded as Ubtao wished.

Artus never learned how the bearers interpreted what happened next, whether they believed Ubtao had revealed his anger through his children or the dinosaurs had been acting upon instinct.

It started when the lone altispinax ceased its roaring. The silence lasted an instant, then the rolling call of other sail-backed dinosaurs came from every direction. Artus looked from right to left and scanned the trees and tangles of vines for signs of movement. Though the creatures sounded close, he couldn't see anything. Then he remembered the coloration of the altispinax on the rocks. In this overgrown part of the jungle, it would blend in with the vegetation.

"Judar," Artus said, "get the bearers to form a circle between those two large trees."

Another roar, close at hand. Artus stared hard at a cluster of frond-heavy plants. The sound seemed to come from there. . . .

The dinosaur opened its mouth to roar again, and the flash of hundreds of daggerlike white teeth gave its location away. Gods, Artus shouted in his mind, they're close! They've probably been lurking around us since we left camp!

The altispinax turned, and its sail caught the sunlight bleeding through the canopy. The dinosaur growled, rolling its red-rimmed eyes. Artus dropped his pack, stepping slowly backward toward the bearers. He could hear the worried murmuring of the Tabaxi as they propped their packs around their position in a waist-high defensive wall.

"Should we climb the trees?" Judar asked, gripping his bamboo pole with trembling hands.

Artus glanced at the closest trees. Their trunks were too fat around, their bark too smooth. The lowest branches lay hundreds of feet off the ground. The men would never be able to climb fast enough or high enough to avoid the dinosaurs.

"We're going to have to make a stand here," Artus said, stringing his bow. "Let's just hope they're not very hungry or—" he nocked a blue-fletched arrow "—that we can prove we're not an easy meal."

The red-eyed altispinax moved forward cautiously, testing the air with its wide nostrils. It casually kicked Artus's
pack. The three claws on its foot tore a hole in the sturdy
canvas as if it were gossamer. With two gulps the dinosaur
devoured the rations Artus had carried there, along with
the rest of his clothes, a spare pair of boots, his canteen,
and the remains of the shredded pack itself. That meager
fare gone, it looked once more at the explorer and his
trapped party.

All around the makeshift fort, the bearers faced sail-
backed monsters with equally ravenous looks in their eyes.
These were smaller than the one that had devoured
Artus's pack, but they also seemed more anxious to get at
the men. The Tabaxi held their bamboo poles out like
spears, prodding any altispinax that got too close. That only seemed to irritate the creatures further, especially since
the sharpened points did little more than scratch the dinosaurs' tough hide.

The brute in front of Artus roared, then started forward
at a jog. As he went to draw the longbow, Artus saw Judar
reaching for him. More precisely, the guide seemed to be
pointing at the now-useless Mulhorandi amulet hanging
around his neck. The white paste that damped its magical
energy shone dully in the perpetual twilight beneath the
canopy. "That can't do anything for us," Artus snapped,
elbowing the slight youth aside.

He fired at the dinosaur twice before it crashed into the
packs. One arrow struck a shallow wound in its wide forehead, right between its eyes. The shaft bobbed as the
creature ran. The second arrow went right into the altispinax's mouth. Blood drooled from the beast's jaws as it
chewed the arrow to pieces.

The altispinax almost leaped high enough to clear the
pack standing between it and Artus. Luckily, it didn't quite

succeed. As it scrambled for footing, the pack fell to bits beneath its claws. More supplies tumbled onto the ground, only to be gobbled up by the smaller sail-backed monsters.

The bearer closest to Artus dropped his pole and gamely hacked at the beast with his machete. Artus himself was forced to use his bow as a club. He slammed it again and again across the beast's skull, waiting for the wood to break. The bow never did shatter, though most would have. The sailor who had sold it to Ibn had been telling the truth; the weapon had been crafted by the servants of the elven court on Evermeet. Such bows, though not created by sorcery, always proved amazingly resilient.

With one snap of its powerful jaws, the altispinax bit through the bearer's bamboo spear. Another snap, and the Tabaxi was dead. The man's scream excited the dinosaurs into a frenzy, like hungry sharks spurred on by blood-filled water. The smaller creatures tore at the packs, while three or four larger beasts tried to climb over the crumbling barricades. Another bearer was pulled from the circle and immediately set upon by a half-dozen dinosaurs.

The red-eyed altispinax turned back to the embattled men, its snout and jaws crimson with blood and gore. It was then that a brilliant flash lit the area, followed by a roar of thunder louder even than the dinosaurs' growling.

For an instant, everything stood still. Artus had the wild, irrational thought that Pontifax was trying to save him, reaching out from beyond the grave to extract him from one last impossible situation. Or maybe Ibn had summoned the Harpers. Then he saw Judar, crouching at the center of the baggage circle. A shiny stone and a handful of gray powder slipped from his fingers.

"You're a mage?" Artus gasped.

But the guide was already on his feet and running. As he passed Artus, Judar grabbed him by the hood. "Quick!" he shrieked.

Drunkenly the dinosaurs stumbled about, shaking their heads or working their jaws in stunned silence. At least it seemed to Artus they were silent, though his ears were ringing too badly to tell for certain. The remaining bearers took advantage of the confusion to escape, too. They ran off in a different direction from Artus and Judar. Before the explorer could signal the surviving Tabaxi to follow, they had vanished.

The dinosaurs recovered soon after. They milled about the remains of the packs and the two corpses in confusion, then charged after the survivors. Artus could hear them breaking through the undergrowth close behind, splashing through the fetid water, churning up the thick mud. Only one of the beasts caught up with Artus and Judar; in fact, it somehow got in front of them. It was a small specimen, nine feet long with a stunted sail upon its back.

Judar was intent on getting the dinosaur out of their way, and quickly. In one fluid movement, the guide reached into his white robes, withdrew a pinch of sand, and tossed it at the dinosaur. As it traveled forward, the sand expanded into the shape of a lion twice as large as a man. The conjured creature struck the altispinax head on. Artus lost sight of the dinosaur, but when the cloud lost its form and the sand settled to the ground, not even a single bone remained.

"Why didn't you tell me you were a mage?" Artus asked as they took off again at a run.

The guide said nothing, only stepped up their grueling pace. Soon the roars of the dinosaurs faded, masked by the cries of birds and other creatures high in the canopy. A short time later, they were out of the swamp. While that meant no more slogging through mud, the undergrowth grew more dense here. Without the bearers' machetes, they were forced to rely on Artus's dagger to hack their way through the thick vines and fronds blocking their path. The going was tough and very slow.

"I want an explanation," Artus said. He dropped the vine he was cutting through and wiped his brow. The day was growing intolerably hot, even with the protection of Theron's tunic.

Judar slumped to the ground. "I really do not wish to discuss it."

"If you'd been honest and told me you had spells at your control, we might have avoided that fight with the alti-spinax altogether," Artus snapped. "Those bearers would still be alive!"

The guide shook his head slowly. "In most Tabaxi tribes, only village elders and those the elders choose as appren-tices may use magic. The bearers would not have traveled with a renegade like me." He turned his large eyes to the explorer. "We would still be at the port."

Artus paused, considering the explanation. He had heard something about Tabaxi mages being protective of their craft, but that still didn't explain everything. "At the start of the fight, you reached for the medallion I wear. Why?"

"I was born with a rare gift. I can see the aura all magical things radiate," the guide offered honestly. "I saw a slight glow from the medallion and thought it might help us." He shifted on his heels, tearing up saw-edged grass one blade at a time. "I am sorry I led you to disaster. My fami-ly's shame seems to no know bounds. First Kwame, now this. . . ."

Artus sank to the ground beside Judar. "Well, magic or no, we'd better try to make it back to Kitcher's Folly by sunset. We should be safe there, at least from the dino-saurs." He looked up at the curtain of greenery surround-ing them. "From there we can go to the port. We'll have to gather what supplies we can along the trail. At least I can still do a little hunting."

Artus had managed to salvage a few items from the disastrous morning: his dagger, his bow and arrows, the clothes on his back, and Theron's map. Judar had nothing but his white robes and the spell components in his pockets. As they struggled on, presumably northeast toward Kitcher's Folly, the guide explained that another explorer had taught him the rudiments of magic. With a few years of experimentation, he had done much to develop those kernels of knowledge. Judar only knew enchantments useful for battle. While that would help protect them from any other menacing dinosaurs, it would do little to speed the trek back to Port Castigliar.

Luckily, the dinosaurs they stumbled upon that afternoon were gentle giants, content to tear up whole bushes and clumps of bamboo with their gaping mouths. The first resembled a monstrous armadillo, though its head was large and broad. Rock-hard circles of bone, like plate armor, covered its body, and blunted spikes patterned its skull. From the brief look Artus got before the beast trundled away into the jungle, he figured the dinosaur to be at least twice as big as the largest elephant, perhaps even thirty-five feet long. Its most amazing feature was not its size, but the bulging knob of bone at the end of its tail. The club splintered trees as the dinosaur walked, demonstrating how formidable a weapon it would be in battle.

They spotted the other dinosaur, or more precisely the other group of dinosaurs, in a clearing at the edge of a small pond. Artus recognized them as a family of stegosaurus. The largest of them, perhaps twenty feet from the tip of its pointed snout to the four sharp spikes at the end of its tail, would have been dwarfed by the armored monster he and Judar had disturbed earlier. An alternating double row of bony, diamond-shaped plates ran the length of its arched back, starting small near its neck, growing larger in the middle, and tapering down again along its tail. Six of the beasts grazed upon the tender grasses at the water's edge. They turned to idly study the two men who pushed out of the jungle, but apart from herding the two smallest behind their mothers, the dinosaurs went about their business as if no one else shared the pond.

The afternoon wore on, and the twilight world beneath the thick jungle canopy began to slide into a more profound darkness. To make matter worse, after hours of walking Artus and Judar were still thoroughly lost. The guide insisted they were moving toward the well-worn trail to the port, but the way remained close to impassable. Artus checked the dagger again and again. It always agreed with Judar's assessment of their direction.

"We will surely break into the more traveled areas tomorrow," Judar assured the explorer, though Artus found little comfort in the guide's words. His predicament had made him rightfully cautious, and Judar's secrecy about his skill with magic had fanned the embers of his suspicions into an open flame again.

They ate a meager meal in silence. After, they rested in the darkness, listening to the calls of the night-stalking creatures. Artus sat with his bow across his lap, two arrows planted point-first in the ground nearby. If anything entered their small camp or passed too close through the branches overhead, he intended to make the beast think twice about attacking. He didn't want to think about what would happen after the arrows were gone. Anyway, it was better to go down fighting.

Artus was soon asleep, the stress and strain of the day dragging him down to oblivion.

A sharp jab in the back woke the explorer, how much later he could not tell. He rolled to the side, grabbing for his bow and an arrow. Holding the bow sideways, he glanced around the camp. Moonlight filtering through the canopy revealed a terrifying scene.

Judar lay face-down a few feet away. Over the motionless guide stood two squat goblins. Artus loosed the

arrow, hitting one of the intruders square in the chest. It
went down with a grunt, its wide mouth moving wordless-
ly. Two more goblins crashed from the bushes, nasty-
looking spears held menacingly forward. The rustle in the
vegetation to his back told Artus that others had circled
around to surround him.

Kneeling as he was, the explorer could look the manlike
creatures straight in the eyes. Their faces were round and
flattened. Broad foreheads sloped down to dull eyes the
yellow of rotten eggs. Noses that seemed uniformly
squashed wandered out to their high cheekbones, toward
their pointed ears. Their skin was strangely mottled with
reds and oranges. Artus had seen goblins before, but never any as wild as these. They wore only torn breechcloths
and a few scattered scraps of leather armor.

The rest of the arrows lay far away from the explorer,
certainly too far to reach before a goblin spear took him in
the back. Artus slid his grip toward one end of the longbow. It had served as a club against the dinosaurs readily
enough. The goblins' skulls would prove easier to break,
too. . . .

He had tensed his legs, ready to lunge, when another
goblin entered the clearing. This one was fully a foot taller
than the others, with a well-tended breastplate of dinosaur
hide covering his torso. He snorted when he saw the dead
goblin warrior, then pointed at Artus.

The shuffle of bare feet alerted Artus to the attack. He
spun around. Two goblins rushed toward him, ready to
grapple him barehanded. It took but one swing of the bow
to send them sprawling. A clear path to the jungle suddenly
lay before him.

Maybe I'll get out of this alive, he thought hopefully.

That hope died quickly. A solid blow to the back of the
head knocked Artus to the ground. Darkness rolled over
his mind, shutting out the night in waves.

"He no challenge for Batiri," the armored goblin said scornfully. He kicked Artus in the side.

The explorer spoke fluent enough Goblin to understand this coarse dialect. "Batiri!" he gasped. Artus's thoughts spun like a raft caught in a maelstrom. Oh gods, his mind screamed, the cannibals who captured Theron!

Then another wave of darkness crashed down upon his thoughts, dragging Artus down to unconsciousness.

* * * * *

Artus awoke in a circular hole in the ground, rain dripping on his face through the bamboo-and-frond roof covering the dank prison. His head throbbed, and his face was wet from the rain and sticky with blood. When he tried to sit up, pain arced through his head like lightning in a stormy sky.

With a groan, he collapsed back onto the dirty straw pallet. Gingerly he touched the top of his head. Three sizeable lumps formed an uneven circle on his scalp. That would account for the blood and the pain, he decided. I got one lump when they attacked, but where did the other two come from?

Vaguely Artus recalled being moved from the site of the ambush to wherever he was now. The Batiri had tied his hands and feet, then strung a pole through the ropes. They carried him this way, just as Artus had seen big game hunters transport their trophies. Each time he awoke, a goblin clubbed him back to unconsciousness. He grimaced. That would account for the other two goose eggs.

"Well?" came a familiar voice from across the squalid room. "You don't plan to just lie there, do you? Be a good soldier and get moving."

Artus stared in amazement, his jaw slack. There, on a broad stump that served as the jail's only chair, sat Pontifax—or at least his ghost. The old mage was pale, and

Artus could see right through him to the earthen wall. His bushy eyebrows were raised in slight amusement over eyes that still shone like phantom sapphires. His mouth was turned up in a smile.

"I—I don't believe this," Artus muttered. He put his hand to his forehead. "They must have hit me harder than I thought."

"Good!" the spirit exclaimed. "It's about time you started being a little more skeptical. Look where you've got yourself by trusting people without making them prove their mettle." Pontifax glanced around and shook his head. "Well, better take the gorgon by the horns and get yourself out of this, my boy. The sun is setting, and the goblins are getting restless."

Artus closed his eyes tightly. "This isn't happening," he said, then repeated it two or three times, mantralike. Sure enough, when he looked again, the specter was nowhere to be seen. He chalked the hallucination up to the welts on his head, a lack of food, and the dire straits in which he now found himself.

Slowly he got to his feet, then waited for the dizziness to subside. Weak light crept into the room through the thatched roof, along with the rain. The circular prison was ten or twelve paces across in the center, with walls about fifteen feet high. No door. No ladder up to the ground.

He wondered for a moment where Judar was. Theron Silvermace had made it clear two fates were possible at the hands of the cannibalistic Batiri—becoming a sacrifice to the thing they worshiped or landing a spot on their menu. Since he was still alive, Artus assumed the goblins intended to sacrifice him. That Judar was nowhere to be seen meant another fate had likely befallen him. Artus forced that thought from his mind and scanned the room again.

The prison seemed more than roomy enough for its meager contents—a straw pallet, the up-ended log, and a few discarded wooden plates. His dagger and his bow had been taken. Since the goblins had burrowed it into the ground, the prison proved cool, if somewhat damp. Water ran down the walls in rivulets, turning the floor into a mire. Artus was a bit surprised the walls hadn't collapsed, considering how much it rained in Chult. A closer examination revealed the source of the prison's stability—a fine net of tree roots held together by bamboo poles.

Exhilaration damped the throbbing in Artus's skull and calmed the hunger raging in his stomach. A plan had presented itself, prompted by the goblins' ingenuity.

The discarded wooden plates were easy to break, cracked as they were from dampness and misuse. One of the fist-sized pieces was sharp enough for Artus's needs. With it, he set about cutting a foothold into the wall, shearing away the roots. It proved more difficult to sever the bamboo supports, but the earth had made them softer than the canes Judar had cut near the altispinax swamp. With a minimum of noise, masked in part by the falling rain, Artus cut two more footholds higher up.

Mud began to seep from the gaps almost immediately, making the climb treacherous. Twice, Artus's feet slipped from the footholds. He landed on his back in the mire, frozen with dread, waiting for a goblin guard to push back the roof to see what had caused the commotion. But the Batiri proved oblivious to Artus's activities. He was soon at the top of the wall, peering cautiously through a hole in the roof.

The prison was situated at the edge of the Batiri camp. Three huge trees towered over the hole, the source of the roots used in the walls. Nearby, a dark line of plants and vines encroached upon the area cleared for the village. That was his path to freedom.

In the other direction lay the village itself, a collection of haphazardly placed huts. Totems of dark wood jutted up

before each building. The man-sized poles were intended
to keep away evil spirits, Artus decided. He'd seen similar
totems in orcish settlements in Thar and kobold warrens in
Ashanath. The sun still struggled to break through the pal-
lid storm clouds overhead, and patches of wan light dotted
the clearing. The goblins were waiting for the sun to give
up the fight and retreat for the evening. Goblins hated sunlight. It made them weak and nauseous.

Artus could see only two Batiri, and they were quite
close.

"Leave be, Balt," one of the warriors snorted. He sat at
the base of a massive tree, not ten feet from the prison. A
spear leaned against the trunk, well out of the goblin's
reach. "Prisoner no get away. I club on head again if he try
to run."

The Batiri with the dinosaur-hide breastplate loomed
over the guard, fury dancing across his features. His grim-
ace revealed a small pair of fangs. "I club you," he snarled.
"You march or you go to Grumog."

The guard was slow to his feet, but he heeded Balt's
warning. Taking up the spear, he marched toward the
prison. This was the chance Artus needed. He ducked beneath the cover of the roof and tensed, waiting for the goblin to get close. The shuffling of flat feet got nearer . . .
nearer.

Artus burst through the fronds and grabbed the guard by
the ankle. Raising his spear, the goblin shouted in surprise,
but he couldn't strike before Artus yanked his foot from
beneath him. With a shriek, the guard toppled onto the
roof. The bamboo supports cracked, then broke under his
weight. The warrior crashed to the floor of the prison
amidst a rain of bamboo splinters and torn fronds.

Balt rushed forward, drawing a wickedly curved scimitar. He lashed out just as Artus pulled himself up from the
hole, but the explorer somehow managed to roll out of the

way. The blade bit into the ground next to Artus's head, and a dollop of mud slapped into the explorer's face. Blinded in one eye by the muck, he tried to kick Balt. The goblin used the flat of his blade to easily divert the awkward attack.

"Escape!" a deep voice bellowed. Then another joined in. "Capture Grumog's bounty!"

These weren't goblin voices shattering the silence, but the gravelly cries of the totems before each hut. The leering, twisted faces on each wooden pole shouted warnings to their masters, calling the Batiri to arms. Balt smiled at the cacophony, certain the village would rouse itself in time to recapture the human . . . if he didn't subdue the man first himself.

Artus saw that confidence in the goblin's yellow eyes. He'll expect me to run now, the explorer realized. Better not disappoint him.

With speed born of exhilaration and more than a touch of fear, Artus rolled away from Balt and jumped to his feet. He took one step toward the jungle, just as the goblin expected, then wheeled around. Balt's guard was down, and he was nowhere near quick enough to block the vicious right hook Artus threw. The punch landed squarely on the warrior's lantern jaw, sending him reeling to the very brink of the pit. Balt dropped his scimitar and windmilled his arms in an attempt to save himself, but it was futile. Artus snatched up the sword and struck the goblin in the chest with one fluid stroke. The dinosaur-hide armor protected Balt from the blade, but not the push backward. He tumbled into the pit, cursing and shouting.

Batiri warriors began to stream out of their dark little huts, spears and small bows in their hands. Arrows buzzed around Artus like angry bees as he pushed into the jungle. He could hear the goblins swarming around their village, shouting orders that could be heard even over the wailing of their totems.

It's pointless to try to outrun them, Artus decided, especially with night coming on fast. Maybe I can hide out until dawn, then make a break for it. That plan in mind, the explorer stealthily scrambled up the nearest tall tree. Shielded by the thick foliage, he observed the goblins without being seen.

To Artus's surprise, only a few scattered groups of Batiri combed the bush looking for him. These hunting parties, made up of ten or more warriors each, beat the bushes and checked behind each boulder in the jungle immediately surrounding the village. A few even scanned the trees, though they acted as if they didn't think it likely the human would hide there.

The remaining goblins milled around the village. A few went from totem to totem, slapping the wooden sentinels to make them stop their shouting. A handful found a rope ladder and were in the process of rescuing Balt and the unconscious guard from the muddy pen. Most just lit torches outside their homes, jabbered, and pointed toward the ruined prison.

As the commotion died down, Artus recognized another sound—a familiar voice pleading for mercy.

Judar's screams filled the air, clear and chilling. Artus couldn't see the Tabaxi guide, but it sounded as if the noise was coming from inside the largest building in the village, an impressive two-story wooden structure with a peaked roof. A gaping pit yawned next to this building, and a white metal gong hung from a wooden stand at its edge. From Theron's story, Artus guessed this to be the lair of the Batiri's god, Grumog.

They're going to sacrifice him, Artus realized. He pushed aside as much of his cover as he dared, trying to catch a glimpse of the unfortunate man. Indecision gripped him, and his conscience prodded him to try something, *anything,* to save Judar. He couldn't just sit by while they tortured him or tossed him to the creature in the pit.

In the end, Artus didn't have to decide. From the tangle of branches and leaves above him came a high trill and the clack of mandibles. He looked up just in time to see a monstrous spider, his equal in size and as hairy as any wolf. As the creature lurched forward, Artus realized why the goblins hadn't given the trees much attention. He also lamented the fact that the Batiri had taken his dagger; for the first time in years he could have used the enchantment that allowed him to control spiders, and he didn't have the blasted thing.

Still, Artus was armed, and his reflexes and years of fighting such lurking menaces saved him. He jabbed up with the goblin's scimitar, skewering the spider. The momentum of the creature's lunge impaled it farther upon the blade, but it also knocked Artus out of the tree. His fall, as luck would have it, was broken by several Batiri. There his good fortune ended, for the hunters were neither killed nor stunned, just bruised and enraged.

He scuffled with them, breaking one goblin's arm and shattering another's knee, but they overwhelmed him by sheer strength of numbers. The only thing Artus felt fortunate about as they carried him back to the village was that no one had thought it necessary to hit him on the head again.

All the while, Judar's screams rang out. The goblins paid this noise little mind as they brought Artus to the center of the village, to the steps of the two-story building he had seen from the tree. The screaming stopped and the doors to the wooden building opened. Shrouded in shadows, two figures emerged. "I'm glad that's done with," one of them said. "My throat is raw."

The words were Judar's, save that the voice was even higher than normal, even more like a woman's. In the gloom, Artus could only make out dark shapes in the doorway. Then a half-dozen torches flared to life on either side of the stairs.

Kaverin Ebonhand stepped from the doorway, his jet-black hands closed in tight fists before him. "This time, Cimber," he said slyly, "I'd say I have you."

Eight

"Kaverin!" Artus screamed. He pulled away from the goblins, even managed to get halfway to the stairs before seven Batiri warriors tackled him from behind.

The red-haired man shook his head in mock sadness. Kaverin was dressed in a loose-fitting white shirt and white pants, with high black boots and a wide-brimmed hat. Above his head, the albino monkey hovered in the air, fanning him with its leathery wings.

"Don't do this, Cimber," Kaverin said as he walked slowly down the stairs. The winged monkey followed his every move. "I've convinced the Batiri queen to sacrifice you to the great and powerful Grumog rather than serve you to her in-laws in a plantain sauce. Don't give her cause to change her mind."

Judar laughed that coarse laugh of his. "May I let this dreadful disguise down now?" At a nod from Kaverin, he closed his eyes and murmured an incantation. At first

Artus thought his vision was blurred by the tears of rage
burning his eyes; Judar's features softened, then slid away
like sand pouring through an hourglass. It was truly sand
that fell from the person who had disguised herself as
Judar, for such was the main component of the Mulhorandi
sorcery Phyrra al-Quim knew best.

The disguise gone, Phyrra rubbed her olive skin and
stretched. She turned to Artus, and her round glasses
caught the light of the torches, flashing like tiny suns.
"Please, tell me they captured you because you were coming back to save me."

Artus forced a calm facade to slam down over his fury.
"Hardly," Artus murmured. "I was knocked out of the tree
by a giant spider."

"They're plentiful in this part of the jungle, from what
the Batiri tell me," Kaverin noted. He knit his smooth
stone fingers together. "The queen will be here in a moment to toss you into the pit. I hope you know how satisfy-
ing this is for me, to see you beaten when you're so close
to the ring. You can go to the Realm of the Dead knowing
you led me right to it—well, you and Theron."

Artus kept his eyes masked. "So that's it. You were spying on Theron. That's how you knew to follow me here."

Idly Kaverin waved the comment aside. His eyes, as always, showed no life, no emotion. "Theron Silvermace
was beneath my notice. I've had agents of the Cult of Frost
trailing *you* for years, Cimber. That's an honor, you know.
Up until recently, they all had orders to gather information,
but leave you alive. Quite sporting, no?"

Phyrra straightened her white robes. Then, dusting
sand from her hair, she came to Kaverin's side. "You'll be
better off dead, Artus," she taunted. "All your friends are
waiting for you in Cyric's realm—Pontifax, Theron—"

Artus's facade slipped. "Theron, too?"

"I had hoped to spare him that sadness, my dear,"

Kaverin gently admonished. "He'd have met up with the batty old fool soon enough."

"I'll see you dead, you bastards," Artus shouted. He struggled against the goblins' hold. "If I have to come back from the grave to do it, I'll—"

Savagely, Kaverin backhanded Artus. A fist-sized bruise purpled on the explorer's cheek, and his ears rang from the pain. "You'll do nothing, Cimber. This is the end." Kaverin removed a small book bound in wyvern hide from his pocket. "I know all your thoughts, all your petty desires, all your sordid little romances. The only thing Quiracus did right was steal this from you. It proved to me you weren't so worthy an opponent after all."

"And you killed him, too," Artus said.

"No, I killed him," Phyrra gloated.

Artus turned to her. "You're going to die at Kaverin's hands, sooner or later, no matter how loyal you are."

Kaverin frowned. "How predictable. Trying to set us against each other." He ran a cold jet hand along Phyrra's cheek, and she smiled. "Phyrra knows full well she's on her way to the afterlife the moment she fails me. She knows, too, I can offer her more power than she could obtain through more . . . legitimate allies. Right, my dear?"

"Of course," she said. Taking a small stick of charcoal from her pocket, Phyrra moved close to Artus. "Don't move, or I'll use your own dagger to cut your eyes out. You don't need to see to be sacrificed to Grumog."

Carefully the sorceress lifted the medallion from Artus's chest. She studied the white casing that had so successfully trapped Skuld, then drew a Mulhorandi picture-glyph on it. The metal vibrated and hummed. Blue fire ran along the chain; Artus could feel it tingling on his neck.

"You don't know how much it galled me to save you from the dinosaurs," Phyrra said coldly. "If you had let me talk the bearers into camping at Kitcher's Folly, the goblin raiding party would have caught us there as planned. Instead, I had to cast a spell to mislead the dagger's compass and trudge through the jungle, pretending to be your trusted servant. . . ."

"Why not just let the damned monsters kill me?" Artus asked. "Better yet, why didn't you just send more assassins to the port?"

"Frost minions are too difficult to conjure here and terribly difficult to maintain," Kaverin replied. "Besides, I've decided I need to murder you myself, to stop your heart beating with the hands you forced upon me. I wouldn't trust anyone else to do it." He tossed Artus's journal into the dirt. "After the minions killed Pontifax, I knew I had beaten you. It was only a matter of sending someone trustworthy to fetch you for the slaughter."

Phyrra lifted the chain from Artus's neck and handed the medallion to Kaverin. Tossing his hat aside, he slipped it over his shock of red hair. "You won't be needing this, Cimber," he said casually. "I thought it a shame to waste such an interesting artifact."

The tolling of a gong brought an appreciative murmur from the crowd of goblins that had gathered in front of the central building. Slowly they began to file toward the pit. The seven warriors who held Artus hefted him over their heads and followed. Kaverin walked close behind, as did Phyrra, once she had picked up Artus's journal.

The pit gaped like a ghastly open wound, mist seeping from it like blood, snaking in long, thin wisps over the ground. A huge gong stood at the widest point, next to a small wooden bridge. A bored young goblin leaned upon the gong's supports. He watched the procession with heavy-lidded eyes, then smacked his lips and raised a cloth-wrapped club. Again he struck the gong. The sound filled the air, echoing back in distorted tones from the pit.

"We ready to offer chow for Grumog?" came a voice

from the throng.

The crowd parted and a female goblin sauntered forward. She had the same general features as the rest of her tribe—mottled red and orange skin, yellow eyes, and a broad, flat nose—but she also possessed a full head of flowing, golden hair, the likes of which would have made any lady in King Azoun's court jealous. In fact, despite her decidedly goblinlike physiognomy, she might have been considered quite attractive.

It was clear to Artus then how Kaverin had managed to win the Batiri to his cause. The queen wore a beautiful silk dress and sported a dozen brooches and necklaces. Her hands were heavy with rings.

"Queen M'bobo," Kaverin said smoothly, in his most polished Goblin. He bowed to the monarch and held out a hand. She took it and gracefully came forward. "This is the scoundrel I was telling you about."

She raised a thin eyebrow. "He not so much." With her finely manicured claws, she pinched Artus's arm. "Not much to eat anyway. OK. We throw him in."

"Wait!" Kaverin exclaimed.

"What wrong?" M'bobo asked.

"You—you can't just drop him into the pit."

The queen thought about it for a moment, then nodded. "You right. Balt! Get Grumog's new stuff."

The goblin warrior with dinosaur-hide armor limped forward. He used Artus's bow as a staff, and the quiver of arrows hung on his back. Without a word, he walked up to Phyrra and jammed a hand into her pocket. She tried to push him away, but he still came away with the dagger the centaurs had given to Artus. "This all," Balt grumbled, holding up the bow and the dagger. He limped to the foot of the bridge and tossed them into the pit, then dumped the quiver of arrows.

"The book, too," Artus said. He gestured with his chin

to his journal, still clutched in Phyrra's hand.

The sorceress started to object, but Kaverin silenced her with a look. "It won't do him any good," he said softly.

She handed the book to Balt, who unceremoniously heaved it into the pit. Then the queen gestured to the warriors holding Artus, and they started toward the bridge. Kaverin quickly blocked their path, drawing the ire of both M'bobo and Balt. "What now?" the queen sighed.

Trying his best to maintain his calm, Kaverin spread his hands before him. "Why don't we kill him *before* we send him to Grumog," he suggested. "I thought you'd allow me to prepare him for—"

M'bobo wrinkled her face in disgust. "Grumog like us, not eat dead food."

The warriors pushed past Kaverin, who suddenly found his carefully designed plan falling to pieces. No matter how dangerous Grumog might be, the creature might prove to be no match for Artus Cimber. He'd certainly shown himself adept at battling such strange creatures in the past. If the goblins tossed him into the pit alive, he might escape. And that just wouldn't be satisfactory, not at all.

Kaverin clubbed two of the warriors with his stone hands. Skulls crushed, they crumpled to the ground. Chaos broke out around the bridge. Goblins hefted spears and bows, but couldn't attack because of the press of bodies surrounding Kaverin. Phyrra lifted her arms to cast a spell. M'bobo, who'd seen enough magic in her time to recognize the threat, clobbered the sorceress with a spear shaft.

Artus broke free of the goblins and pushed to the center of the bridge. He grabbed a torch from the railing, then used it like a club to keep the Batiri at bay. No one dared attack him with spear or bow for fear of killing Grumog's sacrifice. The explorer locked eyes with Kaverin, who was being held by Balt and ten of his warriors. For an instant, Kaverin's cold, lifeless eyes showed a spark of something—anger, surprise, fear perhaps. Artus didn't stick around long enough to find out. Torch in hand, he vaulted over the railing and disappeared into the mist-filled pit.

He managed to slow his fall a little by grabbing an outcropping of rock. That maneuver probably saved Artus from breaking his neck, but the rough stone sheared the skin from the side of his hand and his wrist. His fingers slipped from the blood-slicked stone, and again he fell, rebounding painfully off the uneven wall. The torch was battered out of his hand just before he hit the ground, but fortunately it stayed lit.

The air exploded from his lungs when he landed, facedown atop a pile of clothes; wooden plates, and old bones. The latter cracked and splintered under his weight, slicing dozens of shallow cuts all along his chest. For a moment, Artus gasped frantically, concerned only with breathing again.

Then he saw the glint of four beady eyes staring at him from the shadows.

"Pardon us, old man," came a cheerful voice out of the darkness, "but could you be bothered to point the way to the exit from this drab place?"

Artus grabbed his bow, which lay nearby. It had no string, but that didn't matter. The elf-crafted wood had served well enough as a club before. "Don't come any closer," the explorer warned.

One set of eyes narrowed. "There's no need for that sort of rough stuff. We was only looking for a way out of this trench." This voice was deeper than the other, with a mournful tone that made Artus think of the huge cloister bells in the House of Oghma.

Two dark figures detached themselves from the shadows and came warily forward. At first Artus took them for pygmy bears, for they walked on all fours, had stout bodies and coarse fur. As the two creatures moved fully into the torchlight, though, he saw that they were something else entirely. Short legs supported their chubby bodies, which were half as long as Artus was tall. Their heads seemed to grow right from their shoulders, with rounded ears, flat noses, and bristling whiskers.

The larger of the pair was dark brown, with sad eyes. "I 'ate being stared at," he grumbled. "Better if 'e tried to club me than stare at me."

"Now, now, Lugg," the smaller, gray-furred creature chided happily. He held up a thickly clawed front paw. "The gentleman has obviously never seen a wombat before." He turned vacant blue eyes to Artus, who could only stare at the duo, dumbfounded. "See," he continued. "Completely awed by our unheralded entrance."

Artus shook his head, certain the lumps he'd gotten from the goblins and the blow from Kaverin's fist had rattled his brains somehow. First Pontifax's ghost, now talking wombats. He closed his eyes. That had dispelled the phantom Pontifax quickly enough.

"That won't 'elp a bit," Lugg noted flatly.

The creature was right. When Artus opened his eyes, both wombats still stood at the edge of the junkpile, staring up at him. "You're not Grumog, are you?" he asked.

"Sorry," the gray wombat replied. "Don't know the chap. I'm Byrt, and this is Lugg. Who—"

A bellowing roar echoed up from the lone tunnel sloping out of the pit. It rattled the loose stones in the walls and sent a shower of dirt cascading from the roof. Artus took a quick survey of his surroundings. Mist swirled all around, but he could easily see that the walls of the circular prison were too steep to climb, even if he did want to face Kaverin and his goblin allies again.

"Wait a minute," Artus said. "How did you two get in here?"

Lugg shook his head. "We pushed through that 'ole over there. I don't think you'd fit in it, if that's what you're thinking."

Artus cursed. After snatching up the quiver of arrows, he began to turn over the pile of bones, tattered clothes, old cookware, and broken pottery in search of his dagger—and any other weapons he could find. Byrt quickly joined in the hunt, digging into the possessions of those sacrificed to the goblins' god. "By the way," the gray wombat asked, "for what, may I ask, are we searching?"

Artus spared him a withering look. "Go away," he said simply.

"Good idea, that," Lugg murmured and trundled off toward the hole in the wall.

"Just a moment," Byrt said. "If that was Grumog bellowing a moment ago, he sounded quite large and quite mean—rather like Nora, my kid sister. And if Grumog is indeed anything like her, this fellow may need our help."

Lugg's response to that was a derisive snort. Nevertheless, he turned back around and sat down.

Artus found his dagger inside a cracked goblin skull and his journal resting in a rib cage. Grateful to have them again, he slipped the blade into his boot and the book into his pocket. Whatever Grumog was, it was thorough in stripping the flesh from its victims. In fact, it had tried to eat most of the bones and rubbish, too. There was little in the pile that wasn't scored with teeth marks.

"If it's weapons you seek, here's a spear, in relatively good condition," Byrt called. He bit down on the pole, dragged it to Artus, and spat it out. "Only one previous owner—a headhunter who used it to do in little old ladies on their way to the market. Yours for a song."

Again Grumog's roar rang through the cavern, this time underscored by a rousing cheer from the goblins above. "Ah. That's just the song I had in mind," Byrt chirped and hurried off in search of more weaponry.

"That's a bunch of them Batiri up there, ain't it?" Lugg asked mournfully. "Brrr. Those rotten twisters are a lot of—"

"Look, Lugg," Byrt interrupted. "Why don't you go on up ahead and delay Grumog a bit. You know, use what little grace you still possess to keep him occupied. Dazzle him with fancy footwork and the like."

"What for?" Lugg shouted.

"I just came up with a plan," Byrt said proudly. "You slow Grumog up, and I'll widen the hole enough for our friend here, Master—" He paused meaningfully.

"Artus Cimber," the explorer said, not looking up from ransacking the refuse pile. He had uncovered another goblin spear, a bent and rusted sword, and a small shield made of palm fronds. "Thanks anyway, but I can take care of myself."

"Yeah, maybe 'e don't need protecting," the brown wombat said truculently. "Besides, why me?"

Byrt flashed him a fatuous grin. "Because you would be a mouthful and a half to a starving monster. I would merely be a mouthful. Being a ravenous beast, which would you choose?"

"I'd choose not to go," Lugg grumbled.

Byrt didn't wait for a more serious answer before he set about widening the hole. He tore into the loose rock with his claws, scattering dirt and rubble in a wide arc behind him. Artus wasn't certain, but he thought he heard the wombat whistling a tuneless song as he worked.

At the point where the tunnel opened into the pit, Lugg took up his post as unwilling sentinel and would-be decoy. "I can't see a thing out there," he said.

Just then, the mist grew thicker and a spade-shaped head poked into the cave above Lugg. It was fully equal in size to the wombat, with bulbous eyes and a huge, gaping maw. Teeth like garden spades jutted up around its scaly lips. Mist poured from two sets of gills that flapped along the thing's snaking neck, obscuring the long, serpentine body coiling slowly out of the tunnel.

Lugg yelped and dashed away from the creature. Whether the wombat intended to draw Grumog's attention or not, he did so quite successfully. It slid into the pit in pursuit of the chubby snack, mist hissing from its gills, its thousand small legs pulsing along the walls and floor. As much as Artus could see in the growing murk, Grumog resembled a cross between a reptile and a centipede, with a thin body tapering away to a double-barbed tail.

"Byrt!" the brown wombat shouted. " 'Urry up!"

Grumog arched its back and opened its mouth. Four long tentacles shot forward, groping for Lugg. The wombat scrambled behind a rock, only to have it snatched away an instant later by the tentacles. The gray-green limbs stuffed the stone blindly into Grumog's mouth, then retracted as the creature chewed up the unappetizing morsel. It quickly spit out the remains of the large stone—a few fist-sized rocks and a shower of gravel.

When Grumog opened its mouth to roar again, Artus threw one of the two spears he'd found. The iron-tipped shaft sank deep into the creature's side, and its roar of hunger became a yowl of pain. The victory was short-lived, though. When Grumog couldn't reach the offending spear with its short legs, it used its tentacled tongue to pull the barb from its side. Casually it tossed the weapon away.

Artus glanced over his shoulder. "Lugg's right, Byrt. Hurry!"

"Almost there," came a muffled reply.

Grumog started forward again, this time right at Artus. To slow the beast, Lugg dashed close to its legs. The wombat dodged in and out among the thin stalks, shouting. The tactic clearly annoyed Grumog. The beast halted abruptly, then launched its tentacles at Lugg. One of the quartet of writhing limbs wrapped around his rear legs.

Artus dove forward. Fearlessly he raised the remaining spear high over his head and jammed it into Grumog's tentacles. The beast roared and shook its head, tossing Lugg across the pit in the process. The wombat tumbled end over snout and landed with a grunt atop the junkpile.

Artus, meanwhile, had gotten himself hopelessly tangled in Grumog's tentacled tongue. He had succeeded in driving the spear through two of the four limbs, but also in getting his left leg completely wrapped up. The creature, realizing at last that shaking its head like a broken maraca wasn't going to stop the pain in its tongue, decided to swallow the problem.

"Success!" Byrt noted with satisfaction. He backed out of the newly widened hole just as Grumog started to reel in its tentacles. "Oh my," he said, staring at the monster. "*That* can't be good."

Lugg charged again, biting down hard on the end of one tentacle. This gesture, while uncharacteristically heroic for the wombat, did nothing to slow Artus in meeting his fate. The spear caused so much pain Grumog barely noticed the addition of a wombat bite, and Lugg's sixty pounds was nothing to its thickly muscled tongue.

Closer to the creature's mouth, Artus had let go of the spear and was now hacking away with his dagger. The creature's misty breath rolled over the explorer, choking him with its sour smell. Hanging upside down, gasping and suspended by one leg, it was difficult to do much damage. Still, desperation had granted him surprising dexterity, and he had succeeded in slashing a few minor wounds.

Fortunately for Artus, the spear presented Grumog a momentary dilemma. It was simply too wide to fit in its mouth. The creature tried once, twice, then a third time to pull the shaft in, but the wood held. This was enough of a delay for Artus to right himself and make a sizeable gouge in the ensnaring tentacle. Shrieking, Grumog released him.

The explorer landed atop Lugg, knocking the wombat hard enough to make him lose his grip. Good thing, too, for at that moment Grumog snapped the spear and swallowed it whole. The creature's tentacled tongue shot back into its mouth.

"Quickly, children," Byrt called. "The animal pens are closed for the evening. Toddle to the exit. No stragglers, please, and no feeding the unpleasant local gods."

Lugg spit out a chunk of tentacle and ran. Artus was about to follow on the wombat's furiously kicking heels when he saw his journal had been jarred from his pocket by the fall. He thought to reach back for the book, but a horrifying noise stopped him.

Grumog roared and lunged at Artus, mouth open wide. The explorer managed to dodge the clumsy attack, but the creature did succeed in tearing up a large section of the pit's floor. Grumog chewed up the earthen victim. Sadly, it found no bones to crush, no flesh to rend. It did, however, get a surprise.

Along with the rocks and dirt, Grumog had gobbled up Artus's journal.

When the beast bit down upon the wyvern-hide binding, its spadelike teeth shredded the tough covering—and thus broke the enchantment placed upon the book long ago by the Red Wizards of Thay. Thousands of pages spewed out of the journal when the binding snapped. Grumog tried to push them out of its mouth, but there were simply too many of them. The lizard-thing gagged. Twitching and gasping for breath, it fell over and kicked its feet futilely. Then the god of the Batiri died.

Artus walked silently to the creature's head. Its mouth had been forced so wide by the paper that the lower jaw hung at an impossible angle, broken. A few pages floated free of Grumog's mouth and drifted to the ground. Artus picked up one of these. The top read: *The tale of Elminster at the magefair, as told to me by the Sage of Shadowdale himself.* Most of the text had been sheared off by one of Grumog's teeth.

He crumpled the page and let it fall.

The journal had contained his whole life, everything he'd done as an adventurer and all that he'd learned from the sages and heroes of Faerun. Even when it had been stolen aboard the *Narwhal*, Artus knew somehow he would get it back. Now it was gone for good, irrevocably destroyed.

"That was quite a trick," Byrt said, nosing one of the pieces of parchment. "It goes to show the power of a good book."

The larger wombat trundled to his fellow's side. "Leave 'im alone," Lugg growled. "Can't you see 'e ain't thrilled about this?"

Artus absently gathered up his unstrung bow, a few stray pieces of discarded clothing, his quiver of arrows, and the now-smoldering torch. Without a word, he headed off down the tunnel, backtracking Grumog's trail. The wombats fell in behind him, keeping a respectable distance.

"I think he can help us," Byrt whispered.

Lugg shook his head mournfully. "I don't think *anyone's* likely to 'elp us."

Grinning so broadly all his wide teeth showed, Byrt replied, "Give him a chance, old sport. I think our Master Cimber is a good fellow, if a bit at sea right now." He looked up at the man shuffling down the tunnel, shoulders slumped, head bowed. "Anyway, I think he could use *our* help, poor chap." He picked up the pace, trying to catch up to the explorer.

"I wonder what 'orrible thing 'e did to deserve that," Lugg mumbled, then hurried after the others.

* * * * *

Kaverin Ebonhand leaned back in his chair and placed the back of one hand to his forehead. The black stone remained cool, even in the most unfriendly of climes. Currently, it was doing a fine job of soothing the headache he had developed the moment Artus disappeared into the pit.

"What do you think the punishment is for murdering Batiri warriors?" Phyrra asked, nervously cleaning her glasses with the hem of her tunic.

The decor of the room they occupied suggested many gruesome possibilities. Like much of the goblin queen's two-story palace, the main motif here was human bones and animal skins, though this particular room was rife with skulls. The bleached relics of meals past grinned from the walls, the tables, and even the backs of chairs. Small and large, human and inhuman, they kept perpetual, sightless watch on the prisoners.

Kaverin chuckled bitterly. "Allowing Cimber to escape was the worst punishment they could have inflicted upon me, my dear." He gestured to Feg, and the winged monkey fanned him more fervently.

"He might be dead, you know."

That hopeful statement only turned Kaverin's mood more sour. "Impossible," he scoffed. "You heard the clatter from the pit. Did it sound to you as if that—that—*thing* the goblins worship simply chewed Cimber up? He was armed, for Cyric's sake! Could this Grumog succeed where I have failed, despite the efforts of six long years?"

The sorceress silently returned her attention to the Mulhorandi artifact she had taken from Artus, which still hung around Kaverin's neck. The medallion was very, very old and exceedingly interesting. She had added two more glyphs to the white damper surrounding the silver coin. Now Phyrra took up her charcoal one last time. "I've already broken the enchantment that made it impossible to remove the medallion, as well as the one limiting Skuld's servitude to moments when his master is in danger." She made two quick strokes. "This one will free him from his imprisonment. You'll have a sleepless guardian who never has to leave your side."

With a final cross of the charcoal stick, Phyrra completed the magical symbol. The white casing cracked, then flaked away. Silver light radiated from the medallion. The sorceress covered her eyes, but Kaverin found himself mesmerized. The tiny, four-armed figure on the front of the disk writhed in pain. It grew larger and larger, until it could barely crouch within the confines of the circular prison. The medallion warped and, finally, disappeared in a burst of energy.

When the spots cleared from Kaverin's eyes, he found Skuld standing before him. The Mulhorandi guardian spirit held Phyrra by the front of her blouse. "Your spell made me fail to protect my master, witch," Skuld rumbled. "For that you shall die."

"No," Kaverin said calmly. He dangled the twisted remnant of the medallion before him on its chain. "I, Kaverin Ebonhand, am your master now. Let the woman alone."

His silver eyebrows knit in consternation, Skuld dropped Phyrra unceremoniously to the floor. He planted two of his hands on his hips, rubbed his chin with another, and reached for the medallion with a fourth. Kaverin ducked out of the chain and handed it to him.

"Only the one who wears this has the right to control me," Skuld noted. "You relinquish that right so easily?"

"Of course not," said Kaverin smugly. "The glyphs the young lady added to the disk make you my slave, whether I wear the medallion or not. You must protect me and do my bidding . . . forever."

"Until you die," Skuld corrected. "I will be free when you die." He crushed the chain and the fragments of the silver medallion into a ball.

Kaverin smiled. "Then you will never be free. Moreover, you are going to help me find a ring that will make certain I don't ever have to see the Realm of the Dead again. First, though, we—"

The door to the room creaked open, and Queen M'bobo sauntered in. At her side was Balt, the leader of the Batiri warriors and her consort. While the queen's face showed little emotion, the veins on the general's neck were bulging with suppressed anger. Neither seemed particularly surprised to see Skuld, and they disregarded his presence with the unthinking bravado of royalty. Kaverin understood their confidence; the entire village would tear him to shreds if he harmed their beloved queen.

"We no kill you now," Balt said, disappointment clear in every broken word.

Kaverin bowed and gestured to his silver guardian. "My thanks for your consideration. This is Skuld. He is my manservant, just arrived from parts unknown."

With practiced disinterest, M'bobo eyed the servant. His double set of arms was no more strange to her than the light-skinned humans who had begun to appear in her jungle. "Maybe he do," she murmured. "You meat or metal?"

Skuld remained silent, but Kaverin quickly filled the awkward lapse. "Do for what?" he asked.

"You owe price for warriors. Pay family something good and heavy," Balt replied. Expecting resistance, he raised his chin defiantly and planted the butt of his spear on the wooden floor.

Phyrra stood and dusted herself off. "What about more beads and trinkets?" she asked Kaverin in a Cormyrian dialect meant to baffle the goblins.

He shook his head. It was clear in the goblins' faces that

the time for petty bribery was over. "Name your price," Kaverin told the queen.

Slowly she leveled a scaly finger at the winged monkey. The creature shrieked and hopped to its master's shoulder. "Feg is very valuable to me, and I treasure him greatly," Kaverin said, though his eyes remained as cold and lifeless as his hands.

Balt pointed his spear at the creature. "We go easy. Take monkey and all baggage. That be heavy enough."

"What?" Phyrra exclaimed. "How are we supposed to survive here without any supplies?"

Kaverin sat down, rested his elbows on the chair, and knit his jet fingers together before his face. "You need to be paid something valuable, but also of equal weight to those warriors I killed, is that it?" At M'bobo's curt nod, he sighed. "Skuld, you do not eat. Am I correct in assuming that?"

"I have not consumed a bite of food or swallowed a gulp of wine in a thousand years," he reported proudly, though his filed teeth would have made any casual observer think otherwise.

"And you do not speak unless I ask you to? I find idle chatter very annoying in a traveling companion."

"That is so, master."

Kaverin nodded. "You know sorcery, of course. . . ."

Phyrra al-Quim was a quick-witted woman, and it was only a moment before the direction of this conversation became startlingly clear to her. She pulled a small sphere of pitch from her pocket and raised her hands. The spell she intended never came to pass, though. Skuld grabbed her hands and lifted her from the ground. With his other set of hands, he clamped her mouth shut. Her glasses clattered to the floor. "It is fitting for you to be punished, witch. You caused me great discomfort."

Kaverin gestured casually to Phyrra. "She should be

enough to cover most of the debt," he said. Then he turned to the sorceress. "Sorry, my dear, but you were correct about the supplies. I cannot sacrifice them and hope to un- cover my prize." A frown crept across his thin lips. "It's too bad you aren't heavier, though. I would have preferred not to have lost Feg, too. It gets rather hot without him fanning me."

Gently he nudged Feg off his shoulder, and the winged monkey sailed across the room to M'bobo. "I must insist on the right to use him to spy on my enemies, if the need arises," Kaverin noted.

M'bobo nodded absently, caught up as she was in pam- pering and cooing over the bat-winged ape. For its part, Feg seemed thoroughly disgusted by the whole situation. The monkey cast a longing look back as M'bobo left the room.

Balt called in a contingent of warriors, and they took the struggling mage from Skuld. Phyrra thrashed about, her eyes wide with terror. As she was carried from the room, her gaze fell upon the skulls lining the walls. She screamed, knowing she would become part of that grisly collection— just as soon as the Batiri had their dinner.

"Do be careful to keep her mouth closed and her hands bound," Kaverin called after them.

When the commotion had at last died down, the stone- handed man turned to his new servant. "As I was saying before that costly interruption, we have one more task to complete before we can set off in search of this very impor- tant artifact." He picked up Phyrra's glasses and twirled them idly in his ebony fingers. "We must go down into the pit in the center of the village and see if your previous mas- ter is still alive."

When Kaverin gazed through the glasses, the lenses made his lifeless eyes huge. He blinked and settled the spectacles on a table. "In a way," he said, "I hope Cimber

survived his encounter with Grumog, so we can present
his corpse to the Batiri. It would be fitting to have his
bones set on display in here next to Phyrra's. She would
have wanted it that way, poor girl."

Nine

Artus held the torch up to the tunnel's low ceiling. With his dagger, he probed the packed earth. It looked promising. A few hours of hard work and he might be able to loosen some of the larger stones, perhaps even bring the walls down. The trick would be blocking the passage without burying himself, too.

"We could help, you know," Byrt offered brightly. "Wombats are constructed rather well for excavation. It's our lot in life, really—a burrow here, a furrow there."

"Thanks, but no thanks," Artus murmured.

The wombats had been following him for hours, though they had little choice in the matter. Grumog's tunnel had proved impassable, leading as it did to an underground lake. In silent frustration, Artus had returned to the pit and crawled through the hole Byrt had so helpfully widened during the battle. That was, after all, the only way left to explore.

Artus had done his best to keep the wombats at a distance. That proved simple with Lugg; the brown-furred creature trundled along, minding his own business. Byrt, however, was annoyingly curious and insufferably cheerful. He blurted out a constant stream of questions and inane comments. Still, Artus suspected a keen intelligence lurked behind those vague blue eyes.

"This isn't the place for bringing the house down, you know," Byrt offered, expression blank as ever. Artus, engrossed in studying the balance of stones in the wall, ignored him completely. The little wombat tugged on the explorer's boot. "I don't believe you heard me, old man. I said—"

"I heard you," Artus sighed. He leaned back against the cool stone wall. "Look, I don't have anything against you two, but I really don't want anyone tagging along with me. I have important things to do."

"As do we," Byrt said sincerely. "We need to find a way out of this jungle. You actually don't think we're locals, do you?"

Raising one eyebrow, Artus studied the gray-furred creature. With all the other strange things he'd encountered in Chult, he had, as Byrt suggested, simply dismissed the unique duo as yet another example of bizarre local fauna. "If you're not Chultan, what are you?"

Lugg opened his mouth to speak, but Byrt launched into a complicated tale of thievery and kidnapping on the high seas. The brown wombat shook his head and sat in the shadows, brooding.

"Where we're from, Lugg was a passable second-story man," Byrt began theatrically, "and I was a . . . well, let's just say I made my living as a jack-of-all-trades. A year ago a ship out of the City of Splendors found our island—a happy little place off Orlil, just prefect for wombats. Lugg was burying some loot on the beach when the captain of this pirate ship came ashore. Thinking Lugg would make a wonderful addition to Waterdeep's zoo, he grabbed the poor fellow. When I tried to rescue my comrade—as I am wont to do now and then, being the valiant sort—I was snatched, too."

Lugg snorted. "There you go, rambling on again. That's what got us into all this trouble, if you ask me. You don't know when to be quiet!"

The comments went unchallenged, and Byrt continued blithely on. "The ship was bound first for Refuge Bay, but by the time we sighted this dreadful place, the captain had decided to strand us. That dashed poor Lugg's hopes for a life in show business, and I had left off pining for home and rather looked forward to seeing a city larger than fifty wombats and the occasional odd platypus—though, to be perfectly blunt, I've never met a platypus who wasn't rather odd."

"Awright," the brown wombat grumbled, "that's enough of that. You want I should fill in the rest of the story? I could finish this yarn in ten words or less, I'll bet."

The vacant look fled Byrt's eyes for just an instant. Then he shrugged. "If you'd rather continue, Lugg, by all means do. Your storytelling is better than any sleeping draught, and I need a bit of a snooze. In fact, we could all use a good sleep, if we're to spend much more time in this dratted jungle. . . ."

When Lugg sank back into the shadows, Byrt nodded his approval. "Thank you for that vote of confidence, old man. All money will be gladly refunded if we fail to please." Sidling up to Artus, he continued the tale. "Now listen, for this is where the story gets interesting, like the part of a mystery where the prime suspect is discovered head-down in a vat of malmsey." Byrt grinned, but failed to notice his audience did not share his amusement.

"As I was saying, about a year ago we were left here to

sweat to death—or be eaten by a monstrous lizard, a pack of wild-eyed goblins, or whatever else took a fancy to us. We've also had our share of problems with the Batiri, by the way. We barely managed to escape being their catch of the day, served in a yam sauce with a side of leeks." He shuddered at the thought.

"For a year we've had no supplies and only our wits to rely upon for survival. I, of course, am managing just fine with those restrictions, but Lugg here is at a bit of a disadvantage. It's been a heroic struggle, of course, and so far we've remained unvanquished. However, I believe it's time we got out of the jungle and continued on our trek around the world. All this sight-seeing has made us unhappy with our island, and now we'd like to see what the rest of the world is like."

"Sorry," Artus said, "but I can't help you. I don't know when I'm leaving, and I can't take responsibility for your safety right now."

"But you got to leave this godsforsaken place sooner or later, right?" Lugg asked hopefully. For the first time, his somber mood lightened.

"I don't want—"

"Yes, Lugg," Byrt interrupted. "He doesn't want any companions just now, wombatlike or otherwise. It was really rude of you to presume so." He turned to Artus. "Let me make up for my muddle-headed friend's bad manners. I will do the digging and close off the tunnel between us and the goblins. Shan't take long, but we'd better move up the trail a ways. There's a perfect spot not too far along. I noticed it when we passed through earlier."

"Is the opening to the surface far from there?" the explorer asked suspiciously.

"Actually, yes, very far. It will be quite a toddle—a day or so, I should think—to the portal by which we entered this dismal path."

Artus pondered the alternatives for a moment, then said, "Fine. Let's get this over with."

If possible, Artus's concession made Byrt even more cheerful. The little gray wombat chattered incessantly as they trudged through the murky tunnel. Lugg, too, seemed heartened by the explorer's acceptance. He still walked with his head down, his eyes half-lidded, but there was a bit of a spring in his step that hadn't been there before.

Finally they came to a spot where the passage narrowed. The way was so restricted Artus had to extinguish the torch for fear of burning himself or filling the tight tunnel with smoke. Relying only on his dagger for light, he barely managed to squeeze into the gap on hands and knees. He had never been too keen on close places, but this stretch of tunnel made him border on panic. As he struggled along, the passage narrowed more and more, as if the earth itself were tightening a stony fist around him.

It seemed to take forever, but at last the passage began to widen again. Artus found he was sweating and even trembling a bit by the time the ceiling was high enough for him to sit up straight. "All right," he said, wiping his forehead, "now what?"

"Now you move down the tunnel a bit, and we see if we can burrow our way to victory," Byrt said glibly. "There is mostly packed earth up above. A few well-placed tunnels will probably finish closing off that narrow section."

Artus had his doubts, but did as the wombat asked. Even if Kaverin caught up with him now, this spot would be easy to defend since the goblins would have to climb through one at a time to get at him.

As he took up position farther down the tunnel and settled in to wait, Artus's stomach reminded him noisily that he hadn't eaten in some time. He fished through his pockets and came up a single strip of dried beef, mangled and dirty. At that moment, the jerky bore a striking resemblance to the finest steak Artus had ever eaten. He had the stringy strip halfway to his mouth before his years of traveling stayed his hand. Byrt had said the exit was a day away. While they might stumble across something edible, it was unlikely. Best save the meager ration until later.

Artus turned his attention to taking inventory of the wounds he'd gathered in the last few days. His head ached from the three lumps, though the rain in the goblin camp had washed most of the blood away. His jaw throbbed from Kaverin's stone-fisted punch. That was likely bruised, too. He touched it tenderly and found the cheek swollen and warm. Correction: *definitely* bruised. He had lots of scratches and a few small cuts across his chest from falling atop the junk heap, but nothing serious. His hand was scraped raw from his fall into the pit. All in all, he was in great shape, considering the events of the past few days.

"Awright," Lugg said wearily. "That's taken care of that." The brown wombat was covered in dirt, and his muzzle was scratched and grimy.

"Oh?" Artus said. He stretched and sat up straight. "I didn't hear anything."

As he hurried up the tunnel, Byrt said, "All in good time, as they say. We did our best not to bring the roof down around our round little ears. We're wombats, you know, not earthworms." The gray creature went puffing right past Artus. "I wouldn't dawdle, friends. Wombat construction—or should I say demolition—is not the most exact of sciences."

Artus and Lugg gathered themselves quickly, but not quickly enough. A grating roar filled the air, the sort of sound that makes teeth lock together and hackles rise. Then the ground lurched and a cloud of choking dust rumbled up the tunnel. Fine grit settled over the explorer and the larger wombat, leaving them gasping for air.

"Rather an improvement, I would say," Byrt noted wryly. He had apparently outdistanced most of the disturbance, though his gray fur would have hidden any dirt that settled upon him. "Now we look like a team—birds of a uniform gray color, or something like that."

Artus abruptly turned around. "Wait!" Byrt shouted. "No offense intended. Really!"

"You've done it again," Lugg grumbled, watching Artus disappear into the dust-choked tunnel. "Just like aboard the *Rampage*. You talked and talked and now 'e's 'ad it with us. Probably went back to the cave-in to bury 'imself rather than listen to you any more."

The little wombat was berating Lugg for his sour mood when Artus reappeared a short time later, coated even more heavily with the gray soot. He was coughing, and the dirt had stung his eyes red. With knees stiff from long walks and little restful sleep, Artus kneeled down in front of Byrt. "Thanks for taking care of the tunnel," he said sincerely. "It will take Kaverin days to dig through that mess." The explorer smiled. "I don't know if I should pat you on the head or shake your paw."

"Either will do," Byrt said. "I'm actually quite easy to get along with, you know."

Artus smiled and patted the wombat on the head. When he looked around, the explorer found that Lugg had trundled ahead before he could be treated to the same.

* * * * *

"This happened only a short time ago," Kaverin noted flatly. He wiped the grime from his hands, stared at the pile of rock and earth blocking the tunnel, and stood a moment in thought. "Cimber might have killed Grumog with that blasted journal of his, but he didn't do this on his own. Not in so short a time. There is definitely someone—or something—down here helping him."

"No one else alive in tunnel!" shouted Balt. "Grumog chow everyone we toss."

The goblin general was failing miserably at keeping his rage under control. Upon the discovery of the paper-choked god, Queen M'bobo had intimated it was somehow Balt's impiety that had caused this disastrous turn of events. It was now Balt's task to bring Artus back to the village for punishment. Only in that way would the spirit of Grumog be appeased. If he failed, the general would be the premiere sacrifice to the next god they found.

"The tunnel back by that monster's corpse was widened by something with claws, like a badger," Kaverin explained. He thought it likely Balt couldn't remember the disgusting contents of his last meal let alone the events of that evening, but he needed to keep his would-be allies mollified. If that meant droning on, simply to lull the goblins with his lilting voice, so be it. "Cimber is many things, but a werebadger is not one of them." He turned and raised one jet-black hand to Skuld.

At the gesture from Kaverin, the silver-skinned giant bowed and gave his two torches to Balt. He set to work clearing the debris, crushing the smaller stones to dust, breaking the larger rocks into gravel.

"Let's leave my manservant to his task," Kaverin said. "Besides, I think it's time I interviewed your village elder."

They walked back to a wide spot in the tunnel. There, the goblins had set up a crude command post, complete with supplies that consisted mostly of baskets full of small, chattering rodents and shrieking monkeys. The doomed animals seemed to sense the gruesome fate awaiting them—to become live meals for Balt and the dozen war-riors accompanying him. The general ordered the goblins lounging around the boxed lunches to begin the grueling task of hauling away the dirt and broken rocks Skuld was digging from the cave-in. They grumbled as they formed a ragged bucket brigade, toting sad-looking pails that leaked more than they carried.

This left one lone Batiri, snoring loudly as he slept against a large barrel of water. When Kaverin shook him, the old goblin snorted awake and looked up at the human. His old eyes were bluish white, and his toothless mouth worked continually, like a cow chewing its cud.

From the way the goblin stared at him, Kaverin was certain he was being sized up as a potential meal. "The queen sent you here so we could talk," he said curtly. "I need to know about any human cities nearby."

The goblin nodded and said, "Old stories about great Tabaxi village, about Mezro, eh?" He chuckled. "Bring lots of food here, Mezro. Lots of humans try to find it. Batiri find them first."

Kaverin leaned forward. "Yes, Mezro." The word had a magical quality coming from his thin lips, like the name of a long-cherished lover. That fabled city, lost to modern man, had drawn Theron Silvermace to Chult. Perhaps the mysterious natives who had aided Rayburton in saving him from the Batiri had come from there. A magical city would be a fitting hiding place for the old explorer and the Ring of Winter. "Is it near here?"

Again the old goblin chuckled. "No one seen Mezro, not since long time." The lids of his eyes drooped. "They hide it years and years ago so Batiri not eat them. Only witch doctor . . . T'fima . . . only he know Mezro. . . ." Then the goblin was asleep again, dreaming of the various explorers that had crossed his plate because of the lost city.

Kaverin let the doddering creature sleep. Taking a cup of water from the barrel, he considered the old goblin's revelation, then walked slowly to Balt's side. "Do you know of a Tabaxi sorcerer named T'fima?" he asked. Neither his voice nor his eyes betrayed his excitement.

The goblin general blanched. "We not bother Ras T'fima. He too powerful for us."

"I doubt that very much, Balt." Kaverin smiled wickedly. "But I don't think we need disturb him, just watch his camp. If your elder is correct, and this Ras T'fima knows where Mezro is hidden, he may just lead us right to it."

*   *   *   *   *

Artus and the wombats moved on at a steady pace, but as Byrt had anticipated, the trek to the first opening lasted quite a long time. Luckily, fresh water pooled in many places along the way—often clean and clear—so they could satisfy their thirst. Food was another matter. By the time they had traveled for a few hours, the wombats were almost as hungry as the human. The dried beef was long gone; dusty though it was, to Artus it had tasted like the best venison served in Suzail. Still, the meager portion had done nothing to curb the ache in his stomach.

"The first edible thing we see is doomed," Byrt said as they came to the side tunnel leading to the surface.

The main path continued on, wide and straight, but they didn't give it a second look as they hurried up the sloping spur. Gray light bled sullenly through the leaves and vines covering the jagged crack that served as entrance to the tunnel. The rain had stopped during the night, but a steady patter of water fell from the leaves and the roof. The tunnel opened onto the side of a low mound. Pushing the foliage aside, Artus found himself with a good vantage of a gently sloping hillside.

Byrt tried to muscle past, but a well-placed leg stopped him dead. "See here," he began. "I only—"

"Quiet," Artus hissed. He let the leaves fall back over the opening. "There are a dozen goblins moving through the underbrush out there, a hunting party of some kind.

Back into the tunnel."

After a quick and quiet descent to the main tunnel, Artus looked dazedly at his companions. "They look like Batiri. Have we gone in a circle somehow?"

"No, no," Byrt said, swallowing the mouthful of leaves he had bitten. "There are Batiri all over the jungle, like sand fleas at a beach or civil servants at a cheap pub. It's said among the locals that you can't fall out of a tree without landing on a goblin. . . ."

The weight of exhaustion pushed down on Artus, a feeling compounded by the drain of hunger. "I hate to say this, since I'm almost ready to eat the next beetle that crawls across the floor, but we'd better keep moving. The sun is coming up, so the goblins will be looking for a hiding place. They might stumble across this cave." He shuffled a few steps down the tunnel, using the unstrung bow as a staff. "I'm not strong enough to fight one goblin, let alone a whole hunting party."

Artus thought only about food as he trudged along. At least, that was all that occupied his thoughts until they came upon a stretch of tunnel limned in a strange gold radiance. It sparkled like the purest sunlight, and when Artus stepped into the glow, his hunger-induced thoughts of steak and ale and fresh-baked pies were replaced by other, more jumbled notions.

Confusion began to tug at the corners of Artus's mind, and his thoughts turned to his plight. The explorer pictured himself lost beneath the surface of Chult, in a maze of tunnels that had but two exits—the one at the Batiri camp and the other they had been forced to pass by. The images grew more vivid. He saw himself shriveled from hunger, dazed from lack of water. And for what? He looked around at the golden tunnel walls.

Suddenly Artus was twenty years old again and here to rescue someone. That's right. The tunnel led under the jail

in Surd, where his father was being held before his execu-
tion. The Sembians never took pity on highwaymen, especially those who preyed upon merchant caravans. Besides,
hanging the notorious Shadowhawk would gain the local
lords favor with the country's overmaster.

This was the third time in as many years Artus had found
himself breaking his father out of jail. Shadowhawk, indeed. The old man might have been a real threat to travelers in Cormyr and Sembia a decade ago, but not now. He
was getting too slow for all this "robbing from the wealthy"
stuff.

"It's a good thing no one at the temple of Oghma knows
about you, Father," Artus grumbled. He prodded the ceiling with his staff. Yes, he might want to start digging here.
"The loremasters just wouldn't understand how I could let
you keep on robbing merchants. They aren't too open-
minded, not like Nanda. . . ."

Artus stopped digging into the ceiling with the unstrung
elven bow and put his hand to his forehead. Nanda hadn't
crept into his thoughts for years. He'd been married to her
for only a few months, just after he'd turned twenty. It was
a whirlwind romance, ending in a union approved by neither his parents nor her guardian. That had made it all the
more attractive to both of them. Sadly, those few months
had turned out to be the worst of Artus's life, especially
after he discovered his new bride's secret devotion to
Loviatar, the Goddess of Pain.

No, he wasn't here for his father, and Nanda had left him
fifteen years ago. He wasn't even in the Heartlands now.
The thoughts swirled in his mind. Chult. He was lost somewhere in Chult.

Dazed, Artus looked around the tunnel again. "What am
I doing here?" he hissed.

"Looking for the Ring of Winter," someone said.

Artus looked down, wondering how the wombats knew

about the ring; he hadn't told them about it—at least he didn't think so. "How do you know that?"

He found his two companions in complete disarray. Byrt's eyes were closed tightly and he was walking in a circle, whistling a cheerful tune. Lugg had collapsed onto his side. His eyes were open, but he seemed stunned.

"This is a sorry-looking group, though I'm not one to judge, I suppose."

Pontifax cleared his throat, trying to draw Artus's attention. He stood farther up the tunnel, ghostly and pale, just as he had appeared in the Batiri prison. The explorer took a step toward his old friend, and the phantom backed away. "This way," Pontifax said. "Gather up your two furry cohorts, and come this way."

"Wait," Artus said. "Why are you here?"

"There's no time," the ghost wailed.

"Was your death so—"

Holding up a transparent hand, Pontifax replied, "All that matters right now is that you keep moving down the tunnel. You've got to get out of this golden light. It's some sort of enchantment, a wall of confusion."

That would explain my jumbled thoughts, Artus decided, but not the ghostly mage's presence. But before he could question Pontifax further, the phantom mage disappeared. The explorer paused for a moment and stared at the spot where Pontifax had been. He tried to piece some reasonable explanation together, but found it increasingly difficult to concentrate.

He lifted Byrt—who was still walking in a circle, oblivious to the phantom Pontifax and everything else around him—and tucked the wombat under one arm, along with the unstrung bow. Then he leaned down and grabbed Lugg by the ear. The brown wombat followed along docilely, a blank look in his eyes. It was awkward going. The bow slipped twice and clattered to the ground. Even when it stayed under Artus's arm, it constantly whacked Byrt on the head. That didn't stop the gray wombat from whistling, though.

After a time, the golden light faded and the swirl of confusion subsided from Artus's thoughts. Soon after, Lugg realized with a start that he was being led along by the ear. With a huge frown, he pulled away from the explorer and hurried ahead. Byrt took longer to recover, but Artus found it hard to tell the difference; the little wombat acted strangely all the time. And when Artus asked Byrt and Lugg about the ghostly visitor who had rescued them, both wombats responded with looks that announced their concern for Artus's sanity.

Finally the tunnel ended. The floor here was smooth, the walls more carefully hewn from the surrounding stone. A wide crack split the wall before the tired, hungry trio. That meant release and, hopefully, food.

The low-ceilinged cavern they entered was dark and full of debris. A quick look around told Artus the crumbling stones were the ruins of some ancient structure. Ornate columns lay in pieces near the edges of the room. Heavy, square blocks of granite, used as the bases for long tables, cluttered the center. The wooden tops from those tables, and the shelves that had once filled the iron brackets attached to the walls, had long ago crumbled to dust.

"This might have been a library at one time," Artus ventured. He knelt to study the engravings on a fragment of masonry. The glyphs, which depicted dinosaur-headed men and women, were unlike any he'd seen before.

"Do they serve food in libraries?" Lugg asked, nosing through the rubble.

"No," Byrt replied. "You get books from libraries, not baked goods. That question makes me wonder if you have lived a tome-free life, old man."

Lugg snorted. "All the tomes in the world won't 'elp my

stomach now . . . though I might stoop to nibbling on a picture book of onions and radishes, if one 'appened to present itself."

They continued on, though the next room and the one following proved to be very much like the first—crumbled columns, topless tables, and empty brackets hammered into the walls. Eventually, though, they came to a stout wooden door, around which a halo of light shone brightly. Artus pushed it open . . . and what lay beyond took his breath away.

The room was huge and utterly deserted. Thin stone columns stood at even intervals along the walls, supporting globes that burned with a magical radiance. Smaller globes rested upon each of the dozens of tables set in orderly rows across the floor. Books of every sort stood upon sturdy shelves, row after row, more volumes than even the much-lauded library of the Stalwarts held. Artus slipped through the door and grabbed the nearest book. The words were totally foreign to him—a mixture of symbols and picture-glyphs like the ones on the ruined columns.

"I don't suppose either of you can read?" Artus asked.

"Most certainly I can," Byrt replied. When Artus held the book down to him, he smacked his lips and sighed. "I stand corrected."

All the other books on the shelves nearby proved to be written in the same unusual language. Artus was trying to decide which tome to take for more careful study when the door on the opposite end of the room swung open.

Even at such a distance, the stranger's beard proclaimed him a man, despite the flowing tan robe that hid his frame. Close-cropped and white as snow, the beard met up with the shock of silver hair atop the man's head, making a bright halo around his darkly tanned face. Engrossed as he was in the large volume open in his hands, he didn't immediately notice Artus. He read as he walked, shaking his head in vehement disagreement every few steps.

With his nose buried in the pages before him, the silver-haired man walked to a table close to the still-unnoticed strangers and sat down. He leaned toward the glowing globe at the other end of the table and said something Artus could not hear. Four tiny legs sprouted from the globe, and it ran to the man's side, coming to rest only when it was right next to his book.

It was then that Artus got his first good look at the man. "Lord Rayburton!" he exclaimed. He took a step toward the long-lost explorer, amazement clear in his eyes. "You're alive!"

The book slipped from the table and slammed to the floor as the silver-haired man spun about. Theron was right—the man was a ringer for the statue in the society's study. The famed explorer looked no older than that representation, though the sculptor had captured him at the age of sixty, more than twelve hundred years ago.

At the commotion, the globe light hefted itself from the table and dashed to safety far away from the noise. "Who are you?" Rayburton demanded. His features were sharp, and his mouth turned down in a frown, but kindness lurked in his clear eyes.

Seeing the apprehension on Rayburton's face, Artus stopped and looked down at his torn clothes and the dried blood on his injured hand. "I must look pretty frightening," he said in his best Old Cormyrian. As he put aside the unstrung bow, he added, "I came a long way to find you, sir. My name is Artus Cimber, from Cormyr. I'm a member of the Society of Stalwart Adventurers, an explorer like you."

"Your grammar is terrible for a native speaker of Cormyrian," Rayburton noted. "Do you speak Tabaxi?" he asked, switching effortlessly to that Chultan tongue.

Artus could only shrug and shake his head.

Rayburton studied him carefully, his brows knit in consternation. Finally the hard line of his mouth softened, replaced by a smile that matched the kindness in his eyes. "A Stalwart, you say?" He sighed. "I should have known someone from that bunch of well-meaning crackpots would find me one day. You're a friend of that other fellow, the one we saved from the Batiri when we rescued Kwalu?"

"Yes, Theron Silvermace. He—Crackpots?" Artus stammered. "You founded the society, didn't you?"

"I let them use my name," Rayburton said. "Biggest mistake of my life. I never was one for clubs—just an excuse for back-slapping and group inertia. Rather talk about the past than go out and look for it. And the society's still going you say? Amazing." He lifted the book from the floor. "How do you know me? A portrait?"

"A statue," Artus corrected. "In the main library."

"And how did you get in here?" Rayburton asked. He crossed his arms and leaned back against the table.

Artus had the uncomfortable feeling of being back in the House of Oghma, held captive in the prefect's study because of some transgression. "Through a tunnel," he said. "It led into the ruined part of the library. . . ."

Lugg struggled to the top of a nearby table. He spoke neither Tabaxi nor Old Cormyrian, but he could make himself known quite clearly in the trade tongue known as Common. "Look," he said, "if you two are going to yap all day, we want to know where the kitchens are."

From the floor at Artus's feet, Byrt added his approval. "A meal really is in order. Lugg gets rather cross if he's not fed regularly. Not that he isn't cross at other times. You know, bites when tugged and all that."

"In a moment," Artus said as he studied Rayburton's hands. They were wrinkled and beginning to spot with age. Ink stains covered the fingers of his right hand, the sure mark of a scholar or scribe, but there was no ring to be seen.

Artus stepped forward and grabbed Rayburton's shoulders. "The Ring of Winter," he said, his eyes gone wild. "You have it. That's how you made it snow. It kept you alive all these years."

With one solid shove, Rayburton freed himself. "I don't have the ring." For the first time, anger showed on his kindly face. "If that's what you're here for, you'll go back to the society empty-handed."

Artus felt the world fall away under his feet. Before he knew it, he was sitting on the floor next to Byrt. The little gray wombat looked him in the face, worry in his vague blue eyes.

"But you must have the ring," Artus whispered. "You're still alive. It makes the wearer immortal. . . ."

Rayburton kneeled beside the younger explorer. "The ring didn't keep me alive," he said. "It was the magic in this place. Mezro has quite a lot of wonderful things in it."

"Mezro?" Artus managed to gasp. "I discovered the lost city of Mezro?"

Rayburton's gentle laughter filled the library. "It's hardly lost to the people who have lived here for four thousand years," he noted. "But if you want to put it that way, the Mezroans probably won't mind. I said the same thing when I stumbled across the place, and they haven't thrown me out yet."

He looked into Artus's glassy eyes and mentally catalogued the cuts and bruises on his arms and face. "You've had a time of it, eh?" Helping the younger man to his feet, Rayburton added, "The thing for you now is rest, and maybe a surgeon's attention. After that, we can talk about how you managed to 'discover' Mezro."

Ten

From *The Eternal Life of Mezro* by King Osaw I, called "the Wise" by his beloved subjects: ruler of all Mezro, negus negusti, and bara of Ubtao. Translated to Cormyrian by Lord Dhalmass Rayburton, advisor to the king.

There is no exaggeration in the bold claim that Ubtao founded Mezro. The great god of the Tabaxi built the core of the city himself, the temple and amphitheater rising first from the chaos of the jungle. Mezro was to be the place where all the people of Chult could learn how to pass through the maze of life, how best to reach the heart of all and discover the true nature of the world. It became that. Yet Mezro also became a place where thieves and charlatans preyed upon pilgrims, where men and women and children came to beg Ubtao's help with the most insignificant of problems.

Ubtao created the barae to help him deal with those distractions, to resolve the petty demands of the throng. The seven barae were chosen from the citizens of Mezro and gifted with special powers. Over time, the barae became the rulers and defenders of the city, as well, but that was after Ubtao left the Tabaxi to find their own way in the world.

For it is also true the Tabaxi tried to make Ubtao a household god, a god who had to prove his worth by healing old men of aching joints, by settling arguments over the ownership of goats, by proving each and every day that his power could be used to make life easy. But Ubtao, who created the labyrinth that is this earthly world, made the Tabaxi to live there. He stayed in Mezro to teach them how to best pass through the maze, but he would not destroy the everyday trials that were its walls.

Finally there came a day when Ubtao said, "If the people wish to cry and complain rather than listen to my wisdom, then so be it. I will leave them to wander the halls of life without my guidance." Then he returned to his home in the sky and refused to speak to his people again while they were mortal.

And that is why a Tabaxi must die before he may meet his maker.

The exceptions to this rule are the barae. These seven, the mighty paladins of Ubtao, live forever unless they are murdered or lose their life on the battlefield. Their wisdom and faith in Ubtao shield them from old age and sickness. In return, they must protect Ubtao's fair city of Mezro from all harm.

If a bara is killed, another must take his place within one day. That is the only time a mortal may enter the barado, in the great Temple of Ubtao itself. In the barado, the supplicants gather so Ubtao can choose his new paladin. The one the god chooses is granted some magnificent power. Ras

*Nsi, one of the first seven raised up by Ubtao, was given
the power to muster the dead. Mainu, she of the golden
eyes, was granted control over the waters in the Olung
River, which flows through the city to this day.*

*When I became a bara, on that terrible day when three of
the paladins were slain in defense of Mezro, I was given
the power to remember everything I see or hear. These
memories are safe from time, never to be like the banks
that hold a fast-flowing river, worn away more and more
with each passing year. What I know and what I learn remain with me always, as clear and sharp as the eyes of a
jungle cat on the hunt.*

*It is thus I remember the coming of Dhalmass Raybur-
ton, a lord of the distant land of Cormyr, as if it were yesterday. In truth, he arrived six hundred years ago. He was
like all the other explorers who had come to Ubtao's jungle, certain we were savages who had somehow wrested
our great library and our fine buildings from some more
civilized nation. Unlike the others, he soon saw how blind
he was to the accomplishments of other peoples. And
when he accepted the truth of the matter, he found he had
no desire to return to Cormyr. Within ten years of becoming a citizen of Mezro, Rayburton placed himself in Ubtao's
hands and asked to be made a bara. He was chosen.*

*And that is how Dhalmass Rayburton became the first
paladin of Ubtao not born of the Tabaxi. . . .*

Artus rested the heavy book on his lap and looked over
at Lord Rayburton. The expatriate nobleman returned the
puzzled stare placidly. "I suppose you're wondering about
the time frame," Rayburton said after a moment. "I mean,
the book says I arrived here six hundred years past, right?
Well, King Osaw wrote the history six hundred years ago.
There are more volumes, taking the thing right up to the
present, if you don't believe me."

"Oh no," Artus replied quickly. "It's not that at all. I . . . er, it's just so . . ."

"Amazing?" Rayburton smiled and nodded, making the silver triangle hanging from his right earlobe bob up and down. "Mezro is that and more. It didn't take me long to discover how astounding this place is. Once I did, I couldn't bring myself to leave."

Artus put the book aside, propped himself up in the bed, and glanced around the large room that was presently serving as his hospital quarters. It was clean and filled with light from the open window and the three glowing globes that stood at various posts around the room. A tri-bladed metal fan spun briskly overhead, night and day. Aside from the wide, comfortable bed, the room held a nightstand, a larger table, two chairs, and a chest wrought of some fragrant wood. Colorful paintings of abstract designs— squares and circles and triangles in subtle and intriguing arrangements—hung on the walls.

"Thank you," Artus said in Tabaxi, leaning close to the light globe standing upon the nightstand. The radiance dimmed. Then the globe went dark.

Inside the opaque sphere, a complicated arrangement of gears and levers ground silently to a halt, and the four tiny creatures that worked the device sat down. The light makers, or so Rayburton called them, resembled elves in their slender forms and graceful movements, but they had no faces or other features to distinguish one from another. All the globes in Mezro were powered by them.

"Are you sure these things aren't prisoners?" Artus asked.

Rayburton shrugged. "Whenever someone builds a globe with the proper works inside, they just show up, ready to work. They don't eat, don't sleep. They make light and wait to make light." He stood and peered into the globe. "Near as I can guess, they're some sort of quasi-elemental, and the mechanical setup must summon them or act as a gate to their home plane somehow. Damned useful, whatever they are."

Picking nervously at the corner of the book, Artus turned to Rayburton once more. "So you've lived this long because you are a bara of Ubtao." He sighed. "You never found the Ring of Winter. . . ."

The kindness fled the older man's eyes. "No, Artus. I don't have the ring." Rayburton paced to the window and glanced outside, squinting against the late afternoon sunshine.

"But the society's histories say you were searching for it when you disappeared from Cormyr," Artus pressed. "Can you tell me anything—"

Rayburton turned so the explorer could not see his face. "You seem like a good and honorable man," he said softly. "The Ring of Winter holds nothing for you."

"Then the stories were right. You *were* searching for it in Chult," Artus said eagerly. He pushed himself out of bed and straightened the long, shapeless shirt he wore. "Why did you think it was here?"

When he turned, Rayburton did little to conceal his anger. "You're a fool. The Ring of Winter is a terrible force for chaos and destruction. When I lived in Cormyr, I saw its handiwork—whole villages covered in ice, the people frozen, their faces paralyzed in agony. All the wearer of the ring needed to do was imagine the place under a dozen feet of ice and snow." He studied Artus, gauging the shock that colored the younger man's features. "And that was a minor display, by someone who wanted to let the king know he wasn't the only power in the land. The ring has the might to bring the whole world to its knees."

"I never heard about the ring destroying a Cormyrian village," Artus admitted.

"The chroniclers must have been careful to hide it.

Wouldn't have done the crown much good to look so helpless against dark sorcery, I suppose."

"That story only makes me want the ring more," Artus
said firmly. "Such a mighty artifact should be used for
good, to free people from fear and injustice."

Rayburton smiled weakly. "A noble sentiment, but spoken like lines from a bad play." He laid a hand on Artus's
shoulder. "Most of the people who scrambled for the ring
said things like that, even in my time. But if you hunt for
something long enough, you begin to desire it for no other
reason than to finally possess it."

"Gods, the thing is cursed." Artus sagged wearily back
onto the bed. "It took Pontifax's life, and I'm no closer to
finding the damned thing than I was before. He died for
nothing."

"No," Rayburton said. "There's no curse on the ring
other than the desire it inspires in men like you." He shook
his head. "And me, as you know. I hunted for the ring for
five years before I came here."

"Then you can—"

"I'll tell you nothing else, Artus." Rayburton took the
book from the bedside before the explorer could begin
fidgeting with the binding again. "Give up the quest.
The Ring of Winter is something better lost forever. The
'civilized' lands up north are far too barbaric for such powerful weapons."

Artus stared at Rayburton for a time, trying to find some
new tack to take, some new way to convince him to share
his knowledge of the ring. At last he walked to the basin of
water that rested atop the table. "Cormyr has changed a
great deal in twelve hundred years," he offered, then
splashed his face.

As he perched on the edge of the bed, Rayburton
scoffed, "Changed? We've not seen a trace of that great
transmogrification here. Far from it. The teak merchants

come here and rape the land. Then there are the slavers who prey upon the Tabaxi and the big game hunters who destroy any animal they can find." He threw Artus a towel. "And this Kaverin fellow you mentioned. Is he a herald of this new, peaceful society that has taken root in the Heartlands in my absence?"

The kindliness had returned to Rayburton's eyes, but with it had come an air of smug satisfaction. Artus ignored the question and dried his face and hands.

"The fact that people still read those dreadful books I wrote is proof enough to me that Cormyr is no more civilized now than when I left," Rayburton added. "Those things are filled with thoughtless condemnations of many civilized people—the Shou, the Tuigan." He shook his head. "It makes me sick to think about them."

Artus opened the chest and took out his clothes. They had been cleaned and mended while he slept. "Some learned men are familiar with your books," he said, "but don't puff yourself up with too much righteous indignation. Most scholars—and I count myself among them—recognize your books for what they are. We generously write off your shortcomings as a philosopher as a reflection of your era. There're still some useful things in the books, once you get past all the 'thoughtless condemnations' you dished out."

An uncomfortable silence fell over the room. Rayburton returned to the window to stare out at the quiet side street while Artus shrugged into his clothes. As he pulled on his boots, the younger man said, "I'm sorry for the outburst, but . . ."

"But I deserved it," Rayburton conceded. "It's hard not to grow a little rigid in your thinking after a thousand years, and it's been that long since I spoke with anyone from Cormyr." He looked back at Artus. "Let me show you the city."

"I'm not sure—"

"You might be able to understand why I have such strong feelings about the place if you let me show you around," Rayburton said. "Besides, King Osaw wants to meet with you before he offers you a guide back to the coast."

"I don't know if I'm going back to the coast just yet," Artus murmured. "But your offer is most gracious, Lord Rayburton." He gestured toward the door. "Lead on."

They left the small house that had been Artus's hospital and emerged onto a narrow street paved in cobblestone and lined with one- and two-story buildings. One white wall of the alley gleamed in the light of the setting sun. The other was lost in shadows. Songbirds called from the roofs, the happy sound underscored by the rumble of carts and the murmur of a dozen conversations from a nearby thoroughfare.

As they walked, Rayburton explained that Mezro was laid out in four quarters. They were currently in the heart of the residential area; a young student of the city's healers had volunteered to take Artus in and care for his wounds. The man had been so gentle and stealthy in his ministrations that the explorer had never met him. Artus had awakened after sleeping for a day and a half with bandages on his cuts and the lumps on his head packed in cool compresses. A bowl of fresh fruit and an earthenware pitcher of water rested on the table next to the bed.

Artus and Rayburton followed the alley to the left, then the right. The buildings all looked very similar—white walls and tiled roofs, shutterless windows netted against the jungle's biting insects. Left, then right, then right once more, but still the sounds of the main thoroughfare grew no more distinct. Neither did they become more distant.

"This is like the maze in King Azoun's gardens," Artus noted.

"The whole residential area is a labyrinth," Rayburton

said. "You'd never have found your way out alone."

Artus mopped the sweat from his brow. "The mazes of Ubtao, eh?"

For the first time, Rayburton seemed impressed with the young explorer. "Precisely!" He scanned the ground around the nearest home's back door. "Here. Look at this."

Someone had drawn a maze in a patch of sand scattered around the stoop. The pattern started simply enough, but near one corner it grew quite complicated.

"Let's see . . . the child who drew this must be, oh—" Rayburton rubbed his chin "—eight or nine, I'd say."

"How can you tell that?"

The admiration fled Rayburton's face. "The complexity, of course. Every child learns a simple maze that represents his life. It grows more and more complicated as the years go on. When a Tabaxi dies, he must draw the completed maze for Ubtao. That's how they gain admittance to the afterworld." He stepped around the swatch of sand. "If they fail the test, they come back as ghosts or ghouls or the other dark things to hunt the jungle at night. Needless to say, the Tabaxi practice all the time—in the evenings, usually, after they finish working and the children are let out of school."

"All the children go to school?" Artus asked, a bit taken aback.

Rayburton cocked an eyebrow. "Why not? All children need to learn, don't they?"

"Well, yes," Artus sputtered. "It's just that, in Cormyr, the churches charge a lot to share their knowledge, so only the rich can take advantage of it. Everyone else either becomes a craftsman's apprentice, marries well, joins the army, or ends up a cutpurse."

"So your parents were wealthy?" Rayburton said casually, though there was disdain hidden just below the surface of the question. "That would account for the crest on your tunic, I suppose."

Artus hopped sideways to avoid a large, complicated maze sprawling across the alley. "The crest belongs to the man who gave me the tunic," he said curtly. "I'm no nobleman. Far from it."

"No need to explain yourself to me," Rayburton noted. "I was rich. My father was a lord, as was his father and his father. Gods, we Rayburtons were around when the first elves were driven out of the Cormyrian woods to make way for human settlers." He looked over at Artus and pursed his lips. "Right before I left Suzail for Chult, I did some detailed genealogy work for my sister. Needless to say . . . how to put this . . . my ancestors turned out to be pretty loathsome all the way around, once you got to know them. I've never had much respect for titled families since."

The tension Artus had begun to feel eased at that statement. "Then you would have loved my family. My father was a well-intentioned highwayman. He was quite a good one, too, stealing from the rich and all that. He put me through school that way.

"One day he robbed a caravan belonging to the church of Oghma. He was so impressed with the loremasters, how polite and knowledgeable they seemed, that he used the money he stole from them to enroll me in their school." The explorer frowned. "Somehow, I've always suspected my teachers knew that."

"Your guilt was probably written all over your face," Rayburton observed sagely.

At last they reached the main thoroughfare. At first it appeared to Artus to be like the Promenade in Suzail. The wide street was quickly filling with people, dark-skinned like Ibn and Inyanga back at Port Castigliar. Some pushed carts laden with tools or clothes or food. Others carried their burdens or struggled with children too small for school. The sound of wagon wheels clattering over the cobbles mixed with the chatter of men and women.

When Artus looked more carefully, though, he saw that there was an order to the movement that never showed itself on the streets of Suzail. The people filed past in happy groups, all heading for side streets into the Residential Quarter. They carried with them the tools of their trades—hammers and chisels, books and scrolls, merchants' ledgers and beaded counting devices. They were going home after a long day's work.

There was none of the chaos of Suzail's bustling streets—no vendors hawking wares or teamsters driving their loaded carts through alleys busy with pedestrians. He saw no soldiers strutting through the crowd, no beggars huddled in empty doorways, no ale-soaked dandies careening down the way, singing bawdy tunes. Plowmen and scholars walked together, sharing a joke or a story of the day's labor. The only confusion and bustle in the crowd was brought on by a group of young children running home, books and writing tablets tucked securely under their arms.

The men and women were dressed much the same, in sandals and long white robes Rayburton called tobes. A few men went stripped to the waist, the dirt on their hands proclaiming them farmers. A few women with infants went bare-chested, too, though only Artus seemed to notice them in the crowd. Most of the Tabaxi turned to get a look at the green-clad stranger with Lord Rayburton as they passed.

The bara nodded respectfully to the people who greeted him. At last he turned to Artus. "Each day, just before sundown, this street fills with Mezroans on their way home from the other quarters. It's been this way for four thousand years."

Keeping close to the walls, Artus and Rayburton made their way against the crowd. It was then Artus saw beyond the throng, to the vast fields that lay across the way from the white-walled houses. Neat rows of trees and bushes, vegetables and flowers, ran for miles, broken now and then by a field laying fallow. Small huts stood out against the crops in a few places. Scarecrows kept their stiff-armed vigil against birds that had stopped being frightened of them long ago. At the far end of the fields, the tall trees and tangled growth of the jungle reared up, dark and foreboding.

"This place is huge," Artus said. "How have you kept it hidden all these years? Hundreds of expeditions have come to Chult looking for Mezro, but. . . ."

Rayburton pointed to the line of high palms that marked the beginning of the jungle. "A wall surrounds the city. It's a vast circle—the city, I mean—and the sorcerers here constructed the wall a little over five hundred years ago, to stop the Batiri from raiding."

"And I went under it," Artus said, "without ever knowing it was there."

"Oh, you felt the effects of the wall," Rayburton corrected, "though you didn't know it at the time." In response to Artus's puzzled look, he added, "Lugg and Byrt told me you passed into an area that glowed with golden light right before you stumbled into the ruined part of the library. Then it became hard to think. Well, that light was a side effect of the wall. It's invisible above ground, but there must be some element in the tunnel walls causing an alchemical reaction, making it visible. Do you see?"

It was clear Artus didn't see. Rayburton scowled and tried again, his voice taking on a decidedly pedantic tone. "The wall's not bricks and mortar, it's magic. A sort of, er . . . wall of confusion. Anyone who gets near it without wearing one of these—" he tugged at the triangle of silver hanging from one ear "—becomes hopelessly muddled and wanders away. You did us a favor by stumbling in here; we got the architects to seal off the tunnel so no one else can make the same discovery."

"A wall of confusion. So that's why Theron got lost when he followed you from the Batiri camp," Artus said, more to himself than to Rayburton. The older man let the comment pass without an explanation.

As the crowd thinned, Artus got a look at their destination—the huge temple that rose up at the heart of Mezro. Four wide streets, one at each major point of the compass, emptied into a circular plaza. At the center of this roundabout stood the most beautiful structure Artus had ever seen.

The temple towered over all the other buildings in Mezro. Flying buttresses jutted out from its wall like the elegant, muscular legs of a hunting beast waiting to spring. An arcade of piers marked the first floor, topped by a row of arches. Above these stood a long set of stained glass windows, sparkling like thousands of cut gems before the setting sun. A glittering, golden dome capped the roof.

As Artus reached the edge of the plaza, he noticed something peculiar about the temple. At first he dismissed it as a trick of the light or, perhaps, a warning that his fatigue was returning. "Lord Rayburton, the temple looks like. . . ." He cocked his head. "It only has one wall."

Rayburton nodded. "Amazing, isn't it? No matter where you stand, you see the same wall, from the same perspective. Some sort of dimensional trick, I suppose. When a temple is built by the god it's meant to honor, you should just accept it and marvel."

The closer Artus got to the temple, the more its grace and subtle beauty overwhelmed him. The walls weren't built of stone blocks, but interlocking triangles of crystal. The dark gems looked as fragile as Sembian lace and

glistened seductively. Looking at the walls was like staring
at clouds; the longer Artus gazed at the swirls of light and
shadow, the more fantastic the shapes that appeared before him. At first they were simple things—squares and
circles, half-formed faces and bodies. Then the mace and
hawk crest from his tunic appeared on the wall, broken into
hundreds of tiny images at the center of each triangular
block. At first he thought it was a reflection, but no matter
how much he moved, the image remained still in the
crystals.

The crest warped and twisted, becoming the harp and
moon symbol of the Harpers. That changed swiftly to a pair
of hands, black as pitch and clutched into angry fists. After
a moment, the hands clasped together. The color bled out
of them, and they became the kind, smiling face of Pontifax. Artus reached out, but his friend was gone, lost in a
tangle of trees and vines. The jungle closed in, filling all the
crystals with a deep green radiance.

It was then that a simple image formed against the riot of
trees: a ring, a plain band of gold flecked along the edges
with sparkles of light. No, not light. Frost.

The Ring of Winter.

"It's here!" the explorer cried. "I know it's here."

"Artus!"

The voice came from far, far away. It tugged at his con-
sciousness, but Artus pushed the nagging thoughts aside.
If he stared at the ring in the crystals long enough, if he
focused all his thoughts upon it, he would learn where the
Ring of Winter was hidden.

"Master Cimber! Oh dear, he's gone quite rigid. I hope
you don't have a sizeable pigeon population in this square."

That high, cheerful voice insinuated itself into Artus's
mind and threatened to tear his thoughts away from the
ring. He knew, too, someone was shaking him by the
shoulders. He didn't heed the call, but instead stared at the

ring as it spun slowly in the crystal before him, close enough to touch. *Forget what Rayburton said,* a voice told him. *You've spent your life searching for the Ring of Winter. It's here in Chult. It can be yours.*

A fierce pain in his ankle shocked the siren call out of the explorer's mind. "Hey!" he shouted, hopping backward. In doing so Artus tripped over the large brown wombat, who still had his teeth locked onto his boot.

"Leave it to Lugg to cut to the heart of the matter—or the foot, in this case," Byrt chimed. "Well done."

Lugg released his hold on Artus's ankle. Wrinkling his nose in distaste, he said, "More like extremely rare." He spit and stuck out his tongue. "Feh. That's really 'orrible tasting, that is."

"What . . . what happened?" Artus murmured. He rubbed his eyes. The image of the Ring of Winter remained clear for an instant, then faded.

"A property of the temple walls," Rayburton said. "Rather like a massive scrying crystal. Allows you to see into your own heart. I should have warned you not to look too closely. You've been standing there for the better part of an hour." He extended a hand and helped Artus to his feet. Only then did the dazed and bemused explorer notice the two other people standing between him and the temple wall.

The first was a tall, stern-faced Tabaxi. Like the other Mezroans, he was dressed in a flowing tobe. His was not white, but purple, with small green triangles clustered over his heart. Unlike the others Artus had seen, this man carried a weapon—a war club, which hung at his waist. From the muscles cording the man's bare arms, he could quite obviously wield the knobbed cudgel to good effect.

"This is Negus Kwalu," Rayburton said, gesturing toward the stone-faced Tabaxi. "Eldest son of King Osaw."

Artus dusted himself off and bowed deferentially. He

knew enough about Tabaxi culture to recognize negus as the title reserved for princes in direct line to the throne.

Kwalu's brown eyes narrowed to slits as he studied Artus. He stood perfectly still, a square-featured statue staring at the explorer. From the hard line of the negus's mouth and the crease of concern on his jutting brow, Artus guessed he was not faring well in the prince's silent test.

Finally, the negus offered a few clipped phrases. The tone alone told Artus they were a formal greeting and welcome to the city, though Kwalu hardly seemed pleased to deliver it. Rather than risk offending the man by mangling a reply in Tabaxi, Artus smiled as genuinely as he could and bowed again. Kwalu nodded, then turned on his heels and marched off toward a hugh amphitheater on the other side of the plaza.

For an instant, the explorer was certain he had struggled through the difficult exchange with as much grace as possible. A woman's bright laughter shattered that thought almost as quickly as it had formed.

"You really don't speak Tabaxi, do you?" the young woman said in Old Cormyrian, then laughed again. The sound was clear and refreshing, like a cool spring rain.

Lord Rayburton frowned severely, but that did nothing to silence the woman. She nodded to Artus and said, "My father is too annoyed at me right now to introduce us. I'm Alisanda Rayburton."

She held out a slender hand to Artus, who took it almost without thinking. He found himself staring at the woman with the same intensity he'd shown the images in the temple wall. Alisanda was as tall as the explorer, with the dark skin of her Tabaxi mother and black hair knit into a dozen tight braids across her scalp. Her green eyes shone with a calm self-assurance and a ready wit, things Artus had always valued in his old friend Pontifax, things that instantly beguiled him now.

"You can call me Sanda," she said, her round face lit with a smile, "but only if you give me back my hand."

"Oh, sorry," Artus murmured. He let go of her hand. "So why were you laughing?"

Sanda gestured to Lord Rayburton, who still seemed rather put out by his daughter's actions. "Father told me you came here without knowing how to speak the language. I didn't believe him." She shrugged. "It just seems kind of silly, don't you think?"

Bristling at the insult, unintentional though it was, Artus said, "I never planned to come here. The trip was unexpected."

"Oh, don't mind her," Rayburton said bruskly. "She's terribly rude sometimes. When she gets this way, I try my best to ignore her."

"Speaking of being ignored," Byrt cut in, "how about sharing a bit of the conversation with us. We don't mind being talked down to—no choice, really, when you're as short as we two."

Sanda knelt and scratched behind Byrt's ears. "Sorry. You and Lugg will just have to do a better job of letting us know you're here."

"That's hardly their problem," Artus grumbled, rubbing his ankle where Lugg had bitten him. A set of deep teeth marks marred the boot in a rough circle.

"Sanda has more of an appreciation for animals than most," Rayburton noted absently. He was checking the length of the shadows in the plaza. "That's the power Ubtao granted her when she became a bara—animal friendship, she calls it."

"Oh," Artus said coolly. He glanced at Sanda, suddenly uncomfortable. "How long have you been a bara?"

"Almost five hundred years," she replied. "Not very long, not compared to Father or King Osaw." After a pause, she added, "Still, Negus Kwalu has only been a bara for a hundred years, so I'm not the youngest."

"The negus is a bara, too?" Artus exclaimed. "Gods. When am I going to meet someone here my own age?"

If Lord Rayburton noticed the tension that had settled between Artus and his daughter, he showed no sign of it as he turned his back to them and started away from the temple. "No time to waste," he said. "The sun will be down soon, and I need to go talk to Ras T'fima about . . . well, about some old debts." He stopped and looked back over his shoulders. "Lugg and Byrt should come with me, I think."

"What a wonderful idea, Lord Rayburton," the little wombat said. "I think Artus should spend a little recreation time with members of his own species before we three trek back to the coast together."

"I never said I was going back—"

"Good evening, Sanda," Byrt said, doing his best imitation of a courtly bow. He turned his vacant blue eyes on her. "Your charm and discretion are truly the centerpiece of Mezroan society." With that he hurried after Rayburton. Lugg hefted himself sleepily from the ground and trundled after them, shaking his head.

Sanda watched her father and the wombats cross the plaza, then disappear into a crowd that was beginning to gather around the huge amphitheater. "Shall I show you the rest of the city?" she asked.

"Actually," Artus said. "I think I need to find someplace to sit down and rest." He slumped against the side of the temple, careful not to look too closely at the myriad crystal triangles.

Sanda hooked her arm under Artus's. "I know just the spot. There's a park near the schools—did I tell you I teach history at the schools? No?" She tugged the explorer off the wall and guided him into the plaza. "We can go to the park and talk. In fact . . . I might be able to lay my hands on some Tabaxi primers, if any of the children left them in the classroom."

She has to think I'm a complete boob, Artus decided. Not surprising since she's more than ten times my age. He looked over at the young woman—at least she appeared young. Twenty-five, perhaps. Thirty at the oldest. Sanda caught him studying her and smiled warmly.

"After you've got the rudiments of Tabaxi down," she said, "maybe you can tell me a bit about the Heartlands— you're from Cormyr, right? I only have Father's word to go on for what the North is like, and I think you've already caught on to how cranky and unyielding he can be."

Artus had been caught up in finding some pretext for extricating his arm from hers. But the feeling he had—that he was being led along like a wayward orphan—disappeared in the face of her guileless chatter. "It's a deal," he said, settling his arm against hers. "You give me Tabaxi lessons, and I'll teach you about Cormyr."

Eleven

The dinosaur towered over Artus, its bulk blocking out the sun. It was obviously a carnivore, and a hungry one at that.

On a pair of strong, muscular legs, the monster raised its body to its full height—five times as tall as Artus. The dinosaur's forelimbs were small, more like a pair of bird's claws, and they clutched at the air continuously. Its long tail swished back and forth, stirring up the dust on the barren plain. These details of anatomy fled the explorer's mind when the thing opened its mouth. At their base, its teeth were as wide around as a man's fist, but they tapered to needle points. That's all Artus saw for a moment, those teeth.

"*Zara n'tomo, karth?*" the dinosaur said in a soft, high voice. It reached down with one of its bird-hands and shook the explorer gently by the shoulder.

Artus started awake and yelped in surprise. The five small children standing around him echoed that shout and leaped back a few steps. They were dressed in white tobes, their schoolbooks in one hand, their sandals in the other. All had their hair shaved close to the scalp, though the girls had cut intricate patterns in the curls they had left.

The oldest child—a girl of ten or so—took a tentative step forward and repeated her question. "*Zara n'tomo, karth?*"

"Oh, *Ka . . . neb*—no, uh—*nez . . .*," Artus mumbled, trying his best to remember the Tabaxi phrase for "I don't speak the language." It simply wouldn't come to mind. He shrugged and smiled stupidly.

That seemed to be answer enough to whatever the girl had asked, for the children returned the smile and went their way. Their laughter gave voice to the early afternoon sunshine as they ran across the grass. Soon the children had vanished behind the high shrubs bordering the park.

Alone once more, Artus sat back on the stone bench. He and Sanda had spent most of the night there, talking about Cormyr, Mezro, and any other topic they happened upon. They hadn't given over enough time to common Tabaxi phrases, though Artus had discovered why Sanda found his ignorance of Tabaxi surprising. Lord Rayburton had taught her the basics of a dozen languages; his power as a bara was the ability to comprehend and converse in any tongue, human or inhuman. Over the years, she had come to expect everyone to be able to speak whatever language necessary.

Tabaxi had proved more difficult than the explorer had suspected. In addition to the trade tongue known as Common, Artus spoke four languages. Not even one of them was vaguely related to Tabaxi, however, so he was at a loss to find cognates or any other similarities that would make conversing easier. He remained as he had been on his first day in Mezro—at a loss without an interpreter.

Artus craned his neck and scanned the paths snaking

around the small park, through the flowing shrubs and
dwarf palm trees. No sign of Sanda. At dawn, she had hurried off to ready herself for her job at the school, promising
to return by highsun. She was now almost an hour late.

The explorer was considering a short walk through the
Scholars' Quarter surrounding the park when three burly
Tabaxi, all carrying shields and clubs, appeared on the path.
Their leader, a lanky fellow with a pug nose and custard-
colored eyes, pointed at Artus.

Perhaps the children had warned the city watch about
the scruffy, white-skinned derelict in the park, Artus decided. He tried to remember the words Sanda had taught him
in case of just such an emergency. "*Ka Alisanda Rayburton
wa'la*," he said to the leader of the trio.

The warriors were unimpressed. The pug-nosed one
jabbered at Artus for a moment, his words spilling out so
fast most Tabaxi would have had trouble sorting out his
meaning. The explorer could only shrug and repeat the
phrase, which was supposed to alert any curious locals he
was a guest of Sanda's. If it meant anything to the three
men, they didn't show it.

Finally the pug-nosed warrior stepped forward and
grabbed Artus by the arm. He wasn't rough about it, but
when he pulled the explorer from the bench, there was no
question of resisting. Even if the men hadn't been armed,
Artus wouldn't have argued. The clubs only provided that
much more incentive for him to go along quietly.

"I hope you have a nice prison," he said as they hustled
him out of the park. "I suppose I'll be spending a lot of time
there, at least until Sanda and Rayburton figure out where I
am." Even if they couldn't understand a word he said,
Artus hoped the warriors would pick up on his genial
tone—however forced it was—and decide he wasn't much
of a threat.

They hurried through the cramped streets in the

Scholars' Quarter, past the massive library and the dozens of specialized schools and laboratories that filled that part of Mezro. Clusters of students, both young and old, milled in many places. Some talked and joked, while others buried their heads in books or just ate their lunches, basking in the sunshine before returning to a dark classroom. Artus and his escort drew the attention of most of those they passed; somehow, though, the explorer got the impression the students were reacting to the warriors' weapons, not his appearance.

At last they reached the central plaza and the oddly beautiful Temple of Ubtao. Growing up in Suzail, Artus had learned to navigate the cityscape using buildings as guides. Now a strange directional vertigo washed over him; as Rayburton had warned, the temple's facade appeared exactly as it had when he'd approached from the opposite side last evening.

"Artus!" someone shouted from the crowd gathered at the temple's entry arch. Sanda pushed through the circle of twenty or so warriors and rushed across the cobblestones. "I'm sorry the soldiers had to bring you this way, but Lugg said he would only talk to you. He stumbled into the plaza a little while ago, an arrow in his side."

"Lugg? Who shot him?"

Sanda started to speak, but choked on the reply. It was then that Artus noticed she'd been crying. Her green eyes were glassy with tears and rimmed with red. "Oh, Lugg will be all right," she managed after a moment. "It's my father and Byrt. . . ."

Holding back a sob, she took Artus by the arm and led him to the circle of warriors. At their center, Lugg lay on his back, his stubby legs in the air. Two of the Tabaxi held a canvas square to shade the wombat. Blood matted the brown fur along his left flank and colored the silver triangle that hung from one rounded ear. The arrow that had wounded him lay nearby. The wombat's muzzle was battered and bruised. As Sanda knelt at his side and stroked his cheek, Lugg flinched. "Oi," he murmured. "Let me die in peace, will you?"

"Artus is here," Sanda whispered. "Please, tell him what happened."

Struggling to hold his head up, Lugg turned to Artus. "You've got to 'elp 'im," he said frantically. "The bloody Batiri took Byrt. I tell you 'e's no good on 'is own, not without me to look out for 'im."

Artus got to his knees beside the wombat. "The Batiri took Byrt? How did they get inside the city?"

"They didn't," Lugg answered curtly. "The Batiri grabbed 'im and Rayburton when we went outside the wall to see the witch doctor. I thought it was a bad idea, but no. They—"

"Lord Rayburton, too!" Artus exclaimed. "Lugg, where did this happen? How many of them were there? Which way did the goblins take them?"

The wombat closed his eyes and rested his head on the ground. "I'll tell you, but only if you promise to get Byrt away from those rotten twisters," he hissed through clenched teeth. A spasm of pain shivered along his side.

"Of course," Artus answered quickly.

"Please," Sanda said. Tears had begun to stream down her round cheeks again. "If the hunting hasn't been good lately, the Batiri may—may . . ."

Lugg sighed. "Yeah. I 'eard what the goblins do to people they capture. They tried to grab Byrt and me before. Wanted to make us part of a festival dinner, they did." He rolled onto his side. Wincing, he began his description of the ambush.

Rayburton, Lugg, and Byrt had left Mezro just before sundown, heading for the camp of Ras T'fima. Just why Rayburton needed to visit T'fima was unclear to the wombat, but he did know the matter was urgent.

After a short trek along a jungle path, they smelled the aromatic smoke from a cookfire. They were that close to the sorcerer's camp when the Batiri raiding party attacked. The battle was short, with thirty of the bloodthirsty goblins overpowering both Rayburton and Byrt. Lugg managed to escape. An arrow in his side, the wombat spent the night hiding from the goblins. Only at dawn was it safe for him to leave his hiding place and struggle back to Mezro.

"If the Batiri have had them all night, they could be miles from here," Artus said. "We'd better get after them right away."

Sanda leaned close to Lugg. "Are you certain you were near T'fima's camp? The goblins are never bold enough to go so close to his home. They're terrified of him."

"Yeah, your father was pretty surprised, too," Lugg said. "Maybe they was spurred on by the 'uman with them, or the silver bloke with four arms."

Artus cursed and said, "Kaverin, and he has Skuld now, too." Scowling fiercely, he rubbed his chin. "That might be a blessing, Sanda. Kaverin will keep your father alive for a while, until he's learned what he can from him."

"You know these men who bring the Batiri so close to our city?"

The voice was high and thin, the words spoken in halting Common. Artus looked up at the old man standing over him. Though he was hunched with the weight of many years, his inner strength and wisdom seemed to radiate from him like warmth from the sun. A crown rested upon his wrinkled brow, the platinum blending with his close-cropped hair. His eyes were almost lost in folds of deep wrinkles, but were piercing and intense nonetheless. His clothes were simple—a tobe much like those worn by everyone in Mezro—but a dozen platinum bands encircled his arms.

Artus bowed his head, for this could only be King Osaw. "Your Highness," he said. "I do know of the man who allied himself with the goblins. He commands a spirit with four arms and silver skin."

When Artus looked up, he saw that Negus Kwalu now stood at his father's side. He no longer wore his purple tobe, but a simple breechcloth. A small, square breastplate of dinosaur hide covered his chest, with the tails of six exotic hunting cats cascading down his back. Manes cut from other wild beasts made up the long, stringy cuffs that hung from his calves to his ankles. Black and white feathers jutted out from his helmet at all angles. The prince studied Artus with an unnervingly steady gaze, not a hint of expression on his rugged features.

"If this man allies with the Batiri, he is the same as the things that stalk the dark corners of Ubtao's jungle at night," King Osaw began softly. He studied Artus's face for a moment, then added, "Will you help us to rescue the bara?"

"Of course, Your Highness," Artus replied. "I will tell you anything I can about Kaverin and the silver spirit."

King Osaw nodded, then turned to Sanda and Kwalu, issuing orders in a low tone. When the king was done speaking, he left the circle of warriors and made his way back into the temple. The men who had been using the canvas to shield Lugg from the sun now made it a stretcher for the wounded wombat.

"Don't forget," Lugg said to Artus as he was hefted off the ground. "You promised to save 'im."

"I won't forget," Artus murmured, though he had his doubts there would be anything left of Byrt if they found the Batiri. Kaverin would keep Rayburton alive—at least until he learned what he could about Mezro and the Ring of Winter—but the little gray wombat could only offer cheerful, but inane comments. Kaverin's probably killed him already, Artus decided sadly.

Sanda gestured toward the Residential Quarter. "Kwalu went to get your bow and knife," she said.

"Wait," Artus said, "where are we going?"

"To talk to Ras T'fima," Sanda said. "The Batiri captured Kwalu a few weeks ago, when he was on a hunt far from the city. My father and I raided their camp. Anyway, T'fima was the one who provided the blizzard that gave us cover." She looked away, nervously plucking at one of her braids. "I hope he'll help us again."

"Wouldn't it be easier to go after the Batiri with an army?" Artus asked.

Sanda shook her head emphatically. "The goblins are spread out, but there are many more of them then there are Mezroan soldiers. Besides, we disbanded the army years ago. There was really no need for us to maintain one. People like Kwalu keep the military arts alive, of course, but mostly on a theoretical battlefield." She scanned the plaza, impatient for the negus's return. "That's why we're going to ask for T'fima's help," Sanda added absently. "His magic is worth more than a thousand soldiers."

Artus ran a hand through his hair, which was damp with sweat from walking to the plaza. "T'fima must be some sorcerer to whip up a blizzard in this type of heat," he said. "Wait. Let me guess. He's a bara, right? Two thousand years old?"

"Fifteen hundred years," Sanda said, smiling at Artus's exasperation. "The same as King Osaw, though T'fima was younger than the king when he was chosen by Ubtao."

A slight twinge of disappointment crept into Artus's thoughts; secretly he had hoped to find T'fima had used the Ring of Winter to make it snow. "Yes, well, King Osaw did look like he'd lived through a rainy season or two," Artus noted archly. "How old was Osaw when he became a bara?"

Sanda lowered her voice conspiratorially. "Eighty-five, but don't let that fool you. He's had a gaggle of children over the years—Kwalu was born not much more than one hundred years ago. The negus still acts like a spoiled child sometimes, but he's really—"

The conversation ended abruptly when Kwalu arrived. Not only did the negus carry his own weapons—a broad-bladed spear, dinosaur-hide shield, and vicious-looking war club—but Artus's bow, quiver, and dagger, too. He unceremoniously dumped the explorer's weapons into his arms, then produced another large knife and handed it to Sanda. As Artus struggled to keep the quiver from up-ending, Kwalu started out of the plaza at a loping run.

"We'd better hurry," Sanda said. She stepped to Artus's side and held out a silver triangle. "This may hurt a little." Swiftly she touched the triangle to Artus's right ear, and it fused to the lobe.

"Hey! That really smarts!" Artus shouted. He tried to pull the earring off, but it wouldn't budge. "Look, I'm not sure I want to attach any magic jewelry to myself just now," he said. "I had this medallion stuck around my neck and—"

Sanda turned to follow Kwalu. "It's the only way for you to pass through the city wall without being affected by the magic," she shouted over her shoulder. "We can take it off after we rescue my father."

Artus gave the silver triangle one last tug, cursed long and loud in Cormyrian—after all, no one could understand him, so restraint was unnecessary—then started after Sanda and Kwalu. They were making good time through the streets, and the explorer had to run at top speed to catch them. He was puffing even before they reached the outer edge of the Scholars' Quarter. There the streets trailed off into rubble, the finely tended parks into tangles of wild vegetation.

"When will we pass through the wall?" Artus asked between gasps.

Sanda wasn't even winded. "We already have," she said, taking stock of the explorer with obvious concern. "Artus, you really need to pace your running. Set a stride that will match ours, but won't tire you so. We have a few miles to go yet."

The explorer was in good shape, but running in this sort of heat was something to which he was just not accustomed. Still, Artus did his best to work into a longer, more relaxed stride. Though he couldn't hope to match Kwalu's exhausting pace, he managed to keep Sanda and the negus in sight. That the Mezroans trusted Artus to do so was illustrated clearly by the fact that they never looked back to see if he was still with them.

When vines and bushes began to obscure the trail, Kwalu slowed a little. A short time later, the negus stopped. Without explaining why, he began a careful search of the brush to either side of the path.

Artus didn't particularly care why Negus Kwalu had called a halt. He collapsed onto the ground, arms straight out from his sides. After a moment, he mustered enough strength to pull his hood over his face to block the sun.

"You'd better get up," Sanda said. Even from her voice, Artus could picture the sympathetic look in her green eyes. "Your muscles will cramp up if you stop moving, and we'll be running again in a moment. Kwalu spotted some signs of the Batiri. He wanted to look around and get an idea of the number of warriors in the raiding party."

Groaning, Artus tried to sit up. He groaned louder when he realized he was lying on top of his bow. "Why don't you just bury me here. I'll come back as a zombie or a ghoul. Then I can chase Kaverin back to Cormyr on foot without ever getting tired."

A firm hand grabbed Artus by the arm and pulled him to

his knees. "Don't joke about such things," Sanda hissed.

Artus thought to reply, but Kwalu had started off again toward Ras T'fima's camp. Sanda quickly fell in behind the negus, and Artus started slowly after them. He found out within a few steps that Sanda had been right; the muscles in his legs throbbed with cramps.

It wasn't long before the jungle thinned again, and the trail cleared. Artus assumed they were nearing the camp of the Tabaxi sorcerer, but before he saw any signs of habitation, he heard frantic shouting. It drowned out even the incessant cries of the monkeys and birds in the canopy. At first Artus thought T'fima might be under attack by the goblins. Sanda and Kwalu didn't react to the screams and moans, though. They pressed on through the clutching vines and saw-leafed bushes as if they heard nothing unusual.

T'fima's camp was small—little more than a sprawling hut and a garden situated on the bank of a peaceful, slow-moving river. Part stone, part sod, the hut leaned drunkenly against a tall, thick tree. Its roof was equally haphazard, composed of palm fronds, tin plates, and air. The garden was quite a sight, too; at first glance Artus couldn't tell if there was a single planned crop in amongst the weeds.

The piles of broken stone littering the clearing were the strangest thing about the camp. Heaps of granite and limestone, slate and shale all ran together. They were highest near the hut itself, forming a narrow, waist-high valley that ended at the front door. And at the highest point of these mock canyon walls sat a night-black cat with sharp fangs and exceedingly large claws.

Sanda scratched the animal as she passed, and it arched its back gratefully to accept the attention. It mewed as Kwalu went by, more like a duck quacking than a cat's cry. Even the stone-faced negus paused to pat the guardian absently. As Artus got close, however, the cat hunched its back and hissed. The explorer held out a hand in a show of friendship, but the cat would have none of it. With a lightning-fast swipe, it slashed at the proffered hand, drawing four thin lines of blood along the palm.

"Don't try to get past Neyobu," Sanda called from inside the hut. "Until T'fima invites you in, he'll do everything he can to keep you on that side of the door. And that's more than you might think."

Neyobu eyed Artus malevolently. Then the explorer noticed the three small pearls set in a triangle atop the cat's head. Blue-white sparks flicked from one stone to another as the guardian stared, unmoving, at the stranger. Not to be intimidated, Artus sat down in the valley and returned the cat's unfriendly gaze.

The shouting from the hut never ceased, but it changed tone and intensity when Sanda and Kwalu went inside. Soon the guests were bellowing, too, trying to be heard over the sorcerer's exclamations. Artus could see little of the dim interior, but what he could see was as cluttered as the campsite. Piles of stone and larger hunks of rock seemed to be the hut's main furnishings.

A particularly loud exchange ended with a crash of stone scattering across a tabletop. Then all was quiet. At last Sanda came outside, a smile on her lips and a gem the size of a small bird's egg in her hand. "Open your mouth," she said, holding the red stone out to Artus.

He stared at the gem. "I have to eat a stone before T'fima will let me in? Thanks, but I'll just wait here."

"T'fima doesn't speak Cormyrian or Common or any other language you do," Sanda replied. "Put this on your tongue and you'll be able to speak Tabaxi for three days. It's a carnelian, I think."

The red gem had myriad runes carved into its smooth surface. Artus turned it over in his hand twice, then popped it into his mouth. Like the most delicate of elven candies, the gem melted instantly. However, it tasted more like exceedingly foul orcish goulash or the sole of a soldier's old boot. Since some claimed orcs used discarded shoes in their cooking, the difference might be purely academic.

Artus spit out what was left of the carnelian, which wasn't much. "Gods," he sputtered, "I'll be lucky if I don't get sick. Was that really necessary?"

"He's right. You speak Tabaxi like a native," Sanda said. "Can you understand me?"

Astonished, Artus nodded. "Perfectly.

Grandly, Sanda gestured toward the doorway. "T'fima has a few questions for you."

Artus steered a wide path around the black-furred guardian. The cat watched him go by, then clawed at him playfully as he crossed the threshold. The explorer jumped away from the half-hearted swipe. "I think someone pounded those pearls into his head too hard," he said facetiously.

"Quiet down or I'll pound something into your head," someone shouted from the other side of the huge boulder that stood in the center of the hut. "I put those pearls on that cat four hundred years ago, and he hasn't complained once!"

Artus's initial impression of the hut's decor had been quite accurate. Almost everything in the place was made of stone, or was used to prop up a stone, or was part of some intricate experiment focused, unsurprisingly, on a stone. Glass tubing wound around chunks of crystalline feldspar. Uncut rubies and emeralds churned in beakers full of bubbling liquid. Large rocks served as tables and chairs, though one thick wooden slab was laid across a rock near the door. On it were strewn tools for delicate engraving and dozens of gems, much like the ensorceled carnelian.

And in the center of the hut, as Artus had first noted, stood a monstrous chunk of some sort of indeterminate stone. In a few places, T'fima had carved runes into this central boulder. Mostly, though, it was simply massive and untouched.

A short, fat man waddled around the boulder, as flabby as his furnishings were hard. His eyes were full of barely restrained anger, his mouth gasping open and closed like a beached fish. From the mass of tightly curled hair atop his head to the clenched toes of his bare feet, the man radiated a violent challenge. When he got close to Artus, he stopped and planted his hands on his hips. He trembled like a volcano preparing to erupt before he said, "Well? Why were those fellows spying on me—the goblins and that human?"

The words burst out like magma, full of ready condemnation. Artus was taken aback for a moment. When he gathered his wits, though, his reply was cool and precise.

"The human—whose name is Kaverin Ebonhand—obviously heard from the Batiri you are an important man," Artus said flatly. T'fima's title of Ras meant his prestige rivaled that of a duke in the North. "He must have been watching your camp to see who came and went. Lord Rayburton happened to visit at the wrong time."

"But why take Rayburton?" Ras T'fima asked.

"Kaverin followed me to Chult. He's looking for Lord Rayburton, mostly because of this artifact he was supposed to have—the Ring of Winter."

That comment made T'fima pause. "Never heard of it," he blared, then narrowed his eyes. "Then you're to blame for those goblins lurking around here, tramping through my garden?"

From a darkened corner near the door, Kwalu said, "The stranger may have brought trouble on his heels, but any problems you have with the Batiri are your own doing. You can come back inside the walls of the city any time you wish. After all, you are still a bara, even if you don't act like one."

Artus expected that comment to draw a bitter outburst from T'fima. It didn't. Instead the sorcerer cocked his head and listened for something on the roof.

The explorer looked up. "What's—"

Neyobu dashed into the hut. Artus watched, amazed, as the cat leaped from stone table to stone chair without disturbing anything, then scrambled up the large boulder. Before the explorer could finish his question, Neyobu disappeared through a hole onto the roof, a black blur against the bright sky. The commotion that broke out on the tin part of the roof was loud, but brief. An instant later, the cat dropped through the hole again. He held the corpse of a leather-winged albino monkey firmly in his fangs.

Kwalu detached himself from the shadows to examine the strange catch. "It's not one of Ubtao's beasts," he said, taking the monkey from Neyobu.

"It belonged to Kaverin," Artus said. "He bought the thing from a mage in Tantras. He uses—er, used—it to spy on people." He lifted the monkey's head. "I think he could see through its eyes."

"Lay the thing out on the floor," T'fima ordered. "Spread it out flat on its back."

As Kwalu and Artus arranged the winged monkey, the sorcerer went to the wooden-topped table and snatched up a carving pick and two small pieces of colored quartz with a waxy tinge. He scratched a few runes into each of the stones. "The beast is recently enough dead that it will still be linked to its master," the sorcerer said. "Let us see where he is."

T'fima placed a piece of quartz over each of the monkey's pink eyes. A swirl of color appeared in the air over the corpse. It coalesced into a ghostly image of a two-story wooden building, cold torches lining the stairs to its front door.

"That's the Batiri camp," Artus exclaimed.

"Just as this Kaverin is seeing it now," T'fima added.

The image flowed and changed as Kaverin hurried up the stairs, into the goblin queen's home. Two guards, armed with spears, backed into the shadows of the main hall as the daylight streamed in. Kaverin barely gave them a glance as he rushed toward a door at the end of the hall. A carved human skull grinned from its center.

Skulls lined the room beyond, as well. They covered the walls and rested upon every flat surface, every piece of furniture. In a chair graced with only one such trophy sat Lord Rayburton. The bruises on his face and blood on his tobe told of abuse, but he was alive. A sigh of relief went up from Sanda and Artus.

As Kaverin got closer to Rayburton, Artus found his eyes drawn to the head resting atop the chair. It was a recent kill, missing only some of its skin. Still, the long, stringy hair and round glasses were all Artus needed to see. Phyrra al-Quim had met the treacherous end reserved for Kaverin's closest allies. He wasn't pleased by the sight, but he did feel some vague sense of justice.

Kaverin began to look around the room in a seemingly random pattern, almost as if he were dazed. Artus spotted Byrt, crammed into a wooden cage in one corner; Skuld stood over the imprisoned wombat. The silver giant's eyes were closed, and both sets of arms were folded over his chest. Suddenly Skuld looked up, directly at Kaverin. He wove an intricate pattern in the air before him, his mouth moving in a chant Artus and the others could not hear.

The image disappeared, and the smell of charred flesh filled the hut. The two pieces of quartz flared brightly, burning deep into the monkey's head. In one quick move, the sorcerer picked up the corpse and emptied the stones onto the dirt floor. Then he tossed the dead monkey out the door. An instant later, Neyobu flew outside and descended upon his prize.

"This fellow is clever," T'fima admitted. He picked up the two smoking stones. They crumbled to ash in his hands. "He figured out we were spying on him and had that silver brute dispel my magic. You will have trouble rescuing Rayburton, I think."

"As a bara, it is your responsibility to aid the city and the other paladins who serve it," Kwalu noted stiffly. "King Osaw has sent me to ask your help in the name of Ubtao. Bring down a storm upon the goblins, just as you did to facilitate my rescue."

T'fima lowered himself onto a squat chunk of basalt. He pondered the plea for a time, muttering to himself. Finally he looked up at Kwalu. "No."

Both Sanda and the negus took a step forward. "What?" they shouted in unison.

"The wall still stands around the city, doesn't it?" T'fima said. "I agreed to help rescue Kwalu because the king and Lord Rayburton told me the wall would come down."

"King Osaw offered to bring the matter up before the citizens of Mezro," Sanda corrected. "Which he did. The people voted to keep the wall up."

"That doesn't change things," the sorcerer said. He crossed his arms over his chest. "I left Mezro five hundred years ago and swore not to help again until the wall came down. I won't be fooled into going back on that vow again."

Kwalu grabbed the front of the sorcerer's tobe. "You are a bara," he said. "If the city asks, you must aid us. That is why Ubtao gave you power over the weather."

For a tense moment, the two stood nose to nose. It surprised Artus to see Kwalu back down, but it was the warrior who released T'fima and took a step back. "Old arguments should not cloud the debate now," he said, keeping his anger in check. "All that matters is that you follow Ubtao's law."

Straightening his grimy tobe, T'fima said, "I abandoned

Ubtao's law when I left the city. It means nothing to me—just as the power he granted me means nothing. I use only the magic I can draw from gems now." He turned to Sanda, and his eyes took on an almost pleading look. "I want to help you, but I can't, not while the wall stands. By keeping the city isolated, you are cheating the Tabaxi who live in the jungles out of their heritage."

"You can debate that later, T'fima," Artus said. "Lord Rayburton is in danger right now, and he needs your help."

A tense silence followed, during which T'fima refused to meet anyone's eyes. At last Kwalu said, "We are through here." He gathered up his shield and his weapons, then looked back at the sorcerer. "It would not be a bad thing for you to end your life, Ras T'fima. Then Ubtao could choose a new paladin to replace you, one who would do his duty to Mezro."

Sanda paused before the ras. "Father trusted you. He said you were an honorable man."

"I am," the sorcerer said softly. This time his voice quivered with sadness, not rage. "Lord Rayburton would understand why it has to be this way."

"Well, I don't," Artus said. He took Sanda's arm, and they started toward the door. When he saw Neyobu sitting in the center of the floor, the explorer backed away, bumping into the wooden tabletop. The cat watched him pass, his fangs crimson with the monkey's blood.

Before Artus could leave, T'fima grabbed him. "It's not your place to understand," he hissed. "Just like it's not my place to condemn you for bringing all this down on the city because of some damned ring." He shoved the explorer out the door, slamming it closed behind him.

Kwalu was already at the edge of the clearing when Artus and Sanda got outside. "My father said he would organize a brigade and send them here, but we cannot wait, Sanda. I will leave trail markers, so they can follow us."

The young woman nodded and drew the knife Kwalu had given her. "If we reach the goblin camp while it's still daylight, they'll be sleeping. We can spy on them until the other warriors arrive . . . unless, of course, an opportunity to rescue Father presents itself."

Both Sanda and Kwalu turned to Artus, as if they expected him to hedge at the prospect. He strolled to the edge of the trail that led deeper into the jungle. "I fought my way out of the camp once. Going to spy on them with you two should be as easy as finding a crooked tax collector in Sembia." At their blank looks, he said, "A hungry dinosaur in a swamp?"

For the first time, Artus saw Kwalu smile. The warrior thumped his spear against his shield. "A dead Batiri near Mezro," he corrected. "So you fought your way out of the goblin camp, eh?"

"It was hardly the stuff of bardic songs," Artus said. "But if you're interested, I'll tell you about it on the way."

Twelve

Skuld pressed both sets of palms together and bowed deeply. "The wards are complete, master. No one else may look into this room with magic."

"Fine," Kaverin said. He resumed his pacing, clacking the knuckles of his jet-black hands together with every third step. At last he turned to Lord Rayburton. "You know, milord, I'm beginning to believe you about the ring."

His hands bound firmly behind his back, his legs lashed securely to the chair, Rayburton didn't bother trying to see his captor's face. Kaverin always paced behind the chair, where he remained hidden. Even in Rayburton's time in Cormyr this had been an old interrogation trick; without being able to read body language or expression, the prisoner could use only his ears to judge anything told to him.

"Then you can let me go," the nobleman said. "Byrt, too."

"I'm afraid that's not possible. Your gray-furred friend is

going to be a present to the goblin queen, since the winged spy your fellows killed was technically hers," Kaverin said. He clucked his tongue. "Besides, the goblins are having a victory celebration tonight, and you can't leave before that's over with. They might even serve the talking pig-bear, knowing them. I wonder what he tastes like?"

"Pig-bear!" Byrt exclaimed. "Hardly, sir. I am a wombat. *W-O—*"

Skuld's silver foot descended onto the top of the cramped wooden cage. "Silence, little one. The goblins can eat you whether I pull your teeth out or not."

Byrt opened his mouth to reply, then thought better of it. Sulking, the little gray wombat huddled against the bars and waited.

"Look," Rayburton said, "you believe me when I say I don't have the Ring of Winter. My daughter and the others know I'm here, that I'm alive. They'll come for me. You can count on that. Why not just let me go and avoid a needless battle?"

Kaverin stopped pacing—Rayburton could tell because the clacking of his knuckles stopped, too. "Oh, I have no doubt they'll charge right into the Batiri camp, horns blaring. Cimber is with them, and he is the least subtle person I know."

Finally Kaverin came around to the front of the chair. For the first time, Rayburton saw how exhausted his captor looked. His eyes were ringed by dark circles, his hands trembled from fatigue. Kaverin's voice was a sigh as he said, "Your would-be rescuers may even have the gem-sorcerer with them. They could have the whole population of Mezro with them, and I still wouldn't let you go."

Gingerly Kaverin lifted Phyrra's skull from the back of the chair. He adjusted the glasses and said, "The key phrase, milord, is immortality. Whether you have the ring or not, you've lived for more than twelve hundred years, by my count." He looked into the skull's empty eye sockets; the glasses reflected his own lifeless eyes back at him. "I want to know how you've managed it."

"Never," Rayburton said firmly.

Kaverin yawned and rubbed his tired eyes, then placed the head in Rayburton's lap. "Whatever the secret is, it's something you share with T'fima, since he says he's quite old, too—at least that's what Feg heard before that fanged thing ate him." He scowled at the memory of the image he'd seen through the winged monkey's eyes just before it died—a blur of black fur and razor-sharp claws.

Stoutly, Rayburton fought the urge to flinch from the grisly head or turn away in disgust. "If you want to know, go ask T'fima then," he said. "You'll get the same answer from him, I daresay."

Reaching down slowly, Kaverin took one of Rayburton's fingers in his cold, stony grip. He pulled it backward, just to the point where it strained, but didn't break. "Won't change your mind, will you, milord?"

Rayburton gritted his teeth against the pain and shook his head.

"Quite certain?" Kaverin asked flatly.

Again Rayburton shook his head.

Kaverin didn't ask a third time. He pulled the finger until it touched the back of the prisoner's hand. Rayburton stifled a scream, refusing to give his torturer the pleasure of hearing him cry out.

"Bravo," Kaverin cooed. "Just the sort of control I would expect from a man of your breeding, milord." He gripped another finger. "This will be a challenge, I think."

"You monster," Rayburton hissed through clenched teeth.

Kaverin smiled a predatory smile. "You don't know the half of it." He broke another finger, then grabbed a third. "If it comes to it, Lord Rayburton, I will kill you. Then I'll find your daughter—Oh, don't look surprised. The lovely young woman mentioned her relation to you in T'fima's hut, before my spy was so rudely slaughtered." Twisting the finger sideways, he added, "Maybe she'll be more cooperative."

"Why don't you just ask me?" Byrt chimed from his cage. "I'm a regular font of knowledge. License to lecture granted by the College of Bards on Orlil, order of fabulists. No literary masterpiece too obscure for our attention. Rules of grammar enforced with spirit—root words are a wombat's specialty, don't you know."

"Take that idiotic thing outside," Kaverin said coldly. "Give it to the queen's guards."

As Skuld hefted the cage, Byrt pressed against the bars. His blue eyes were locked on Rayburton. "You'll need to keep him alive if you want to cash in on his fountain of youth, Kaverin." When the stone-handed man ignored him, the wombat added, "Ask him what it takes to become a bara of Ubtao. The benefits are quite good, from what his daughter told me."

"No!" Rayburton lurched forward, making the chair scrape ahead a foot or two. Phyrra's head rolled from his lap and bounced off Kaverin's leg before coming to rest under a table. "Don't tell him," the bara cried.

Kaverin held up a hand, and Skuld paused at the door. "Why would Rayburton's dear daughter tell *you* anything important?"

Glancing up at Skuld, Byrt said. "This will take a while, so you might as well put me down." When the silver giant didn't move, the wombat shrugged. "Suit yourself, but don't blame me if one arm is longer than the other three from holding me up so long."

"Do not try my patience," Kaverin said. "I do not brook fools easily."

"Why would you ever—" Byrt swallowed the rest of the

retort. "Sanda told me because she likes animals, has a gift for dealing with them, you might say." He looked at Rayburton apologetically. "Like her dad, she's a bara of Ubtao—a sort of mystical guardian of Mezro on behalf of the god. In return for serving the public good, they are granted eternal life."

"Don't tell him anything else!" Rayburton shouted.

"Quiet, old man," Kaverin said. He backhanded Rayburton without so much as looking at him, then strolled to Byrt's cage. "So why do I have to keep him alive, now that I know the secret?"

Byrt cleared his throat. "When a bara dies, Ubtao chooses his successor from everyone who presents himself at the temple in the city's center—" he leaned close to Kaverin and lowered his voice conspiratorially "—but you've got to go to the temple to be considered. You see the obvious problem, of course?"

"Of course," Kaverin admitted. "If I kill him before I'm in the temple, ready to undergo the ceremony to become a bara, the good people of Mezro would be sure another candidate got there before me." He paced a few steps, then looked back to the wombat. "I don't suppose you'd be willing to tell me where the city is or how it's hidden?"

Byrt's blue eyes took on a haze of vagueness. "Sorry, I'm just a tourist in these parts. If you let me go right now, I would be utterly lost."

"Then how did you find the city in the first place?" Kaverin asked.

"Couldn't tell you," Byrt said merrily. "It was all Artus's doing. Lugg and I were in a daze, but he found us shelter from the storm and put a thatched roof over our heads. Frightfully bright fellow, Artus. I hear you two go way back."

Kaverin gestured to Skuld. "Give him to the queen."

"I protest!" Byrt cried as he was carried from the room.

"You might show some gratitude. After all, I saved you the
trouble of breaking any more fingers—"

The slam of the door cut off any further pleading.
Kaverin strolled to a long couch that faced his prisoner. "I
guess I'll have to keep you alive, at least until we get into
the city and test out the pig-bear's claim." He clacked his
knuckles together. "And as far as finding Mezro is concerned, we'll just wait for your daughter and that idiot
Cimber to try to rescue you. Then we'll simply follow them
back to the city."

"Why are you doing this?" Rayburton rasped.

"I told you before, milord. The key is immortality."
Kaverin stretched out on the couch. "Since I know your
secret, I'll share one of mine—not anything that would give
you a weapon against me, of course. Just some information
that'll let you know how serious I am about solving this
little mystery. . . ."

Kaverin's voice trailed off and his head dropped to his
chest. He started awake instantly and turned his attention
back to Rayburton. "I don't suppose you've ever been
dead," he said. "I have, thanks to Cimber and that bloated
mage Pontifax. They murdered me about three years ago.
The authorities in Tantras even called it murder." He covered another yawn with one jet-black hand. "I don't begrudge them that. We'd been destroying little parts of each
other for years—I'd send an assassin after Cimber, he'd
gather evidence of wrongdoings and have all my associates
arrested. My killing Pontifax's wife sent them both over
the edge. Looking back, it was bad judgment on my part.
Still, you can't undo the past. Cimber and Pontifax swore a
vendetta against me, caught me in a tavern without my
bodyguards, then blew me into a hundred pieces."

Kaverin studied Rayburton's face, watched contentedly
as horror mixed with the pain. "So down to Hades I went,
to the Realm of the Dead. When you were in Cormyr, the

Lord of the Dead was Myrkul. Not any longer. That's Cyric's domain now." He snorted. "It's a good thing that homicidal maniac killed Myrkul and took his godhood, because he was willing to cut a deal with me: I get to live out the rest of my life, just as if Cimber hadn't caught me in Tantras, but only so long as I sow chaos and destruction in the North. That's why I'm after the Ring of Winter. No other artifact in the history of the world has such potential for destruction."

"I never found the ring," Rayburton snarled. "You won't find it here."

"But there had to be a reason you were in Chult looking for it," Kaverin said. He held up his hand. "But that's something we can discuss later. Where were we? Ah, yes. My deal with Cyric." Lashing out with one stone hand, he shattered a skull resting atop the couch. "The price for all this was a bit steep, I've come to find out. When I do die, I go straight back to Cyric for an eternity of torture."

Rayburton saw a glimmer of some weird emotion flash in Kaverin's dark, lifeless eyes. It was gone as soon as it had appeared, though.

"That's another reason for me to possess the ring—eternal life. But even that would be a torture of sorts, thanks to Cyric. . . ." Kaverin smiled mirthlessly, then fell into a drowsy reverie. From the frown on his face, Rayburton assumed it was far from pleasant.

After a few moments, Kaverin's breathing became regular and deep, his chest rising and falling in a steady rhythm. He did not wake this time, though Rayburton soon wished he had.

The first indication of the horror that was to come was the smell of sulphur. The stench grew so strong it seared Rayburton's lungs and made his eyes tear. Next came the sound of wailing. The murmur never became very loud, just audible enough for some of the individual shrieks and cries for mercy to rise above the hellish rumble. The chorus of the damned made the hair stand up on the back of Rayburton's neck. Panic swelled in his chest, muffling his heartbeat, threatening to choke the air from his lungs.

Finally they came. On either side of the sleeping Kaverin, two huge figures appeared out of the air. Their heads were lupine, with slavering jaws and glowing red eyes. Coarse hair bristled in a mane from between their pointed ears down their backs, but the rest of their bodies were plated with armorlike scales. Each had a pair of human arms ending in clawed hands. These they rubbed together like a miser considering his hoard. Four other limbs, more akin to a spider's legs than anything human, waved and clutched the air. When the beasts moved toward the sleeping man, it was on a snake's writhing body. They pulsed forward and, gripping the couch, leaned over Kaverin.

Rayburton tried to close his eyes, but the ghastly sight had burned into his thoughts. The two creatures, monstrous denizens of the Realm of the Dead, moved closer to the sleeping Kaverin. Yet they didn't so much as lay a taloned hand on him. No, they did something far more terrible.

As Kaverin slept, the denizens whispered in his ears, describing the horrors of the Realm of the Dead and the awful fate that awaited him when he died. The sleeping man twitched and groaned, but stayed lost in slumber. Such was the part of their deal that Cyric didn't reveal to Kaverin on the day he made his pact; so long as he lived, these creatures would visit him every time he slept. Even if he found a way to prolong his life, the stone-handed man would be given a bitter taste of his eventual fate each time he drifted off to sleep.

All that afternoon Lord Rayburton shared in the nightmares those creatures conjured in Kaverin's mind. The sweet voices spoke of tortures and promised terrors beyond belief. They whispered of a world of agony without end, an eternal life filled with misery and suffering, all at the hands of the dark god Cyric.

No matter how loud Lord Dhalmass Rayburton screamed, the voices of the denizens came to him clearly, as if their words were meant for him, too.

* * * * *

Since leaving Ras T'fima's hut an hour past, Artus, Sanda, and Kwalu had moved toward the goblin camp at a steady pace. The jungle had thinned, the tangles of trees and vines giving way now and then to clearings filled with saw-edged grasses, squat palms, and strange creatures. Docile dinosaurs lumbered about, tearing up huge mouthfuls of greenery. Kwalu showed no fear of these gigantic lizards, and they in turn watched unafraid as the trio passed.

Only when he spotted a quartet of dinosaurs running through a clearing did the negus order the party to take cover. These beasts stood twice as tall as Artus and ran on two legs. Their tails stuck out straight behind them like rudders, allowing them to balance as they charged across the field. The most frightening thing about them was the scythelike claw hooking up from each foot. It was clear to Artus that they used these in combat, probably hopping up and tearing at each other like giant birds.

The respect Kwalu showed these monsters surprised Artus, for the negus seemed truly fearless. He had warmed to the explorer considerably after hearing of his escape from the Batiri camp, even offering cryptic hints as to some of his own fantastic adventures. Few predatory beasts had escaped his spear and club, few places in Chult had remained closed to his wandering. He was never specific about his feats, though. His modesty simply wouldn't allow him to stoop to anything even close to bragging.

Though Kwalu appeared tight-lipped to Artus, Sanda was amazed at how talkative the negus had proved to be with the explorer. For her part, she never seemed at a loss for a comment or question. Her mood never darkened for long; she'd even recovered from her worry about her father, convincing herself and the others that they would certainly rescue him in time. Artus found her self-assuredness a welcome beacon, warning him away from the shoals of despair. At least, he welcomed it most of the time. At other moments, Sanda's breezy dismissal of problems seemed frivolous, her mocking tone rather mean-spirited.

"I make you uncomfortable, don't I, Artus?" Sanda asked bluntly as they tore through a particularly thick curtain of vines. A smile tugged at the corners of her mouth. "I would have thought you too worldly to be intimidated by an older woman."

The comment flew straight and true, dead on target to the heart of the matter. Artus could only wince at the sting, though, for Sanda had seen right through him. To deny the truth would be pointless. "You should understand my discomfort," he said. "I mean, I find myself wondering how you see me—like a child or a fool. Don't you ever wonder how we mortals see you? Doesn't that make it hard for you to live with us?"

"Of course," Kwalu said. The negus looked up from the trail marker he was leaving for the Tabaxi troops that King Osaw was sending after them. "That's the reason you've met so many barae in such a short time. We tend to stay together. Why choose a hunting partner who can only keep up with you for twenty years or so?"

"How lonely," Artus said.

"Oh, any isolation is self-imposed," Sanda offered

cheerfully. "The king doesn't have a problem becoming close to 'mortals,' as you call them. Most of the barae have, at one time or another."

"Not me," Kwalu said proudly.

Sanda bowed. "Except Negus Kwalu," she corrected. "The rest of us have had friends, lovers, and children pass away, all while we remain untouched by the scouring winds of time." A cloud passed over her bright features as she looked at Artus. In reply to his unvoiced question, she added, "Two sons and a daughter. Actually, grandchildren, too, and great-grandchildren. I stopped keeping track. It made me too sad to see them as infants and watch them die of old age, all without much noticing the passage of the years myself."

In silence they came to the edge of a wide field. Above the general cacophony, a chorus of high-pitched cries rang out. Desperation gave an edge to the shrieks, a panic that grew as the cries were repeated. The source of the calls remained hidden, though, for the grass in this particular clearing stood taller than Artus's waist.

Cautiously Kwalu started out from the cover of the trees, Sanda and Artus close behind. They had stumbled across creatures hidden in tall grass before: rabbits or deer or even an occasional huge snake or hunting cat. These the negus frightened away by slapping the flat of his spear against his dinosaur-hide shield. The resulting boom sent most animals scurrying for cover.

Kwalu expected the same ploy to work this time. As the grass began to part a little farther ahead of the trio, he slammed his spear to his shield. But instead of running, the unseen animals darted forward. The wake they left in the grass gave Artus no doubt they were heavy creatures, and their cries sounded uncomfortably similar to the yelps of the altispinax that had attacked his expedition in the swamp. The explorer nocked an arrow to his bow and braced himself to fire.

The creature that galloped out of the grass was only frightening in its enthusiasm at finding someone else in the field. It was a dinosaur, but not like the other monsters Artus had encountered in Chult. It stood two feet tall at the shoulder, and twice that from the tip of its tail to the small horn on the end of its beaklike snout. A bony frill protected its neck, and two larger horns jutted from its head. These horns were blunt, not yet grown into the awesome weapons they'd one day become, but Artus still jumped back when the dinosaur took another galloping step toward him.

"Quickly," Kwalu cried. "Get away from them!"

The bellow that erupted from the jungle made Artus's heart skip a beat. The crack and clatter of trees falling before some charging giant followed, along with a low tremor that shook the entire field. Immediately the four dinosaurs answered the call with sharp cries of greeting.

Artus turned and saw Kwalu standing, shoulders back, chin out. As the negus faced the tree line and the source of the awful, ear-splitting roar, the four little dinosaurs raced past him. "Gods," Artus murmured. "They're babies."

The guardian of the four young creatures breached the tree line. It shared the basic shape and features of its young, but it was ten times as large. Its horns were fully developed—as long as Artus was tall and tapered to deadly points. Opening its beaklike snout, it roared a challenge. The teeth in that cavernous mouth were not the jagged knives of a carnivore, but the dinosaur didn't need such weapons. If it wanted to kill the humans, it merely had to trample them beneath one of its four huge feet.

Trees crashed to the ground, shoved out of the way as the dinosaur charged. The young creatures wisely scattered out of the way, but evidently Kwalu did not share that wisdom.

"Run!" Artus shouted.

Calmly the negus lifted his broad-bladed spear and threw it with all his considerable strength. The weapon flew, lodging just below one of the monster's eyes. The wound didn't even slow the beast down. It rampaged forward, closing half the distance between itself and the doomed men with three steps. Kwalu didn't retreat an inch, instead reaching for a small leather box that hung at his belt.

Artus saw then how futile it would be to run. Unless he'd started to move long before the dinosaur broke through the tree line, it could catch him in a half-dozen thunderous steps. The explorer glanced over his shoulder, hoping Sanda had possessed the sense to bolt at the first rumbling footstep. At the same time, he reached back for an arrow from his quiver. Kwalu was right in that much—better to fight until the end.

He never got to fire that arrow. The sight of Sanda, stretched out in peaceful repose before the charging dinosaur, made him fumble the shaft back into the quiver. She hadn't moved a single step. Neither had she drawn her weapon for a final, hopeless stand. No, Sanda had lain back in the grass and fallen asleep.

Certain that bizarre sight would be his last, Artus braced himself for the crushing weight of the dinosaur's foot. Yet the roars of the guardian and the thunder of its charge had stopped. Only the calls of the young, pleading and submissive, rang out over the clearing.

When Artus turned around again, the dinosaur stood close enough for him to reach out and touch the leathery hide of one leg. Nearby, Kwalu leaned against another thick leg, idly adjusting his grip on his shield. "It is a triceratops, I think," the negus noted. "The young must have got separated from the herd. They usually travel in large groups."

"What?" Artus sputtered. He looked up at the dinosaur. It had taken another step toward him, blocking out the sun with its massive frill and horns.

"Sanda has control of the beast," Kwalu offered calmly, gesturing toward the woman with his club. "That is the power Ubtao granted her. She can possess any warm-blooded creature, bend its will to hers."

"But this is a lizard!"

"It is a dinosaur," Kwalu replied. "A child of Ubtao. It is like a lizard, but its massive heart pumps blood as hot as yours or mine."

The negus turned to his fellow bara. "We should move her," he said, shooing away one of the baby triceratops that had begun to nibble at the fringe around his calf. "She cannot control this brute for long."

Artus slung his bow over his shoulder and picked up Sanda. As he draped her limp arms over his shoulders, lifting her on his back, he stared up at the full-grown triceratops. The creature nodded and turned one huge eye toward him. As Artus watched, the black orbs filled with color—the same green as Sanda's eyes. Shaken, he looked away.

When Artus caught up with Kwalu again, the negus was fast approaching the far end of the clearing. He seemed unaffected by the incident, unfazed by the gruesome death he had nearly met. "You knew Sanda was going to do that," the explorer said. "Take over the triceratops, I mean."

"No," Kwalu answered. "I was not thinking of her bara power. I am glad she did."

"Yeah, I'm glad too." Artus shifted Sanda's weight on his back. "Kwalu, if you didn't know she was going to use her power. . . ."

The negus patted the small leather box at his hip. "I have a power of my own, Artus." He let the comment stand, refusing to elaborate even after the explorer asked him directly. All he would say was, "Perhaps you will see me use it against the Batiri. They captured me unprepared to call upon Ubtao the time your friend, Theron, found me a prisoner in their camp. Never again."

At the edge of the clearing, Sanda began to stir. "It was unfair of you to make Artus carry me by himself, Kwalu," she murmured sleepily.

"I do not think he wanted to share the burden," the negus noted. "He did not ask my aid, so I assumed he enjoyed the task."

Artus had not asked for Kwalu's help because the young man was royalty, and one simply didn't demand that a prince stoop to manual labor, at least not in the Heartlands. That was the majority of the reason, anyway. Suddenly self-conscious, he shuffled his feet and shifted his bow from one hand to the other.

But Artus wasn't the only one unsettled by the negus's offhand remark. An uncharacteristic wave of embarrassment struck Sanda, and she hurried past both Artus and Kwalu. "We'd best hurry," she mumbled. "It'll be dark in a few hours."

* * * * *

Sanda kept ahead of the others all afternoon. Only when they reached the outskirts of the goblin camp did she slow down enough for them to speak to her. By then, she had brushed aside whatever was bothering her. Though Artus was curious about her reaction, he let the subject rest until a more convenient time.

Kwalu immediately took up a position at the base of a tree. He detached the dinosaur skin from the bone frame of his shield and rolled the thick hide up into a bundle, which he used as a makeshift camp chair. The frame he folded and hid in the leaves. With his club resting across his knees and one hand on the leather box at his belt, he sat motionless, watching the camp and counting the war banners staked outside the huts and tents.

When Artus went to take up his own position, Sanda held him back. "Unless the goblins spot us and raise an alarm, don't even think about starting a battle," she whispered. "If a sentry gets too close, try to drag him into the bushes before fighting in the open."

It seemed like common sense to Artus, but he nodded politely, as if the bara's orders were full of useful revelations. Before she turned away, he said, "When Kaverin shows himself, watch where he goes. He knows we were spying on him from T'fima's hut, so he might have moved your father from the queen's house."

Sanda paused and took Artus's hand. "Just stay out of sight until the warriors get here. If they arrive before sundown, we'll storm the main building. If not, we'll fall back into the jungle and come up with another plan."

Stealthily Artus moved through the undergrowth, settling for a post a few yards from Kwalu. He sat with his longbow at his side, the arrows planted tip-down in the ground near his feet. This was an old army practice Pontifax had taught him upon returning from the Tuigan Wars. The Cormyrian archers had used the time-saving trick to good effect in their battles with the barbarians.

The goblin camp was much the same as Artus had seen it last. A few guards hid in the shadows of Queen M'bobo's two-story palace. Others squatted in the doorways of various huts or lounged against the leering totems stationed throughout the camp. Artus grimaced when he saw the wooden totems; their screeching alarm rang fresh enough in his ears for him to dread disturbing them again.

One thing had changed in the Batiri enclave. In many places, tattered, sagging tents were staked out next to the huts. Artus could see warriors fast asleep under these dirty bivouacs, piled together like dozing lions. Their spears had been planted outside the tents, much in the same way the explorer had planted his arrows—point-down and ready for quick use. Banners marked with crude symbols announced which clan occupied each part of the camp.

The sun was fading fast, and there was still no sign of the Tabaxi warriors King Osaw had promised or Kaverin himself. Without knowing precisely where Rayburton was hidden, it was pointless to charge into the camp; Artus patiently bided his time by counting the goblins and learning their clan symbols. Sanda didn't share the explorer's patience. As dusk began to settle on the camp, she climbed a nearby tree, perhaps for a better vantage.

"I hear somethin', I do," the closest of the Batiri guards murmured. He was a short brute, even for a goblin, with one fang missing and a jagged gash across his face. He squinted in Sanda's direction. The woman hung motionless and silent, only half-hidden by the brush. Raising his spear menacingly, the goblin started toward her. "What're you there, hidin' in the tree?"

Why doesn't he call out the other guards? Artus wondered, grabbing his bow and nocking an arrow. He centered his aim on the guard's throat; if the arrow struck true, it would stop him from crying out. The guard took another step forward, then another.

Just like when they captured me last time, Artus thought bitterly. Only there's no spider to—

He let the arrow slide to the ground and pulled his dagger from his boot. Concentrating on the softly glowing stone set in the hilt, he whispered, "Come down." In the leaves high above, something trilled a loud reply to the magical summons.

A monstrous spider crawled partway down the trunk toward Sanda. Like the thing that had knocked Artus from his hiding place when he'd first escaped the Batiri camp, this one was easily as large as a man. Hair as black as midnight stood up like a porcupine's bristles all along its body and legs. Its eyes were equally as black, though Artus could catch little flickers of light from them as it moved slowly down the tree.

Using the enchantment on his dagger, he ordered the spider to leap from the trunk, through the thin veil of vines and leaves, and into the goblin camp. Without hesitation it did as it was told, landing right in front of the guard. The goblin shrieked, but he didn't run. He stood nose to mandibles with the spider, skewering it on his spear before the creature had a chance to run or attack.

The guard raised his prize over his head and carried it proudly toward his hut, to the general disinterest of the other goblins. They were trying their best to keep out of the light, catching a few moments of stolen sleep before M'bobo arose from her beauty rest and left her palace. There'd be no rest for them then. Only Balt was a harder taskmaster than the goblin queen. Every Batiri in the jungle knew of the general's cruelty, his unfailing dedication to order and discipline.

So when Balt emerged from his hut before the sun had set, the slouching, snoozing guards bustled themselves to attention as swiftly as possible. The general, imposing in his dinosaur-hide breastplate, stormed around the camp. He slapped some guards, pulled the spears, bows, and arrows out of the hands of others. After inspecting the spear tips or bowstrings or arrowheads, he always threw the weapon into the dirt and berated the soldier for sloppiness. Artus had seen Cormyrian generals do the same thing at the royal parade grounds in Suzail.

Settling himself for a long evening of waiting, Artus kept his eyes on the goblin camp and dug into his pocket for something to eat. He tossed a handful of dried fruit into his mouth. When he tried to chew the mix, he bit down on something hard and sharp and was forced to spit out the offending morsel. It was a gem, long and tapered to points at either end.

How did that get in there? he wondered, then sifted through his pocket again. He came out with two more gems, precisely the same as the first. Holding them up to catch the last of the daylight, he found writing across the sides. The Tabaxi word for "lightning" was spelled out in clear block letters. Did I pick them up at T'fima's hut by mistake?

Artus dropped two of the gems back into his pocket and took to examining the other. Its brilliance and sharpness, its color and clarity all proclaimed it a diamond. With his thumb Artus felt the tooth that had discovered the gem in his dinner. Yes, he'd chipped it all right.

So caught up in his study of the gem was Artus that he didn't notice the absolute hush that fell over the Batiri camp. Only when a shriek of terror rang out, followed by a cacophony of shouts and curses and prayers, did the explorer look up.

"Aiii!" one warrior cried. "The spirits rise against our clans!"

Sanda turned to Artus and hissed, "They can see you!"

Artus couldn't see how. He hadn't moved since taking up his post. The leaves hadn't suddenly dropped off the plants around him. Bemused, he tried to cover himself. It was too late. Balt and his most fearsome warriors were charging across the camp, right toward Artus, Sanda, and Kwalu.

The strange thing was, when the trio stood to meet the first wave, the goblins faltered. It was as if they had seen something else in the jungle. Unfortunately, that hesitation lasted only an instant. Balt waved his scimitar like a riding crop and battered his men into a frenzied charge. The goblins came on, screaming for blood and revenge for the death of their god.

Artus and his companions didn't have time to ponder

how they'd been spotted. And standing as they were, with
their backs to the jungle, they couldn't see the sad, phan-
tasmal figure of Sir Hydel Pontifax behind them. The ghost
hovered above the ground for a moment, hands held out to
Artus. By the time the battle started, he had faded reluc-
tantly into the growing twilight.

Thirteen

The Batiri warriors were close enough for Artus to see the fury in their yellow-tinged eyes and the glint of the fading sun off their razor-sharp spear tips.

Unflappable even now, Negus Kwalu lifted a single locust from the small leather box at his waist and raised the twitching insect high over his head. "Defend Ubtao's great city against the creatures of this village." With Batiri arrows darting around him, he gently released the locust toward the goblin line.

A dark curtain shot up between the Batiri and their intended victims, a wall that moved toward them with astounding speed. Balt had been running too hard to even slow down. He plunged into the curtain, his wickedly curved scimitar slashing before him. The metal blade made it through, as did the general's dinosaur-hide breastplate. The armor protected only a skeleton, though. The bones clattered to the ground in front of Artus, the skull snarling at him with yellowed teeth.

The single locust was now ten thousand, and the droning wall of insects devoured everything in its path. The first rank of goblin warriors died without even having a chance to scream. Nothing save the metal tips of their spears and their gleaming white bones remained. The plants that trailed into the village were devoured, as were the closest huts. The locusts destroyed the wooden bridge spanning Grumog's pit and the supports for the gong standing beside it. Then the the insects scattered through the camp, swarming everything in sight.

Queen M'bobo emerged from her palace and stood framed in the doorway. "Stand and fight!" she cried. An instant later she retreated, a dozen locusts crawling in her blonde locks or latched onto her skin.

The totems shouted and moaned as the insects chewed into them. Wooden faces contorted in pain, the sentries could only creak back and forth ineffectually to dislodge their attackers. The goblins, on the other hand, scattered around the camp, frantically slapping the ravenous locusts away from them. The huts offered no protection, for their thatched roofs disappeared as quickly as the insects found them. A few goblins waved torches or flaming blankets, but the entire village would need to burn before this tack could be truly effective.

Artus lowered his bow. "Let's go!" he shouted. "To the palace!"

Sanda and Kwalu followed the explorer into the camp. The locusts flew around them, but somehow knew not to attack the humans. Few goblins ignored the insects long enough to turn their spears or arrows upon the raiders. One unfortunate warrior, a young goblin with bright orange skin, fell to the ground before Kwalu, pleading for his life. Locusts clung to his back, and a hundred small wounds dotted his legs and face. The negus shoved him aside and raced toward the palace.

The Batiri that recognized Artus fled from him in terror. They called him "Grumog's Bane" and "God Slayer," as they scrambled out of his path. Perhaps that was why the goblins acted so strangely when they first spotted us in the bushes, Artus decided.

The trio had just reached the edge of the wide review area before the queen's home when the double doors burst open and Skuld stepped onto the landing. A cloud of biting locusts covered the silver-skinned giant, but just as quickly the insects plummeted to the ground, dead. His skin, it seemed, was as poisonous as his disposition. Skuld leaped down the stairs, landing flat-footed in the dirt between Artus and the palace. Holding his arms straight out to his sides, the guardian spirit began to spin.

A funnel cloud formed swiftly, drawing in the locusts from all over the camp. That wasn't all. What thatch and straw had not been destroyed by the swarm flew across the camp. Leaves, loose arrows, bits of clothing—all these shot into the whirling cloud. The few standing totems toppled, mouthing curses all the way to the ground. The doors of the palace slammed opened and closed. Across the village, smaller goblins felt the tug of the cyclone and anchored themselves to whatever was close at hand. If they screamed for help, no one heard; the whirlwind roared like a hundred wagons rattling at full speed over a cobblestone street.

Artus and Sanda clung together against the wind, while Kwalu merely planted his feet and closed his eyes. It was as if the negus had rooted himself into the earth. Leaves and sticks battered him, the whirlwind grew more intense, but still Kwalu remained unbowed.

Finally Skuld slowed, then stopped. Debris and dead locusts began to rain down upon the village like hail. "It is over, master," the silver giant shouted.

Kaverin Ebonhand appeared in the doorway. To one side
he was flanked by M'bobo, to the other by Lord Rayburton. The bara's hands were bound, and a gag filled his
mouth. The bruises on his face could have only come from
a beating, but the wild, fearful look in his eyes told of far
more terrible tortures.

All across the camp, the goblins were helping their
wounded comrades and gathering weapons. None were
willing to attack the humans that had brought the locusts
down upon them, despite the orders M'bobo screeched
from the palace door. When not a single warrior lifted a
spear or bow against the intruders, she called for Balt to
whip the soldiers into line. No one had the nerve to tell her
the general was even less likely to jump to her command
than they were. Instead, the tense and fearful Batiri gathered in a wide circle around Skuld and the humans.

"Put down your weapons and give yourselves up,"
Kaverin shouted, holding one empty hand out in a gesture
of peace. "You won't be hurt—and the old man won't be
hurt any worse than he already has been—but only if you
surrender right now."

Artus raised his bow and fired, aiming for Kaverin's
heart. The arrow would have split that wellspring of evil in
two had Skuld not been there. The guardian spirit flexed
his powerful legs and leaped into the air, as high as the
second-story landing where Kaverin stood. The arrow bit
into his chest. With the feathered shaft sticking out of him,
Skuld dropped back to the ground. He plucked out the arrow with one of his four hands and crushed it.

Smiling viciously, Kaverin said, "I wouldn't have believed that offer either." He curled his hand into a fist.
"Give up now, or I'll send Skuld after you. Either way,
you're dead, but Skuld will make what little time you have
left truly horrible if he has to come get you. Mulhorandi
tortures are among the world's most painful, you know."

Sanda drew her long-bladed knife, and Kwalu brandished his war club. For a moment, Artus hesitated. Then he dropped his bow. The barae looked at him, astonished.

"Showing your true colors at last, eh Cimber?" Kaverin gloated. Rayburton tried to run forward, but a stone hand clamped down on his shoulder. "Kill the two natives, Skuld. Save Cimber for me. I am, after all, a man of my word."

The disappointment in Sanda's eyes wounded Artus to the core, but there was no time to explain his plan—even if he knew exactly what to expect. The explorer reached into his pocket for one of the diamond slivers. The gem felt slippery in his sweaty fingers, but he gripped it tightly and held it up before him. He glanced at Skuld; the four-armed guardian was running toward him, gnashing his filed teeth.

Artus said the Tabaxi word for lightning.

The flash that followed blinded everyone who was looking at the explorer and drove the goblin circle back. It should have blinded Artus, too, but somehow his eyes were spared. Something to do with the enchantment on the gem, he decided later. At the moment, his mind was set on controlling the crackling bolt of lightning that had appeared in his hand.

The heat from the lightning washed over Artus in waves, singeing his hair and reddening his skin. Sparks snaked around his arm and slithered up to his shoulder. There was no pain—no serious pain, anyway—just an immense feeling of power. He turned the bolt in his hand, holding it like a javelin.

Skuld rubbed his eyes with the heels of two hands, holding the other set up to ward off attackers. When he took his hands away, he glared at Artus. "That cannot help you," he snarled, then started forward again.

"Let's find out," Artus said. He hurled the lightning bolt. In the instant before the bolt struck Skuld, a silver shield appeared in the guardian spirit's hands. He held it before him, braced with both sets of arms. Then the lightning hit, and shards of silver exploded into the air. Skuld looked down in amazement to where the shield had been a moment earlier. Fingers had been blown off three hands, half the wrist from the fourth. The bloodless wounds glistened like polished glass.

Then Skuld's gaze wandered from his ragged hands to his chest. The lightning had burned a gaping, charred hole right through him. Eyes wide with surprise, the silver guardian stiffened and fell backward. He lay there, twitching and gasping, his filed teeth making him look like a beached piranha.

"You're next, Kaverin!" Artus pulled another of the diamonds from his pocket. At a word it burst into a bolt of lightning.

The goblins standing between Artus and the palace scattered, and Sanda ran forward. "Let my father go!" she cried.

Kaverin clutched Rayburton's throat with one stone hand. "Don't be ridiculous," he snarled, lifting his hostage off the ground and positioning him like a shield.

"Sanda, get back!" Artus shouted. He stepped forward and raised the lightning bolt.

"Throw it, Cimber." Kaverin shook Rayburton like a doll. "Let's see if those bolts destroy human shields as efficiently as they do mystic ones."

A murmur from the milling goblins tore Artus's attention away from Kaverin. In the locust-littered dust, Skuld was struggling to his feet. Shiny new silver flesh had replaced his missing fingers and mended his shattered wrist. A puckered scar marked the spot where the hole had gaped in his chest.

That wasn't the only thing sending ripples of unrest through the mob, a fact Kaverin realized at the same time as Artus. "I don't think they like you aiming a killing bolt at their beloved monarch," Kaverin said. He moved in front of M'bobo, keeping Rayburton as his shield, of course. In his best Goblin, he shouted, "The raiders want to kill your queen!"

Fear held the Batiri in a strong grip, but their loyalty to their ruler was stronger. A few warriors moved to Skuld's side, helping the four-armed guardian to his feet. Others closed ranks before the palace, blocking Sanda and Kwalu from the stairs. Without warning, an arrow flew from the mob, cutting into Artus's shoulder. The explorer cried out and stumbled back. A steadying hand from Sanda prevented him from falling or dropping the lightning bolt.

Seeing Artus wounded broke the spell of terror holding the goblins at bay. They swarmed forward, ready to finish the work the lone archer had started. Kaverin's howl of laughter could be heard even over the din of the Batiri charge.

Artus threw the lightning bolt at the ground. The explosion blasted chucks of earth and rock into the front rank and opened a wide pit in their way. It slowed the charge enough for him to follow Sanda and Kwalu into the mob of goblins standing between them and the jungle. The fighting was furious, but they cut and smashed a swath through the Batiri line. The trio raced into the jungle, bruised and bleeding, a horde of yowling cannibals on their heels.

Kaverin pulled Rayburton down the palace steps and hurried to Skuld's side. "Follow Cimber and the others," he snapped. "Make certain one of them stays alive long enough to make it back to Mezro." As the silver-skinned giant turned away, Kaverin added, "And leave a trail along the way—just in case Cimber has any more tricks up his sleeve and you don't come back."

Skuld touched the shiny scar on his chest. "If this is the worst Cimber can do, he is a dead man." He bowed and dashed into the jungle.

Frowning, Kaverin watched his servant disappear into the night. "I said the same thing myself a hundred times before," he muttered.

Torches flared to life around the shattered village as the goblins set about the unwelcome task of gathering the dead and patching together their homes. M'bobo supervised the work from the palace steps, pointing out tasks with Balt's scimitar. "We need more Batiri real soon," she said to Kaverin. As if to emphasize the point, two young goblins tossed a locust-ravaged corpse onto a pile of bodies next to Grumog's pit.

"Can't you call in the other warriors?" Kaverin asked. He forced Rayburton to sit on the stairs at the queen's feet. "You said there were hundreds of smaller Batiri villages all over the area."

"They no come if we can't promise chow or good pillage," M'bobo replied. She pointed at the gory pile of bodies. "Hey! Hurry up and burn 'em. You want they should get up again?"

Kaverin's flame-red eyebrows drew together in puzzlement. "Get up again?"

After watching a warrior set a torch to the pyre, the queen said, "Yeah. Jungle full of walking dead. Sometimes Batiri get up if you don't burn 'em quick. Sometimes they don't, though." She brushed aside the topic with a wave of the scimitar. "So, can you promise chow?"

"Of course," Kaverin said smoothly. "If you gather enough warriors, I'll promise you all the Tabaxi in Mezro. There should be enough humans there to feed your warriors for a whole year."

Queen M'bobo licked her gray lips in anticipation and called for her runners.

* * * * *

Artus scratched furiously under the bandage on his shoulder. The arrow wound wasn't serious, but the poultice applied by the Mezroan surgeons felt like nothing so much as ants crawling over his skin. "Look," he said, "whatever his reasons, T'fima slid the gems into my pocket. I think he wants to help the city. He just won't admit it."

Sanda nodded her agreement, but Kwalu remained unconvinced. Since returning to Mezro a few hours past, they had been arguing the point—that is, when they weren't catching an hour of desperately needed sleep or being attended by surgeons. Now the three crossed the moonlit plaza surrounding the Temple of Ubtao, bound for the council chamber to see King Osaw.

"It was only a guilty conscience that made him give you the lightning gems," Kwalu noted sourly.

"We wouldn't have escaped the goblin camp without them," Sanda said. "At least they gave us a chance against Skuld."

Kwalu ran his thumb over a chip in his war club. Somewhere in the jungle lay a goblin's corpse with a corresponding dent in its skull. "Our own fighting skill freed us from the goblins, that and my father's warriors. If they hadn't arrived when they did, the goblins would have overrun us for sure."

That was something Artus disagreed with strongly, but there was no more time to argue. The temple door stood before them. No guards or attendants flanked the portal, no torches set it off from the dark crystal walls of the weird structure. Somehow, though, an inner radiance lit the yellowish brown wood. The inlaid panels depicted men and women living within a labyrinth of vines. Around some corners lurked dinosaurs, around others gorgeous fountains and quiet pools. At the center lay the temple itself—Artus squinted and leaned closer. Three tiny figures, positioned just as he, Sanda, and Kwalu were, stood at the temple door. The explorer was never certain if his eyes had deceived him, for at that moment the negus pushed the temple door open.

The eyes of Mezro's greatest heroes fell upon Artus as he entered the temple. Statues lined both sides of the long corridor, gigantic figures carved in glossy black stone. On one side of the door, a woman danced at the heart of an inferno, flames trailing from her hair and curling from her fingers. Across from her, a young boy held his arms to his side, soaring above stone clouds. Eagles swooped around him, talons extended, beaks open in joyous cries of war.

"These are the barae who have gone to Ubtao," Sanda whispered reverentially. "The ones on the right side are the seven original paladins."

As Artus followed her toward a darkened arch at the end of the hall, he glanced up at the other statues in the Hall of Champions. An old man held a hammer over an anvil, a razor-sharp spear tip in the making. Next to him a woman raced a jaguar along a stony path, both charging forward at full speed. Other men and women cast in equally fantastic poses looked down on him with steady gazes, unseeing yet full of understanding. There were empty pedestals farther up the hall, one on the right and a half-dozen to the left. These, Artus assumed, were reserved to honor barae who were still alive.

From behind one of these pedestals Lugg appeared. "You ain't got 'im back, 'ave you?"

Artus stopped before the brown wombat. "No," he sighed. "They stopped us before we could rescue Byrt or Lord Rayburton."

Lugg hung his head. "That's it, then," he said mournfully. "Poor little Byrt's for it now. They've probably cooked 'im up already."

"Don't give up hope," Sanda said. She knelt down and scratched behind the wombat's ear.

At the end of the hall, Kwalu paused. "The king is waiting," he said.

The explorer couldn't bring himself to tell Lugg he had little hope for finding Byrt alive, but from the look in the wombat's eyes, it was clear he understood.

Kwalu, Sanda, and Artus passed through the arch together. The explorer was amazed at the audience chamber that lay on the other side. The arch had been dark, but color and light filled the room beyond.

The walls of the triangular chamber were made of stained glass, and even though the sun had gone down hours ago, light poured through the windows in boldly slanting rays. A mosaic covered the floor, depicting the entire city of Mezro. As on the main door to the temple, tiny figures moved on the mosaic, going about their business beneath the feet of the counselors. In the center of the room, where the mosaic temple stood, King Osaw sat in a huge throne. He was alone in the cavernous room.

The king regarded the negus, Sanda, and Artus with hooded eyes as they kneeled before him and told of the attack on the Batiri village. When they described how they had escaped back to Mezro, however, he covered his withered face with his hands. "Kaverin Ebonhand is coming to Mezro," the king said. "He will lead the Batiri here and bring our city down around us."

"Impossible," Kwalu snapped. "The wall hides the city. Even if he wanted to, Kaverin could not find us."

"Why do you think the silver-skinned one let you return here, untouched?" Osaw asked. He turned clear eyes to Artus. "This Kaverin is a clever man. If, as you have told me, he seeks immortality, he will raze the city to find the secret of the barae. Lord Rayburton must have told him how he has lived so long."

Sanda leaped to her feet. "Father wouldn't reveal our secrets, even if Kaverin tortured him."

"There is no disgrace if he did, Alisanda," the king replied, motioning for her to sit. "Your father is a wise man, but he feels pain like anyone." He looked distractedly at the mosaic. "Right now, I miss his counsel greatly."

Tapping his war club on the floor impatiently, Kwalu said, "There is no danger to Mezro. Even if this scoundrel finds the city, he won't be able to pass through the wall."

King Osaw smiled, a mixture of warmth and patronizing acceptance for his son. "As always, Negus Kwalu, your courage makes you believe yourself invincible. You will find that no wall can stand against every foe."

Finally Artus spoke up. "When they were captured, both Byrt and Lord Rayburton wore the earrings that neutralize the wall. Kaverin or Skuld will certainly figure out how they work, given time."

"Then we must prepare for war," the king concluded. "Kwalu, you must bring the citizens together to stand against the Batiri." The negus nodded his agreement, and Osaw turned to Artus. "You, Master Cimber, must go as my messenger to Mainu, the bara who controls the river that borders the city to the south and west. Tell her Mezro has need of her and explain the threat. If she can promise to hold the Olung River against the Batiri, we can focus our defenses to the north and east."

Artus touched his forehead to the floor, then stood. "Of course, Great King. I shall go at once."

"Sleep first," Osaw said. "But only until dawn. You must not appear ragged to the bara of the river. She loves pomp and ceremony more than anything in this world."

Sanda stood, too. "I will go into the jungle and search for one of Ubtao's Children, a beast that will be worthy of fighting for the city."

"Take a dozen warriors with you, Alisanda, and do not go far," the king commanded. "You will be needed to defend the city."

Osaw stood, ending the audience. Artus and the others left the king pacing across the mosaic, hands clenched behind his back.

In the entry hall, Sanda offered an abrupt farewell. "Wish me luck." That said, she headed for the door.

"Wait!" Artus shouted. He rushed down the hall to her side. "I wish I were going with you."

Sanda looked deeply into Artus's eyes, then suddenly dropped her gaze to the floor. "Remember what I said about spending time with mortals. That applies to you, too, Artus."

In silence Artus watched Sanda leave. When the explorer turned around, he found Kwalu watching him. The negus had a mask of casual disinterest on his face, but the odd look in his eyes told another story. "She would not be so blunt if she did not care for you," he said simply, then turned back to the archway. "I am going to a meditation chamber. I'll meet you here at dawn."

"For what?" Artus asked.

"I will school you in the etiquette of Mainu's court," the negus offered over his shoulder.

Just before Kwalu disappeared under the arch, Artus said, "Where are you going? I didn't see any door leading out of the audience chamber."

"There is only one door inside the temple." Kwalu pointed at the darkened archway. "It takes you anywhere you wish to go, to any of the thousand rooms Ubtao built for his followers."

After the negus had gone, Lugg trundled out from behind a pillar to sniff at the archway. "If we have to wait 'ere till morning, I wonder if this thing leads to any kitchens 'ereabouts?"

Artus stared at the empty pedestals, wondering which of them was reserved for Sanda. "I think I'll just go to get some rest," he said.

At the door to the plaza the explorer paused. He'd never find his way back to his quarters alone, not through that maze of alleys. Besides, it wasn't really fair to leave the wombat on his own. "Why don't you come with me, Lugg. I know a park that has some interesting shrubbery, if you've a taste for that sort of thing."

*   *   *   *   *

The meeting with Mainu that morning was brief and extremely formal. It was also held underwater, at the bottom of the murky Olung River.

As King Osaw had told Artus, the Olung bordered Mezro to the west and south, curving gently through three of the city's quarters. In many places the mystic defensive wall ran parallel to the river, in others right on top of it. The animals that made their home in or around the muddy water didn't seem to notice. Hippos wallowed near the shore, watching kingfishers dive for minnows and other small fish. Turtles and crocodiles basked in the sun, rolling languidly into the water if anyone got too close. They sent ripples across the round leaves of water lilies as they submerged.

Such was the domain of Mainu. From a sumptuous court at the bottom of the river, she ruled the Olung for ten miles to either side of the city. The bara was undoubtedly the strangest Artus had met, and how he came to be in her presence proved stranger still.

Just after dawn, Artus had set off from the Temple of Ubtao. Lugg shied away from trudging to the river on such a sunny day; like goblins, wombats preferred to travel by night. At the riverbank, the explorer called out a ritual greeting and, dressed in his tunic, boots, and pants, waded into the water. After two or three steps, the bottom fell away. Artus plunged into the tepid river, gasping in a mouthful of muddy water as he sank.

After the panic subsided, he found himself breathing the stuff. Artus was used to it now, though the river had the same grimy quality as the air around the metalcrafters' market in Suzail. The oddest thing was coughing, which he did frequently. With each hack, he sent a jet of bubbles swirling around his head.

Artus was trying his best to muffle just such a coughing jag when Mainu finally responded to his plea for aid on behalf of King Osaw.

Artus Cimber of Cormyr, she said, her voice flowing across his mind like the river's gentle current, *we are greatly saddened by this news. As we are loyal subjects of Ubtao and of King Osaw, negus negusti, we will do everything we can to help defend Mezro.*

Mainu paused, her long hair floating around her like a veil of seaweed. She was a thing of the Olung, of that there could be no mistake. Her face and her body were nothing more than a more profound darkness within the murk of the river. She swayed and rocked with the current, held in place by long, thin fingers that gripped the throne with fierce strength. Only her eyes seemed out of place—bright and glowing like the sun.

The bara turned those golden eyes on Artus, who knelt before her turtle-shell throne. *We thank you for delivering this message, Master Cimber, and express our hope you will aid Mezro against the Batiri. If you do, we will afford you the honors due a warrior of Ubtao. The creatures of the Olung will bow to your wishes, and the waters of my river will do you no harm.*

Artus kowtowed, touching his forehead to the carpet of flowing green leaves. The kind offer sent a wave of relief over him; the soldiers flanking Mainu's throne were as awe-inspiring as any he had ever seen. A strange mix of human and lobster, the guards were girded in black shells, very much like a knight's most impressive plate armor.

Their hands were massive claws, and their tiny eyes extended upon long stalks. *You honor me with your kindness, great mistress of the Olung*, Artus replied, just as Kwalu had coached him.

At a slight flick of Mainu's chin, the lobster-men moved forward to escort Artus back to the shore. The explorer rose and bowed again. *King Osaw thanks you, Mainu, as will all of Mezro when this war is over.*

The mistress of the Olung took in Artus's gratitude without expression. *One thing before you go, Master Cimber*, she said. *Is this threat to Ubtao's city great enough for the king to summon all the barae to the cause?*

I do not know all of King Osaw's plans, great mistress of the Olung, Artus replied politely.

Mainu nodded. *Perhaps that will be your next task, Master Cimber, to contact the other bara, the one you have yet to meet. If you are asked to deal with the outcast, remember that he will do anything for Mezro—and that is what makes him truly dangerous.*

The lobster-men flanked Artus as he walked back to the bank. Once out of the river, the explorer found himself dry and the water miraculously gone from his lungs, though he coughed out river silt most of the way back to the temple. Kwalu met him at the temple door, a sheaf of battle plans tucked under his arm.

"What can you tell me about the seventh bara?" Artus asked as he and Kwalu entered the Hall of Champions. "I mean, Mainu mentioned something about an outcast. That's who she meant, right?"

The negus stopped dead in his tracks. "As far as you are concerned, there are only six barae—my father, Lord Rayburton, Sanda, Mainu, T'fima, and me. The reasons why we do not speak of the other, not even his name, are too complicated to go into now. It should be enough that we do not want him in the city again."

"But—"

Kwalu turned on his heels and strode off toward the archway. "Perhaps we can discuss the matter after we drive Kaverin and the Batiri back to the jungle." The negus glanced at Lugg, who was curled into a ball in front of one of the statues, snoring. "I must report to my father. If you want to wait here, I will inform you of our plans for troop placement when I'm done."

The wombat snorted awake. "Well?" he demanded. "What are you doing to get Byrt back?"

Artus traced the name of one of the fallen barae with his finger. "We are going to wait for the Batiri to attack us," he sighed.

"But they might kill 'im before then! Poor Byrt!"

"Look, I didn't say I agreed with the plan, but I'm not in charge here." The explorer paced to the next statue. "In fact, the more time I spend in the city, the more certain I am that I wouldn't want to be."

The brown wombat scuffed back and forth. "With all these barae about, you'd think they could just fly in and grab the two of 'em from Kaverin."

Artus snorted. "If the barae could get along, they might be dangerous," he said. "T'fima won't help because he's pouting about the wall, and there's another bara the king and the others won't call because he did something they won't talk about."

"What other bara?" Lugg asked. "If there's someone else 'anging about with magical powers, the king should bury the 'atchet and let 'im in for the scrap."

Shrugging, Artus moved on to the next statue. "Kwalu wouldn't tell me his name." He paused and looked at the six statues on the right side of the hall. These were the original barae, the ones chosen and empowered by Ubtao himself. But one of the pedestals was empty. "The seventh bara," Artus whispered. "Gods, he must be powerful if he was one of the first."

His eyes flew from one statue to another, taking in the magical gifts of the fallen barae. What did Ubtao give to the last of the original paladins? Artus wondered.

A passage from King Osaw's book, *The Eternal History of Mezro*, came back to him then: *The one the god chooses is granted some magnificent power. Ras Nsi, one of the first seven raised up by Ubtao, was granted the power to muster the dead. . . .*

Artus ran down the right side of the hall, checking each statue. *Tabiaza . . . Anzi . . . Zimwa.* "That's it," he said, joining Lugg before the empty pedestal. "Ras Nsi."

"No!" Kwalu shouted. The negus raced from the archway toward Artus, but it was already too late.

A pool of darkness opened beneath the explorer's feet, and he fell. For a time—he couldn't tell how long—all light and sound disappeared from the world. He moved through a void so absolute he couldn't be sure he wasn't dead.

At last he tumbled back into the world, landing with bone-jarring suddenness in the center of a wasteland. All around him the ground was broken and barren. Charred stumps of trees littered the land for miles in every direction. The sound of wood cracking and trees crashing to the ground drifted in from the distance, while vultures wheeled in the sky overhead, waiting patiently for their bounty. From the stench of rotten meat that filled the air, Artus was certain there was plenty of carrion to be had.

"Oi, get off me," came a muffled voice.

Artus rolled and found Lugg pinned beneath him. The wombat was covered in soot and dirt from the blasted ground.

"Where are we?" the explorer asked. He adjusted the bandage on his shoulder and struggled to his feet.

"Maybe we should ask them poor sots over there," Lugg offered.

Coming toward them was a group of ten men. They moved with painful slowness over the broken ground. As they got closer, Artus drew his dagger. Human and goblin walked together. Their eyes were white and rolled back in the sockets. Cuts and scrapes and the steady working of decay had turned their faces into ghastly masks of death. Some were missing fingers or hands or whole arms. Others had twisted, broken bones jutting from their legs.

"Zombies," Artus hissed. And from the way the undead goblins drooled at the sight of the explorer, he was certain they hadn't lost their taste for living flesh.

Fourteen

Queen M'bobo stared mutely at the ten-foot-tall warrior standing before her. The hulking thing resembled the lizard men she'd seen near the Olung River—scaly skin, massively muscled limbs, and clawed hands and feet—though this beast lacked a tail. Its face was narrow, with a nose that jutted forward like a cutter's bowsprit. Unblinking white eyes returned the goblin's disbelieving gaze, and it moved its beaked snout silently. On one of its tiny, shell-like ears, a silver triangle dangled.

"Fly?" M'bobo scoffed. "It no look like it can run!" She shifted her lion-skin parasol to shade her face from the bright sunshine.

Calmly Kaverin Ebonhand patted the lizard-thing's shoulder. "Skuld stumbled across this fellow when he was tracking Cimber and the others back to Mezro," he said. "There are only about one hundred of them nearby, but I think they'll make excellent scouts and useful front-rank

248

troops." He rattled off a long series of guttural clacks and rumbles, then gestured to the nearest tree.

The scaly giant tilted its head like a curious parrot, growling deep in its throat. Bowing to Kaverin and the goblin queen, it lumbered to the nearest tree. The creature used its claws like the crampons on a mountaineer's boots and swiftly climbed hand-over-hand to a spot high off the ground. There, just below the canopy of leaves, it held one arm out and screeched long and loud. Then it let go of the rough bark.

M'bobo fluffed her golden locks and watched in impatient silence, waiting for the brute to plummet to the ground. But the creature did not fall. It hung in the air as if suspended by thin wires. Kaverin smirked, reminded of the actors he'd seen portraying gods on the stage in Tantras, hanging from the rafters by complicated harnesses. Yet no actor could match the amazing feat the lizard-scout performed next. Its form blurred, skull melting into a beaked head with a rudderlike crown, legs shriveling to thin stalks ending in talons. While its body stayed the same length, the creature suddenly sported leathery wings at least eight feet from tip to shoulder. Again the scout shrieked. It floated forward, then folded its wings and crashed up through the canopy. Only the silver earring distinguished it from the other pteradons cutting through the afternoon sky as it sailed away.

Kaverin sighed in satisfaction. Once Skuld had reported Mezro was hidden behind a magical wall of confusion, it had proven easy to discover the key to breaching it—the triangular earrings both Rayburton and the wombat wore. Now the invasion seemed to be only a troublesome, potentially bloody inconvenience. With the earring Skuld had taken from Byrt, the flying scout would be able to pass close to Mezro and take stock of the preparations. As he and the queen walked through the camp, Kaverin decided the

Mezroans could never muster a defense equal to M'bobo's ever-growing horde.

Goblins from all over the area had swarmed to the queen, and more were filling the camp with each passing hour. The Batiri throughout Chult recognized M'bobo as their leader, though most lived in large hunting groups that rarely saw the monarch. Now all these disparate clans, each hundreds of warriors strong, were crammed together, huddled out of the daylight beneath makeshift huts or massive tents wrought of dinosaur hide.

Fights were frequent and savage, so much so the goblin camp resembled a gladiatorial arena more than an army outpost. Almost everywhere, pug-nosed Batiri wrestled and poked and punched. Fingers and hands were often claimed as trophies, but the goblins rarely killed each other. When a goblin died, the body wasn't butchered for food, but left to rot in the sun. This might have been a show of respect, but Kaverin suspected the Batiri simply understood the smell of fresh carrion quickly attracted dozens of scavengers—hyenas and small carnivorous dinosaurs, vultures and wolf-sized rats. All these dim-witted creatures proved easy targets for the goblin spearmen and archers.

Kaverin and M'bobo passed one group of Batiri as they brought down a two-legged dinosaur that had been drawn to the camp by the stench of corpses and refuse. Each warrior was missing an eye, a wound that proclaimed him a member of the Gouged Orb Clan. The one-eyed savages used their spears to keep the creature at bay, holding its long neck and snapping jaws away from them, while others pelted the beast with stones and arrows. The dinosaur toppled, and the goblins swarmed forward to club it into unconsciousness. Kaverin could not help but notice the warriors of two other clans standing in the shadows of their tents, waiting for the battle to be over so they could lay claim to the prize.

"If we don't hurry, the army may well destroy itself," Kaverin announced, moving briskly away from the impending scuffle.

M'bobo shrugged and idly twirled her parasol. She was quite a sight with her beautiful blonde locks tumbling over her armor wrought of human bone, a delicate parasol in one hand, a battered scimitar in the other. With practiced disinterest, the queen surveyed her rowdy subjects. They all bowed at her passing, even stopping their fistfights long enough to show deference. "They do what I say," she offered at last. "They love me."

Hardly reassured by the proclamation, Kaverin rubbed his tired eyes and let the subject drop. The sooner they attacked, the better. And once Mezro was in his cold stone hands, he would find a way to rid himself of the queen. Perhaps the end of the war will find M'bobo with a Tabaxi spear in her back, Kaverin mused. It won't matter who throws it, just so long as the goblins think the weapon belongs to Mezro's defenders. . . .

"What I'd like to know, old man, is how you intend to replace the chunk of ear you took when you stole my earring. It was a present, you know—the jewelry, not the ear—so you absconding with it like that was really bad form."

Kaverin gritted his teeth at the sound of the inane voice. "Haven't you killed that chattering pig-bear yet?" he hissed.

M'bobo frowned. "We saving him for victory celebration. Fatten him up so all get a piece."

With his cold, lifeless eyes, Kaverin took in the scene. Byrt slouched in a makeshift bamboo cage with wheels on the bottom. Palm fronds shaded the little gray wombat from the sun. A colorful, fragrant cornucopia of vegetables lined the cage's floor, and a large gourd served as a chin rest while Byrt rambled on at Skuld. "If you had to take it—and I suppose you had your reasons—you could have asked," he chattered. "Manners make the . . . er, what are you exactly, if you don't mind me prying?"

The silver-skinned giant wisely paid the wombat no mind. He sat cross-legged, his back against a stout tree. To one side of the spirit guardian lay a jumbled pile of fist-sized stones; to the other was spread a mountain of silver triangles. Sweating goblins continuously hurried into the clearing with buckets of rock. After emptying these into one pile, they loaded up with silver and rushed off to distribute the earrings to every warrior in camp.

"Quiet, Skuld," Byrt hissed at the top of his lungs. "Here comes your master. Don't want him to know you're giving away all the company's trade secrets, the formula for the secret displacer beast sauce and all that."

"Get that idiot out of my sight," Kaverin rumbled. "And keep him away from me, if you want him to live till the victory feast."

As M'bobo ordered two warriors to transport the still-chattering wombat to her tent, Kaverin moved to Skuld's side. Mechanically, the silver guardian took a stone in each of his two right hands, then pressed the rocks between his palms. After muttering an ancient Mulhorandi incantation, he tossed a pair of newly made silver earrings onto the pile at his left.

"How many to go?" Kaverin asked, toeing the mound of earrings with one dusty boot.

"Two hundred or so." Skuld blinked slowly and tried to shake off the pall of boredom that had settled over him. "How many more goblins will we need, master? Let me use my magic for more than changing stones to enchanted silver, and I will conjure a hundred ensorceled gunstones, more powerful than the one your foe used to stun the dragon turtle. We can level all of Mezro, lay waste to—"

"Which is exactly why we need the Batiri troops more

than your explosives," Kaverin corrected. "Don't worry, Skuld. You will be my most potent weapon in the conquest of the city." He lowered his voice and leaned close to the silver giant. "But we need the goblins as spear-fodder, to keep the Tabaxi mages and warriors occupied so you and I can destroy them from a safe distance."

"Hey, Kaverin. He not look so good."

Kaverin turned to find M'bobo standing over the prone form of Lord Rayburton. The bara had his hands bound behind his back and his feet anchored to a boulder by a sturdy chain. He was asleep, though whatever rest he was getting was far from peaceful. He twitched and groaned, caught up in some terrible nightmare brought on by the horrible things he'd overheard the wolf-headed denizens describe in the queen's palace.

Kaverin felt a smile make its way to his thin lips. "We must keep him alive for a few more hours," he said softly. "Only until we can overrun the city and take control of the temple."

M'bobo stuck out her bottom lip as she considered the comment. "Few hours?" she said at last. "We attack before sun goes away?"

"We have the earrings necessary to outfit all your troops," Kaverin noted casually. "We have enough soldiers to defeat their army. We have Skuld. . . . Of course we attack before sunset." He scanned the canopy for signs of the winged scout. "All I'm waiting for is the pteradon's return, so we'll know where to focus our initial charge."

"But goblins hate sunlight!" the queen said. "We never fight wars in daytime!" She held her parasol like a shield against a slant of sunlight cutting through the palm fronds.

"That's the best reason of all to attack now," Kaverin said. "They'll be expecting us to wait until nightfall." At the queen's worried look, he added, "Don't concern yourself, Your Highness. I guarantee you the army will be ready for its victory feast by morning."

"Maybe I'd better give pig-bear more plantains," the goblin queen murmured, then wandered away.

Kaverin slumped against the boulder anchoring Lord Rayburton in place. He watched the pale nobleman toss in his sleep, shredded by unseen claws, bitten by ghostly, venomous fangs. Kaverin's soul had been so blackened by hate and obscured by his lust for power that he did not pity Rayburton, though he realized how horrible the bara's nightmares were. The sight of the tortured prisoner only goaded him on. The shared pain reminded him of how desperately he needed to capture the Temple of Ubtao and become an immortal. Only then could he avoid the ghastly fate the Lord of the Dead had in store for him.

Sleep tugged at Kaverin's weary mind, too, and for an instant he nodded off, just long enough to again hear the corrupt voices of the denizens. He jerked awake and tried to push the fearful images from his mind, but they wouldn't be banished. He hurried off to set the army in motion, hoping that the blood of Mezro would wash the Realm of the Dead from his mind, that the screams of the conquered Tabaxi would drown out the insidious, hellish voices of the denizens—if only for a little while.

*   *   *   *   *

Artus was astounded by how fast Lugg could run. As the explorer charged through the wasteland, the wombat hustled along at his heels. Lugg even found the breath to mutter curses as he ran; Artus could only wheeze and gasp like a fractured tea kettle.

"That's all," the explorer whispered, falling to his knees. An hour of running was enough, his exhausted limbs shouted. The rest of his cramped body was inclined to agree.

Looking nervously over his shoulder, Lugg came to

Artus's side. "They're pretty far back now, but they ain't stopping."

That was the trouble with zombies. You might be able to run from them easily enough, but as long as they could see you, they'd follow tirelessly. And so this pack of ten had done for the past hour. After sizing up their chances of defeating the shambling creatures, Artus and Lugg had bolted toward the distant tree line. The long-dead humans and goblins had lumbered after them, groaning and waving their arms stiffly.

"I need to rest," Artus said. "Just for a moment." He let himself slump to the ground.

Lugg pawed uneasily at the dirt. Like the rest of the area, the soil here was as lifeless as ash. "Yeah, awright," he murmured. "Not too long, though."

The wombat watched the zombies. The dark figures moved steadily on the flat terrain, occasionally stumbling over the few dead tree stumps standing in their way. The dead men walked only in a straight line, it seemed. That would be the key—put something between you and them, something they couldn't clamber over. Lugg scanned the area. A few more stumps. Some shallow pits here and there. No, there wasn't anything that would serve, not close at hand.

The tree line remained distant, as if it were receding as quickly as they could run toward it. Apart from the squawking of the vultures wheeling ominously overhead and the groans of the zombies, the only sounds came from those faraway trees. Wood split and palms toppled noisily. If anyone in the hidden logging camp had heard Artus's calls for help, they'd chosen not to answer. Not that Lugg blamed them. If he didn't like the explorer so well, he'd wish himself well out of this jam, too. The worst part about it was the sun. Lugg hated being caught outside during the day more than anything.

"Come on, then," the wombat said, squinting fiercely. "We'd best be off again."

"Right," Artus mumbled. He tried to push himself up, but his arms wobbled and he collapsed back to the ground like a felled oak.

"This is worse than watching after Byrt," Lugg said truculently. "Like bloody children, the both of you." He nudged Artus with his snout, but got only a grunt for a reply. Narrowing his eyes, he bared his teeth to nip the explorer into action.

Fortunately for Artus, he chose that moment to roll over. "Are they close?"

"Too close for my 'appiness," the wombat grumbled.

With a grunt, the explorer pushed himself to his knees. The zombies had closed the distance to their prey by half, but that still left a comfortable enough lead for Artus and Lugg. They started off again toward the tree line, the wombat trundling at a steady pace, the human staggering like he was undead himself.

Artus pulled his hood over his face. The breeze blowing across the plain was hot and smelled of smoke and decay. "How long can you keep up this pace, Lugg?"

"As long as it takes before I'm off the menu for that lot what's following us." The wombat glanced back at his companion. "As long as it takes for us to get back to rescue Byrt."

"We'll get back to Mezro in time to save him," Artus said sincerely. They had regained their earlier pace, loping forward at a good clip. "Byrt's safe. I—"

The promise was lost on the breeze as Artus sank to his waist in a pool of loose ash and thick, gummy water. He thrashed about for a moment, but that only mired him more soundly. Stand still, his mind cried, though his limbs threatened to lash out frantically. The quicksand rose over his stomach.

Lugg skidded to a halt, still on solid ground. "Grab 'old," he said. The wombat bowed his head and edged toward the explorer.

Artus warned him to stay back. The ash now covered half his chest. Its stench was overpowering, and the explorer had to fight to keep from gagging. Where the soot had splashed over his wounded shoulder, it burned like molten metal.

"I won't let you sink like a scuttled boat," Lugg said. He narrowed his beady eyes. "You won't get out of rescuing Byrt that easy."

Slowly Artus shook his head. "You need to have solid footing," he said as calmly as he could. With slow, deliberate movements, he pulled an extra bowstring from his pocket then reached toward his boot for his dagger. That got him a mouthful of bitter ash, but he managed not to drive himself down too much deeper. As quickly as he dared, he tied the string to the dagger and tossed the blade toward Lugg. "Take hold of this with your teeth."

The wombat did as told, grabbing the dagger in his mouth. When Artus wrapped the sturdy cord around his hand, Lugg began to back slowly away from the sinkhole.

"That's it," the explorer murmured, letting himself be dragged toward solid ground. "Just a little farther. . . ."

Artus felt his foot bump against something solid—the ground, he hoped fervently. The ash was up to his neck, but it seemed at that instant it would get no higher. Then something grabbed the hood of his tunic. Artus thought a branch below the mire's surface had snagged him, but as Lugg pulled him forward and the ash receded from his shoulders, he saw it was a skeletal hand, the bones and cartilage stained gray by the filthy water. He wanted to reach around to free himself from the ghastly thing, but he didn't dare let go of the bowstring.

"Pull, Lugg!"

The wombat's vitriolic reply was thankfully muffled by the dagger and his clenched teeth.

A second hand reached up from the muck, dripping fetid water. It reached around and tried to get a hold on Artus's face. Bony fingers pressed into his mouth and nose and eyes. Suppressing a scream, Artus shook his head violently. The prodding hand slipped away, four thin scratches marking its wake. Finally it settled for a viselike purchase on the explorer's shoulder.

At last, Artus's feet found solid ground. He slipped and scrambled out of the quicksand, releasing the bowstring as he went. The skeleton clung to the explorer's back like a desperate child, arms on his neck and shoulder, legs wrapped around his waist. It was little more than bones and tendons, with cracked ribs and twisted feet. The skeleton's lower jaw was gone—a good thing for Artus, since the undead creature was trying frantically to bite him, rotten teeth scraping over his neck and back.

With the sudden release of tension on the line, Lugg lost the dagger and tumbled backward, snout-over-tail. He landed on his wounded side. "I wish I'd never left the island," the wombat said mournfully.

When Lugg righted himself, he saw Artus grappling with the skeleton. The explorer had found his knife and was using the handle like a cudgel. He brought the blunted end of the weapon down on the creature's skull, the blow sending a spider web of cracks through the gray bone. "Enough!" Artus shouted. "Enough!"

With its sharp, bony fingers, the skeleton clawed at Artus, tearing bloody ribbons from the backs of his hands. But the pain did not penetrate the fury clouding the explorer's mind. Again and again Artus struck, crushing the weird life from the bones. Like a monstrous crab, the skeleton tried to scrabble backward into the mire, but Artus shattered its arm and pinned its legs in place with his weight. Another blow caved in its skull, and the skeleton clattered lifeless to the ground.

As Artus wiped the stinking water and ash from his face, the pack of zombies came toward him with slow, deliberate steps. He flipped the dagger around in his hand. Holding the blade out like the most mighty of enchanted swords, he stood. "Where is your master?" he shouted.

The decaying creatures shambled forward, moaning and clutching the air before them. They were close enough for Artus to see the glaze of starvation in their eyes. Still he did not move.

"We'd better get running," Lugg said, hiding behind Artus's grime-covered boots.

The explorer shook his head and reached into his pocket. The third of T'fima's enchanted diamond slivers slid reassuringly into his palm. Carefully he raised the gem, ready to transform it into a lightning bolt. "No more running, Lugg." He turned back to the zombies. "Where is your master?" Artus shouted. "Where is Ras Nsi?"

It was as if an invisible wall had suddenly been thrown up before the zombies; they stopped in midstride, throwing back their heads to wail in agony. The deafening, unearthly chorus rang out over the blasted plain. Then the zombies turned their wide eyes back to Artus and started forward again.

The explorer opened his mouth to shout the name again, but a gentle hand on his shoulder shocked the air from his lungs. "There is no need to call me, Master Cimber," said a cool, soothing voice.

His reflexes had been honed by years of facing untold dangers and his nerves were frayed raw by the afternoon's confrontations with the walking corpses. Without thinking, Artus slashed at the man behind him. The move was executed expertly, with the skill of a Shou ninja, and the enchanted dagger ran a razor-straight course across Ras

Nsi's throat. The knife had barely left its target before Artus fell back, rolling to a defensive crouch a sword's length away. He brandished the blade before him in one hand, the diamond sliver in the other.

Ras Nsi ran the fingertips of one hand along the knife's path—no blood, not even the slightest nick marked the steel's passing. "A palpable hit," he said quietly. "That would have killed most men. Well done, Master Cimber."

The bara's eyes glowed like red-hot steel, so brightly that Artus found it difficult to look him in the face. The rest of his features were soft, even decadent—a weak chin hidden by a neatly trimmed beard, a pate as bald as a vulture's egg, a flat nose that only emphasized the man's inexpressive mouth. But those fiery eyes told Artus any weakness he saw in Ras Nsi was illusory.

Nsi did not wear the tobe so common in Mezro or the rougher, more basic garb of the Tabaxi villagers. He was clad handsomely in cotton trousers, a loose-fitting brocade shirt, and the flowing blue cape of a Cormyrian nobleman. His high leather boots were spotlessly polished, and the rapier hanging at his hip glinted in the sunlight. A ring on his left hand held a small triangular gem, as green as the hills of the Dalelands in spring. Artus felt his thoughts being drawn into the stone, just as he had when staring at the walls of Ubtao's temple. He shut his eyes tightly and focused on his anger.

Holding the palms of his hands together, Ras Nsi bowed. All the time, he kept his fiery eyes on the explorer. "You have found the lost bara of Mezro. Your weapons are not needed." When Artus sheathed the dagger and slipped the diamond sliver back into his pocket, the bara asked, "Your traveling companion—is he the one known as Byrt or Lugg?"

"Lugg, thank you very much," the wombat said sourly.

Artus glanced at the zombies that had been trailing him.

The ragged pack had thrown themselves to their knees. Even now they bowed to Ras Nsi, their pitiful groans filling the air. Artus turned back to the bara. "How do you know who we are?" he asked warily.

Ras Nsi smiled. "Do we have to play that game? You may take it for granted that I know a great deal. Not everything, but—" he held his hands apart in a mock embrace "—I would be Ubtao if I knew all that transpired in the jungle. I am merely his most ancient and humble servant."

"If you know so much, Master Nsi," the wombat said, fearlessly stepping up to the bara, "then 'ow about letting me know if Byrt's still kicking about."

The zombies cried out when Lugg said their master's name, and Ras Nsi scowled. "Do not speak my name aloud again," the bara snapped, small tongues of flame dancing from his eyes.

The wombat backed up a step, but did not look away. "Sorry—er . . ."

"Your Excellency," the bara prompted. He rubbed his chin and studied Lugg for a moment. "Your fellow is still alive—as is Lord Rayburton." Before Artus could ask how he knew, Ras Nsi added, "If you found me, you must know that Ubtao granted me the power to raise the dead. The power would be rather limited if I could not sense when something died in the jungle, don't you agree?"

Artus straightened his grimy tunic. "If you know about Rayburton, then you know why I'm here."

A strange, almost taunting smile on his lips, Ras Nsi said, "I have my suspicions, but dare not believe them." He grabbed the edge of his cape and lifted it theatrically from his side. "But let us retire to my home, where we can settle this matter in the appropriate style."

With a swirl of the bara's sky-blue cloak, they were gone.

Fifteen

Ras Nsi's home stood at the heart of a very mobile and spectacularly effective logging operation. For miles in every direction, his slaves tore up the Chultan landscape. Elementals summoned from the Plane of Earth—mighty creatures of stone and dirt that could move through the ground as easily as men walk upon it—used their stony hands to uproot trees of every sort. Behind these hulking brutes, gangs of zombies trailed with lethargic steps. The undead slaves dragged the trees back to waiting caravans and bundled the massive cargo onto sledges. Finally, dinosaurs of various species dragged the trees back from the camp and moved them along a wide road toward the coast. In ports all along Refuge Bay ships waited to take the precious wood north.

The sound of trees splintering and crashing to the ground filled the air, along with the shrieks of the birds and apes and other tree-dwellers routed by the destruction.

The whole camp stank of decaying flesh, shattered wood, and overturned earth. Zombies were constantly being crushed by the elementals or the dinosaurs or the falling trees. Just as quickly as they fell, the walking corpses were replaced by newly risen dead. Overhead, vultures and other flying scavengers circled. As soon as the crews moved far enough forward, they would swoop down to claim whatever carrion had been left behind.

In this way, over hundreds of years, Ras Nsi had created the broad, blasted plain upon which Artus and Lugg had found themselves that morning. The scar never seemed to heal. The bara's crews were too efficient for that.

In the center of this chaos sprawled Ras Nsi's palatial home. The building resembled many of the stately houses so common in Faerun's wealthier cities. Four towers capped in spires marked the corners of the huge structure, and a low wall surrounded the courtyard spreading before its front entrance. Arrow loops and stained glass windows dotted the white stone in patterns that appealed to the eye in a dozen subtle ways. Banners floated from poles atop the towers, their bright colors making them stand out against the sun-bleached sky like brilliantly plumed birds. From an open upstairs window, the gentle music of a string quartet lofted upon the hot, humid air.

The entire estate—grassy courtyard and all—was borne upon the backs of two dozen monstrously huge, long-dead tortoises. It was the job of these unfortunate skeletal creatures to keep the estate moving through the jungle at a steady, creeping pace, just ahead of the elementals and the zombies and the falling trees. The gentle swaying of the house was apt to bring fond memories of time at sea, to those who enjoyed such things.

Yet Artus wasn't remembering his days aboard the *Narwhal* as he stood in his newly clean clothes, framed by a large window in Nsi's audience hall. No, the former Harper was thinking on the injustice of the place—the enslaved dead men, the massive destruction of the jungle. "And you do this all for the betterment of Chult?" he asked coldly, turning back to the outcast bara.

"For the betterment of Mezro," Ras Nsi corrected. "In the end they are the same, but you must see that Ubtao chose the citizens of Mezro as his messengers in the world. The rest of the Tabaxi—" he dismissed them with a wave of his hand "—savages. It was their kind that drove Ubtao back to the heavens four thousand years ago."

The bara paced nervously back and forth before a velvet-lined throne, his boots rapping an unsettling rhythm on the polished floor. Like the rest of the room, the chair was imported from the North—from Suzail, in fact. He caught Artus studying the furnishings. "I do a great deal of business with Cormyrians, Sembians, and other northern merchants. Occasionally they send me gifts."

Fine crystal chandeliers hung from the ceiling. Oak tables and chairs brought from the Dales filled the center of the room. The audience hall was very much like a dozen Artus had visited in Cormyr. Only the painting that hung over the large fireplace was different, surprising. In garish colors, ghastly blues and greens and grays, it depicted men and women being pulled into a grassy mound by bloodless hands. If the rest of the hall was meant to soothe visitors from the North, the painting was intended to remind them of their host's power.

"I control the Refuge Bay Trading Company, which owns the *Narwhal*," Ras Nsi said proudly. "That's how I knew who you were—well, one of the ways."

Artus was suddenly glad Lugg was fast asleep in the shadow of the cold hearth. He was finding it difficult to hide his growing disdain for the bara, and he was certain the wombat wouldn't be nearly as diplomatic. "I still don't see how this is helping Mezro," the explorer noted.

Slowly Ras Nsi unhooked the rapier from his belt and hung it over the back of his throne. "Money," he said, a patronizing tone to his voice. "The more money I control, the greater network of servants, the grander things I can do for Mezro—once King Osaw and the others see the error of their ways and allow me to return to the city."

The bara sank into the embrace of his throne. "By Ubtao's blood, they were fools," he chuckled. "I end a three-hundred-year-long war, save Mezro from destruction, and they banish me."

"A war that lasted three hundred years?" Artus gasped.

"They sent you here without telling you of my great crime?" Ras Nsi asked sarcastically. His sun-bright eyes flashed. "They must be embarrassed by their foolishness, especially now that the city is in such grave danger."

Ras Nsi began his tale. He stared into the green stone on his ring as he spoke, as if it were calling forth his memories of the ancient battles.

"The war started about eighteen hundred years ago," the bara told Artus. "That was long before the wall encircled the city. We didn't need sorcerous protection then. Mezro boasted the mightiest army in the world, and every Tabaxi who had the heart to be a warrior flocked to the city to prove his mettle.

"There was another large tribe of humans in Chult then—the Eshowe—and they were our sworn foes. They mocked Ubtao, worshiping the rain and the sun, calling upon local spirits for spells." Nsi sneered and reached behind him for a short-handled spear hanging on the wall. Holding the broad blade toward Artus, he added, "But their local gods could not help them against our righteous armies. For three hundred years we fought, driving the Eshowe farther and farther into the wild parts of the jungle, the valleys where creatures from before time still dwell in dark caves."

The bara tapped the spear against his palm, digging the sharp tip deeper and deeper into his bloodless flesh. The wounds healed instantly. "The Eshowe found just such a beast," Ras Nsi said, his voice strained with excitement. "A creature as tall as the highest spire on the Temple of Ubtao, its body wrought of blinding smoke and choking fog. They made a deal with the creature, promising the souls of all the slain to its greedy stomach, for it fed upon bravery, and the Tabaxi were known throughout Ubtao's jungle as the bravest of all men." He sank the spear into the arm of his throne. "The Eshowe led the beast back to Mezro for a final, desperate attack."

A look of sadness passed across the bara's features, though his eyes still blazed with an infernal light. "They sacked the city before we could defeat them. Our homes, our fields—all burned. Just the temple and a few of the buildings in the city's heart were left standing." Ras Nsi sighed. "Of the seven barae, only I survived. The others all died crushing the Eshowe and the beast. We were the victors, but at a terrible price.

"For the next decade, I hunted the few Eshowe that survived the fight, tracked them with my zombies. I burned their homes and slaughtered their children. And each Eshowe warrior I killed was raised up to fight against his brothers." He gestured casually to the weird painting. "That depicts the last of the Eshowe being killed. There are no more of them in Chult."

Ras Nsi stated the gruesome facts with inestimable pride. Artus shuddered at the claim, his throat constricting. It was clear now the bara was blind to the horror of his actions.

"By the time I returned to Mezro, the legion of dead Eshowe trailing in my wake, Osaw had been made king, with Mainu and that bleeding heart T'fima serving as his most trusted advisors." The bara scowled. "When they saw what I had done, they banished me from the city. 'Your murderous ways are not honorable,' T'fima proclaimed at my trial. They were fools, but I had no choice but obey. Osaw was the rightful king and leader of Mezro. I would have done anything to help the city, and they turned me away!"

The bara glowered for a moment, staring at the screaming men and women in the painting. "I warned them that other enemies would arise, that there was a void in the jungle hierarchy. I have watched the Batiri rise up over the last thousand years. The war Mezro faces now could have been prevented long ago, had they only let me wipe out the goblins, too. But now I will remedy that mistake."

"Forgive me, Ras Nsi," Artus began slowly, "but King Osaw did not send me to ask for your aid. I came on my own."

Furious, Nsi jumped to his feet. "What?" he shouted, brandishing the spear before him. "They don't want me back? Not even now?"

Artus stood his ground, keeping his gaze locked on the bara's face. "I cannot speak for the king. I thought you might be able to help, that the reason for the rift between you and the other barae might be minor enough for us to reason it out. Even T'fima—"

"T'fima is no bara," Ras Nsi snapped, tiny curls of fire leaping from his eyes. "He fell from grace long ago, when he first left the city. Ubtao stripped him of his powers."

The house lurched to a stop. The sweet music of the string quartet, drifting down to the audience hall from somewhere else in the estate, ceased suddenly. So did the sounds of the logging camp. An unearthly wailing rang out, as if the zombies could sense their master's fury.

Ras Nsi drank in the sound. He closed his eyes, let his head droop forward, and held his arms out at his sides. The hellish cacophony seemed to calm him, and when he opened his eyes again the angry fire had subsided a little. "Forgive me. I had thought myself beyond such disappointment," he said coolly. "I had thought you a messenger of the king. I should have known better. . . ."

Nodding absently, Artus murmured, "T'fima isn't a bara? He doesn't have the power to control the weather?"

"Osaw and the others have not held the ceremony to replace him because they do not know he lost his power," Ras Nsi said. "As one of the original seven, my link to the city is far more vital than theirs. I could sense it when T'fima fell away from his duty. It was like he died."

In the empty hearth, Lugg stirred and snorted awake. "Oi. What's all the shouting about?"

"Time for us to go," Artus told the wombat.

Ras Nsi rubbed his chin with one thumb. "Not just yet, Artus Cimber." He narrowed his eyes until they were mere slits of light. "I know a great deal about you and this Kaverin Ebonhand who has taken up with the Batiri, but there is one thing I have not been able to discover. Tell me that, and I will transport you back to Mezro."

"Perhaps," Artus replied impatiently.

"Why did you come to Chult? What are you after?" He dropped the spear to the floor. With a thud, it stuck there.

Artus turned toward the door. "That's a private matter, Your Excellency. Something that does not concern Mezro or Ubtao," he said. "Thank you for your hospitality, but we really should be going."

"Are we going to 'ave to *walk* back to the city?" the wombat asked as he got stiffly to his feet. "We don't even know where we are!"

"Lugg is quite correct," Ras Nsi said, slouching back into his throne. "You will be days getting back to Mezro on your own. The battle will be quite over by then."

"Then I won't be able to help them fight the Batiri," Artus said coldly. "Will you stand in the way of that just because I won't answer your question?"

Outside, the sounds of toppling trees had resumed, and the string quartet had taken up their instruments again on the upper floor. Ras Nsi stood. "Of course you are correct," he said. "You are fighting for Mezro, and I would be a fool to miss this opportunity to aid the city—even indirectly." With a grand gesture, he swirled his sky-blue cloak.

Artus and Lugg began to fade, like the ghostly Pontifax that had haunted the explorer's mind from time to time in the jungle. Before Artus disappeared, though, Ras Nsi said, "It's the ring, isn't it? The one Rayburton brought to Chult from the North? He always was afraid of people like you coming here to hunt for it."

The bara didn't need to hear Artus's reply. The shock on the explorer's face told him everything he wanted to know.

*   *   *   *   *

Artus and Lugg found themselves in the Hall of Champions, standing before the empty pedestal that might one day hold a statue of Ras Nsi. The place was deserted, save for the mute stone heroes, but far from silent. Sounds of a fierce battle came from the plaza. Shouted orders entwined with the screams of the wounded. The sharp clatter of steel against steel rose above the rumble of magical thunder. The fight for Mezro had begun.

"By Tempus's spiked glove," Artus cursed and started toward the door, Lugg at his heels.

In the plaza and throughout the ancient city of Mezro, the scene was chaos, the noise almost deafening. Dozens of pteradons filled the sky, silver orbs clutched in their talons. The flying reptiles soared over the heart of the city on broad leathery wings. When they passed over a group of Mezroan warriors or an important building, they dropped the magical bombs Skuld had given them. The explosions that followed lit the twilight sky and momentarily drowned out the cries of the warriors injured by the blasts. Shards of the shattered buildings and cobblestone from the broken streets ripped through the air, adding to the growing league of the Tabaxi dead.

The city's defenders met the airborne assault with balls of fire and sheets of arrows. In places, magical shields spread like umbrellas over the troops. The bombs exploded against the glowing barriers, filling the sky with fire. Mezroan warriors mounted upon huge butterflies sailed after the pteradons, spearing them with lances or tangling nets around their heads and wings. From time to time one of the reptiles dropped from the air. The creature always changed as it fell, reverting to a form roughly human, though brutish and armored with scales.

From the temple's doorway, Artus could see little of the battle on the ground. Many of the Mezroan sorcerers had taken up positions around the sacred building's single side. They wore the traditional tobe, but also half-cloaks colored in rainbow hues that continually changed. Some of the men and women huddled in tight groups, while others dealt with attacks from the air. A young woman with a mesmerizing pattern of blood-red lines drawn upon her face and arms wielded a long whip of sunlight. With it she battled a pteradon that was trying to fly close to the front ranks. Wherever the brilliant lash struck, it seared the lizard's flesh, leaving its chest scarred and its wings ragged.

Beyond the circle of mages, a line of Tabaxi warriors stood against the goblin horde. They wore wild crowns of feathers and bands of silver and gold on their arms and legs. Dinosaur hide covered their chests. No armor protected their backs, only the tails of exotic jungle cats. There was no need for more than that; Tabaxi warriors never turned away from a foe.

The spearhead of the Batiri attack seemed to come from the northeast, the Scholars' Quarter, well away from the river and any help Mainu could provide. For now, the Tabaxi seemed content to hold a front against the goblins, to keep them away from the temple and the Residential Quarter. Men and women fought side by side. They carried steel-tipped spears, war clubs ridged with sharp studs, and large, diamond-shaped shields. Tiny Batiri arrows stuck out from those shields as thickly as trees stood in the jungle, but only a few shafts got past the wall of tanned hide. The warriors took their wounds stoically, but they fought with fury—as the hundreds of goblin corpses littering the plaza before them proved.

"That ghoulish bloke would 'ave a lovely time 'round 'ere," Lugg said breathlessly. "Good thing no one invited 'im along." He looked up at the explorer. "How are we going to find Byrt in all this?"

The question went unheard. "Look, Lugg, you might want to stay inside the temple. You'll be safe there." Artus scanned the assembled mages and warriors for some sign of Negus Kwalu or King Osaw.

The brown wombat stood a moment on the temple's doorstep. The crash and clatter of the battle frightened him, but not enough to paralyze him into inaction. "Awright, Byrt," he murmured, his beady eyes solemn. "If Artus plans to forget his promise, I'll come to find you on my own."

"Did you say something?" Artus asked. When he looked down, Lugg was gone. "Must have followed my word . . . for once," the explorer noted with surprise, turning his gaze back to the ranks of sorcerers and warriors.

Finally Artus spotted a triangular platinum banner rising above the throng. He looked closer and saw a faint shield of light glittering in the gloaming, arched over the banner and the men gathered around it.

Artus pushed his way through the crowd, coming at last to a tight knot of warriors. "I've important news for the king," Artus shouted, hoping to be heard over the din of lightning bolts and magical explosions.

A calloused hand reached through the throng and guided the explorer through the guards. "We thought we would never see you again," Kwalu said. The negus wore his battle regalia, and had a wild look in his eyes.

"His Excellency was quite hospitable," Artus replied, carefully avoiding Ras Nsi's name. "You're right about him being a madman, though. Where's Sanda?"

"Alisanda has yet to return from her hunting expedition," King Osaw said sadly. "We fear her captured."

Kwalu frowned. "Never. She is too crafty to be caught by goblins; she knew they were preparing for war."

A shiver of dread ran up Artus's spine, but he reminded himself that worrying about Sanda would do her no good. If she were a prisoner of the Batiri, the only way he could help her, and the rest of the city, was to fight.

Briefly the king explained how the goblins had begun their assault a few hours ago, while the sun was still bright in the sky. Such tactics were unheard of, and while the Mezroans were not caught completely off-guard, they were surprised enough for the Batiri to push their way into the Scholars' Quarter. The goblins must have used scouts or spied upon the bara magically, for they were staying far away from the river, out of reach of Mainu's aquatic minions.

It was also clear the Batiri objective was the Temple of Ubtao, for they never launched any attack that might seriously damage the building. Even the pteradons directed their bombs away from the temple. "We have used that against them," Osaw concluded. "If we know they will not harm the temple, we can make it the locus for our army. They dare not direct killing magic against us here, and our warriors are capable of striking ten times for each goblin arrow loosed."

"What about Kaverin?" Artus asked. "And Skuld? I'm surprised that silver monstrosity hasn't shown himself yet."

Kwalu jerked a thumb toward a circle of ten mages. They stood arm in arm, heads bowed in fierce concentration. "We have not seen Kaverin Ebonhand, but our best mages have the silver one trapped," he noted proudly.

"Skuld is a being of such immense magical strength that the sorcerers could sense him coming toward Mezro," the king added. "The moment he entered the city, they conjured a powerful cage of energy and sent it after him. He got no more than a dozen steps into the Scholars' Quarter before they captured him." Osaw bowed his head. "We have not had need of the spell in hundreds and hundreds of years, not since the Eshowe led a thing of darkness out of the jungle to strike us down. . . ."

The king's words trailed off, and Artus turned to the circle of mages. Capturing Skuld may have been easy for them. Holding him prisoner was obviously a different matter. Sweat beaded upon their brows, and many of them gritted their teeth in concentration. One man, his short beard white with age, swayed where he stood. A boy helped to steady him, whispering encouragements to the exhausted mage.

Suddenly, shrieks of pain and horror went up from the sorcerers, underscored by a peal of triumphant laughter that rang out over the din of battle. At the far edge of the Scholars' Quarter, a silver-skinned figure grew larger and larger, until at last it towered over the libraries and schools. Skuld looked down at the chaotic streets and laughed again, his filed teeth glinting in the twilight.

The ten bars of energy around the giant had expanded to contain him. Each of Skuld's four hands grasped a snaking

bar, wrenching it first this way, then that. He tried to twist
them apart, smash them, even bite them to pieces, but
nothing seemed to work. His laughter turned to shouts of
rage. Cursing, he grabbed one bar with all four hands and
shook it violently.

This time only one member of the sorcerous circle cried
out—the white-bearded old man. As Skuld battered the
band of energy, the mage quivered and quaked. A thin line
of blood snaked down his arm, a line that matched the frac-
ture in the hissing band of light in Skuld's grip. When the
bar broke, the mage's arm snapped. The bone jutted out
like a spear tip, but still he kept his place, held up by the
shoulders of those to either side him.

"I can help against Skuld," Artus said, "maybe even stop
the goblin attack, but I need to get to Ras T'fima. Can the
army spare a flying mount to take me to his camp?"

"There's no need for that," Kwalu said. "Hard to believe, but T'fima came to help us."

"He's here?" Artus shouted. "Where?"

"Near the Residential Quarter," the king said. "He's
guarding the old people and children until they can—"

The explorer bowed perfunctorily and raced away. King
Osaw and Negus Kwalu watched Artus until the crowd of
warriors swallowed him. "Perhaps he will be able to convince T'fima to do more than shepherd children tonight,"
Kwalu said bitterly. "We need his power over the weather
if we are to drive the Batiri out of Mezro. I don't know why
he came back if he did not plan to use the powers Ubtao
granted him."

The king shrugged. "Mezro inspires odd loyalties, and
not all of them are grounded upon worship of Ubtao." He
looked back to where Artus had disappeared into the
throng. "Have faith in that. If Artus cannot sway T'fima,
he may be able to discover some other way to aid the city."
Osaw nodded. "Yes, I think that very likely indeed."

* * * * *

Arrows rained down around Artus as he charged behind
the Mezroan lines, toward the Residential Quarter. The
warriors' shields protected the army from the shafts fired
low to the ground, but the mages could keep their magical
barriers over only the most important people in the rear
ranks. This left the land in between the sorcerous protection a prime target for the Batiri archers, who fired blindly
over the front ranks in hopes of hitting someone.

The growing darkness compounded the danger. If you lit
a torch, an archer could aim for the light. If you tried to
move about in the dark, you were likely to shatter an ankle
in one of the holes opened by the pteradons' bombing raids
or slice apart an arm or leg on a weapon dropped by a
wounded warrior. Still, the darkness wouldn't be a problem
for long; from the red glow to the east, Artus guessed that
the goblins had set fire to the crops farthest from the river.
The blaze would spread quickly, lighting the night with its
hellish radiance.

"Hey! Look out there!"

A pteradon swooped low over the front rank of warriors,
too fast for anyone to land a solid blow with spear or club.
The birdlike reptile opened its beak in an angry squawk—
just enough for Artus to get a hold on its lower jaw.

The fin radiating back from a pteradon's skull was very
much like a ship's rudder, so when Artus yanked the raid-
er's head down, it lost control of its flight. That, coupled
with the explorer's weight, made the flying lizard spin out
of the air. Together Artus and the pteradon rolled across
the cobblestones. Talons scraped at the explorer's legs and
stomach, while the creature's wings buffeted his face and
arms. Before the pteradon could think to bite his fingers
off, Artus wisely let go of its beak. By that time, the two
were so tangled together that they continued to tumble

across the plaza as one.

That was a fortunate thing, since the pteradon finally lost its grip on the bomb it had been clutching in one taloned foot. The silver egg bounced once, twice, then exploded. Artus didn't see the burst of flame, but he heard the roar and felt the wave of fire and barrage of cobbles that struck the pteradon. He understood in that instant why the Mezroan warriors favored dinosaur-hide armor; the flying lizard wrapped angrily around him shielded him from the blast.

The pteradon itself was not so well served by its hide. The blast sent a fragment of the pavement through its skull. It took four warriors to drag the thing's limp corpse from atop Artus, even with him straining against its bulk from below.

"Was anybody hurt?" the explorer puffed as he climbed out from under one ragged wing. He looked around. A few injured warriors were being helped away, but they were still walking.

A young boy stared at the explorer in awe. "Nobody was hurt too bad," he said. "You bounced enough times for everyone to run."

Artus rubbed his shoulder. The scuffle hadn't done much good for the arrow wound he'd gotten at the Batiri camp. "Have you seen Ras T'fima?"

"I can take you right to him," the boy shouted happily. Lifting a small, round shield of studded leather over his head, he hurried away. Every few steps he looked back, to be sure the explorer was still with him.

They found T'fima near the edge of the maze of buildings and alleys that made up the Residential Quarter. The boy took one look at the mage, nodded to Artus, and ran back toward the temple. T'fima was as volatile as ever, shouting instructions at anyone who got close and gesturing broadly with his fat-fingered hands. Bits of gravel clung to his tightly curled hair, and dirt covered his tobe.

A small army of old people, wounded warriors, and very young children flooded past T'fima on their way to their homes. It would be safer for them there, since the goblins would surely get lost in the twisting, turning streets. In case any Batiri got past the contingent guarding the district, a handful of warriors were passing out clubs and daggers to the people who could wield them. Artus had no doubt the goblins would be in for quite a surprise if they ventured into the narrow lanes.

T'fima himself had a globe of blue light caught between his hands. He lifted it gently over his head, as if it were wrought of some fragile crystal, then let it go. The globe floated there until the sorcerer pointed toward a group of one-eyed goblins massing for an attack. With a high, shrill whistle, the light flew toward the Batiri. It struck them, but didn't explode or burst into flames, as Artus had expected. The globe splashed over the first dozen goblins like soft summer rain. After the shock wore off, the stunned cannibals laughed and raised their spears.

In a show of contempt, T'fima turned his back on the Batiri and went about directing the defense of the Residential Quarter. Artus drew his dagger and moved to intercept the goblin pack before it could take advantage of the sorcerer's bravado.

Yet as soon as the Batiri took a step forward, blue light began to leak from their empty eye sockets. Their leader tried to shout an order, but only magical radiance poured out over his black tongue. He seemed to choke on it, dropping his spear to clutch helplessly at his throat. The others never got the chance to shout. Before they could open their mouths, they burst like overfull wineskins, their corpses disappearing in a flash of blue before the first drop of blood hit the ground.

Artus grimaced at the gory sight, but could not fault the

sorcerer for effectiveness. The goblins the globe had missed retreated, leaving the Mezroans to continue their work.

"Give her a dagger!" T'fima was shouting as the explorer got close. He pointed at an old woman. "She couldn't lift a club, let alone hurt someone with it. At least with a blade she might get lucky and blind someone!"

"Ras T'fima," Artus said, placing a firm hand on the sorcerer's shoulder.

Slowly the ras turned. "We have things to do here," he rumbled. "Either give us a hand or get out of the way."

"I want the Ring of Winter," the explorer said, lowering his voice just a little.

"And I told you before I don't know anything about it!"

People had begun to turn toward the mage and the stranger. Artus glanced at the upturned faces. Fear held a tight grip over many of these people. It wouldn't do to challenge their protector openly. "I know you aren't a bara," Artus whispered to T'fima, leaning closer. "The master of the dead told me. You've been using gem magic to keep yourself alive—just like your cat—and you used the ring to cause the blizzard that saved Kwalu."

T'fima's eyes got as large as full moons. Muttering, he slipped a hand into the pocket of his tobe. Artus was faster, though. The explorer grabbed the last of the diamond slivers and said the command word. A bolt of lightning appeared in his hand, illuminating the area with cold white light.

"I'm not your enemy," the explorer hissed.

T'fima shook his head. "How can I be sure of that?"

Turning away from the sorcerer, Artus heaved the lightning at the distant goblin line. The bolt sizzled just off the ground. A few of the more observant Batiri in its path scattered before it struck. Two dozen charred corpses was all that remained of those that didn't.

"I've hunted for the ring for a decade," Artus said, forcing calm into his voice. "I've wanted to turn its power to good. Now there's another reason for me to have it—to save Mezro, to rescue Lord Rayburton and Sanda and the others from the goblins."

The sorcerer took his empty hand from his pocket and waved away three warriors who were obviously coming over to see what the argument was about. "And who'll be there to rescue the city from you once you get the ring?" T'fima growled. "Rayburton couldn't control it. That's why he brought it here—he froze an entire village solid in Cormyr. Killed hundreds of people. That's why he gave it to me to hide, so he'd never be tempted to use it again."

Artus closed his eyes. The disaster Lord Rayburton had told him about—he had caused it! "Ancient history," he heard himself say. "Besides, I'm not Rayburton."

"I froze the jungle for miles around, made it snow for three days instead of the hour I had intended." T'fima grabbed the front of Artus's tunic. "Don't you see? I could control weather once—that was Ubtao's gift to me—and yet even I couldn't bend the ring to a good cause!"

Artus pushed T'fima away. "The reason you used the ring was so Osaw and the others wouldn't discover you weren't a bara any longer," he said. "If Kwalu was killed, they'd hold the ceremony to install a new paladin to replace him. Ubtao would have chosen *two* new barae, not one, and then they would have known."

T'fima's fury had returned, and his round form quivered in anger as he rumbled, "If they know I'm not a bara, then the Tabaxi outside the wall will have no voice in the councils. The wall will stay up forever, and they'll be robbed of their heritage!"

A grating sound, like metal shivering into a thousand fragments, rang out over the city, and Artus spun around to see Skuld break through another of the bars on his magical cage. The guardian spirit rolled his eyes and snarled like a straight-jacketed lunatic.

"There'll be nothing left of Mezro once he gets free," Artus said. He pointed to Skuld, who was sawing away at another bar with a glowing fragment from the one he had just broken. "And if the Ring of Winter is here, the man who controls that monstrosity will have it."

Ras T'fima bowed his head. "After I used it to cause the blizzard, I went to the temple and tossed it into the barado. No one goes in that room unless they're electing a new bara, so I thought it would be safe. . . ."

When T'fima looked up, Artus was already gone.

"Keep the children away from the arrows!" the sorcerer snarled at a wounded warrior who was distributing weapons. After the woman hustled the two toddlers away from the arrows, T'fima glanced toward the temple. A wave of sadness swept over him; since there were just six active barae, the only way for Artus to escape the barado once he'd entered would be to pass Ubtao's test. If he succeeded, he would be the new bara of Mezro—and have the Ring of Winter. If he failed, Ubtao would kill him.

At the moment, Ras T'fima wasn't certain which would be worse for the city.

Sixteen

 Artus stood in the Hall of Champions, poised before the archway that led everywhere in the temple. The boom of magical explosions and crash of sorcerous lightning rocked the place. Now and then swirls of hot air rushed through the hall as someone opened the door to the plaza. These newcomers scrambled past Artus and disappeared through the arch to some distant room, seeking medicine or weapons or a hiding place from the advancing goblin army. The explorer paid no attention to them. He stared into the absolute darkness bracketed by the arch, preparing himself to meet a god.

The Mezroan history written by King Osaw and translated by Lord Rayburton had been very clear about that: to enter the barado was to come face to face with Ubtao. It was forbidden for anyone to trespass in the sacred room—other than to take the test to become a bara. Of course Artus had no intention of devoting himself to this strange

god or his city. He wondered, then, what Ubtao would do
to him. Anything he wanted, the explorer decided at last.
Ubtao was, after all, a god.

Fortunately, he didn't seem the fire-and-brimstone sort,
or a raving lunatic like Cyric or Loviatar. "Maybe I'll get a
few prayers to repeat, or a good deed to do," Artus murmured hopefully, remembering his days in the temple
school in Suzail. Then he stepped through the archway.

For a moment Artus thought he'd been transported to
the wrong room. He'd expected a magnificent hall filled
with music and light, with a tremendous throne at one end
and dinosaur guards all along the walls—they were called
Ubtao's Children, after all. The god would come down to
the throne as a ball of light. He—she? it?—would then
speak in a voice like a thousand trumpets blaring in harmony, demanding the reasons for Artus's boldness. The place
would be thrillingly opulent, demanding instant respect and
awe.

Instead, he found himself in a dimly lit room, eloquent of
neglect. A small, sourceless circle of light drove the gloom
away from the center of the room, but darkness cloaked
the walls and ceiling. The air was stale and oppressively
humid. Artus stepped into the light. Not daring to offend
the deity, he waited expectantly for something to happen.

A small girl emerged from the darkness, a gentle smile
on her lips. Her face was round and cherubic, her tobe a
stunning shade of blue. Like the other children of Mezro,
she had her hair cropped close, with intricate patterns cut
into it. *Who would become a guardian of my city?*

The words weren't spoken aloud, but sounded inside
Artus's head. "I am here to retrieve something left in the
barado, great Ubtao," the explorer said. He dropped to one
knee and bowed. "The Ring of Winter. It was hidden here
by Ras T'fima."

This place is only for my barae. I have time only for those who would be champions of my city.

The words held no anger, but when Artus looked up, the little girl was gone. A Mezroan warrior now stood before him. The young man had proud defiance in his eyes. He held his war club in a firm grip, and his voice rumbled in Artus's head like a thunderstorm.

"I am fighting for Mezro," Artus offered quietly.

But you will not become a bara. The warrior melted into the form of a matronly old woman with jet-black skin and hands worn from years of hard work. She turned away and walked slowly back to the darkness at the edges of the room. *You must come with me now,* she said in a sad, tired voice, keeping her stooped back to the explorer.

"Come with you?"

Yes, came the calm, steady voice of a middle-aged man. He had the face of a teacher, full of self-assurance and a slight look of knowing arrogance. His tobe was unkempt, his beard in need of trimming. *There is no reason to give you the test if you aren't interested in becoming a bara. My law says you must be taken up to my home in the sky, since you failed to satisfy my challenge.*

Artus was on his feet now. "If those are my only choices, I will take your test," he said firmly.

Ubtao paused and ran a hand through his beard. *So be it.*

The small circle of light expanded, blinding Artus for a moment. When he could see again, he looked out across an endless field of glossy black stone. A star-filled sky, silver tears on a vast canvas of velvet, stretched overhead. Gently the starlight rained down upon the field. Artus felt the radiance wash over him like cool rain. The nagging pain in his shoulder vanished, as did the ache of the myriad other small wounds he'd gained on the expedition.

The silver light swept across the stone. Wherever it touched, it left a complex pattern of lines and angles and curves. Artus saw shapes emerge from the jumble—a book, the partly unraveled scroll that symbolized Oghma, the crest of the Scribes' Guild of Cormyr, Pontifax's badge of honor from the crusade. These glowed a little more brightly than the rest of the maze, but their light was like a candle to the sun compared to two other shapes Artus could discern before him.

A simple circle dominated the center of the pattern, within it the harp and moon symbol of the Harpers—at least, an incomplete version of the Harpers' symbol.

The world is a labyrinth, and the true followers of Ubtao know the pattern that represents their life. When they die, they must recreate that maze, spell out their past for me. This time there was no avatar to give a face to the voice inside Artus's head. *To be a paladin of Ubtao, a bara of Mezro, you must know more. You must complete the maze long before you die, look ahead to the pattern that will be your life in the years and decades to come.*

The explorer felt his heart sink. No wonder there were so few barae chosen; who could look out over his past and divine his future so accurately? Sanda, obviously. And Rayburton. And all the other barae.

Setting his jaw in grim determination, Artus kneeled and ran a finger along a smooth curve. Thankfully there were some recognizable patterns in the riot of silver, some unfinished symbols he could easily complete. Best to start there, at the obvious. Maybe the rest would fall into place after that.

When he took his finger away from the floor, it was coated in stardust. The line he had been touching remained unchanged, but the radiance clung stubbornly to him. He curled the finger into his palm and made his way to the pattern's center.

"The first thing to do is draw a line across the Harpers' symbol," Artus whispered. "There's certainly no need to finish it." His voice sounded hollow and small on the silent plain.

Now that he was closer, he could see the circle bordering the Harpers' symbol was incomplete, too. Here and there, gaps broke its perfect form. This had to be the Ring of Winter. Nothing else had been so important to his life. As he reached down to complete the ring, something about the design jangled Artus's thoughts; he stepped back and looked at the maze again.

If the Ring of Winter had been his life's quest, why was the Harpers' symbol the true heart of the pattern?

I've given up on them, he reminded himself. I haven't been in contact in years with most of the other members I knew. The Harpers' ideals and methods were important to me once, but I'm just not that idealistic anymore. Artus sighed raggedly. Then why do I want the blasted ring? he thought. To use it for good? To stop scum like Kaverin from exploiting it for his own gain? That's the Harpers' fight, too.

"Maybe closing off the Harpers' symbol would be a mistake," Artus said. "Maybe that part of my life isn't over just yet. Maybe. . . ."

The solution struck him then. No matter what pattern he drew, it would be wrong. The moment he walked out of the barado, he could decide to become an active Harper again. He could just as easily decide to work against them. Life may be a labyrinth, he realized, but you never have walls before you, not unless you create them. The only real pattern is the one you leave behind you, the immutable decisions—right and wrong—that mark the wake of your passing.

"It's done," Artus announced. He looked out across the plain. "Whatever I add could be wrong—or right. All I have to do is decide to make it so."

The past champions of Ubtao appeared out of the velvet-black sky. The statues could never do these men and women justice. They stood in a semicircle around Artus, quietly studying the explorer, their eyes still alight with the passions that drove them in life. Here was the bara that could control fire, bathed in snaking bands of flame; the master of the raptors, arms outstretched as he floated off the ground, an eagle at his side; the weaponsmith, his wrinkled face and arms singed by forgefire, a well-worn hammer in one hand, a magnificent spear in the other.

Only the most wise can see through the illusion of fate, came a soothing voice. It seemed to fall from the midnight sky itself, carried on tiny bursts of stardust. *You are worthy to be a bara of Mezro.*

"But I . . . can't accept that honor," Artus said.

A murmur of disapproval ran through the gathered barae, but from Ubtao there was silence. The barae showed their disappointment with icy stares and grim frowns.

Perhaps you can tell us your reasons, said the woman wrapped in flames.

The old weaponsmith was not so kind. *He insults Ubtao and the city! It is our duty to end his life!*

Artus pointed toward the Harpers' symbol at the center of the glowing pattern. "There are other cities in the world that need protection, other peoples who need to be defended against creatures like the Batiri," he said. "I will fight for Mezro, but not exclusively. I cannot be a bara."

The assembled heroes faded from view, followed quickly by the starry sky and the vast stone plain. Once more Artus stood in the modest chamber. At the heart of the faint circle of light, the explorer looked up into the silent darkness above him. "I need the ring," he said. "Please, let me take it and go."

One who is wise enough to pass my test should know I never would have prevented you from doing just as you wished. My law is simply that, my law. You must follow it only if you choose to do so, only if you give me that power over you.

To Artus's right, not a dozen steps away, the Ring of Winter floated in the darkness. The simple band of gold turned slowly, and it seemed to Artus the faintest glimmer of starlight winked seductively off its frost-flecked curves. With a trembling hand, he reached out for the artifact, the thing that had consumed a decade of his life.

Holding the ring was much like gripping the magical lightning bolts conjured from T'fima's ensorcelled diamonds; the gold band vibrated with power. It also burned Artus's fingers with its intense cold. Frost crept down his forefinger and thumb, then worked its way across his palm. Artus hardly noticed, so stunned was he to actually hold the fabled Ring of Winter.

How long he stood there, Artus could not tell, but his entire hand and half his arm were covered in a thin coat of ice when he next realized where he was. He flexed, sending a shower of ice fragments to the floor. Then, clutching the Ring of Winter in a numb fist, he ran for the door.

When Artus stepped through the archway into the Hall of Champions, he was greeted by the groans of the wounded stretched out beneath the statues. Bodies almost hid the floor, and the explorer had to pick his way carefully to avoid treading on any of the unfortunates.

"Help me here!"

The plea came from a young woman at Artus's feet. She was wrestling with a boy, trying in vain to keep him still while she straightened his broken leg for splinting. The boy would have none of it. He thrashed about, shouting, "I must go back to the battle. They need me!"

When Artus kneeled to grab the boy, he saw it was the same bright young man who had led him to Ras T'fima. "You can't get back to the fight unless you let them help you," he said.

The boy calmed a bit, and when the woman pulled his leg straight, he only cried out a little. Tears of pain in his eyes, he forced a half-smile. "I'll be better by the afternoon. You'll see."

Artus hurried on, the cold eyes of the statues following his progress. A strange feeling stole over him as he glanced back at the unblinking stone faces; perhaps they really were watching him now, gathered in Ubtao's home in the sky. He heard their displeasure in the moans of the wounded, saw their disappointment in the staring eyes of a dead warrior's corpse.

I'll change their minds soon enough, Artus vowed as he pushed open the door to the plaza.

The burning fields lit up the night, and by that light Artus could see the city was in ruins. Gaping holes pock-marked some buildings in the Scholars' Quarter. Others had been reduced to rubble, only stray pillars marking the site of their glory. Goblin archers lined the roofs of the few buildings still standing. They fired flaming arrows at the human warriors and set more buildings ablaze back toward the library. Overhead, pteradons soared unopposed through the shroud of smoke, shrieking in triumph.

The line of Mezroan defenders had retreated, almost to the point where the warriors had their backs to the temple wall. Corpses littered the ground, hundreds upon hundreds of goblins and men. The fierce adversaries were often locked together, their bodies frozen in some violent pose.

The defensive line had almost collapsed completely near the Residential Quarter; even as Artus watched, the Batiri were massing for an attack on the labyrinth of buildings, last refuge for most of the city's helpless. Kwalu must have moved to that part of the battle, for a swarm of locusts seemed to be the sole thing holding the goblins at bay.

Only a few mages were scattered amongst the

defenders. Even the circle of sorcerers intent on keeping
Skuld hostage was nowhere to be seen. The reason for
their absence quickly became clear.

From behind one of the more complete buildings bordering the plaza, Skuld backed into view. The silver-skinned
giant had broken out of his magical cage, but doing so must
have cost him a great deal of power. He stood just over one
story high, about a third as tall as he'd been when Artus
saw him last. He still had a malicious gleam in his eyes. The
blood on his hands did not seem to be his own.

A dinosaur stepped from behind the building now, carefully pacing Skuld, matching each move the spirit guardian
made. It was an allosaurus, one of the most vicious of
Ubtao's Children. Thirty-five feet from its snout to the end
of its thick tail, the creature resembled the monster from
Artus's nightmare that morning in the park. As it walked
upright through the wreckage on two sturdy hind legs, it
clawed the air with its tiny front paws and twitched its tail
nervously. Deep-throated growls rumbled from its mouth.
It snarled and gnashed its rows of teeth, as sharp and as
deadly as Skuld's.

"Sanda!" Artus shouted, for this could only be the work
of her bara powers. The allosaurus was carefully stalking
Skuld, squaring off against the giant to keep him away from
the mortal troops. The bara was likely hidden somewhere
safe, so she could control the beast without too much danger to herself.

The two giants rushed together then. The allosaurus bit
down hard on Skuld's shoulder as they met, the attack's
ferocity lifting the silver guardian off the ground. Skuld
countered quickly. He dug the fingers of three hands into
the dinosaur's sides, and blood gushed out to cover his
forearms. Skuld had not escaped without injury, though.
The thick silver ooze that passed for his own flesh coated
the allosaurus's snout.

Artus shouted the bara's name again and slipped the Ring
of Winter onto his finger. The battling titans, the human
warriors, the entire city of Mezro vanished from his sight.
A blinding, white landscape replaced the jumbled conflict.
Pillars of jagged blue ice broke the horizon in places, and a
vast, smooth plain stretched away forever to the right, the
remains of an ocean frozen solid. The sun flashed rainbows
through fist-sized snowflakes drifting on the wind. A music
of sorts came to him, the soft whisper of that falling snow
and the jangle of ice dropping to the ground.

There was no voice, no siren's call telling Artus to lay
waste to the world, but the explorer knew he could turn
the lush jungles of Chult into this beautiful, icy domain. He
had that power now. The Ring of Winter had granted it to
him. And if Chult was not enough, then he could bend
Faerun to his will, as well. Cormyr, Sembia, the Dales—all
these could be buried beneath leagues of ice and snow, so
deep no explorer would ever find them again. Any who
questioned his right to rule could be dealt with in just such a
manner, the entire world if need be. The Realms could be
his until the end of time, for the ring granted immortality,
too.

Though Artus never would have believed himself tempted by this, he was. The ring promised nothing, demanded
nothing. But the explorer could envision the world as he
had always dreamed it might be, a place free from war and
tyranny, all peoples liberated from want and ignorance. He
could make it so, force the world to match his vision—or
break it all to pieces in trying. He could free every country,
every town or village, from evil.

But he could never free them from his own terrible
reign.

With that realization, the snow-filled world began to fade
from Artus's eyes just a little. All his life, he had fought for
freedom. That was why he'd joined the Harpers, a band

dedicated to nothing more passionately than the right of
every individual to forge his own way in the world. And that
was also why he'd sought the ring, to make certain it
wasn't used to banish liberty from the world. If he had
been too impatient to see why the Harpers favored caution
and a temperate use of their influence on the world, it had
been the zeal of his youth blinding him. Now that he possessed the power to change everything, he saw the neces-
sity for that caution.

Artus looked out over the city of Mezro once more, con-
fident and determined that he could wield the ring's power
responsibly. Only an instant had passed since he'd put on
the frost-flecked gold band. Skuld and the allosaurus were
still locked in battle. The goblins had yet to charge the
Residential Quarter. Fires raged unchecked in the fields.
The Batiri horde was slowly overwhelming the tired defenders around the Temple of Ubtao.

With a graceful sweep of his hand, Artus traced a line in
the air. A wall of ice a dozen feet high sprang up from the
pavement. It ran the length of the plaza, cutting the goblin
horde in half, breaking the advance on the temple. The battles continued closer to the sacred building, but the human
warriors rallied at the sight of the wall, just as many goblins
panicked at being cut off far from their fellows. The cannibals tried unsuccessfully to scramble up the slick barrier,
only to be cut down by Mezroan warriors.

At the edge of the Scholars' Quarter, Skuld had driven
the allosaurus back. Gory wounds scored the dinosaur's
hide, and a huge piece of the silver guardian's shoulder had
been torn off. But Skuld's wounds knit themselves quickly.
Before the dazed and wounded dinosaur could steady itself
from the last skirmish, the silver giant was completely
healed and ready to charge again. Like the battle with the
mages' cage, though, this cost Skuld; even as he healed,
he shrank just a little.

Artus crossed his hands over his chest and concentrated. A wide pillar of ice rose from the ground, lifting him up over the battle. "Skuld!" he shouted. "Leave the beast alone."

The booming voice caused a momentary lull in the fighting, as many—human and goblin alike—looked up to see what powerful new combatant had entered the fray. Before the echo of the challenge had died in the plaza, three pteradons were soaring toward Artus. They dove straight at him, ready to knock him from his high perch even if they couldn't get his soft flesh into their beaks.

Calmly the explorer watched the flying reptiles as they drew closer. When they were over a somewhat deserted section of the plaza, he pointed at their wings and coated them with ice. Paralyzed, the pteradons could not ride the air currents that kept them aloft. Like game birds with arrows through their hearts, the shape-shifters plummeted from the sky one by one and crashed to the ground.

Skuld smiled with savage glee. "So my great savior is not dead." He turned from the allosaurus, which slumped against the building. "I have not yet thanked you for taking me from those ruins in Cormyr."

In four or five steps, Skuld was over the wall. Crushing both goblins and Mezroan warriors, he strode to the pillar. He snatched the explorer from his perch with one hand. "Hah! Where are your powers now?" he shouted, holding his captive high over his head.

Triumphantly, he leaped back over the wall, a dozen Mezroan spears sticking harmlessly out of his legs and feet. With no regard for anyone or anything in his path, Skuld made his way to the plaza's edge. There, in the remains of a ruined building, Kaverin Ebonhand and Queen M'bobo had their headquarters. The two directed the battle far from the fighting, far from any danger. Two camp chairs sat side by side, bracketed by guttering torches and tables laden with food and pitchers of wine. In the squalor behind the leaders, Lord Rayburton lay chained and gagged. Ten goblin guards, armed and armored better than any others in the motley Batiri horde, stood watch over the prisoner.

"I have him for you, master," Skuld announced proudly. Artus's body was still, his legs hanging as limply as a rag doll's. At the sight of Kaverin, though, the explorer began to struggle against the silver guardian's grip.

Kaverin leaped to his feet. "Kill him, you idiot! He has some kind of magical artifact that lets him control ice, some wand or—" His dead eyes went wide with amazement. "Cyric's blood," he whispered. "He found the ring!"

Skuld tightened his fist, but it was as if Artus had suddenly been shielded by some powerful armor. The silver guardian clapped another hand over the one holding his prisoner, but that didn't help either. Perhaps I should just bite the nuisance's head off, he decided. That's always effective.

But when Skuld tried to pull his hands apart, he found them locked together. A cold more profound than any he'd felt in his fourteen hundred years began to seep into his fingers, climb up his arms. He felt his limbs stiffen, his hands grow absolutely numb. In desperation, Skuld pulled at the frozen arms with his other set of hands. The fists holding Artus cracked, then came apart with a loud snap.

The explorer rolled off the giant's frozen hands and tumbled through the air. As he fell, he touched the Silvermace family crest on his tunic. The diving falcon sewn in white on the green cloth flapped its wings and loosed its hold on the spiked mace. The raptor was a thing of thread no longer, but a creature of ice. It pushed away from Artus, instantly growing as large as the explorer. With its cold talons, the ice falcon snagged Artus's tunic and lowered him gently the rest of the way to the cobblestones. Then it circled up into the sky.

"This time, Kaverin, I'd say I have you," Artus said
slyly. He held up his hand, letting the torchlight glitter off
the Ring of Winter.

A line of ten-foot-tall spikes shot up between the command center and the rest of the Batiri horde. Seeing themselves cut off from the rest of the troops, the guards lifted
M'bobo off her feet and set her down next to Rayburton.
They surrounded their queen, holding their spears out
menacingly to form a spiny circle that resembled some sort
of deranged land urchin. Rayburton tried to struggle to his
feet, but M'bobo kicked his legs out from under him. "You
not going anywhere," the queen said, brandishing her
scimitar.

The bara slumped to the ground with a muffled groan. He
turned once more to Artus, but the explorer couldn't decide if the sadness in Rayburton's eyes was the result of his
mistreatment or the fact someone had recovered the Ring
of Winter.

Kaverin Ebonhand didn't run, neither did he let his surprise show. Calmly he placed his stone hands on his hips
and said, "You 'have me' no more than I had you in the
goblin camp."

A pair of silver hands grabbed Artus by the shoulders and
spun him around. Another pair slammed into his sides,
cracking ribs and sending daggers of pain through his
lungs. Artus tried to call upon the powers of the ring, but
the barrage of fists was so fast he couldn't concentrate.
Blow after blow rained down upon him, battering his head,
his arms, his chest. Desperate, the explorer reached out
to shield himself, but Skuld grabbed his hands.

"You can't use the ring if I tear your arms off," the spirit
guardian said gleefully. He stood little more than ten feet
tall now, his magical energy having been drained in repair-
ing the wounds wrought by both the dinosaur and Artus.

As he spoke, Skuld yanked the explorer's arms up and pulled him from the ground. All the while, he drove his other two fists into the man's ribs, hammering away like a dwarf in a diamond mine.

Though the pummeling was painful, it was not as furious as Skuld's first assault. Artus focused his thoughts through the haze of pain. He could feel the ring's power coursing through him, knitting broken bones and healing the muscles torn by Skuld's attack. And as the spirit guardian cocked his free arms back for a killing blow, Artus struck.

A set of muscular arms made of crystal-clear ice sprouted from the explorer's side, blocking Skuld's attack. The silver-skinned giant found all four hands caught in globes of ice that tightened like vises each time he moved. He howled in frustration, but that quickly turned to a panicked cry for help. The ice was spreading up his arms, paralyzing him as it went.

"Master!" Skuld shouted. "I will be slain!"

Kaverin had already foreseen that possibility. With a spear he had snatched from one of the goblin guards, he charged silently forward. Artus could not turn, could not see the attack coming. Certain of victory, Kaverin raised the spear to strike.

The spearhead never reached its mark.

With a shrieking war cry, the ice falcon dropped from the sky. It tore the weapon from Kaverin's grasp, knocking the redheaded man onto his back. The falcon snapped the wooden shaft in two, then sailed back into the night to circle protectively, high over its creator.

From the cobbles, Kaverin looked up with dead, lifeless eyes at Skuld. The spirit guardian gnashed futilely at Artus with his filed silver teeth. His arms, torso, even his legs were coated with ice. Skuld's head remained free, but it only moved sluggishly from side to side. His breath turned to steam in the chill air. Then that, too, stopped, and the silver earrings on the guardian's ears ceased to jangle.

Artus stepped back to study his handiwork. Skuld stood rigid, his arms held menacingly before him—just like the statue he and Pontifax had found that day in the Stonelands, only much larger. Perhaps that's why the Skuld statue was in those ruins; someone had trapped the treacherous spirit guardian and left him to stand forever in the rubble—until some unfortunate stumbled across him, of course. Artus couldn't let that happen again, not after all the suffering Skuld had caused.

The explorer reached up for the spiked mace sewn onto his tunic, the last remnant of the Silvermace crest. The mace disappeared from the cloth and appeared in his hand, as formidable a weapon as any forged with flame. Artus had to strike Skuld only once. The paralyzed giant shattered like glass.

Artus turned, only to find the goblins hustling their queen back to the safety of the jungle. She was cursing them for their cowardice, but not struggling very hard to get away. They'd left Rayburton behind, wisely assuming the powerful human would leave them alone if they did.

That gave Kaverin a hostage, as well, and the leader of the Cult of Frost now stood next to Rayburton, the broken spear held up to the bara's throat. Blood ran in a thin line down Rayburton's neck. "The point is too deep for you to make it so cold it shatters, or to throw a collar of ice armor around his throat to stop it from harming him," Kaverin said.

Artus dropped the mace and took a step forward. Kaverin dug the spear tip deeper into the bara's throat. The thin line of blood became a small but steady stream. "I won't be foolish enough to ask for the ring," Kaverin said, "just my life." For the first time, Artus heard fear in his old adversary's voice—fear and barely hidden madness. "The prize is yours, so you've nothing to fear from me any more."

"You're right," Artus said flatly.

Without the slightest movement, Artus conjured a fierce winter wind. The icy blast struck Kaverin in the chest like a hammer's blow. It lifted him away from Rayburton, bearing him backward until he hit the partial remains of a wall. There, a dozen hands of ice grabbed him. His arms straight out from his side, his legs held apart, Kaverin hung from the brick wall.

Artus cut the ropes binding Rayburton's hands and gave the bara his dagger. The gem that gave off a continual radiance flared like a miniature sun when Artus held the weapon, but died back to its normal glow once Rayburton took it in his twisted fingers. "Artus," the bara said, using his gag to staunch the flow of blood on his neck. "Please. Take the ring off before you lose control."

"I know perfectly well what I'm doing," Artus replied. He turned his back on Rayburton and walked slowly to face Kaverin.

The leader of the Cult of Frost looked wistfully at the Ring of Winter. "So close," he murmured. "So very close." Then the expression vanished from Kaverin's features. "I could have destroyed the entire world, you know."

A rapier appeared in Artus's hand, a long barb of ice tapering to a needle point. Silently he continued to move toward Kaverin.

"Let me free," Kaverin said, struggling against the hands holding him to the wall. "At least let me die with some dignity, not like a madman, chained so he won't bite the headsman."

Artus paused. "So you can die with honor? Be a 'good soldier' like Pontifax?" he asked. With a lightning-quick strike, Artus drove the rapier through Kaverin's heart. "You wouldn't know how."

The scream had yet to die on Kaverin's lips when the

two wolf-headed minions of Cyric appeared to either side of the dying man. They grabbed his jet-black stone hands with their spider's legs and yanked him free of the icy restraints. "The Lord of the Dead sends his thanks, Artus Cimber" they said discordantly, their voices rising over Kaverin's scream. Then the denizens were gone, a stench of brimstone marking their passing.

Artus turned back to Rayburton. "Go to the temple," he said wearily. At a gesture from the explorer, the ice falcon swooped out of the sky and grabbed the bara. "The goblins will scatter without their leaders. Tell the king and Kwalu, if you can find them."

"But what about you?" Rayburton cried as he was lifted from the ground.

"I have a promise to keep."

* * * * *

Lugg hid in the embrace of a tangled, rather odoriferous thorn bush, just beyond Mezro's magical wall. Two gangs of Batiri battled in the small clearing before him, vying for a sack of flour and three mangled chickens. Of the twenty or so goblins that had started the skirmish, only five remained. They were battered and bloody, so exhausted from the fight that they could barely heft their spears.

The flour and the chickens were the dregs of the supplies the goblins had massed for the assault on Mezro and everything they'd pillaged from the city before the fight turned against them. Lugg wasn't sure what had happened to bring on the Batiri defeat. From the shouts of the retreating warriors, he'd heard that Skuld had been destroyed and some human demigod had broken the charge on the temple with a wall of ice. That was good news, at least. Maybe Artus had found that ring he was looking for.

The thought of the explorer brought a pang of regret and

an equal feeling of anger to Lugg. He was still rather annoyed at having to rescue Byrt on his own.

After leaving Artus, Lugg had made his way across the battle-torn city, mostly by hiding in the rubble of shattered buildings until the goblin patrols passed. At first he hadn't much of a plan for finding Byrt, then inspiration tapped him on his furry shoulder. He realized the goblins wouldn't use Byrt in battle and that the little gray wombat was of no value as a hostage. That left him the unpleasant fate of becoming part of the Batiri foodstock.

It was a relatively simple matter to find the location of the goblins' baggage train. By keeping to the shadows, he could watch for the troops transporting supplies to the front lines, then reverse their trail. The sleuthing took Lugg through the Scholars' Quarter, to the place where the Batiri had first entered Mezro. The goblins' supply stockpile was located just outside the city's magical wall.

At the moment, Lugg had the sinking feeling he wouldn't find Byrt here, even if he'd been part of the supply train earlier. Toppled wagons and empty crates littered the area, along with the corpses of fifty or more Batiri. For the past hour, the clearing had been the site of a dozen bloody skirmishes, just like the one going on at that moment before Lugg's beady eyes. The winners had taken whatever they could carry. The losers had been left to rot.

The wombat winced as a goblin fell into the dirt, a spear sticking out of his forehead like a unicorn's horn. The battle was over. With a savage whoop of victory, the surviving Batiri carted the chickens and the flour into the jungle.

The shrieking of birds and chattering of monkeys vied with the diminishing sounds of battle from the city's center. It was difficult to hear over the din, so Lugg was particularly cautious about moving into the open. It wouldn't do Byrt a bit of good if he got captured now, when he was the only one who cared enough to look for him.

At last the wombat trundled out of the thorn bush, sniffing to clear his nose of the lingering, sickly sweet smell. "They must have carried 'im off, too," Lugg said mournfully. "What a bloody rotten way to go—walking groceries for cannibal goblins." He stuck his head into an empty barrel, looking helplessly for some clue that might lead him to his friend. "Still, that's not as bad as what that pirate captain wanted to do with us after 'e'd decided the zoo wouldn't want us. Four-legged footstools indeed!"

Lugg fairly shook with anger at the indignity he'd been subjected to aboard the ship that had stolen him and Byrt from the little island near Orlil they'd once called home. To his surprise, he found he missed the squalid place more and more. It was certainly paradise compared to Chult, if for no other reason than its complete lack of goblins.

"This is what we get for trusting 'umans, I suppose." Lugg paused to pull a sharp bit of stone from his paw. "Still, I thought Artus was more of a chum. We saved 'is life, after all. But what does 'e give us in return? The rotten twister lets me and Byrt fend for ourselves with the goblins."

"That's hardly charitable on your part, old sport."

The familiar, cheerful voice came from a nearby bush. It took a minute of frantic uprooting for Lugg to get to the source, but when he finally did, he found Byrt sitting contentedly in a bamboo-barred cage. Fresh fruits and vegetables packed the prison. From Byrt's chubby cheeks, it seemed he had been well fed during his captivity.

"The Batiri were very hospitable," the gray wombat said, nibbling on a large yam. "One of them hid me here, hoping to come back later I suppose. I strongly suspected his motives, of course, but I figured you would free me from any bubbling pots before things got too hot."

Byrt looked at his friend with vacant blue eyes. "Artus has his hands full, I'd wager, so don't be so hard on him.

That Kaverin fellow who was after him—" he mocked a shiver "—quite a rotten piece of work. His descendants will be embarrassed for generations. I can just see his great-grandson now, pelted by overripe summer squash in the schoolyard for having such a blighted family tree. . . . Very sad, indeed."

Years of traveling with Byrt had given Lugg the uncanny ability to block the little wombat's voice from his mind. Anyone who'd spent time with Byrt knew how useful this was. And Lugg did just that as he set about gnawing on the thick ropes holding the cage together. In fact, he focused his attention so completely on the task that he didn't hear the sound of unstealthy feet moving across the clearing or Byrt's frantic words of warning. Only the sharp prick of a spear in his rump managed to tear Lugg away from his rescue efforts.

"Don't poke 'em! Just grab 'em and c'mon!"

Lugg spun around and came face to face with the tip of a half-dozen goblin spears. The Batiri warriors were more heavily armored than the others the wombat had seen; their breastplates and helmets actually looked as if they might turn a blow aside. And behind these daunting adversaries stood Queen M'bobo, frowning at the delay in their escape and fluffing her beautiful golden hair.

"Well," she snapped. "Get on with it!"

The warriors stepped closer, and Lugg bared his teeth in a fierce snarl. The brown wombat backed up to the bars of Byrt's cage. When one of the Batiri, braver than the others, took a tentative step forward, Lugg sprang. He grabbed the spear in his mouth and wrenched it from the goblin's hand.

"I could have told you that would happen," Byrt chimed from inside the cage. "He can be terrible protective of his friends. And speaking of friends, did you know we are on quite good terms with the muckety-mucks of the fair city you just tried to renovate by uncontrolled fire?"

M'bobo snorted in a decidedly unladylike manner. "They all busy fighting. 'Sides, who cares about two pig-bears?"

"If you turn around," Byrt said, smiling vacuously, "I believe you'll find out."

The queen of the Batiri glanced over her shoulder, wary of some silly trick. When she saw Artus standing right behind her, she really wished the wombat had been trying something devious. M'bobo yelped in fear, which brought the attention of the guards to the slayer of the silver giant. They, too, gaped in surprise.

Lugg spit out the spear. "Awright, you lot," he rumbled. "Beat it."

The goblins didn't need to be told twice. As one, they dropped their weapons and retreated into the jungle. For a time, the queen's angry shouts could be heard over the jungle's usual cacophony.

Artus kneeled beside Lugg. "I should be angry with you, coming out here on your own like that. I told you I'd rescue him."

"Lugg's always had a problem trusting people," Byrt offered. He licked his lips and bit into a large onion. "I think it's something from his childhood. I, on the other hand, never doubted—"

A horrifying shriek and the rustle of something moving quickly out of the jungle stopped Byrt short. An instant later, Queen M'bobo erupted from the trees. Her armor was bloody, her right arm ragged from some vicious attack. She looked like nothing so much as a weird comet shooting across the ground, her golden hair a glittering tail in the moonlight.

Artus braced himself for an attack. "Stay behind me," he shouted to Lugg.

The goblin queen didn't get three steps into the clearing before she tripped over the corpse of a Batiri killed in the skirmish for food. At least, it seemed as if she tripped. As Artus watched, the gruesome corpse wrapped its arms around M'bobo, pinning her to the ground. Four dark shapes reached out from the tangle of bushes and vines. The bony, decaying hands entwined themselves in the queen's beautiful, flowing hair. They dragged her screaming back into the jungle.

"She's little more than a wild animal, Master Cimber" came a cool, soothing voice from the darkness. "Moreover, she's an enemy of Mezro. She's not worthy of your pity."

Two eyes, glowing like red-hot steel in the shadows, caught Artus's attention. It could only be Ras Nsi.

"If I can't defend Ubtao's city from the inside, I'll do what I can on the outside." Something flowing and as blue as a midsummer sky passed through a shaft of moonlight. Artus could hear the hush of the zombie lord's cloak as he turned to follow his minions into the jungle. "Tell them that, the king and the others. I am still a bara, whether they wish to believe so or not."

Artus stood in silence for a moment, then called a dagger of ice into existence and set to work on Byrt's cage. From time to time as the explorer worked, a goblin charged out of the city. They were as uninterested in confronting Artus as he was in battling them. He felt tempted to stop the wretches from rushing into Ras Nsi's killing embrace, but the feeling was fleeting. The Batiri had earned that doom by attacking Mezro, and it wasn't his place to save the goblins from themselves.

"Let's get back," Artus said as the sturdy cage finally gave in to his dagger. "There'll be a lot to do. Sanda and the others will need our help." He smiled when he thought of telling the beautiful bara about the ring's ability to grant immortality to its wearer.

Slowly Lugg shook his head. "I still can't believe we

won."

Taking a last bite of the store of food from his prison, Byrt said, "I don't know how you can continue to be so utterly cynical, Lugg. As I was mentioning before Queen M'bobo's untimely arrival and even more untimely departure, I never doubted Artus and you would rescue me and save the city." He grinned victoriously. "And, as usual, I was absolutely correct!"

Lugg looked up at Artus. "I 'ate it when 'e gets like this. We won't 'ear the end of it for days. Isn't there something you can do? You've got that ring now, right?"

The little gray wombat was chattering away in his inane voice about how everyone would be much better off if they'd stop worrying about things and listen to him. Artus glanced at the frost-flecked gold ring on his right hand, then at Byrt's vacant blue eyes.

"Sorry, Lugg," Artus sighed, "but I guess there's a limit to what even the Ring of Winter can do."

Epilogue

Almost half of Mezro was destroyed by the Batiri raid. The crops for an entire year had burned to the ground. The Scholars' Quarter lay in ruins, though somehow the Great Library remained intact. Cracks snaked across the building's rose marble facade and a few of the columns gracing its portico had been broken, but the vast storehouse of knowledge, the books and papers of four thousand years of Mezroan history, had been miraculously spared.

The dead were interred in the Temple of Ubtao, in a vast mausoleum that held the remains of every man, woman, and child ever to live in the blessed city. The room was lined with statues and plaques commemorating the dead, some incredibly ornate, others powerfully simple. The ceremonies to honor the fallen defenders lasted weeks, and even the vital work of rebuilding the city was put aside to give homage to the slain.

The goblin corpses inside Mezro's walls never rose to join Ras Nsi's army. The renegade bara showed that much respect for King Osaw's ancient pronouncement, though every corpse left outside the city vanished within hours. No one had any doubts where they had gone. Osaw decided that to add more bodies to Nsi's corps would be foolish, so the remaining Batiri dead were either burned or given over to Mainu. The strange bara distributed the bodies amongst her minions, who had held the Olung River so well that not a single goblin managed to cross it. The piranha and lobster-men devoured the corpses greedily, leaving nothing for the zombie lord's army.

With the barae's help, the task of cleaning the city was made easier. Sanda directed various dinosaurs in the movement of large stones. Kwalu used his locusts to destroy any buildings ruled unsafe by the council. Even without his bara powers, T'fima proved invaluable. He healed even the most life-threatening wounds with his gem magic.

For his part, Artus used the Ring of Winter in a hundred ways to aid in the restoration of Mezro. He created braces of ice to steady walls and roofs until they could be repaired, coated the ground with slick sheets so great burdens could be moved more efficiently, and many other more mundane things. Byrt and Lugg stayed at the explorer's side constantly, at least until he managed to convince the wombats they could help the city more by entertaining the children wounded in the conflict.

Finally, after weeks of back-breaking labor, the citizens of Mezro rested. At highsun they gathered in the plaza around the Temple of Ubtao, ready to give thanks to their leaders and their god. The mood was understandably somber. Food was becoming scarce and many friends and loved ones were painfully absent.

The stout-hearted Mezroans found ample reason to celebrate anyway. Their city was safe, the goblin horde turned back to the jungle, and a new bara had been elected. Ras T'fima had admitted to his deceptions shortly after the fight, and Ubtao had chosen a young girl to replace him. The girl had left the barado with the awesome power to control plants, and her work with the devastated fields had already begun to pay off.

Near the door to the temple, Lord Rayburton and Ras T'fima shared a mug of t'ej and looked out over the throng. The amber, fermented honey was almost too sweet for Rayburton, and he wrinkled his nose after each sip.

"What I don't understand," the old explorer said, "is why Artus can control the ring when it turned against us."

Ras T'fima shrugged. "Maybe we turned against it. I think it has an agenda of its own, that it was created for some purpose."

"Such as?" Rayburton poured the rest of his t'ej onto the cobbles and leaned closer, cradling his splinted fingers.

"To do good," Artus said. He stood behind Rayburton, Sanda and the wombats beside him. A new beard covered his jaw, making his brown eyes seem even darker. Except for the green tunic Theron had left for him, his clothes were ragged and worn from his weeks in Chult. "I can sense it. The ring was created to be a force for good."

Rayburton fell silent. Artus now knew the full story of how the old explorer had discovered the Ring of Winter in the wilderness near Shadowdale. For a time Rayburton had controlled the artifact. Then, when a Cormyrian nobleman refused to let him conduct a dig on his property, Rayburton tried to use the ring to frighten the noble and his serfs away. Instead of driving them off the land, he buried the entire village and the noble's estate in ice, killing everyone for miles around. Frightened and ashamed of the murders, he came to Chult, hoping to hide the Ring of Winter so it could never be used again.

"That must be the reason!" Ras T'fima shouted, his

chubby face flushed from too much t'ej. "I have to admit, I was trying to defend my secret with the ring. I wanted to save Kwalu, of course, but that wasn't—" He drew his lips into a tight line and lowered his booming voice. "Has Kwalu forgiven me yet, Sanda?"

She smiled warmly. "He would forgive you anything, just so long as you keep fighting for Mezro."

Raising his mug, Ras T'fima nodded. "Now that they've agreed to lower the wall, they'll never get rid of me. By the way, Artus, thanks again for your help in the council."

"It's only right," Artus said. "The Tabaxi cut off from the city are at the mercy of the Batiri and the zombies—and the other dark things in the jungle. They should be able to turn here for protection."

Lugg stamped his foot impatiently. "Are we ready to go or not?" he grumbled. His ears were ragged from children tugging on them, his whiskers bent and twisted. Not that he didn't like the tykes, but they were tougher on him than the Batiri.

Sanda hugged her father. "He's right. We should go." Her green eyes filling with tears, she held Lord Rayburton close. "We've already said our good-byes to King Osaw and Negus Kwalu."

"Look, Sanda—" the old explorer began.

"You don't have to say it again," she noted. "I'll be careful of the thugs and murderers and lunatics in Suzail."

"If Kaverin Ebonhand is representative of the people Artus knows from the North," Byrt chimed merrily, "he should be able to point out the really dangerous chaps in the city by name. They probably spend a lot of time in his rooms, practicing knife throwing and trading stories of heists."

"What I was going to say," Rayburton began again, scowling at the little wombat, "is that you should keep an open mind. I believe Artus about the changes that have occurred in the Heartlands since I was there last. You should be able to learn a lot, and the more a bara knows of the world, the better she can serve Ubtao."

Artus shook hands with T'fima and Lord Rayburton. "We'll return soon," he said, taking his dagger from his belt.

In the days following the battle, Artus had discovered the Ring of Winter boosted the magical abilities of anything he held. His dagger had proven to be invaluable with its newly heightened powers. The gem on its handle, meant to give off a faint light, glowed like a star if he wished it to. More importantly, the dagger not only acted like a compass, but could instantly transport Artus and up to five others to whatever location he pictured in his mind.

His dagger held before him, Artus closed his eyes and called an image of his home in Suzail to the fore. He lived alone, in two small attic rooms near the harbor, which he rented from a fletcher named Razor John. The place was packed to bursting with books and trinkets from Artus's travels. Stacks of notes and unanswered correspondence lay atop every flat surface. On the shelves, the spines of books propped up small statues of long-forgotten gods and ancient heroes. Towers of worthless copper coins from various states no longer in existence served as paperweights, as did oddly colored stones, rusted daggers, shoes, and even a medal awarded the explorer by King Azoun and the Society of Stalwart Adventurers for his contribution to the study of Cormyrian history.

When Artus opened his eyes, he, Sanda, and the wombats stood in the midst of this riot of parchment and junk. The room smelled like musty old books, something Artus had never really noticed until now. He went to the tiny window and opened it. A chill wind blew in, setting a few pages sailing about the room like crazed kites.

"I think it was easier to get around in the jungle," Byrt

said, trying to climb over a stack of notes on the possible whereabouts of the Ring of Winter. The wrinkled, ink-splattered parchment kept slipping out from under his feet. After five tries, he gave up and slid back to where he had started.

"You can be back in Chult in a flash if you're not happy here," Artus said absently as he went to the rickety front door. A note bearing the seal of the Harpers lay partway in the room.

Sanda came to the explorer's side, her arms wrapped tightly around her. It was cold here, colder than it ever got in Chult. "What is it?"

"A note requesting my presence at the inquest into Theron Silvermace's death," Artus sighed. "I was probably the last one to see him alive." He frowned and folded the note. "They suspect me, I would imagine, especially since Theron and I argued that last time I saw him."

"What will you do?"

"I'll go, of course," Artus said. "I think it's time I re-established my ties with the Harpers. Now that I have the ring, I can do a lot of good. I just wish I weren't going back to them under this sort of cloud."

"That's all been taken care of, my boy. I told the Harper council what happened with Kaverin's frost minions, and they believed me. I make a very convincing witness these days."

A ghostly figure drifted out of a large stack of books to the center of the room. It was Pontifax, or had been Pontifax. He was translucent and pale, though his sapphire-blue eyes had kept the slightest hint of color. To the shocked look on his old friend's face, he raised his bushy eyebrows. "Yes, it really was me you saw all those times in the jungle."

Artus stammered a reply, but Pontifax held up a stubby-fingered hand. "I didn't explain earlier because I couldn't control when I came and went. All I could do was pop in whenever possible and wait for Ubtao to yank me back to his house."

"Ubtao?" Sanda asked. "What's he got to do with this?"

"A fine question, my dear," Pontifax said. "As Artus undoubtedly told you, I was killed in Port Castigliar by Kaverin's frost minions. I closed my eyes for the final time, and next thing I knew I was standing in a dark room with all sorts of strange glowing lines on the floor. This voice says, 'Complete the pattern of your life.' Naturally I had no idea what he was talking about—it was Ubtao, if you hadn't guessed." The ghost held up his hands. "I failed the test, so I was sentenced to become a ghost. Hardly a military trial, I must say."

Artus finally found his voice. "Wait a minute," he said. "You always worshiped Mystra. Why didn't you go to her realm when you died? I thought that was the way it worked."

"That's the way it's *supposed* to work," Pontifax corrected. "I'm caught in some sort of bureaucratic mix-up. Ubtao says I'm doomed to be a ghost. Mystra says I'm not. That's why I can't control when I come and go. If one of the gods gets it into his or her mind to chat about the matter—which is far too frequently, if you ask me—I'm instantly transported to their palace. And there I sit, waiting for days on end for the archangels or whatever to usher me in to their boss."

Artus shook his head. "You're not in pain, are you? I mean, is there anything we can do?"

Pontifax paused, then said, "No pain. Actually, not much of anything. In all it's mostly dull, being dead. At least it is right now. Maybe after they get my status sorted out things will liven up, so to speak." He sighed in exasperation. "They could take a cue from the military. I'll bet Torm's afterlife isn't like this. You wouldn't find Tempus putting up with—" And then he was gone.

"I'm glad all of you saw that," Artus murmured. "At least I know that I wasn't just imagining him."

"But what if we're all as mad as you?" Lugg offered truculently.

Byrt was staring wide-eyed at the spot where Pontifax had been floating. His gray fur was flecked here and there with white, and Artus could almost swear the bristles around his snout were standing as straight as lances. "Oh my," was all the wombat managed before his vague blue eyes rolled back in their sockets and he slumped onto the pile of parchment.

"Unbelievable," Lugg crowed. "We've finally discovered a way to keep 'im quiet! Quick, Artus, write down the date."

Artus picked up a stack of blank pages and looked at them nostalgically. "I think I'm done with journals for a while, Lugg," he said, dropping the paper back onto his cluttered desk.

Sanda slipped her hand into Artus's. "My thoughts exactly. You'll have decades to write your memoirs, now that you have this." She twisted the Ring of Winter playfully. "Don't you think you should live life a little first?"

"Absolutely," Artus replied. He ran the back of his hand along the gentle curve of her neck and kissed her softly. "And when I do get around to writing this all down, it'll be that much more interesting."

FORGOTTEN REALMS®
FANTASY ADVENTURE
▪ THE HARPERS ▪

The Night Parade
Scott Ciencin

Myrmeen Lhal, the seductive ruler of Arabel, enlists the aid of the Harpers to rescue her long-lost daughter from the Night Parade, a shadowy group of creatures that feeds off human misery and fear. **On sale now.**

Crypt of the Shadowking   Mark Anthony

Iriabor of a Thousand Spires, richest of the Caravan Cities, has fallen under the dark sway of the Zhentarim. The fiery Harper agent Mari Al'Marin and the cynical ex-Harper Caledan are all that stand between the evil group and the domination of a rich and thriving city. Only a quest for long-forgotten magic might provide the means of defeating the Zhentarim's plot.

Crown of Fire   Ed Greenwood

Shandril possesses the deadly magic of spellfire, but the wizards of Zhentil Keep covet her knowledge. With the aid of companions Narm and Delg, and occasional help from Elminster the Wizard, Shandril must escape the Zhentarim and turn her powers against them.

Soldiers of Ice   David Cook

Journeying north in defiance of the Harpers, Martine of Sembia finds herself trapped in the snowbound valley of Samek, kept company by gnomes and an ex-paladin named Vilheim. There she finds love and war as the outnumbered gnomes defend their valley agianst an advancing horde of savage gnolls.

BIGGER, BETTER, MEANER AND MORE OF THE VERY BEST FROM SSI!

EYE OF THE BEHOLDER II: THE LEGEND OF DARKMOON is a graphically based AD&D® computer fantasy role-playing saga.

This exciting sequel to *EYE OF THE BEHOLDER* gives you stunning pictures, realistic animation, 3-D "you-are-there" point of view *and more!*

A bigger adventure means more to explore, people to meet, clues to learn and mysteries to unravel! Better graphics and improved "point-and-click" interface make playing even easier.

There are lots of new, smarter, meaner monsters — some of the nastiest ones are human!

Available for: IBM and AMIGA.

Visit your retailer or call 1-800-245-4525, in USA & Canada, for VISA /MC orders. To receive SSI's complete catalog, send $1.00 to:

STRATEGIC SIMULATIONS, INC.®
675 Almanor Avenue, Suite 201
Sunnyvale, CA 94086